THE TOLPUDDLE WOMAN

THE TOLPUDDLE WOMAN

E. V. Thompson

LONDON NEW YORK SYDNEY TORONTO

This edition published 1994
by BCA
by arrangement with
HEADLINE BOOK PUBLISHING

CN 8342

First published in 1994
by HEADLINE BOOK PUBLISHING

10 9 8 7 6 5 4 3 2 1

Phototypeset by Intype, London
Printed and bound in Great Britain by
Mackays of Chatham PLC, Chatham, Kent

BOOK ONE

Chapter 1

Lying in bed in the darkness, a blanket drawn up to his chin, Wes Gillam lay very still. The creaking of the flimsy wooden bed frame might cause him to miss something of the heated, albeit one-sided discussion going on downstairs.

Although there was a floor between the two rooms, he was able to hear every word that was being spoken. Sounds from the cottage's single downstairs room followed the narrow path taken by the yellow lamp-light between warped floorboards. They also reached him through gaps as wide as a man's wrist above and below the ill-hung door at the foot of the stairs.

The discussion between his parents was about Saul, Wes's nineteen-year-old brother. Always the subject of contention between them, matters had become much worse of late. Indeed, they had talked of little else for days.

'It isn't right for the boy to be out at such a time of night,' declared Eli Gillam, heatedly. 'The darkness is a cloak for the devil's deeds. What is our Saul doing that can't be done in the good Lord's light? That's what I'd like to know!'

'He'll be with his friends, Eli. Sam Standfield's just back from working in Exeter. Saul and the others will want to be hearing all about life there.'

Rachel Gillam took on the role that had increasingly fallen to her in recent weeks: that of conciliator between father and son. But Eli Gillam was a lay preacher in the Methodist Church. He was not an easy man to turn aside from a subject he had chosen to attack.

'I don't want a son of mine listening to whatever Sam Standfield has to say about the goings on in any city. Saul has enough wild ideas in his head without having young Standfield put more there.'

Rachel knew her husband's views on sinful city life and she chose to remain silent. But any hopes she might have entertained that Eli would drop the subject were quickly dashed.

'Are you quite sure Saul is with the Standfield boy? He's not gone to Southover to meet the young girl who's living over there

3

now? The one folks are all talking about?'

Upstairs, Wes held his breath as he waited for his mother's reply. He knew Saul *had* gone to Southover to meet the girl of whom his father disapproved so strongly. His mother knew it too.

'Now, Eli. Describing a girl you hardly know in such words is unchristian. Saranna Vye may be a little wilder than many of the girls around here, but with her background that's hardly surprising. Her father was a brave soldier who died fighting Napoleon, as well you know. He left her mother to bear the child on a battle-field in Spain. They've been living near London since then, as far as I can make out. I know they were returned to the parish because they'd become vagrants, but there's many good folk these days who've lost work and home. You can't expect a girl like that to be the same as one who's never known anything but a dirt-floor cottage in Tolpuddle.'

'She's been around these parts for long enough to learn Christ-ian ways. John Makepeace is the minister on the Southover cir-cuit. He's as good a preacher as you'll find anywhere in Dorset. If she went to chapel and took to heart the message he preaches I'd have nothing to criticise. That reminds me, have you seen the list of preachers for this week? I can't remember where I'm supposed to be preaching on Sunday. I know I promised to go to Dewlish in the afternoon . . .'

Upstairs, Wes relaxed. His mother had managed once again to avert a full-scale family argument. Tomorrow he would try to talk to Saul, yet again. Ask him to make an effort to meet their father halfway. Not to flout his authority for so much of the time.

It would not be easy. Saul and Eli Gillam were too much alike. Both were strong-willed men, each convinced his own opinion was always the right one. If only they were able to tackle prob-lems together they would be a formidable force. As it was, their paths were more likely to lead to a violent collision.

Wes turned on his side. The thin yellow light leaking through the floorboards touched Saul's bed. At right angles to his own it was no more than a hand's breadth away and the same distance from the top stair. The sleeping space occupied by the two brothers was not so much a room as a narrow landing.

Wes had a sudden twinge of sympathy for the brother who was barely three years older than himself. It was not much of a life for a young man who wanted to improve his lot. Saul had always resented the lack of opportunities in the Dorset village of Tolpud-dle. In a town he might have found what he sought.

Unfortunately for Saul, the manor of Tolpuddle had been bought by the Reverend Edward St John. A suspicious, irascible man, he had a particularly lucrative living in nearby Hampshire.

He also had a deep distrust of working men with ideas above their station in life, and was convinced they were highly dangerous to the established social order and smooth running of the country.

Edward St John held the same view of Methodists. An ambitious man from a Methodist family was anathema to him.

St John did not live in his manor, but as landlord of most of the Tolpuddle lands, he wielded a great deal of influence. Sufficient to ensure that not only was Saul Gillam unable to advance himself, but no one in Tolpuddle dared employ him. Saul had been unemployed for almost a year.

Instead of sympathising with his eldest son, Eli Wesley *blamed* him for the predicament in which he found himself. Eli firmly believed there was a place for everyone in the order of things. Despite his own obvious intelligence, Eli was himself no more than a farm worker, with few possessions to show for a lifetime of hard, uncomplaining work on a Tolpuddle farm. Nevertheless, as a staunch Methodist, Eli Gillam was content to look forward to a better life that would be his in the hereafter.

Wes must have dozed off. He awoke with a start, immediately aware of raised voices in the downstairs room.

'. . . I'll ask you once again: where have you been? No one who's up to any good is abroad at such an hour of night.'

'Oh? Then perhaps you should tell the squire from over at Affpuddle. I passed him along the road just outside Southover. The smell of brandy was so strong as he went by it's a wonder the horse wasn't staggering.'

'What gentlemen get up to is nobody's business but their own – and what were you doing over at Southover? I thought you'd gone to see Sam Standfield. Were you visiting that Vye girl again? I've told you before, I'll not have it, do you hear me?'

'I said nothing about seeing Saranna Vye.'

'No, but then, it's not a name that's likely to be mentioned in any respectable family hereabouts – and what other reason would you have for being at Southover?'

'As a matter of fact there *was* another reason. I heard Farmer Pearse was about to begin harvesting. I went to Southover to ask him for work.'

Eli eyed his son uncertainly. 'Joseph Pearse is a good man. Has he agreed to take you on?'

'No.'

'You've no doubt spent all this time pleading with him to give you work?' There was heavy sarcasm in Eli's voice.

'It wouldn't have served any purpose. His mind was made up. So I spent the rest of the evening at the Vye house instead.'

'I knew it! You can make all the lame excuses you like, but the only reason you went to Southover was to see this Vye girl. I'm ashamed of you. Ashamed that a son of mine can stand before his father and tell such lies to his face.'

'I'm not a liar, Pa.' Saul spoke so quietly that Wes only just caught the words.

'Oh? Then perhaps you can explain why all your attempts to get work take you in the direction of Southover? At the same time you can tell me why you never succeed but always end up at the house of that Vye girl.'

'I'll tell you if you really want to know, but you'll find the truth less to your liking than you seem to think.' Wes could tell by his brother's tight voice that he was angry – and it boded ill. Saul Gillam's temper was notorious in the district.

Rachel Gillam knew the warning signs too. 'Now that's quite enough from both of you. If you carry on like this you'll wake young Wes and he has to be up early to go to Dorchester for Widow Cake. Off you go to bed now, Saul.'

'No, Rachel. He's not escaping so easily tonight. Let the boy have his say. I want to know why neither Joseph Pearse nor anyone else will give him work.'

'Eli . . .'

'He's right, Ma. It's time he knew why Joseph Pearse wouldn't take me on. *You're* the reason, Pa. You and your preaching ways that have upset every landlord and every vicar for miles around here. Since it's "honesty" you're looking for tonight, *that's* the reason I haven't been able to find work for a year. First the Reverend St John, and now James Frampton who owns most of the land that St John doesn't, have issued warnings to their tenant farmers. Take on a Methodist preacher, or any member of his family, and they can look elsewhere for a farm when their leases come up for renewal.'

Saul's revelation was followed by a silence that lasted so long that Wes was forced to expel his pent-up breath in a rush of sound that he feared could be heard downstairs. Then his father said angrily, 'You're lying, Saul. No man would refuse another work because he comes from a God-fearing Methodist family.'

'How would you know? You can't see farther than the door of your precious chapel. Besides, you've worked all your life for Thomas Priddy. He's his own man, and a Methodist too. If you're really so keen on learning the truth, I suggest you leave his farm and try to find work elsewhere – as I have. You'd soon learn that your narrow-minded, holier-than-thou attitude doesn't impress anyone outside your own church.'

'Saul! How dare you speak to your father like that?' Rachel Gillam made a last desperate attempt to prevent the yawning gap

6

between her husband and her son from widening any further.

'It wasn't my idea, Ma. But it's high time he knew that not everyone believes all that's good in the world stems from the Methodist Church. Jesus Christ wasn't a Methodist – but I'll wager he had a lot more understanding and tolerance than any Methodist I've ever come across in Tolpuddle.'

'Hold your tongue, boy! I'll not have such vile blasphemy uttered in this house. You'll apologise this instant!'

'What for? For telling the truth? I thought you set great store by honesty.'

'You heard me! Apologise this instant or . . . or you can leave this house.'

'You don't mean that, Eli. He doesn't mean it, Saul . . .' Rachel pleaded to father and son in turn.

'Let him tell me that for himself.' Saul spoke tight-voiced.

'I've said all I'm going to say on the matter. You'll apologise for your words or you can leave this house first thing tomorrow morning.'

'He didn't mean anything, Eli. You made him angry, that's all. Please . . .'

Wes could imagine his mother's face, screwed up in anguish and torment. Arguments between Saul and their father had always been a part of family life, but they had grown worse in recent months. Far worse. He knew his mother had been dreading something like this happening.

'Saul, tell your father you're sorry. Please. For *my* sake . . .'

'No, Ma. In spite of what he's said about me, I'm *not* a liar. I can't say what I don't mean. I'll leave in the morning. I'm going to bed now. I'll see you before I go . . . Goodbye, Pa.'

The stairs creaked beneath Saul's weight and when he reached the landing he undressed swiftly and angrily. Wes said nothing until he heard the bed complain under the weight of his older brother.

'Saul . . . you won't really leave home? You won't go away?'

'You still awake, Wes? If you've been listening you'll know what's been said. It can't be unsaid now.'

'I don't want you to go, Saul. Neither does Ma. Nothing will be the same without you.'

'I'll miss you and Ma too, Wes. But that's the way it's got to be.'

'Pa will have calmed down by morning. He'll ask you to stay.'

'Don't wager anything on it, Wes. Have you ever known Pa to admit to anyone that he's wrong about anything? He'll never even admit it to himself – and certainly not to me. But go to sleep now. You've an early start in the morning.'

Wes lay in an unhappy silence for a long time before asking

7

quietly, 'Where will you go, Saul? Will you stay with Saranna and her ma?'

'I don't know either of them well enough for that, even though Pa thinks I do. Besides, their cottage belongs to our vicar. If he heard I was staying there he'd likely put them both out. Don't worry about me. I'll be all right. Go to sleep now.'

There was movement in Saul's bed as he turned over to face away from Wes.

From downstairs, the sound of voices came to Wes for a very long time. Wes heard his mother crying and was so unhappy he believed he would never sleep.

His last waking thought was that this was the worst night he could ever remember during his sixteen years of life in the tiny Tolpuddle cottage.

Chapter 2

Wes was awakened in the early morning by the sound of someone tapping with a long stick on the outside of the small landing window.

The window was standing open. Scrambling as quietly as he could from his bed, Wes hissed, 'All right, Arnold. I'm awake.'

He needed to repeat his statement three times, his voice becoming progressively louder before the knocking ceased and a slow voice from outside called cheerfully, 'I didn't think you'd sleep for long after my knocking!'

Arnold Cooper was a very simple soul.

As Wes dressed in the darkness, his mother made her way from the bedroom off the landing.

'I'm sorry if I woke you, Ma.'

'You didn't wake me. I've been lying awake the whole night.' As she reached the top stair Rachel Gillam added in a low voice, 'I'll let Arnold in. I left the fire banked up last thing. I'll boil a couple of eggs for you both before you go out.'

'I'll be all right, Ma. I don't need anything.'

'Of course you do! You can't go all the way to Dorchester on an empty belly – and Arnold certainly won't have had anything to eat.'

Arnold lived with an ageing grandmother who was as simple as himself. For much of the time he needed to take care of *her* wants.

When Wes had almost completed dressing, he heard a sound from Saul's bed.

'You awake, Saul?'

'I couldn't sleep even if I felt like it. Not with the noise you and Arnold made between you.'

'You've thought about things, Saul? You're not leaving today?'

'I've thought about everything, Wes, but I haven't changed my mind. I can't stay here. Pa thinks it's my fault I haven't found work. It isn't. I can do a day's work as well as anyone else when I'm given a chance, but no one will give me that chance. Time and time again I've been turned down when they learn I'm the son of Eli Gillam, the well-known Methodist preacher. The only way I'll

9

ever get work is to go right away from Tolpuddle. To where they've never heard of Pa.'

'What will you do for money?'

'Don't worry about me, young Wes, I'll get by. You stay here and take care of Ma – Pa too. One day he's going to learn that the Methodist Church can't stand up to the combined might of both landlord and the Church of England. He'll need you then.'

Wes rummaged beneath his bed and pulled a cloth from inside one of the shoes placed there. There was a dull jingling of coins as he emptied them from the cloth to his hand. He put one coin back then, after a moment's hesitation, added it to the others.

'Here, Saul. Take this. It's almost five guineas. It will keep you going for a while. I hope you'll find work before it's gone.'

'Are you sure, Wes? I'll pay you back one day.'

'That's all right.'

Wes tried to sound cheerful. Even though the money was all he had to show for five years of working.

'Come here, young brother.'

Saul Gillam hugged Wes to him roughly. 'You take care of yourself, you hear?'

'You, too. Let us know where you are, if you can. For Ma's sake.'

Wes clattered down the stairs before he made a fool of himself.

It was still dark when Arnold and Wes made their way from the Gillam cottage. In sharp contrast to Wes, Arnold was in a replete and happy mood.

'I like eggs.'

'So I noticed. You ate four.'

'We don't have 'em at home. Gran says chickens are more nuisance than they're worth.'

'Remind me to give you some eggs from home when we get back from Dorchester. Our hens are still in full lay and we've got more than we can sell.'

'I'd like that.'

They tramped along the narrow lane in silence for a few minutes before Arnold spoke again.

'How many of Widow Cake's pigs are we taking to market?'

'Three sows, the boar, and eighteen weaners.'

'The sows and weaners'll be no trouble. I'm not so sure about that old boar. He's a bad-tempered old sod.'

'That's why Widow Cake's getting rid of him. He ran her out of the pig-pen last week. Don't worry, we'll put a rope through his nose-ring and keep him tied inside the cart. He'll be no trouble to us, you'll see.'

They turned off the lane into a rough, rutted track that led to a small farm. The farm was owned by Thomas Priddy, the employer of Eli Gillam. He was loaning them a horse and high-sided cart to transport Widow Cake's pigs to Dorchester market.

The horse was old and had a tendency to bite but Wes successfully harnessed it, backing the animal between the shafts of the cart by the light of a cheap, spluttering candle. With Arnold sitting in the vehicle and Wes walking at the horse's head, they made their way through the still-sleeping village and beyond, to where Widow Cake had her cottage, surrounded by its own land, up the hill to the north of the small village.

The wagon had not been in use for many months and one of the wheels screeched with an ear-punishing noise that made Wes wince. The darkness about them amplified the sound. He was convinced they would bring every one of the three hundred or so inhabitants of Tolpuddle from his or her bed.

It still wanted half-an-hour to dawn, but Amelia Cake was waiting impatiently at her kitchen door. She launched into an immediate complaint about the 'tardiness of today's young men'.

'There's not one of you wouldn't rather lie abed than be up and about earning an honest shilling . . . Now I suppose you'll both be expecting me to give you breakfast before you begin work?' She held up a lantern as she spoke, peering at each young face in turn.

Arnold hesitated, tempted to say 'Yes', but Wes replied for both of them. 'No, thank you, Mrs Cake. My ma made breakfast for both of us before we set out. We'd have been here sooner but I don't think the horse has been worked for a long time. It took a while to harness up.'

'A likely story!' grumbled the widow. 'Well, don't waste time now you're here or everyone will have bought all they want by the time you get my pigs to the market.'

As Arnold had predicted, the boar proved the most difficult of the animals to load. Annoyed at being woken at such an early hour the irascible animal peered from tiny eyes, seeking someone, or something, on which to vent its bad temper. The only thing that came to view in the pale yellow light from the lantern was the pitchfork wielded by Wes in an attempt to pass one of the prongs through the ring in the animal's nose.

The boar brushed the fork aside time after time until Wes threw down the implement in disgust. Reaching out, he grasped the disgruntled animal by the tail. Outraged, the boar rounded on him, but this time Wes was the quicker of the two. In one swift movement he grasped the ring in the creature's nose.

The big boar squealed angrily, but although its body writhed in outrage, the animal kept its head still, aware of the pain any violent move would bring.

'Quick, Arnold, get that rope tied to the ring and we'll load it on the cart.'

'All right . . . but make sure you keep hold of him while I'm doing it.'

Arnold attached the rope and a few minutes later the large, ill-tempered animal was led up the ramp formed by the cart's tail-gate. Secured to the cart, the boar was boxed in by a couple of planks of wood.

Now it was the turn of the sows and the weaners to be loaded. Wes feared the squealing of the young pigs would bring men running from the village to find out what was wrong. One sow refused point-blank to enter the cart, but Arnold's great strength was brought into play. Cornering the two-hundred-pound animal, he lifted her bodily into the cart before the sow had time to recover from her surprise.

The remainder of the pigs behaved comparatively well and Wes breathed a sigh of relief when the tailgate was lifted to secure the animals.

Widow Cake had been highly critical of the two young men's efforts in loading the pigs and had gone into the house shortly before the last sow was loaded. She now reappeared bearing a small bundle, wrapped in a piece of muslin.

'Here's the bread and cheese I was going to give you for break-fast, together with a bit of fat bacon. You can eat it along the way – but be sure to bring the muslin back. If you don't I'll deduct it from your day's pay. And don't try to cheat me over the sale of the pigs or you'll find yourselves before the magistrate. Remember, I'll be checking up on you . . .'

Widow Amelia Cake was still threatening the dire conse-quences of dishonesty when the cart passed through the gateway. Soon her voice was lost in the squealing of the cart's ungreased axle and the noisy protests of the vehicle's load.

Chapter 3

Wes and Arnold said very little to each other for the first half-hour of the journey to Dorchester. For much of this time Arnold happily munched his way through the bread and cheese unexpectedly given to them by Widow Cake. Wes hardly noticed. He was sunk deep in thought about the situation at home and the effect that Saul's leaving would have on life there.

He knew his mother would be particularly hard hit. She loved her home and family, and was deeply distressed by the rift that had developed in recent months between Saul and his father. She had tried all in her power to head off their arguments, but there seemed to be a sad inevitability about it all. As though an ultimate clash of wills needed to happen.

Wes would also miss Saul desperately, although the two brothers were very different. Wes had an insatiable thirst for knowledge. He had learned to read at an early age and had borrowed books from anyone fortunate enough to possess them.

Saul, on the other hand, was wise in the hurly-burly of everyday life. Practical and tough, he had come to Wes's rescue on more than one occasion when others would have bullied him for his lack of worldliness.

Eli Gillam had always hoped his bright younger son would find his future as a minister in the Methodist Church. But Wes had little interest in the religion that was so much a part of his father's life. He much preferred discussing with Saul the implications of the Trades Associations that were springing up in the industrial towns to the north.

Saul was scornful of book learning, but he was knowledgeable about the growing calls for parliamentary reform that were sweeping the country. He believed the working men of England should be given more say in the running of their country.

'There's still a piece of cheese left. Do you want it?' Guiltily Arnold held up a small portion of tooth-marked cheese.

Soft grey light was seeping into the sky to the east and Wes could see greed in conflict with more generous emotions in Arnold's expression.

'You have it. The breakfast Ma gave us has set me up for the morning.'

The cheese disappeared into Arnold's mouth before Wes finished speaking.

'Thank you, Wes,' he mumbled past the cheese. Swallowing hurriedly, he added: 'How much money do you think we'll get for the pigs?'

'Depends on the market. Probably not more than four-and-six or five shillings a score for the sows – say two pounds each if we're lucky. We might get a shilling or two more for the boar. He's a pretty good one. The weaners should fetch four or five shillings apiece.'

'How much is that altogether?' Arnold looked at Wes, his expression revealing the awe he felt for those able to count in such figures.

'We should return to Tolpuddle with something between ten and twelve pounds for Widow Cake.'

Arnold's awed whistle blew an errant crumb from his lip. 'That's a fortune! More than I'll ever earn in all my life!'

Wes smiled. 'Not quite, Arnold. How much does Widow Cake pay you now?'

'A shilling a day.'

Wes received the same sum from their employer, but he worked for six days a week. Arnold was employed only on a casual basis.

'Then by working every day for a full year you'd earn more than that.' Talking to Arnold was a way of shaking off the gloom of his own thoughts and Wes asked: 'What would you do with such money?'

'I'd marry Mary Riggs.'

Arnold replied so swiftly and positively that Wes turned to look at him. Mary was a warm and generous young girl, much liked in the village where she lived and worked.

'Have you and Mary talked about this?'

Arnold coloured up and nodded. He had replied to Wes automatically. He wished now he had thought before speaking. He was *always* wishing he had paused to think before speaking.

'I haven't ever said anything to anyone else. Neither has Mary.'

'Well, you're a dark horse and no mistake, Arnold.' Wes grinned at his companion's discomfiture. 'Don't worry, your secret's safe with me – and I'm very pleased for both of you. Now, will you go back and check that the boar's tied up safely. He seems to be hammering about a bit . . .'

They were encountering more market traffic now. Horses; wagons; herdsmen and shepherds with their charges. All were

14

converging on Dorchester for the last big market of the year.

This was primarily for the sale of animals. Had it been the beginning of the year there would have been almost as many young men and girls as animals. Standing about in self-conscious groups, they would hope to hire themselves out for whatever tasks a prospective employer had in store for them.

But this was autumn. Always a bad time of the year for work, it had been made far worse in recent years. New machines had been developed to take on the arduous but hitherto well-paid task of threshing. It was a state of affairs that was causing increasing anger among the farm labourers who saw their families going hungry. Such agricultural progress benefited only those who had never known want.

Soon they reached Dorchester. Here the roads were so busy Wes needed to concentrate on the job in hand.

The animals exhibited for sale were all in the one long street, grouped according to species. There were many cattle on offer, but at this time of the year they were more likely to be bought by a Dorset butcher than by a farmer. Money would need to be spent to feed them on a farm during the long winter months that lay ahead – and there was little money to spare in the rural communities.

There was the occasional bull here, past its prime and unlikely to fetch much money. Interspersed among the larger animals were sheep, chickens, and ungainly complaining ducks. There were also pigs – and today these were in great demand, fat pigs in particular. Salted or smoked, a pig was enough to keep a household in meat for the winter months. Even the weaners would have put on sufficient weight by Christmas to satisfy the most greedy family – and still leave enough meat to sell at a profit.

Yet prospective buyers were cautious. They passed slowly along the whole row of pig-sellers, selecting carefully before commencing their bargaining.

While Arnold remained in line to have the sows and a weaner weighed by the official weigher, Wes went around the various vendors in order to get an idea of the selling price. He was pleasantly surprised to learn they were averaging five shillings and sixpence a score weight – and sellers were not accepting offers less than five shillings. Hurrying back to Arnold, Wes was in time to help with the weighing and pay the required fee before finding a place for the cart among the other prospective sellers.

Wes's first sale was a good one. Ten weaners were sold for three pounds. This was quickly followed by the sale of the largest sow, after some hard bargaining, for two pounds, twelve and sixpence.

Not long afterwards a gentleman came along accompanied by a

labourer who seemed to know a great deal about pigs. They were very interested in the boar. In answer to the gentleman's questions, Wes assured him the boar was: 'In his prime and had never been known to sire less than ten in a litter.'

'I'll give you two pounds for him.'

Wes's indignation was not feigned. 'I've just sold a sow for more than that, sir. This boar's worth more than a fiver. I couldn't let him go for less.'

'Here. Look at this. This is one of his piglets. Ain't that a beauty?'

Arnold lifted a wriggling weaner and held it up close to the gentleman's face.

A look of irritation was the reply, but when he realised Arnold was somewhat simple the gentleman increased his offer to Wes by a full pound.

He eventually sold the boar to the man for four pounds after another prospective customer came upon the scene and expressed an interest in the irascible beast.

Paying Wes the money, the man said, 'I hope he's as fine a breeding boar as you say, that's all. I'll send a couple of men to take him away before the end of the market. I'll have a receipt too, if you please. Make it out to Lord Chideock.'

By noon, Wes had twelve pounds two shillings and sixpence in the soft leather purse he carried in his pocket. He still had a sow and eight weaners to sell but was confident they would go before the day was over. He was well satisfied with the day's business. Taking sixpence from the bag, he handed it to Arnold. 'Go and buy us two threepenny pies. Even Widow Cake can't begrudge us that after what we've made for her today.'

Impressed by Wes's extravagance, Arnold went off to buy the pies. He had not been gone for more than a few minutes when a young girl wandered along the line of carts offering pigs for sale. About Wes's own age, she was slim, dark-haired and dark-eyed.

She stopped at the cart containing Widow Cake's pigs for longer than she had at the other carts and Wes wondered at her interest. She did not appear to be a buyer. She was an attractive young girl, although on closer inspection it was apparent that her print dress was faded with age. It had also been let out at the seams on more than one occasion. The dress was far too small and bore evidence of having been repaired here and there. She was also barefooted. This was not unusual in the countryside, but most people put on shoes to attend a market in town.

Looking up from her examination of the pigs, the girl ignored the curiosity she saw in Wes's gaze. 'How much are your weaners?'

'I've just sold ten for three pounds. That makes them six shillings each.'

'*Six shillings!* That's downright robbery! I'll give you two shillings for the one with a black mark on its back.'

Wes had already singled out the weaner with a black mark as being the best of those remaining in the cart. He shook his head, 'Why don't you ask right out for me to *give* it to you?' Looking from her dark eyes to her bare and dirty feet, he added, 'Are you a gipsy girl?'

'No – but what if I were? Would you offer me a weaner in return for taking me to the alley behind the Antelope Inn? Isn't that where men take their whores on market days?'

'I wouldn't know.' Wes was embarrassed by the down-to-earth bluntness of the barefoot girl.

The girl saw the colour flare up on Wes's cheeks and said suddenly, 'All right. Give me the weaner now and you can take me down the alley – but you'll need to wait until dark. I'll not lift my skirt in broad daylight for anyone.'

Still scarlet-faced, Wes managed a grin. 'By nightfall I'll be sitting at home. If I give you the weaner I've no doubt you will be too, and having a good laugh at my foolishness.'

The girl shrugged indifferently. 'Please yourself. You're not the only one in the market offering pigs for sale, you know.'

As she walked away Wes thought he could detect disappointment in the way she carried herself. She had probably come to Dorchester especially to buy a weaner. On many recent market days two shillings would probably have been sufficient. There would have been few days in recent years when prices had been so high.

The girl paused by a group of three rough-looking men not far away. At first Wes thought she was talking to them. Then he realised she was looking in a cart close to where the men were standing. Probably inspecting more pigs.

Unexpectedly the girl turned around and returned to where Wes stood.

'Hello, again.' He grinned cheerfully at her. 'Have you come to increase your offer – either of them?'

'I'm here to do you a favour – although I don't know why I'm bothering. Have you taken a lot of money today?'

Wes frowned. 'What's that to do with you?'

'Nothing at all – but those three men over there seem to think you're worth robbing. The one with the red neckerchief is a pickpocket. He'll steal your purse and pass it on to one of the others straightaway. Then, if he's caught, there'll be nothing to prove it was him.'

Having imparted this startling information, the girl walked away before Wes could gather his wits together sufficiently to make a reply.

He looked towards the three men. They were rough-looking characters of a type that roamed the countryside in great numbers. Sleeping wherever nightfall found them, they survived by begging or stealing. Since the end of the war with Napoleon many ex-soldiers and -sailors had been reduced to tramping the roads of England. Few had any prospect of employment. Most discovered they were unwanted in parishes where their names had once been spoken of with pride.

Eli Gillam had brought his family up to regard such men with compassion and Wes was not convinced the girl had overheard their conversation accurately. Nevertheless, the men were still talking together and it seemed to him they were deliberating avoiding looking in his direction.

At that moment Arnold returned with two huge pies, beaming in anticipation of the unexpected feast.

Before Arnold could say anything, Wes removed the money bag from his pocket. Keeping his large and slow-thinking companion between himself and the three men, Wes swiftly stuffed the bag inside Arnold's shirt.

'I want you to take care of this for a while, Arnold. I don't know the truth of it, but I've been told that three men are planning to try to steal it from me. Don't look around now, but it's the three men standing near the grey horse, behind you. I believe the smaller of the three – the one with the red neckerchief – will try to do the stealing. Stay close to me and keep a watch on what's going on.'

For a few moments Arnold was so excited he forgot about his pie – but only for a few moments. The aroma of cooked beef and flavoursome gravy escaping from Wes's pie as he bit into it drove all other thoughts from the head of the simple young lad.

Halfway through his pie, Arnold looked up and stopped chewing.

'They've gone!' he said, speaking past a mouthful of pie crust.

'Good!' Wes too was enjoying the rare treat provided by the meat pie. 'I thought that girl might have got it wrong.'

The words were hardly out of his mouth when there was a sudden commotion nearby. The crowd parted and two men emerged. Quarrelling violently, it seemed they were about to come to blows.

It took a few moments for Wes to realise the quarrelling men were two of the three vagrants pointed out to him by the girl. Before he had time to consider the reason for their actions there was a loud shout from Arnold.

Wes turned around to see Arnold with his arms wrapped around the third vagrant, lifting the man clear of the ground.

'It happened just like you said it would, Wes. While you was watching the other two this one came up behind you and had his hand in your pocket. You didn't even feel him doing it, did you?'

'It's a lie. I was just walking past, minding my own business when I was grabbed. I ain't done nothing. Ah!' The man's protest ended in a painful gasp as Arnold tightened his grip.

'We'll call the constable and see whose story he believes, shall we?'

'Don't do that, young sir, I beg you.' The vagrant's bluster disappeared. 'I'm an old wounded soldier fallen on hard times, that's all. It won't happen again, I promise you.'

'It won't happen again if you're transported,' said Wes, uncompromisingly.

'It won't be transportation or the hulks for me, this time. It'll be the gallows for certain. You wouldn't do that to me, young sir. Say you wouldn't.'

Wes had come to Dorchester to sell Widow Cake's pigs. He had no wish to involve himself in the trial of a man for attempted pickpocketing. All the same . . .

The decision was taken out of his hands. The would-be thief suddenly wriggled free. The next moment he was literally running for his life through the crowded market place, scattering men, women and children before him.

'You deliberately let him go.' Wes voiced the accusation to Arnold.

'Well . . .' Arnold shifted his weight from foot to foot, uncomfortably. 'He didn't take nothing. Would *you* have seen him hang for nothing more than putting his hand in your pocket?'

'You're too soft-hearted, Arnold. But you're right. We couldn't see him hang. Come on now, we've still got a pig and eight weaners left to sell.'

Wes saw the girl passing through the crowd about half-an-hour after the incident with the pickpocket and he called to her.

'Have you bought yourself a pig yet?'

'No.'

'If you still want the weaner with the black spot, she's yours for two shillings.'

Stopping before him, the girl said suspiciously, 'If you're thinking of meeting me in the alleyway after dark, you'd better forget it. I won't be there.'

Wes grinned. 'Neither will I. No, you've saved me from having all the money I'd taken stolen. If the pigs were mine I'd give you

19

the weaner, but Widow Cake would take me before a magistrate if I did.'

A few minutes later Wes was adding two shillings to his bag of takings and the delighted girl was disappearing into the crowd clutching the protesting young pig.

Only when she had disappeared from view did Wes realise he had not asked her name, or where she was from.

Chapter 4

The market day at Dorchester had been a great success. Prices had fallen away a little during the afternoon, but Wes managed to sell the remainder of Widow Cake's pigs. He was returning to Tolpuddle with seventeen pounds, four shillings and sixpence for the widow. It was far more than he had expected to make.

Some of Wes's pleasure disappeared when Widow Cake took the money he had made and asked him suspiciously whether he had kept any back for himself and Arnold.

'I've given you more than half-as-much again as I expected the pigs to fetch at market – but, yes, I did keep some back. I spent sixpence on two meat pies. One for me and the other for Arnold.'

'Why did you need to buy pies? I gave you bread, cheese and fat bacon before you left here this morning. You shouldn't have needed anything more to eat.'

'We were hungry. Arnold had eaten the bread and cheese by the time we reached Dorchester. If we'd waited until we both got home we'd have gone more than twelve hours without food.'

Angry with his employer's meanness, Wes turned away and spoke to her over his shoulder. 'Arnold will stay and do anything that needs to be done. I need to return the horse and cart before dark. It's Sunday tomorrow. I'll be here to feed the animals and read the Bible to you.'

'Are you so rich now that you are happy to go home before you've been paid wages for your day's work? Here, take this – and don't be late in the morning. There's no pigs to be fed, but there's the chickens, and the ducks . . .'

She put money into Wes's hand, and then passed some to Arnold.

'There are *two* shillings here.' Arnold said, looking at the money he held in his hand. At the same time Wes realised she had given him *three* shillings. It was much more than their usual daily rate.

'If you don't want it you can give it back. You've made five pounds more than I was expecting, so we'll all go to bed happy tonight. Mind you, with the pigs gone there'll be less work to do

21

about the place. I'll need to consider cutting your pay.'

Walking home, after returning the cart and stabling the horse, Wes jingled the coins in his pocket happily. He wondered whether he should have said anything to Widow Cake about selling one of her weaners to the girl in the market for two shillings. He decided he had been right to say nothing.

The Gillam cottage was not a happy place without Saul and the manner of his leaving had placed a strain upon the family. Rachel blamed her husband for driving her elder son away. Eli, for his part, refused to acknowledge any responsibility for the behaviour of his wayward son.

The morning after the market was a Sunday and Eli set out at dawn to begin his long circuit of the Methodist churches, carrying out the Lord's work.

Wes was sitting at the table eating his breakfast when his father left the house. As Rachel Gillam watched her husband walk along the garden path to the gate, she tangled her hands in her pinafore in anguish.

'What's happening to our family, Wes? I wish I knew where our Saul is. What do you think he's doing?'

'He's only been gone for a day, Ma. I doubt if he's had time to do anything yet.'

'Do you think so, Wes? Perhaps he's changed his mind about leaving home. If he's not gone very far he might be staying at Southover, with that Vye girl.'

'I don't think so, Ma. I spoke to him about her before he left. I'm pretty certain he doesn't know her as well as you and Pa believe.'

'He wouldn't tell *you* if he was going to stay with her! He'd know I'd find out, sooner or later – and so would your father. They might have fallen out, but Saul wouldn't intentionally upset him in such a way.'

Wes did not agree with her. Saul and his father had been locked in bitter argument for months. Matters had reached the stage where neither of them would make any attempt to avoid hurting the feelings of the other. But Wes kept his silence.

'Will you go to Southover when you're done at Widow Cake's, Wes? See if our Saul is there and ask him to return home?'

It hurt him to see his mother pleading in such a manner, but he would be doing her no favour if he allowed her to hold out false hopes.

'Ma, I really don't believe Saul is there. He'll be farther away than that by now.'

'*Please*, Wes. For me?'

22

He wiped his plate clean with the last scrap of bread, and sighed. 'All right, Ma, if that's what you want. I'll go to Southover when I'm through at Widow Cake's.'

'What's the matter with you this morning, Wesley Gillam? If I didn't know different I could be forgiven for thinking that Bible you're reading from is written in a foreign language. What's the matter with you, boy? What's on your mind? Is something wrong at home?'

Dressed in her Sunday clothes, Widow Cake sat in her armchair beside the fire. Although she no longer attended the Tolpuddle church, she always wore her Sunday best on the Sabbath.

'Do you hear me, Wesley? I asked you what's troubling you? Your mind isn't on the word of the Lord, that's quite certain.'

'It's nothing, Widow Cake. I'll try to concentrate more.'

'Don't tell me it's nothing. You've a face that would turn cream sour. Reading the Bible and not making a word of sense of what you're reading is worse than not reading it at all. Is it that brother of yours?'

Wes's start of surprise gave Widow Cake the answer to her question.

'I thought so. He was seen leaving the village yesterday with a bag of his belongings on his shoulder.'

'Which way did he go? Was he heading towards Southover?'

'I don't know which way he was going, only what I've been told. But from the size of bag he was said to be carrying I'd say he was going a sight farther than Southover ... And he wasn't alone, you know.'

'Who was with him? Saranna Vye?'

'I don't know any Saranna Vye. Your brother went off with Jonathan Galton. There's a pair for trouble, if ever there was one. Your father may preach of the peace of the Lord in his Methodist chapels, young Wesley, but there's precious little of it been passed on to that brother of yours.'

'Saul is all right. If he'd been able to get work he'd have settled down as well as anyone else.' Wes repeated the excuse he had heard his mother give for Saul over the years.

'I wouldn't expect you to say anything else, you being his brother. All I can say is I'm glad *I'm* not his poor mother, that's all.'

Widow Cake took the large leather-bound Bible from his hands and lovingly opened the front cover. Inside were recorded the births and deaths of five generations of her family. She could not read, yet she knew the names and details written here by heart.

Looking at the writing for a while, she closed the book again.

'But I'm nobody's mother. Mine is the last name that will go in this Bible. Put it back on the shelf where it belongs, then you can go. It's been a poor reading today, and no mistake. I might just as well have gone to one of those Methodist chapels where your father preaches. I can't abide them white-washed walls, and I prefer to have a man of learning preaching me a sermon, but at least I'd have had a decent reading from the Bible.'

Chapter 5

The cottage where Saranna Vye lived with her mother stood beside a muddy and ill-maintained lane on the side of Southover farthest from Tolpuddle. The cottage was in no better condition than the lane. Its thatch was sagging and ragged, while the woodwork around doors and windows was unpainted and rotting away. A profusion of flowers grew in front of the house, but the remainder of the garden was tangled and neglected.

Wes knocked on the open front door. When no one answered, he stepped inside. Compared to the outside of the cottage it was surprisingly clean. There were even a couple of small threadbare mats on the hard-packed dirt floor. He called up the stairs, but still no one replied.

He was walking round the house to the kitchen door when he heard the squealing of a young pig. The sound was coming from the far end of the tangled garden. Then he heard a girl's voice, talking coaxingly.

Heading towards the source of the sounds, he was in time to see a girl shooing a pig into a sty that was even more dilapidated than the cottage. The girl had her back to him. When the pig was safely inside the sty, she pulled a broken gate to and fastened it as best she could with a piece of rope.

'That's not going to keep a pig in for long . . .'

Wes's comment came to an abrupt end as the girl turned around to face him. He had met her in Dorchester market the previous day.

It was the girl who had bought one of Widow Cake's weaners from him for two shillings!

Each looked at the other in amazement for some moments. Suddenly blood rushed to the girl's cheeks. 'What are you doing here? If it's because of what I said I'd do if you let me have the weaner cheap, you'd better go away again – and quick! My . . . my father's in the house. He's big man with a violent temper. If you don't leave right away I'll call him.'

'If you're Saranna Vye, I know you're lying. Your father was lost in the war against Napoleon – and there's no one in the

25

house. I know because I went inside and called. You're here on your own.'

The girl looked about her quickly and Wes gained the uncomfortable impression she was looking for an improvised weapon with which to drive him off the premises.

'My being here has nothing to do with the pig. I didn't know you and Saranna Vye were the same person. I came to see if my brother was here, or if you have any idea where he's gone.'

Saranna still appeared uncertain of him. 'Why should I know where your brother is? Who are you?'

'Wes Gillam.'

'You're Wes Gillam? Saul's brother? He's spoken about you often. He says you're the brainy one of the family. But Saul's not here. Our landlord is Reverend Warren of Tolpuddle. I expect you know him? He'd throw us out if we took in the son of such a well-known Methodist preacher as your father. We couldn't risk that. We had too long without a roof over our heads.'

'But . . . Saul's spent a lot of his time here with you. He told us so himself. It was the cause of many of the arguments he had with Pa. Pa doesn't think . . .'

Wes broke off in sudden confusion, but Saranna completed the sentence for him. 'Your pa doesn't think I'm suitable company for the son of a pious Methodist preacher. Well, hadn't *you* better be getting off home, Wesley Gillam, before he learns you've spent a few minutes with me?'

'Pa and me don't argue the way he and Saul did. It doesn't alter the fact that Saul himself told me he came here often.'

'He came visiting, yes – but not always to see me or Ma. He came most often when Uncle Richard was here.'

'Why should he come to visit your uncle and tell everyone he was visiting you?'

'Because my uncle is Richard Pemble, the Trades Association organiser, from Kent. He's not my real uncle, he was a soldier in the army with my father, in Spain. Now he's going around the country trying to bring all the Friendly Societies and Trades Associations together in one huge movement. He would talk with Saul and some of the other young men from the village about starting a Friendly Society, or a Union for Farm Labourers, here in Dorset.'

'I've heard of Richard Pemble. Didn't he used to be a Wesleyan lay preacher?'

'He still is.'

'You're right about my pa's reaction had he known Saul was coming here to see *him*. I've heard him say that Richard Pemble should be banned from every Methodist church in the country.

26

Pa thinks your uncle's a rabble-rouser, stirring up trouble for other Methodists.'

'And Uncle Richard says that men like your father are "land-owner's lackeys". He says it's a preacher's duty to stand up for the rights of working men. To make them see they're entitled to a fair day's pay for a good day's work.'

'That's what Saul said to Pa many times. Now I know where it came from! It didn't go down well in our house, I can tell you. But . . . do you know what Saul's doing now? Has he told you where he's heading?'

'He came to the house and spoke to Ma when I was at Dorchester yesterday. He's heading for Kent, with one of his friends from Tolpuddle. They've gone to find Uncle Richard.'

'Why?'

'Saul said he wants to help him in whatever he's doing.'

'How will he do that? Saul's no great speaker – or even a deep thinker. He's strong and determined and there's no one tougher, but he's too easily led to be able to persuade others to do what he says.'

'Uncle Richard isn't looking for men to do any thinking for him, or tell others what to do. He's far too fond of doing that for himself. He wants men like Saul, who'll do exactly what he tells them, without thinking too much about it.'

'Saul doesn't think too much about anything he's supposed to, but he's not the best person in the world for doing what he's told.'

'That's what I think, but Uncle Richard doesn't want to hear the opinions of others. He'll just have to learn it for himself.'

'That's all very well for Richard Pemble. If they fall out it's our Saul who'll be a long way from his home and family, not your uncle.'

'Do you always run around looking after your brother? I'd have thought he's big enough to take care of himself.' Saranna spoke mockingly and Wes found her scornful expression hard to face.

'Saul doesn't need anyone to run around after him – but it's no good telling our ma that. He left home after a big row with Pa. She asked me to come here to see if he was staying with you.'

'Well, he's not.'

Wes thought he had seldom met a girl so naturally aggressive as Saranna Vye. 'Do you have an address in Kent for Richard Pemble?'

'No. I don't think Ma has, either.' Saranna's manner softened a little. 'You can wait and ask her for yourself, if you like. She helps with the cooking at Reverend Warren's house on a Sunday, but she should be home in an hour or so.'

Wes shook his head. 'It doesn't really matter. Kent will seem as far away as the moon to Ma. I'll just tell her Saul has gone to find work with your uncle. If ever there's an urgent need to find out any more, I'll know where to come.'

He nodded to where the weaner had its nose through the gap between the sty gate and the post that held it. Both gate and post were shaking alarmingly. 'If you don't fix that sty you're going to lose your two-shilling pig.'

'She's already got out twice. I've tried to fix the gate but I can't.' She looked at him hopefully. 'I don't suppose you could fix it for me? I'll make you a cup of tea while you're doing it . . . It's good tea. Ma gets all the used tea leaves from the vicarage.'

Saranna Vye's arrogance of a few minutes earlier had been replaced with the wheedling tone of voice used in Dorchester the day before, when she was trying to persuade Wes to sell the pig to her.

Remembering that occasion and aware she was trying to use her charm on him, he said mischievously, 'You made a much more interesting offer yesterday, when you wanted to buy the pig. Isn't it just as important to you to want to keep her?'

'I've already told you, I never intended keeping that part of the bargain. If that's the sort of person you are then you needn't bother, Wesley Gillam. I'll find someone else to fix it for me, don't you worry.'

Wes thought the high colour in Saranna's cheeks made her look even more attractive than usual, but he realised his comment had not been taken as the joke he'd intended.

'I'll fix it for you – for a cup of tea. Do you have any tools?'

There was an outhouse with a door as ricketty as the pig-sty gate. It contained a number of ancient tools. Most were either rusty or broken, but by using a broken-handled sledge-hammer Wes was able to secure the gate post and improvise a temporary hinge in place of one that was patently beyond repair.

When the task was completed, he sat on the ground holding the cup of weak tea Saranna had made for him. She sat on a nearby stone that had once been part of a farm roller, nursing a metal cup.

'Do you work anywhere?' Wes asked the girl.

'No. I worked for a while in the kitchen up at the vicarage at Affpuddle, but the vicar's son couldn't keep his hands to himself. After I'd scratched his face when he cornered me in the scullery, he had me dismissed.'

She shrugged. 'We're hard up, but not *that* hard up.'

When he had finished his tea, Wes said, 'You really do need a new hinge for that gate. I think there's an old one at Widow Cake's – that's where I work. They were her pigs I was selling in Dorchester yesterday. I'll ask her for the hinge and come over and fit it for you next Sunday, if you'd like me to?'

Saranna hesitated before saying, 'All right.'

Walking home from Southover, Wes found he was thinking far more about Saranna than he was about the main purpose of his visit to the Vye cottage.

He had a feeling that Saranna did not trust him and was surprised to find it mattered to him. He also believed she was misunderstood by men like his own father.

Saranna Vye was a girl who had been brought up without a father. She and her mother were living in as much poverty as anyone he knew and life had not been easy for them. While they were drinking their tea Saranna had told him that her mother had worked in the house of an army officer wounded in France. The officer's home was close to London. When he died the house had been left to a cousin who promptly turned Saranna and her mother out on to the streets.

Wandering the countryside, they had tried for a year to obtain work. Then they had been picked up by a magistrate and sent back to the parish that was considered to be their home, as required by the laws of the land.

Fortunately, a farmer at Southover was the father of a man who had died in Spain during the same battle that claimed Saranna's father's life. The two men had been friends since childhood. He gave Saranna's mother work in the house and she also helped out in the dairy.

The vicar of Tolpuddle, the Reverend Warren, allowed her to live in the old cottage he owned in exchange for a day's work from her on Sundays and an occasional evening when he was entertaining.

Wes thought about Saranna's positive manner. It had probably been brought about by the fact that both she and her mother were natural targets for unscrupulous men. She had probably learned the hard way that being too trusting was a mistake she could not afford.

She had already showed him that she would take no nonsense and it seemed to him Saranna Vye had earned a reputation that was totally unjustified. Had his father met her for himself and not relied upon gossip, he might not have objected quite so strongly to his eldest son visiting the Southover cottage.

Wes dismissed the thought with an unconscious shrug of his shoulders. Once something was implanted in his father's mind it was well-nigh impossible to prise it out again. Besides, he and Saul were two of a kind. If they resolved their differences about Saranna Vye then they would no doubt have found something else about which to argue.

Of more immediate interest to him was finding out just how

friendly Saul and Saranna had really been. He suspected they might have been closer than Saranna had led him to believe.

Chapter 6

When Wes arrived for work at Widow Cake's cottage the next morning there was no sign of his employer, but he was not concerned. On days when her arthritis was particularly troublesome it sometimes took her an hour or more to get out of bed and put on her clothes. On such mornings she was particularly bad-tempered and he had learned from experience to keep out of her way.

After releasing and feeding the hens and ducks and cleaning out their houses, he made his way back to the shed beside the house where the tools were kept. A hedge at the far end of the hay meadow needed trimming and re-laying. If his employer was in a bad mood it would be a good place to be working.

There was still no sound from the cottage when Wes emerged from the shed carrying the tools. He frowned. Widow Cake was exceptionally tardy today. Even on a bad morning she could usually be heard clattering pans in the kitchen by this time, complaining to no one in particular about her many aches and pains.

He was carrying a billhook, pruning-knife and sharpening stone. Placing them on the path, he made his way around the cottage to the back of the house. Here he found the kitchen window standing open.

There had been a little rain in the night and when Wes looked inside he could see small pools of water on the window-sill inside the room. For the first time, Wes became concerned for Widow Cake. It was not like her to leave a window open when there was the likelihood of rain. The widow was also so fussy she would have wiped up any rain that entered through an open window, the moment it was found.

'Are you up and about, Mrs Cake?' Wes shouted through the open kitchen window.

When he received no reply, he made his way to the front door. He intended calling the same question up the stairs, which rose from the entrance hall, but the door opened only a couple of inches. Something was behind it. Something heavy . . .

Hurrying back to the kitchen, Wes climbed through the window and made his way through the house to the front door. He immediately found the reason why the door would not open. Widow Cake was lying on the floor behind the door.

At first, West thought she was dead. Apprehensively, he stooped over her. He was greatly relieved to see her breast rising and falling in time with her shallow breathing.

She was lying on a cold, stone floor and, gripping her beneath the armpits, Wes pulled her to the kitchen. Here he laid her on the rug in front of the fireplace. It was the best he could do. Widow Cake was a stoutly-built woman and far too heavy for him to lift to the settle in her best downstairs room.

He could see now she had a cut on her head, just above the hairline. The blood had dried, but it looked ugly. She felt cold too. Lighting a fire would warm the kitchen, but that would take time. Hurrying upstairs, a part of the house where he had never been before, Wes saw a bedroom door open. The bed showed signs of having been slept in, so it registered with him that she could not have lain unconscious for the whole night. Taking a blanket and patchwork eiderdown from the bed, he carried them downstairs and placed them over Amelia Cake.

He was in a quandary now about what to do. His mother would know, but the Gillam cottage was some distance away, in Tolpuddle itself. He did not like to leave Widow Cake for so long. However, he could do nothing more here.

Hurrying from the house to the lane outside, the first person Wes saw was Charles Hammer, the village constable. He was leading a ribby, sway-back stray horse in the direction of the village, no doubt heading for the pound.

After listening in frowning concentration to Wes's garbled and excited description of what he had found in the cottage, the constable said, 'Where's Widow Cake now?'

'Lying on the carpet in the kitchen, still unconscious.'

'I'd better go and have a look. Take this horse to the pound for me, then go off and find Magistrate Frampton at Moreton House. Tell him what's happened and say I'm looking into it.'

'But Moreton House is four miles from here! Shouldn't I fetch someone to have a look at Widow Cake to see how bad she's hurt?'

'There's not a doctor between here and Dorchester. She could be dead by the time he arrived. Go and fetch Magistrate Frampton, he'll know what should be done. Ride the horse there, if you want to. It might as well be doing something useful as eating good hay in the paddock. Off you go now – and be quick. I'll take charge of things here.'

Wes had less confidence in the ability of Charles Hammer to

32

'take care of things' than the constable had in himself. Before setting off to Moreton House he called in to see his mother and told her what was happening.

Rachel Gillam had her arms immersed to the elbows in a washing tub but she immediately began drying them. 'You get off to Moreton House,' she said to her son. 'Charles Hammer is a fool, but he's not a man to cross. I'll go on up to Widow Cake's cottage and see if there's anything I can do for her. Off you go now.'

Moreton House was a grand mansion to the south of Tolpuddle. Standing beside the River Frome, it was approached by a long curving drive.

The house itself was large and four-square and Wes pulled up the plodding, head-drooping horse halfway along the driveway, suddenly unsure of himself. He was hesitant about going boldly up to the impressive front door, but felt his message was too important to pass on to a servant.

'Who are you? What do you want? Have you come to see my grandfather?'

The voice of a young girl startled him. She was seated on a swing hanging from a branch on the far side of a huge tree, set in the midst of shrubs and surrounded by lawns. Preoccupied with his errand, Wes had not seen her, but he was relieved to find someone who might help him with his dilemma.

'I've come to speak to Magistrate Frampton.'

'That's my grandfather. Does he employ you? If so you should address me as Miss Josephine. He'll be very cross if you don't.'

'I don't work for Magistrate Frampton.' The young girl was probably no more than fifteen years old and Wes tried not to allow the arrogance in her voice to influence the manner of his own reply. 'I've come with an urgent message for him, from Constable Hammer of Tolpuddle.'

'It can't be so terribly urgent if you rode here on *that* animal.' Josephine Frampton looked disdainfully at Wes's saddleless mount. 'You'd have probably arrived sooner had you walked.'

'Do you know where I can find Magistrate Frampton?' asked Wes, stiffly. He had thought he cut quite a dash riding through the countryside on a horse.

'No,' said the girl unhelpfully as she pushed with her feet to set the swing into motion once more. 'Go to the servants' quarters, at the rear of the house. They might know. There again, they might not.' Swinging back and forth, she turned her face away from him.

There was a hitching post at the front of the house, but Wes thought it inadvisable to tie the horse there. He led it around the side of the house. Before he reached the kitchen door a sash window was raised on the ground floor and a man looked out.

'You there! Boy! Where d'you think you're going, eh?'

'I've been sent from Tolpuddle by Constable Hammer to find Magistrate Frampton, sir.'

From the manner of the man at the window, Wes was fairly certain he had found the man he was seeking. The man's next words confirmed his belief.

'I'm Magistrate Frampton. What's it all about?'

Pulling the horse away from the grass of the immaculate lawn, Wes explained, 'I went to work this morning and found Widow Cake lying on the floor of her house. She's unconscious and has a nasty gash on her head.'

'So? The woman probably had a fall or something.'

'That's what I think, sir, even though the kitchen window was wide open. But I believe Constable Hammer suspects someone got into the house and attacked her.'

'Does he now? Well, that's entirely another matter. Very well. Go back to Tolpuddle. I'll come there as soon as I can. Where does this Widow Cake live?'

After giving the magistrate directions to the widow's cottage, Wes turned to return the way he had come, but Magistrate Frampton called to him once again.

'Boy!'

'Yes, sir?'

'Not the front way. Use the servants' gate, at the back of the house. Remember it if ever you need to come here again.'

'Yes, sir.'

As Wes was leading the dejected horse along the servants' path to the gate, the girl he had last seen on the swing suddenly emerged from the bushes and stepped on to the path in front of him. Her unexpected appearance startled the horse. Showing more energy than it had at any time during the journey from Tolpuddle to Moreton, the animal jerked its head violently, pulling the bridle rope free from Wes's hand.

As the horse looked for a way of escape, Wes called to the girl, 'Don't let it get past you!'

'Only if you say, "Please, Miss Josephine". Go on, say it, boy.'

'I haven't got time for your silly games . . .'

Wes advanced cautiously towards the horse which was looking about uncertainly. He had almost reached the animal when Josephine suddenly snatched off her bonnet and flapped it violently.

It was all the nervous animal needed. Swerving past Wes it ran back the way it had just come, but this time it left the gravel path. Cantering across the smooth green lawn beside the house, it left hoof-sized pot-holes in its wake.

Wes ran after the animal, expecting at any minute to hear Magistrate Frampton bellowing at him from the window where he had appeared earlier. But the only sound was the laughter of Josephine Frampton.

The unexpected burst of energy displayed by the horse lasted only until it reached the far boundary of the lawn. When a breathless Wes caught up with it, the animal was busily cropping the short, rich grass.

As he gripped the bridle rope, Wes looked back. His stomach churned at the sight of the hoof-deep tracks across the otherwise immaculate lawn. For a moment or two he toyed with the idea of returning to inform Magistrate Frampton of the incident.

He decided against such a course of action. He had only met the magistrate once, but James Frampton had not impressed Wes as being the most tolerant and understanding of men. Besides, to do so would have meant leading the horse back across the lawn and increasing the damage already caused. Better to leave well alone and put off the inevitable confrontation.

Wes rode away from the house via the main entrance. Using the servants' gate would have meant passing the house – and possibly meeting up with Josephine Frampton once more.

He thought he heard the young girl's voice calling to him as he reached the lane, but he did not turn round. He would be happier if he never saw the magistrate's precocious grand-daughter again.

Chapter 7

Wes turned the horse loose in the pound before making his way to Widow Cake's cottage. The escape across Magistrate Frampton's lawn seemed to have drained what little energy had been lurking in the animal's gaunt frame. Wes had been obliged to walk the last mile to Tolpuddle, tugging the ancient horse behind him like a reluctant puppy on the end of a lead rope.

Amelia Cake had regained consciousness. She was now seated slumped in a wooden armchair in the kitchen. The fire was alight and Rachel Gillam was making a cup of tea.

Constable Hammer was also in the kitchen, seemingly unable to stand still in one spot for more than a few minutes. He was desperately eager to question Widow Cake, but the importance of his office meant nothing to Rachel Gillam. He could question the widow when she had drunk a warm, sweet cup of tea and had gathered her wits about her. Not before.

'Did you find Magistrate Frampton? Is he coming here?' Hammer greeted Wes with the eager questions as he entered the kitchen.

'Magistrate? What nonsense is this, Charles Hammer? Why should I need a magistrate?' Amelia Cake raised her head to speak, but the movement caused her intense pain and she placed the fingertips of both gnarled, arthritic hands to her temples.

Rachel Gillam was pouring hot water on to tea leaves inside four cups. Glancing through the window, she said, 'If your magistrate is overweight, has a red face and rides a fine grey mare, I'd say that's him outside, tying his horse to the gate.'

'You don't need me here.'

Even as he spoke Wes was making for the kitchen door, but Constable Hammer reached out and caught his arm before he could escape.

'You stay right here, my lad. You're a material witness. I'll need you to tell the magistrate exactly what you found when you arrived here, this morning.'

'What's he on about?' asked Amelia Cake irritably. 'I wish someone would tell me what's going on in my own house.'

'You just rest here awhile, Widow Cake,' said the constable importantly. 'Now Magistrate Frampton's here you'll know soon enough. He's the senior magistrate for the whole Dorchester district.'

Returning his attention to Wes, Constable Hammer said, 'You wait here with Widow Cake too, Wesley Gillam. I'll go and meet Magistrate Frampton.'

'What's that man up to?' asked Amelia Cake. 'I never have thought much of him, even though I've had little to say to him before today. Just as well too. He's even more of a fool up close than he appears to be from a distance. Pass me that cup of tea, will you, dear? My head's ringing like a blacksmith's anvil.'

Rachel hardly had time to hand a cup to the seated widow before Magistrate Frampton swept into the kitchen with the parish constable in his wake.

When he saw Wes, an expression of cold anger crossed the magistrate's face. Wes's spirits sank. He realised the damaged lawn had been discovered and blame accurately apportioned.

'I hoped I would meet up with you again. I'll speak to you in a few minutes, young man. First of all, what's been happening here?'

'I think we have a felony on our hands, sir,' explained the constable. 'Young Wesley Gillam is employed by Widow Cake. He came to work this morning and found this window in the kitchen open. He thought nothing of it until Widow Cake failed to put in an appearance. When he came looking for her, he found her lying just inside the cottage door with a very nasty gash to her head – as you can see for yourself.'

The magistrate glanced at the widow who stared up at him with an expression of pained bewilderment on her face.

Addressing the constable, he said, 'Do you think it was burglary? Who would have committed such an act? In my opinion the cottage is too far off a main road for it to be the work of a passing vagrant.'

'Ah!' Glancing at Rachel Gillam, the constable looked away again quickly. 'Two young village lads left their homes rather suddenly yesterday, Mr Frampton. No one seems to know where they've gone. One of them is the brother of young Wesley here – and son of the lady who's been tending to Widow Cake. If you ask me . . .'

'My Saul had nothing to do with this, Charles Hammer – and don't you dare try to say he did.'

'Be quiet, woman!' Magistrate Frampton gave Rachel Gillam a stern, courtroom glare. '*I'll* decide who has or has not anything to do with this matter. There's been a burglary. A serious felony. Constable Hammer . . .'

'Charles Hammer has no more sense than he had the day he was born.' This time the scornful interruption came from Amelia Cake and Magistrate Frampton's stern frown made no impression on her. 'What's all this stupid talk of a burglary? Isn't it bad enough for a poor widow-woman to fall downstairs and hurt herself without having a lot of foolish folk come filling her house with their noise and stupid chatter.'

Magistrate Frampton looked at the woman suspiciously. 'Are you saying there has been no burglary? Or is this merely an attempt to protect someone you know from the due process of the law.'

'I'm telling you, I fell down the stairs. I gave my head an almighty crack and all this foolish chatter is doing nothing to help the headache it's left me with.'

'But . . . the open window?' The village constable clutched at a fragile straw to justify his actions in calling out the most senior magistrate in the county of Dorset.

'That's the reason I came downstairs. I was baking cakes last night and left them in the oven too long. I opened the window to let the burnt smell out of the kitchen. When I was abed I woke, heard the rain and remembered the window was still open. I came downstairs in too much of a hurry and caught my foot in my nightdress. I'm not too steady on my feet at the best of times. I should have known better.'

Now it was the turn of the unhappy constable to be the target for a disapproving magisterial glare. 'Couldn't you have ascertained the facts before calling me out from my home – and giving this young idiot an opportunity to gallop his horse across my lawn?'

The magistrate flicked a hand in the direction of the 'young idiot' and Wes's hopes sank, but the misery of the constable was not over yet.

'I'm sorry, sir. I thought . . .'

'You did nothing of the sort. As a result you've wasted a great deal of my time. I'll be sending a letter to your parish clerk, you can be certain of that.'

Having dealt with the cringing parish constable, Magistrate Frampton now turned his attention to the unhappy Wes.

'You . . . Wesley Gillam, is that your name?'

'Yes, sir.' Wes hoped the fear he felt did not show. James Frampton was a very important man – and Wes had, albeit unwittingly, caused damage to the magistrate's property.

'With a name like that you'll be a Methodist, I've no doubt?'

'We're a Methodist family, yes, sir.'

'I might have guessed it. If there's trouble anywhere in the district there'll be a Methodist involved somewhere. What d'you mean by galloping your horse over my lawns – and after I'd told you to take it away from the house through the servants' gate?'

'I didn't gallop it across your lawn, sir. Someone . . . *something* frightened it. The horse broke free and went across the grass.'

Wes thought it inadvisable to lay the blame for the horse's actions upon the magistrate's grand-daughter.

'How it happened doesn't matter. It was your damned horse that caused the damage. I'm not paying a gardener good money to put right a mess you've made. I doubt if you have the money to pay him so you'll come and work at Moreton for a week to pay your debt. You understand?'

Before Wes could reply, Amelia Cake said, 'He'll do nothing of the sort! Wesley Gillam is employed by *me* and I have need of him here. Especially now.'

'Then will *you* pay for my gardener's time in putting right the damage caused by the boy? After all, he came to Moreton on your behalf.'

'He went because a stupid village constable sent him there. By rights *he* should be the one to pay. Constables and magistrates are ready enough to take money from honest folk, but I've never heard of either one giving any away. If you want Wesley to come and do work for you then you'll have to make do with Sunday afternoons. That's the only time I can spare him from here.'

For a moment it seemed Magistrate Frampton might argue with Amelia Cake. However, now she was in full possession of her senses once more she proved her expression could be every bit as intimidating as his own.

The magistrate shrugged. 'Very well.'

Scowling at Wes, he said, 'For the next three months you'll come to Moreton House on a Sunday afternoon when you've finished here and work until dusk. I'll tell my gardener to expect you this Sunday. Don't think I'm likely to forget, either. If you fail to turn up I'll have you arrested and brought before my court charged with causing wilful damage.'

Having humbled the village constable and delivered justice to Wes, Magistrate James Frampton placed his hat firmly upon his head and passed out of the house, heading for the vicarage. Since he had ridden all this way on a fool's errand he would pay a visit to the Reverend Warren. He should at least obtain a brandy or two to warm himself for the return journey to Moreton.

Chapter 8

When Magistrate Frampton and Constable Hammer had left Widow Cake's cottage, Rachel Gillam expressed her anger at the arrogance of the magistrate and the outcome of his visit.

'Who does he think he is, coming here and throwing his weight about? He treated us all like dirt. Sneering at Methodism and dishing out punishment as though he was in his courtroom. He should have praised our Wes for carrying out his public duty. Instead, he's been punished just for letting that old horse walk over a patch of grass. As for believing our Saul would break into a house and rob someone!'

'Magistrate Frampton can't change what he is,' replied Amelia Cake. 'He was brought up to behave like that. The one I blame is Hammer. If he hadn't jumped to stupid conclusions, a magistrate wouldn't have been brought into this in the first place. The trouble with Hammer is he wants to make a name for himself. A constable can't do that in a law-abiding village like Tolpuddle.'

The two women aired their grievances as Rachel Gillam bound up Amelia Cake's ankle. The widow had twisted the joint in her fall down the stairs and it was swollen to twice its normal size. As they talked, Wes carried in logs from the woodpile in the yard, stacking them beside the fireplace.

'There, that should be easier.'

Her task completed, Rachel Gillam stood up. 'You'll need a stick for a while, to help you get around. If I was you I'd rest that ankle as much as you can for a few days.'

'That's all very well,' grumbled the widow, 'but there are things that need doing about the house. Who's going to do it? I suppose you couldn't help me out?'

'I'd like to, but I'm working at East Farm for the next few weeks. That reminds me, I should be there now!'

Moving to make way for her son, entering the kitchen with another armful of logs, Rachel Gillam added, 'Perhaps you can find a girl from the village, although offhand I can't think of a reliable one who isn't already fully employed.'

'I know one.' Wes spoke without thinking and immediately

regretted his impetuosity. He should have waited until his mother had left the cottage and spoken only to Widow Cake.

'Oh! And who is this young lady of leisure who's known to you and not to me?' Rachel Gillam fixed her son with a look that meant she intended getting a straight answer from him.

'It's Saranna Vye . . . from Southover.' As his mother opened her mouth to voice a protest, Wes added hurriedly, 'She keeps her own cottage absolutely spotless, Ma. I saw inside there when I went to see her yesterday. You'd say so yourself if you saw it . . . honest!'

'I sent you there to find out if she knew anything of our Saul, not to look around her house and learn her life story. That girl's trouble. If your father found out you'd had anything to do with her he'd go for you the same as he did for Saul. She's never been taught any good Methodist principles.'

'Neither have I,' retorted Amelia Cake. 'But no one's dared to question *my* principles – and they'd better not, if they know what's good for them! I'll remind you, Rachel Gillam, that we aren't all narrow-minded Wesleyans in this village. Who I have to help me in *my* house has nothing to do with that husband of yours. Go and find this girl, Wesley. Bring her here and let me have a look at her.'

Wes looked at his mother who stood tight-lipped across the kitchen. She stared directly ahead of her, disapproval written in every line of her body.

'It's no good your looking to your mother. She can tell you what to do when you're at home. For as long as you're *here* you're working for me and *I* tell you what to do. Go on, don't stand there gawping, boy, or the day will be over before you bring me this girl. She'd better understand right away that I have no intention of giving anyone a full day's pay for less than a full day's work.'

Wes's mother followed him from the house. Once outside, she said, 'You're a fool, Wes. You know nothing of this girl, yet you recommend her to come and work in Widow Cake's house. For all you know she could be a thief – and you'd probably be blamed for bringing her to the house.'

'I believe she's honest, Ma.' After a moment's hesitation, Wes told his mother how Saranna had prevented Widow Cake's money from being stolen from him at Dorchester market.

'You told me you'd never met the girl when I asked you to go and speak to her about our Saul!'

'I didn't know she was the same girl then. She never told me her name when we met in Dorchester. But I really do think she's honest, Ma.'

Only partly mollified, Rachel Gillam said, 'I hope she is, for

41

your sake – and for mine. I've lost one son, I don't want to lose another. Off you go now, before Widow Cake starts on you again.'

Outside the gate Wes and his mother went in different directions, but Wes had not gone far before his mother's voice brought him to a halt.

'Wesley! Say nothing of this to your pa. The less he hears about this girl the better it will be for all of us. He blames her for Saul leaving home. Nothing anyone says will make him think any different.'

Saranna was in the scullery of the Vye cottage at Southover when Wes called on her. She had just finished the family washing and was wringing it out over an iron-hooped wooden tub.

She was surprised to see him, but gave him a warm, welcoming smile. 'Have you brought the hinge already? You said you wouldn't be bringing it until Sunday. I thought you worked in the week.'

'I do, but Widow Cake's had a nasty fall down the stairs during the night and hurt her ankle. She was talking of getting a girl in to help in the house until she was better. I suggested you might do it. She's sent me to see if you'll help her out.'

Saranna's face lit up in a delighted smile. 'That was nice of you. I could do with work, we're desperately short of money right now. When would she want me to start?'

'Straight away. In fact, if you get there quickly enough you might even get a full day's pay from her.'

Saranna hesitated for only a few moments. 'All right – but you'll need to help me hang these clothes on the line first.'

Ten minutes later Wes and Saranna were hurrying along the narrow country lanes, heading for Tolpuddle and the cottage home of Amelia Cake.

'What's she like, this Widow Cake?' Saranna put the question to Wes.

He shrugged. 'She's been a widow since soon after the Napoleonic Wars and is badly crippled with arthritis, although she won't admit it most of the time. She's bad-tempered, mean – and expects anyone who works for her to cram two days' work into one.'

Saranna looked at Wes uncertainly. 'I'm not so sure you *were* doing me a favour when you suggested I should come and work for her.'

'She's all right, really.' Wes gave Saranna a wry grin. 'Her talk is a lot harsher than her actions. Just when you think you can't take any more she does something unexpected and everything's all right again. I've worked for her these last five years, so I suppose I know her better than anyone else.'

'Doesn't she have any children of her own?'

'No, nor relatives in this part of the country. Her husband was a regular soldier. They met when he was away in barracks somewhere. He brought her to Tolpuddle when she was a young girl and then she went with him when he was with Wellington's Army.'

'That's what my ma did. She only came back to England with me because my pa was killed.'

'You'll have to speak to Widow Cake about it. You might even find she and your ma knew each other out there.'

Saranna had little time that day to question Amelia Cake about life with Wellington's Army. The widow complained bitterly that Wes had taken advantage of her good nature by spending so long fetching Saranna from Southover. Nevertheless, both her employees were given a full day's chores to perform.

Saranna worked hard until well after darkness fell. When she finally left the cottage there was a cold drizzle and she shivered. She wore only her thin, patched dress.

Wes had left work more than half-an-hour before, but Saranna found him waiting for her beneath a twisted oak tree in the lane.

'I thought you'd gone home ages ago.' Saranna's voice revealed something of the weariness she felt. She firmly believed she had been given tasks to do that had not been tackled for at least a year.

'I waited to see how you'd got on with Widow Cake. Did you speak about the war?'

'There was no time to *talk* about anything. At least, not so far as I was concerned. I don't think Widow Cake ever *stopped* talking. "Do this." "Do that." "Shift this chair." Then: "Shift it back again." It seemed that every time I turned around she was standing behind me. The only time I ever stopped was when I remembered I ought to breathe now and again. She's lucky I never kicked the other leg from under her!'

'She was following you around to make sure you could do things the way she wanted them done. Once she's satisfied you can, she'll leave you alone.'

'Unless she decides she doesn't want me working for her any more.'

'If she was going to dismiss you she'd have done it today. No, you've passed the test. You'll be all right now.'

'Is that why you waited? To see if I was still going to be working for Widow Cake tomorrow?'

'I . . . I suppose so.'

'Why? Because you were frightened of being told off by her if I didn't suit?'

'No! I just wanted to make sure everything was all right. That you didn't take too much notice of her grumbling at you all the time. She doesn't mean it, you know. She's got a kind heart, really.'

Saranna's sniff might have been a result of the cold air of the evening, or an expression of her feelings for Widow Cake. 'She has a funny way of showing it, that's all I can say.'

'But you will be coming back to work at the cottage again tomorrow?'

'Will it matter to you whether I do or don't?'

Wes was silent for a long time as he wondered how he should answer her question. He eventually settled on the truth.

'Yes, I think it will.'

'Then you'll be happy to know I'll be there in the morning. See you then, Wes.'

'Yes. I'll see you then.'

Walking home in the darkness, Wes found he was grinning fit to split his face. He decided it must be because he had done something to help the girl who was Saul's friend.

Chapter 9

'With all the land you have here you ought to keep a cow, at least.'

'What do you know about it, girl? Why should I want a cow – unless it's to make more work and expense for myself?'

Saranna and Amelia Cake were in the kitchen of the widow's cottage. The young girl was scrubbing the kitchen table while her employer sat in a fireside chair, her hands resting on the top of a walking-stick.

Having the eyes of the critical widow-woman upon her was unnerving. Saranna had made the remark as much to divert Amelia Cake's attention as anything else.

'With a cow you would have your own milk, could make butter and cheese, and sell the occasional calf.'

'No doubt I'd be unknowingly supplying the Vye and Gillam households with milk, butter and cheese too.'

'My ma gets all we need from the farm where she works at Southover – and I can't see Wes taking so much as a chicken's egg that didn't belong to him.'

'How would I pay for this cow and all the food it'd eat during the winter months? Or hadn't such a thought crossed your mind?'

It had not, but Saranna had a quick brain. 'You might not have to pay for it at all. My ma works for Farmer Hooper and he was saying only the other day that he has more milk cows than he needs right now. He'd like to get rid of a few of them and run some heifers, for beef, but he really needs a bit more land. If you were to let him graze his heifers in your fields for part of the year, he'd probably give you a cow as payment. My ma would make sure you got a good one that'd give milk for a long time.'

'And what about feeding the cow in winter, when the grass isn't growing? I've yet to meet the animal that can live on fresh air.'

'This has been a better year than usual for hay. Farmer Hooper has plenty to spare. He'd probably throw in winter feed with the cow. In future years he'd no doubt be only too glad to grow hay in your fields, and leave a stack behind large enough for your own cow.'

Amelia Cake was still mulling over Saranna's suggestion when

45

there came a heavy knocking at the front door of the cottage.

As Saranna put down the scrubbing brush and began rinsing her hands in the bowl of soapy water, Amelia Cake put her weight on the walking-stick and struggled to her feet. 'Someone at the door is no excuse for you to stop working. Get on with that scrubbing, I'll go – and don't forget under the edges of the table top. I'll inspect it when I come back. If it's not the way it should be you'll be a few pennies short at the end of the week.'

Saranna smiled at the departing back of Amelia Cake. It had not taken her very long to realise that the widow's irascible manner hid a vulnerability that she kept from the world. Saranna had only been working for the widow for a few days, but she was already fond of her.

Pausing in her scrubbing, Saranna heard Widow Cake talking. After a while there was another voice. This one deeper, more coarse. Curious, Saranna left the scrubbing brush on the table and went to the door which led from the kitchen to the small front hall. Cautiously, she peered around the door, but Widow Cake caught the movement.

'Saranna, I have no time for beggars, but I won't see an old soldier – a *wounded* old soldier – go hungry when there's bread in my larder. Go and fetch the half-a-loaf on the top shelf, and some cheese. There's a piece on the slate slab. The rind's going mouldy, but the cheese itself is all right.'

Instead of doing as she was told, Saranna came from the kitchen to the door. Peering out, she saw a tall, long-coated man wearing a black eye-patch and in need of a shave. He wore a long, army watch-coat that might once have been grey. Patched and dirty, it was now of an indeterminate colour. Only one leg reached from beneath the watch-coat to the ground and the beggar maintained his balance with the aid of a makeshift wooden crutch.

'Morning, missie. The blessing of an old soldier upon you . . .'

Before he finished speaking and much to Widow Cake's astonishment, Saranna slammed the cottage door in the face of the 'ex-soldier' and rammed home the bolt fitted to the inside of the door.

'What . . .?

Widow Cake called for an explanation but Saranna was running for the back door. Calling out as she went, she cried, 'Don't open the door to him – and shout for Wes!'

Before she went out through the kitchen door to the garden, Saranna snatched up a heavy kitchen broom. Once outside she followed the advice she had given to her employer and began shouting for Wes as she headed for the chicken pen.

The ragged man leaning over the fence of the chicken run had two chickens in his hands. The neck of a third hung limply from a gap between two buttons of his jacket. When he turned and saw the loudly shouting girl rushing at him brandishing a broom he dropped the chickens he was holding. One flapped feebly on the ground, the other staggered drunkenly away to crash into the fence, complaining raucously.

The man turned to run but a blow from the broom knocked him to the ground. An ill-secured button parted company with his jacket and the third chicken dropped lifeless to the earth.

The hapless would-be thief scrambled awkwardly to his feet. Stooping low and shielding his head with both arms against the blows that Saranna rained upon him, he fled in the direction of the cottage gate.

Wes arrived in time to see the two beggars fleeing along the lane. The wounded ex-soldier was running as fast as his chicken-stealing companion, the 'amputated' leg miraculously restored to him.

'Well, I never did! He had his leg tied up under that coat of his all the time!' Amelia Cake looked at Saranna with grudging admiration. 'How did you know, girl? And what made you suspect there was another of 'em round the back of the house after my chickens?'

'Ma and me was on the road for a while, Mrs Cake. There aren't many tricks I haven't seen, believe me, and that one's an old dodge. Besides, I'd seen the man who was at your door before – only he had two legs when I last set eyes on him! You would have recognised him too had you seen his face, Wes. He was one of the three men who was planning to steal your money at Dorchester market on Saturday.'

Amelia Cake looked from Saranna to Wes and back again sharply. 'What's all this? You never said anything to me about someone trying to steal your money . . . or was it *my* money?'

'It was your money.' Wes would not meet her eyes. 'I didn't say anything because they never succeeded, thanks to Saranna. Arnold had the money tucked inside his shirt and the thief put his hand into an empty pocket.' He shrugged. 'So there was really nothing to tell you.'

'What do you mean, *nothing*? Unless I'm mishearing things, Saranna saved me from losing more than seventeen pounds. Do you think I'm so mean that I wouldn't have given the girl a reward? Is that what you think of me?'

'I don't want a reward, Mrs Cake. I got that when Wes let me have a weaner for two shillings. I don't want anything more.'

'You sold a weaner for two shillings when they were fetching six, and never thought to tell me?' Amelia Cake's lips formed a thin, tight line. 'I think you've been taking too much upon your

47

shoulders, young Wesley Gillam. Far too much – and to think I gave you extra pay! I've a good mind to stop that – and the four shillings I lost on the pig – from your wages.'

Saranna was confused by the swing of Widow Cake's moods and dismayed by the trouble she had caused to Wes. 'I'm sorry you're upset, Mrs Cake. I . . . I can't pay you anything extra for the weaner, but I can let you have it back . . . if that's what you want?'

For a moment Widow Cake's expression softened, but it was so fleeting that an onlooker might have been forgiven for thinking he or she had been mistaken.

'What I want is to get at the truth. It seems to me there's a lot been going on behind my back that I don't know about – including Wesley's eagerness to have you come here and work in the house . . . but I've been standing on this leg for far too long. Help me back in the house. You can make me a cup of tea, girl. While I'm drinking it the two of you can tell me the whole story from the very beginning. I've no doubt there'll be a few questions for you both to answer . . .'

Wes was late completing his chores at Widow Cake's cottage that night. Saranna had left more than an hour before, but she was waiting for him further along the lane.

There was a heavy drizzle and she came to him from the shelter of the hedge. Clasping his arm, she said, 'I'm sorry I got you into trouble with Widow Cake, Wes. Truly I am.'

'It wasn't your fault. She's just a mean old woman, sometimes, that's all. I expect it's been bothering her that she gave me an extra couple of days' pay when I got back from Dorchester market. This just gave her an excuse to take it back. I expect she'll feel happier now.'

'Perhaps, but she's told me she'll think seriously about getting a cow. That will make work. We should both be able to keep our jobs with her.'

There was silence between them for a few moments and Wes would never know how hard Saranna was wrestling with her conscience. Suddenly she took his hand and pressed three coins into it.

'What's this?'

'It's the money Widow Cake took back from you. She said I had more right to it than you, seeing as how it was me who stopped you being robbed. That if it had been left to you you'd have come back to Tolpuddle without anything. Pigs or money.'

'What she says is true.' Wes spoke gruffly, aware that her fingers were still clutching his clenched hand. He also remembered how desperately she had wanted the weaner at the market and had given him all the money she possessed to buy it. 'You've a lot more right to the money than me.'

'No. It would have been different if she hadn't taken it from you to give to me. I can't take it now. It wouldn't be right.'

Wes was torn between the knowledge that he had given all the money he possessed to Saul when he left Tolpuddle, and an awareness that Saranna too had nothing.

'I'll tell you what we'll do. We'll share it.' He opened her fingers and placed a coin in her hand. 'There's a shilling for you and I'll keep one for me and give you sixpence when I get change. Is that fair?'

'It's more than fair, Wes. It's very generous. Thank you.'

Their hands stayed together for a long while as they walked on along the lane towards the Southover junction where their paths would take them in different directions.

Behind them they would both have been surprised to see Widow Cake seated beside the kitchen fire in her cottage. She was smiling to herself as she rocked gently back and forth in her chair.

From a window she had seen Saranna settle herself in the hedge to wait for Wes. Amelia Cake had a shrewd idea of what the young girl intended doing with the money that had been taken from Wes and given to her.

The thought pleased the widow. Young Wesley Gillam and Saranna Vye were a well-matched couple. They reminded her of herself when she was a girl and of Henry Cake, the young soldier she had followed to the battlefields of Spain. The man she would willingly have followed to the very ends of the earth had he asked her to. Henry would have understood her actions today if no one else ever did. She hoped he might also have approved of them.

Chapter 10

On Sunday when Wes went to Moreton for the first of his after-noon 'punishments', Saranna was waiting for him halfway along the lane from Widow Cake's cottage.

When he expressed surprise at seeing her so far from the Vye cottage on her one day off work, Saranna shrugged. 'I finished all the work at home early and came to see Ma. She's working at the vicarage in Tolpuddle today. I was going to help her, but Reverend Warren has guests and his wife told me she doesn't want to see me about the kitchen looking like this.'

The day was cold enough for Wes to be grateful for the fustian jacket he wore, but Saranna had on only a short-sleeved frock. It had been made for a much smaller girl and although she was slim enough to get into it with ease, it was far too short for her. Today she wore her long black hair loose and it hung beyond her shoulders. With her dress and her dark skin, he thought she might easily have passed as a gipsy.

He handed her the hinge he had obtained from Widow Cake's shed, promising to call in on his way home from Moreton House and fit it to the gate of the sty.

As they walked along the lane together Saranna glanced up and caught him looking at her. Wes said quickly, 'There's a chill wind today. Aren't you cold wearing only a dress?'

'I don't feel the cold. Ma says it's because I was born on the side of a mountain in a snowstorm. She says that after surviving that I need never fear any kind of weather ever again.'

'Was that in France?'

The little Wes knew about Saranna had been gleaned from the conversation of others, and the outline of her life she had given to him, some days before.

'I don't really know. Neither does Ma. It might have been Spain or France. It was in the mountains somewhere between the two countries.'

'Was your pa with you then?'

'No. He was in some battle. Ma says he must have been killed

50

about the same time as I was born. He never saw me and I never knew him.'

'Things must have been hard for your ma over there after you were born.'

Wes built up a picture in his mind of Saranna's mother tramping through the snow carrying a baby through the far off mountains of France and Spain, leaving her husband in a grave behind her. He had heard from Widow Cake of some of the hardships of following an army when it was campaigning. After Saranna's birth, her mother would not even be following it in order to be with her husband. It must have been a dreadful time.

'Ma doesn't talk about it much now. When she did, she'd say that it happened so often that the army wives looked after each other. They all knew it might be their turn next. The worst time was probably when we returned to England. No one wanted to know a soldier's widow with a young baby to support and she couldn't get any help. She had a hard time then, I know.'

'Why didn't she come straight back to Tolpuddle?' Wes knew the Vye family had been in Tolpuddle for less than two years.

'Ma wasn't too certain of the welcome she'd get. She ran off from home when she was my age to be with Pa. She felt she couldn't return penniless and with a baby to support.'

'So what did she do?'

'All sorts of things. She worked in some big houses in Kent and Essex for a while, but Ma was too pretty – and she was a widow. If there was a man in the house he'd be convinced Ma must want to jump into bed with him at the earliest opportunity. Usually his wife would think so too, and we'd have to move on. Then one day the master of one of the houses thought he might be luckier with me than he was with Ma. She heard me screaming and came in and hit him with a lamp. It knocked him unconscious. I think the lady of the house was more upset about the broken lamp than she was about her husband, but we had to leave in a hurry. Ma worked for an officer who'd been wounded in France, but then he died. For a long time we were on the road, moving from one place to another.'

Wes cast a quick glance at Saranna. He felt she was leaving a great deal unsaid. Probably the true story of her own life would never be told.

'What made you come back to Tolpuddle after all that had happened to you?'

'We had no choice. Eventually, Ma and I were picked up for vagrancy and taken before a magistrate. He could have sent us both to prison. Instead, he heard Ma's story and took pity on us. He said the parish where someone is born is responsible for

51

looking after their own paupers, so he sent us back here. Ma learned that both her parents had died of cholera soon after she went away, so we stayed in the workhouse for a month. Then Ma managed to get work on Southover Farm and Vicar Warren of Tolpuddle let us have the cottage we're living in now.'

'You've had a pretty hard life,' said Wes sympathetically.

'Perhaps. But I'd rather that than be like some of those who live in Tolpuddle and Southover. They'll never travel farther than the churchyard.'

They walked on saying very little for a while before Saranna suddenly asked, 'Have you heard anything from Saul since he went away?'

'No.'

Her words came as a surprisingly painful reminder to Wes. Saranna was Saul's sweetheart, not his. Working with her and meeting her occasionally like this, they had begun to build up an easy relationship. It pushed her association with his brother into the back of Wes's mind for most of the time. When Saranna gave him a quizzical glance he realised his answer had been far more curt than had been intended. He hastened to add an explanation.

'You're more likely to hear from him through your uncle or one of his friends. Saul can't write very well, so any news of him will have to come through someone else.'

Wes looked at Saranna who was fingering a piece of honey-suckle she had just plucked from the hedgerow. 'Have you heard from him?'

'No, but someone who knows Uncle Richard called in on us last night. He was on his way to Weymouth from Chatham in Kent. He said that Uncle Richard's stirring up a lot of trouble there. So much that it's already spilled over into Sussex.'

Alarmed that Saul would become involved, Wes said, 'What sort of trouble?'

'A lot of farm labourers will see their families go hungry this winter because the farmers have bought or hired threshing-machines to do the labourers' work. Men are angry about it. Uncle Richard is urging them to take matters into their own hands and smash up the machines. Some are beginning to listen to him. They're forming gangs and going about the countryside ordering farmers to turn their threshing-machines over to them. Those who refuse are having their ricks and even their barns burned down.'

'Do you think Saul is with them?'

'He'll hardly have reached Kent yet, but I've no doubt that he'll join one of Uncle Richard's gangs once he gets there. Mind you, dear Uncle Richard won't be *personally* involved. When the

52

arrests begin he'll be able to prove he was miles away from wherever trouble was breaking out.'

'We can't let Saul get involved in something as dangerous as that. What can we do about it?'

'Absolutely nothing – unless you ask your pa to pray for him. Saul always used to say he's pretty powerful at preaching.'

'The less Pa knows about Saul's involvement with Richard Pemble, the better it will be for everyone. I don't want Ma to hear about this, either. We'll just have to hope Saul will have enough commonsense to keep out of trouble.'

Even as he was speaking, Wes knew his brother was not likely to walk away from such trouble as Richard Pemble was stirring up in the south-eastern counties. The situation could have been tailor-made for young men like Saul. Men who resented the near-absolute power that landlords possessed over their lives. Who had fallen foul of those who held such authority over them and been left with a smouldering hatred of their 'betters'. Saul would relish an opportunity to strike back.

The troubles in Kent and Sussex and the part that Saul might be playing in them dominated the conversation between Wes and Saranna during the remainder of their walk to Moreton House.

At the gate to the large house, where the path to the back of the house separated from the main drive, Wes suddenly groaned.

'What's the matter?' Saranna was concerned, thinking he had suddenly developed a pain.

Wes pointed to where a swing dangled from the branch of a single oak tree in the middle of the house's extensive lawns. Josephine Frampton was seated on the swing, rocking it gently back and forth.

'She's the matter. Magistrate Frampton's grand-daughter. It's her fault I'm here today, working as a punishment. She frightened the horse I'd ridden here from Tolpuddle and made it bolt across the lawn. I was hoping I wouldn't see her again.'

'She doesn't seem to be looking this way. If you hurry you might be able to reach the house without her seeing you.'

Acting on Saranna's suggestion, Wes set off for the house. He was halfway there before Josephine Frampton, bored with swinging back and forth, decided to spin around, twisting the ropes of the swing together. She saw Wes heading for the house and called out to him, at the same time waving.

Wes made no response. There was no telling who might be watching from the house. He did not dare contemplate the punishment the all-powerful magistrate might mete out to a young labourer who behaved too familiarly towards his grand-daughter.

Josephine rose from the swing seat immediately. Setting out

to head off Wes, she suddenly noticed Saranna and stopped to watch her.

Just inside the gate, Saranna was creeping stealthily along the river bank. Crouching low, she appeared to be attempting to hide from someone or something.

Josephine hesitated for a few moments, then she changed direction and made for Saranna. She would be able to find Wes later. First she wanted to satisfy her curiosity about this unknown girl's strange behaviour.

When still some yards from Saranna, she called, 'What are you doing? This is private land, you know. If you're poaching . . .'

'Shh!' Saranna held a finger to her lips. When the other girl drew closer, she whispered, 'I'm not poaching. There's a young otter down there, in the river. He's not much more than a baby now, but when he grows bigger he'll catch more fish than all your poachers. All the same, he's very sweet.'

'Where? Where is he?' Josephine asked eagerly. 'I've never seen an otter. Is he very big?'

'No, he's no bigger than a kitten – there he is!'

'I didn't see him.' Josephine's voice revealed her disappointment.

'He's just gone into the reeds, down here.'

Saranna dropped to her knees on the river bank and Josephine hitched up her expensive, frilly dress and kneeled beside her.

The river bank was very steep here. As both girls leaned over to catch any movement in the current-bowed reeds Saranna called, 'There he is . . .'

In pointing, Saranna bumped against the other girl, knocking away one of the arms supporting her weight. With a loud scream, Josephine tumbled headfirst down the steep bank, completing a somersault before she hit the water with an almighty splash.

She came up spitting water but as soon as she was able she opened her mouth wide and let out a series of ear-piercing screams. They continued until the unfortunate girl slipped in the mud of the river bed and she went under again.

When she came up this time there was genuine terror in her eyes. 'Help me! Help me, please – I can't swim.'

In truth, she was in little danger. The river at this spot was extremely muddy, but not particularly deep. However the bank was steep and it would prove difficult for her to climb out.

Reaching down, Saranna said diffidently, 'Give me your hand.'

Josephine reached up eagerly but her hand was so muddy she slipped from the other girl's grasp.

'Rinse the mud off in the water then give me your hand again. Quickly!' Saranna could see people running from the direction of the house. She did not want to be around when they arrived, but she could not leave Josephine in the river. The girl was in such a panic anything might happen.

When she slipped from Saranna's grasp, Josephine's head had gone beneath the water once more and she was almost hysterical, but she reached up towards the outstretched hand.

This time the grip held. Slowly, with much effort, Saranna hauled the other girl from the water and up the bank to safety.

Lying gasping on the river bank, Josephine was less than grateful to her rescuer. 'You . . . you . . . pushed me!' She was shivering with a combination of fright and cold.

'Don't be so silly. You slipped. It was lucky I was here to pull you out. If I hadn't been, the current would have washed you downriver and you'd be halfway to the sea by now.'

Saranna was exaggerating, but the people from the house had almost reached them. Before making good her escape she needed to convince Josephine she had fallen in the river by accident. Saranna was well aware that Josephine's grandfather was Magistrate Frampton. He would not be above putting out a hue-and-cry for her if he believed she had pushed his grand-daughter into the river.

The first to reach the scene was a servant. By now Josephine's teeth were chattering so much she was unable to speak. She began crying with the cold, the tears tracing a path down her mud-stained face.

The servant took off his coat and placed it about the bedraggled girl's shoulders. When a woman arrived on the scene, Josephine wailed, 'Mama!' and ran to her.

The woman, immaculate in a velvet dress, held her wet and muddy daughter at arm's length, an expression of distaste on her face.

Saranna edged away. A much older man had reached the scene now and she guessed this was Magistrate Frampton. He was listening to the shirt-sleeved servant who had been first on the scene. Observing her moving away, he called, 'Girl! Come here.'

Bracing herself for what he might say, Saranna advanced to where the man stood, breathing heavily from his unaccustomed exertions.

'You're not a Moreton girl. Where are you from?'

'From Southover . . . sir.'

'I knew I hadn't seen you around here before. D'you know who I am?'

'You must be Magistrate Frampton . . . sir.' Subservience did not come easily to Saranna.

'That's right. I'm also Josephine's grandfather.' He nodded to where the coatless servant stood, listening to the conversation. 'Robert tells me you pulled her from the river. Might even have saved her life, he said. What was she doing so close to the river, d'you know?'

'She was watching a young otter.'

'An otter, you say? Well, I'll be damned! There hasn't been an otter on this stretch of the river for years. I'll have to get the dogs along here.'

Reaching into a waistcoat pocket, the magistrate drew out three golden coins. He replaced one and handed the other two to Saranna. 'Here, girl. This is for your promptitude in saving my grand-daughter. Run along home and change now. You're almost as wet as she is. Off you go.'

Hiding her delight and disbelief, Saranna snatched the coins and dropped the magistrate a brief curtsey. Then she ran off, afraid he might change his mind.

Chapter 11

'If I'd been told to choose someone who deserved to fall in a river, Miss Josephine would have been my first choice.'

Len Cull, head gardener to James Frampton, made the comment to Wes, a faintly smoking pipe clenched between his teeth. He and Wes were watching the wet and weeping Josephine Frampton returning to the big house, surrounded by a retinue of family and servants.

The head gardener wore his Sunday church clothes. It was the only day he had off in the week, but he had been told to meet Wes and put him to work upon his arrival at Moreton. It was a chore he resented, and he knew where to lay the blame for the disruption of his day off.

'She might have drowned,' said Wes. He was wheeling a barrow in which were the tools he was going to need for the afternoon's work.

'True,' said the gardener, unrepentant. 'Although they do say as how the devil looks after his own. Besides, you have no cause to feel sorry for her. If it wasn't for her you wouldn't be spending the next dozen Sundays working in Mr Frampton's garden. You'd most likely be out walking some nice young girl instead.'

'Did you see her frighten the horse?' Wes had not seen the gardener nearby when the incident had occurred.

'Is that what she did? No, I didn't see that, but it doesn't surprise me. What I do know is 'twas her as told her grandfather you'd put your horse to a gallop across the east lawn.'

'But that's a lie!' Filled with indignation, Wes told the Moreton head gardener exactly what had happened.

The gardener nodded acceptance of Wes's story. 'I don't doubt a word of what you've told me, young Gillam, but Miss Josephine is a convincing young liar. Her stories have cost me two of my best young gardeners – and lost them their reputations. Neither of 'em will ever get work hereabouts again, that's certain. Her mother knows what she's like, I'm certain of that. The only one who either can't, or won't, see her for what she is seems to be Mr Frampton. Yet he's quick enough to call a man or a woman a liar when he's on the magistrates' bench, mind. I think he enjoys sitting in judgement on some poor soul who's done no more than catch a rabbit for the pot, so his family won't starve.'

It seemed the gardener would bare more of his soul, but he caught the expression on Wes's face and came to an abrupt halt.

'I've done enough talking for one day, but don't forget my warning: keep well clear of Josephine Frampton. Unless you do, you'll find yourself in the sort of trouble that'll bring you far more grief than working at Moreton House for a dozen Sunday afternoons. Miss Josephine will have someone's neck stretched on the gallows one day, you mark my words. Make certain it isn't yours.'

With this dire warning, Len Cull led the way to a huge pile of earth. Wes was instructed to pass it through a sieve and mix it with grass seed. Then he had to carry it in the wheelbarrow and fill the holes made by the hooves of the frightened horse.

Much to his relief, Wes saw no more of Josephine Frampton that day. Late in the afternoon as he toiled on the lawn, a young servant girl took pity on him and brought him a cup of tea: 'Laced with a little something.' She told him the magistrate's grand-daughter had been put into a warmed bed – 'With a goose-grease poultice bound on her chest.'

Wes was unused to alcohol and the 'little something' was suf-ficiently strong to catch at his breath and make his eyes water. But it was so warming he downed the lot.

Dusk was falling before Wes finished his first day's task. By the time he had cleaned the tools and put them away it was quite dark. He was also weary, but he had promised to fit a hinge to the Vyes' pig-sty.

Arriving at the small cottage Wes met Nancy Vye, Saranna's mother, for the first time. She was in the earth-floored kitchen surrounded by an aroma of cooking that made Wes's mouth water and he remembered he had eaten nothing since breakfast.

Nancy Vye was much younger than he had imagined she would be, taking into account the many things she had done during her lifetime. Then he remembered that Saranna had told him her mother had run away from home and been married when she was no more than Saranna's own age. Nancy Vye was an attractive woman and she had the same black hair and dark skin that her daughter possessed.

'So you're the young man Saranna's been telling me so much about this last week!'

Nancy Vye eyed him critically. 'There's not much flesh on your bones, is there?'

'I'm kept too busy ever to grow fat,' replied Wes, with a weary grin. He had taken an immediate liking to Nancy. She had a smile that was capable of blunting the most cutting words.

'Well, you may not have your brother's brawn, but from what I hear you have the brains for both of you.'

'Unfortunately it needs more brawn than brains to fit a hinge to a sty door,' said Wes. 'Do you have a lantern?'

'Saranna will fetch it while I make a drink for you. When you've done I'll have something waiting for you to eat – no, don't argue. It's the least I can do. You've done a great deal for us. First you let us have the pig at a very low price, then you got work for Saranna with Widow Cake. She's a grumpy old biddy, I'm told, but there's not much to be happy about when you're a soldier's widow. At least she speaks to Saranna as one human being to another, which is more than you can say for most of those she's worked for in the past. Most of those I've worked for too, come to that.'

Wes would have argued more forcibly about staying at the cottage for a meal but the appetising smell of cooking kept him silent. While she was talking, Nancy Vye was bustling about the kitchen making a cup of tea. Placing a steaming mug on the table in front of him, she reached up to a shelf at the side of the window. A bottle was hidden behind a number of large jugs and she lifted it down.

Pouring some of the contents into Wes's mug, she said, 'There, that's something that was brought all the way from France for me by a night-trader. He dropped it in on his way to make a delivery to a magistrate in Dorchester.'

'A smuggler? Here!'

'I suppose folks would call him that, although he works as hard as anyone else I know for his living. I've never heard of his hurting anyone while he's doing it – and you won't find a better drop of brandy anywhere. It'll keep you warm while you're fixing the sty.'

Wes tasted his tea and grimaced. 'It's certainly strong.' It was even stronger than the laced tea he had been given at Moreton House. Nevertheless, Wes decided he liked the unaccustomed taste even though his father would not have approved. Eli Gillam would not allow alcohol in the house. He was constantly warning his sons and the congregations to whom he preached about its dangers.

Wes took another sip. It was certainly warming. He could feel it flowing from his throat down towards his stomach.

'Here's Saranna with the lantern. Off you go – and take your tea with you. Don't be too long, I'm cooking supper now.'

Outside, while Saranna held a candle-lit lantern for him, Wes wrenched the broken hinge from the gate of the pig-sty and began to fit the new one.

As he was trying to line the hinge up with the remaining one, the lantern suddenly shook, casting shadows over the work.

'Can't you hold it still?' Wes had reached a critical stage and he spoke more irritably than he intended.

'I'm sorry . . . I'm a bit cold, that's all.'

'Have some of this.' Wes handed her the cup containing the tea and brandy and she took it gratefully. Sipping some, she said, 'Ma's put plenty of brandy in this. You must be in favour!'

Wes was holding a number of nails in his teeth and he could only grunt in reply.

'Did you have any trouble with Josephine Frampton today?'

Taking one nail from his mouth, Wes knocked it in the wood of the gate. He spat the remainder into his hand before replying. 'None at all. She fell in the river and spent the remainder of the day in bed. It was just as well from what the head gardener was telling me. Magistrate Frampton's already got rid of two gardening boys because of her.'

'What did they do?'

'Nothing. She made up stories about them. I've learned it was she who told her grandfather about the horse going across the lawn, too.'

'Then she deserved her ducking.' Saranna decided to say nothing about her part in the incident, or the reward it had brought her.

Wes had been working for about ten minutes when Nancy Vye called from the house that supper was ready.

'I'm almost finished.' Wes hammered in the last nail, checked that the hinge was firmly attached, then hung the gate on the post. It swung easily and Saranna expressed her delight.

'Now I won't have to go searching for that old pig when I come home from work every night. We might even be able to grow some vegetables in the garden too.'

'I'll give you some help with that, when it's light enough to work in the evenings.'

'Your pa might have something to say about you working here, but it would be nice if you could.'

The supper served up by Nancy Vye was a bacon pudding. It tasted every bit as good as the aroma in the kitchen had promised. Wes cleared his plate in a manner that was to Nancy Vye's satisfaction, then washed it down with the last of the watered brandy that had accompanied the meal.

By normal drinking standards, Wes had not had an exceptional amount to drink, but he was unused to it. When he stepped out-side the cottage into the cold evening air he felt things begin to spin about him.

Saranna was watching Wes closely, as she had been during the latter part of the meal. Now she said, 'I'll walk to the village with you.'

'You don't have to . . .' Wes's tongue felt twice its size. 'You'll get cold.'

'I'll borrow Ma's shawl.'

'I must say thanks to your ma . . . for the meal. It was lovely.'

'You've already thanked her *and* you've said "goodbye" twice. Come on, give me your arm.'

Saranna tucked Wes's elbow firmly in the crook of her arm. Satisfied she could support him should he become too unsteady in the darkness, she led him towards Tolpuddle.

Her caution proved well-founded. There was never any fear of Wes collapsing along the way, but occasionally his legs seemed to lose their direction. On more than one occasion Saranna needed to pull him back to the centre of the narrow lane.

Wes seemed unaware of her efforts. He chattered away happily, talking at greater length than he could ever remember. He told her of his family, of the books he had read, and how he hoped that one day he would be more than a labourer, working for Widow Cake.

'If you don't sober up before your pa sees you, I doubt if you'll survive the night. Saul used to say he's very strong against drunkenness.'

'I'm not drunk!' Wes said indignantly.

'Not by normal standards, no. But we're talking of what your pa will say.'

'He won't be home yet. He's preaching at Dewlish. He always gives them a sermon they remember for the rest of the year.'

They had passed the mill on the outskirts of Tolpuddle and were within sight of the light in the window of the Gillam cottage when Saranna suddenly brought Wes to a halt.

'You should be all right now.'

'Are you leaving me?' Wes sounded disappointed and Saranna was pleased.

'We've both got to work tomorrow and I must help Ma to clean up tonight.'

'I enjoyed having supper with you and your ma. It . . . it wasn't just the food, either – though that was good. Really good.'

'You must come again. Ma likes you. She said so.'

'I like her.' With a sudden burst of unexpected courage, Wes added, 'I like you too, Saranna.'

'Do you?'

Saranna was standing very close to Wes and when he reached out and pulled her to him clumsily, she offered no resistance.

He kissed her on the lips and her mouth responded to his. He pulled her closer until, excited beyond all caution by the feel of her body pressed against his, he moved his right hand from the small of her back. Placing it first on her hip, he then slipped it down between their two bodies.

She pushed him away so roughly he almost fell backwards. 'Don't do that! I'll not be mauled by anyone when they've been drinking – not even you, Wesley Gillam, do you understand?'

Gathering his scattered wits together, Wes stuttered an apology but suddenly realised he was talking to the night. Saranna had gone.

Had he not been so befuddled by drink, and unhappy at Saranna's abrupt departure, Wes might have pondered on the import of her parting words. Instead, he found that without her he needed to concentrate on putting one leg in front of the other in order to walk a straight path to the door of his home.

Chapter 12

'It's a good job your father's out late tonight. If he saw you like this he'd give you such a thrashing I'd be without two sons tomorrow, not just one. Bend over now. I'm going to pour another jug of cold water over your head. I don't know what they put in that tea at Moreton House, I've never seen anyone in such a state. It's a wonder you got home at all.'

Wes gasped as the water from the jug cascaded over his head. He had told his mother only of the drink he had been given at Moreton House. Nothing of stopping at the Vye cottage.

'That's enough, Ma. I'm all right now, really I am.'

Blinded by the water and with only the light escaping through the partly open kitchen door to guide him, Wes reached out in an attempt to locate the towel.

Stripped to the waist, he was standing on the garden path at the rear of the cottage. He had been subjected to his mother's rough-and-ready method of sobering him up quickly. The knowledge had been acquired at second-hand and it was the first time she had needed to put it into practice during the whole of her married life.

'*You* may think you're all right, young man. You won't be if your father sees you like this, I promise you that. I dread to think what he'd say.'

'You know very well what he'd say, Ma.' His hair no longer dripping water, Wes handed the towel to his mother, exchanging it for a rough-textured shirt which he pulled on over his head before following her through the kitchen door. 'But he isn't right about everything, you know. Saul told him that before he left.'

'That's quite enough from you. I won't have you talking about your father like that. He . . . we *both* are trying to bring you and Saul up to become good, God-fearing young men.'

'*You've* taught us about goodness, Ma. About having respect for other people. It's Pa who's done the "God-fearing" bit – and why? Why should we all *fear* God so much? I read the Bible to Widow Cake every Sunday and there's as much in there about love as there is about fear. In the chapter I was reading to her today it said that "God is love". It said nothing about God being fear. Why doesn't Pa teach us more about love and less about fear? If he had then Saul might still be here with us.'

'I said that's enough of such talk, Wes.' As Rachel Gillam spoke tears sprang to her eyes. Her heart ached for the son who had left home so abruptly. 'Your father is as loving as any man you're likely to find anywhere. I won't have you saying otherwise. He finds it hard to let it show, that's all. There are lots of men like him – but most are not half as good. He feels things as deeply as anyone, Wes – and more than many. Saul's leaving home has hurt him very deeply – as it would if he'd seen you in the state you were in when you came through the door. He's devoted his life to God, but that doesn't mean he loves us any less because of it.'

'Well, I wish he'd show it more, that's all.'

'Love's a two-way thing, young Wesley. You'd do well not to forget that. You can begin your side of it by never coming back here in such a state as you have tonight.'

'All right, Ma. I'm sorry.' Wes knew he had upset his mother with his talk of Saul. Now he put his arms about her and gave her a hug. 'It won't happen again.'

'Then we'll let it pass this time. But you'd better get to bed as soon as you've had something to eat. Otherwise your father will want to know why you're sitting here in the kitchen with your hair soaking wet.'

'I'm not hungry. I . . . had something to eat there.'

Wes did not specify where 'there' was. He hoped his mother would accept it without question. She had been upset enough tonight.

'Not hungry?' Rachel Gillam seemed surprised. 'Oh well, perhaps it's just as well. We don't want you being ill during the night. The best thing you can do now is go up to bed, before your father gets home.'

Lying in his room in the darkness, Wes thought of all that had happened that day. There was one particularly vivid memory in his mind. Everything else quickly fell away as he re-lived the moments when he kissed Saranna. The feel of her lips against his and of holding her body in his arms. The memory turned sour when he recalled the manner in which she had left him.

Remembering, he felt deeply ashamed. Not only because of what he had done, but because Saranna was his brother's girl. Saul had gone away, but one day he would return to Tolpuddle and resume his place in her life.

The thought of this threatened to tear Wes apart. He wanted Saul to return because he missed his brother greatly. The family

64

was incomplete without him and, as a result, Rachel Gillam was desperately unhappy. Saul was her eldest son. Her first-born.

With Eli out of the house so often, going about the Lord's business, many of the duties of the man-about-the-house had fallen upon Saul's shoulders. Wes had assumed some of them, but it was not the same. He realised he was no more than his brother's stop-gap – for everyone.

Wes felt suddenly depressed. He was second best to Saul in the Gillam household – and second best with Saranna. He felt thoroughly miserable.

To make matters worse, every so often the room would begin to swim about him. When this happened he would sit bolt upright. Focussing all his concentration on a sliver of light coming up between two floorboards, he would stay still until the room righted itself and ceased its movement.

Wes thought sleep would evade him but when he heard voices he realised they had awakened him, although they were not particularly loud. In fact, he needed to concentrate to hear what his mother was saying. Not so with his father. Eli Gillam's voice would carry to the farthermost corner of a chapel from the pulpit even when he tried to whisper.

Both parents were in bed, in the adjacent, doorless room. As Wes listened, his father said, 'It's immoral, Rachel. The Duke of Wellington and his government should pass a law making it illegal.'

Such was the guilt weighing upon Wes's conscience that he immediately thought his father was talking about alcoholic drink. But there were other matters on Eli Gillam's mind.

'I've heard talk of them cutting wages in other parts of the country, but never put much store by such gossip. Then Thomas Priddy stopped me as I was on my way out to the chapel this afternoon. Told me he was going to have to dock a shilling a week off my money! I was flabbergasted, I don't mind telling you.'

Wes's mother murmured something that he could not make out and then Eli Gillam was talking once more.

'I did, and in no uncertain terms, but I protested in vain. He told me it was either that, or he'd have to put me off altogether and find a lad who'd come cheaper. After all these years of working faithfully for the man he tells me that I'm lucky to be keeping a job at all!'

Once again Rachel Gillam's reply was inaudible to her listening son.

'He says it's because the price of produce keeps dropping while the cost of farming continues to rise. It seems there's been a meeting of all the farmers and landowners around these parts.

65

They've all decided they have to cut costs. Their way of doing it is to bring in threshing-machines so they can lay off men in the winter. Those men who are still employed will have their wages cut. Nine shillings is to be my wage in future, Rachel. Every man employed on a farm hereabouts will have a shilling knocked off his weekly wage. We're more fortunate than many. With Wes's wage and what you bring in we'll manage, even if we do have to economise on one or two things – but what will happen to men like Tom Cross? He's six young children and a sick wife. How is he to manage with only nine shillings a week coming in? They find it difficult enough as it is.'

This time Rachel Gillam's reply reached Wes. 'What about poor relief? Won't they be entitled to claim that from the parish?'

'I doubt it very much. Those who hold the purse strings of parish relief are the same men who are cutting wages. They're hardly likely to give back in poor rates what they've saved in other ways.'

'What can we do? We can't see them starve. That's not Christian . . .'

'All that can be done is to pray for them – and all the others like them.'

'Prayers won't feed young children, as any mother will tell you.'

'We must trust in God, Rachel. He moves in a mysterious way, his wonders to perform. Who are we to doubt him?'

'I'm glad I'm not Tom Cross's wife, that's all. I'd want more than prayers for my children. That reminds me, while you're praying for the Cross family, I hope you'll offer up a prayer for our Saul too.'

'You've heard from him?'

Wes wished Saul could have heard the eagerness in their father's voice.

'No, but I've been thinking about him a lot lately, especially with all the rumours I've been hearing about the trouble going on everywhere. Farm labourers burning ricks and destroying those threshing-machines you just mentioned. He left here full of resentment and could easily fall into bad company.'

'I don't believe that of him, Rachel. Not of any son of ours. He's had a good Christian upbringing. Saul wouldn't get mixed up with any lawbreakers.'

'I hope not, Eli. I pray every night that he won't . . .' For a moment Rachel Gillam lost control of her voice. When she could speak normally once more, she said, 'I keep remembering what he was like when he was a small boy, no more than two or three years old. You'd take him to chapel with you sometimes if you were preaching in Tolpuddle, carrying him on your shoulders. The two of you seemed so happy together. So happy . . .'

Her control faltered once again and Wes heard her crying. His father was speaking once more now, comforting her, his voice softer than Wes had ever heard it before.

Later still, as Wes was dropping off to sleep once more, he heard the creaking of the bed in the adjacent room and the sounds of his mother and father making love.

It was a sound Wes had heard many times before. He turned over in the bed, his eyes hot. He felt ashamed. Not because of what they were doing, but ashamed they could not enjoy a degree of privacy when they made love.

Chapter 13

Wes went to work at Widow Cake's the next morning feeling apprehensive about having to face Saranna. Much to his surprise, she behaved as though nothing had happened.

He should have been relieved. Instead, he was at first puzzled and then aggrieved. He had lain awake for at least part of the night worrying about what had happened between them. Yet it seemed to be a matter of so little concern to her that she had forgotten it already!

He was not able to speak to her until the midday break. He was eating a piece of cold potato pie, seated on the stump of a tree he had felled the previous year, when Saranna brought him a cup of tea.

'I thought you might like this,' she said. 'It's got lots of sugar in it. It should help your headache.'

'I haven't got a headache,' declared Wes, indignantly.

'You deserve one,' retorted Saranna, unsympathetically. 'What did your father say about you returning home the worse for drink?'

'He didn't know,' replied Wes. 'Ma had me out in the garden, pouring buckets of cold water over my head. Anyway, I was in bed by the time he came in.' After a momentary pause, he said hesitantly, 'I'm sorry about what happened last night, Saranna. When we reached my cottage. I want you to know . . . it had nothing to do with the drink I'd had.'

'That's a pity, Wes. I was hoping that what you did was *entirely* due to drink.'

'But . . . you said you wouldn't be mauled by me *because* I'd been drinking.'

'I won't be mauled by anyone, drunk or sober. If it wasn't drink that caused you to do what you did, it can only complicate things between us. I didn't want that to happen.'

'I'm sorry,' Wes apologised, his brother in mind. He believed Saranna's remarks sprang from the same source.

'Bring the mug with you when you come to the house.'

Without further reference to what had passed between them,

68

she turned and hurried back to the cottage.

Saranna was not waiting for Wes when he left work that evening, or on any other evening that week. He saw her most days at Widow Cake's cottage, but only when their employer was present or within hearing. There was no opportunity to talk to her in private and Wes felt thoroughly miserable.

The next Sunday he left the widow's cottage after his Bible reading and made his way towards Moreton House. It was time to perform another afternoon's punishment set by James Frampton. Much to Wes's surprise, he found Saranna waiting for him at the end of the lane leading to her own cottage.

'Hello, Wes. Do you mind if I walk with you as far as Moreton House?'

'Of course not! But I thought you weren't talking to me because of what happened, and what was said . . . last week?'

'What made you think that? Was it because I haven't waited for you in the evenings? That had nothing to do with you. Ma hasn't been too well. I had to get home quickly each evening and do the work she usually does. She's a lot better now and gone to work at Reverend Warren's today.'

Wes could not make up his mind whether or not she was telling him the truth, but it made no difference. He was happy to have her with him once more.

'You should have said something. I might have been able to help in some way.'

'My ma has always said it doesn't do to take your troubles to work with you. It's not what an employer pays you for and they don't really want to know. Talking of Widow Cake, has she told you that Farmer Hooper went to see her on Friday night? He's agreed to let her have a cow.'

'She's said nothing to me.'

Wes was hurt by the omission. Widow Cake had taken to confiding in him over most things during recent years.

'She's a deep one and no mistake,' said Saranna. 'And shrewd with it. After all the discussion we had about getting a cow that was already giving milk, she finally persuaded Farmer Hooper to let her have a cow that's almost ready to calve. That way she'll have milk in a couple of weeks anyway, and a calf to sell in the spring, when it should fetch a good price.'

'There'll no doubt be more work for me, but I can't see any more pay resulting from it . . .' Wes passed on the information he had overheard from his father the previous Sunday night.

'This is exactly what Uncle Richard foresaw. He told it to Saul and he says it to anyone else who'll listen. I would hate him to be proven right.'

'My father also said that arson and the wrecking of threshing machines is spreading. Would that be Richard Pemble's doing?'

'Not personally, though he's bound to be behind it.'

'I'm worried about our Saul getting involved in all this. Have you heard anything from him?'

Wes found it increasingly difficult to ask questions of Saranna that called attention to her relationship with Saul. Had he been absolutely honest with himself he might have admitted to a feeling of jealousy, although this was not an emotion to which he was accustomed.

'Everything we hear comes from men who are on the road. They don't rush from one place to another, so any news is a long while in arriving.'

They continued talking of the possibility of the troubles reaching Tolpuddle until they came within sight of Moreton House.

'I wonder if Josephine Frampton will be there today?' Wes spoke apprehensively.

'You shouldn't let her worry you so much,' said Saranna. 'Anyway, she has someone with her. While I was waiting for you I saw her and Fanny Warren in a carriage together heading this way.'

Wes felt a great sense of relief. He *was* concerned about Josephine's interest in him, whatever the reason. It was not only as a result of the head gardener's warning. Wes sensed for himself that the girl could cause trouble for him. Serious trouble. But Fanny Warren would keep a check on her. Fanny was the daughter of the vicar of Tolpuddle. A kindly, good-natured girl, she occasionally called upon Widow Cake, bringing fruit from the vicarage orchard.

'Ma told me to ask you back to our house for supper tonight, on your way home.'

Wes hesitated, remembering the outcome of his previous visit to the Vye cottage.

'There are one or two little jobs you could do for us if you did call in.'

'All right. I expect it'll be about the same time as last week.'

Josephine Frampton was not on the swing when Wes made his way to the house, but his relief was short-lived. Given the task of raking all the gravel paths and drives around the house, he was on a path through an area of shrubbery when she appeared. Fanny Warren was with her.

'Look! There's a patch here you've missed. You'd better do it again.'

'Yes, Miss Josephine.' Wes inclined his head to the Tolpuddle vicar's daughter before walking to the section of path indicated by Josephine Frampton. It had been raked as efficiently as the remainder of the path, but he knew better than to argue and went over it once again.

'Boy, can you read?' Disappointed that he had obeyed her so meekly, Josephine Frampton put a foot on the rake he was holding, and kept it there until he looked up at her.

'I can, miss.'

Josephine Frampton was holding a writing book and some pencils. Laboriously she wrote in the book and held it up for him to see. 'Tell me what it says.'

The words on the page, written in a large scrawl, were, 'I am a stupidd fool'.

Wes read the words, but said nothing.

'You said you can read. Why don't you tell us what the words say?'

'It's not my place to tell a young lady that she's written she's a fool, miss. But may I point out that "stupid" is spelled with only one "d" and not with two?'

Josephine Frampton swelled up until Wes feared she might explode. Then she said, 'How *dare* you be so impertinent? I'll tell my grandfather . . .'

'Oh, come on, Josephine. Stop behaving like an idiot. You brought that on yourself – you know very well you did. Come on, if we don't hurry up and do something soon it will be time for me to go home again.'

With a last malevolent glare, Josephine Frampton hurried after her friend, much to Wes's relief. He had over-stepped the mark again with Magistrate Frampton's grand-daughter. He knew he had Fanny Warren to thank for his salvation.

As the two girls walked away, Josephine Frampton said petulantly, 'I'll get my own back on the boy for being so cheeky. You see if I don't.'

'You'll do no such thing, Josephine. You tried to make Wesley Gillam look foolish and it didn't work. If you'd known him better you wouldn't have tried.'

'*You* know him?' Josephine gave her companion a surprised glance.

'Of course I do. Tolpuddle is far too small for everyone not to know everyone else who lives there. Wesley is very bright. My father often says that if he were a member of our church instead of being a Methodist, he would have singled him out for special attention. Perhaps even helped him to go away to school in order to better himself.'

71

'He's a Methodist? Ugh!' By over-reacting, Josephine sought to regain some of the esteem she felt she had lost in the eyes of this quiet, self-assured young vicar's daughter. 'My grandfather despises Methodists. He says they haven't the learning to preach Christianity. All they do is stir up trouble among the lower classes.'

'My father wouldn't go as far as to say that, but he does feel they're misguided. He believes they would do better to persuade their members to attend a proper church on Sunday.'

Josephine looked back to where Wes was still busily raking the gravel on the path behind them. 'I wonder what he'd do if he were made to go to a proper church? Do you think he'd throw a fit or something?'

'Now you're being silly again. Come on, show me the pony your grandfather has bought for you. My father says I might have a new one for my next birthday . . .'

Josephine fell into step beside the Tolpuddle girl, but before they were out of sight her glance went back to Wes. She would find some way to pay him back for making her appear a fool in front of her friend. Nobody got the better of Josephine Frampton.

Chapter 14

'What are your feelings towards Wesley Gillam?'

Nancy Vye put the question to her daughter as they prepared supper together in the kitchen of their cottage.

Saranna shrugged a little too emphatically. 'He's just someone I work with, that's all.'

Nancy had been looking inside the pot that rested on top of the fire. Banging the lid down, she turned to face her daughter. 'This is your mother you're talking to, girl. Not some stranger who doesn't understand your ways, and your moods.'

'I like him,' Saranna conceded grudgingly.

'Better than that brother of his?'

'They're so different from each other there's just no comparing them. You must have noticed that for yourself, surely?'

'I notice a lot of things. What I'm seeing right now is that you're wanting to keep two young men dancing to your tune. Two brothers. It's a dangerous game, my girl.'

'I certainly don't have Saul Gillam dancing to my tune – and never have had. Besides, he's gone off to goodness knows where. He might not be back for years.'

'But has he gone off expecting you still to be here when he *does* come back?'

'Nothing was ever said.'

'There are some things that don't need to be put into words, as well you know.' Nancy Vye crossed the kitchen to lift down a herb jar from a high shelf as she was talking. Returning to the fire, she continued, 'I'll ask you again. Is there anything between you and Saul Gillam, or have you set your cap for his brother?'

When Saranna did not reply, her mother said, 'Perhaps I've got it all wrong. Perhaps it's neither of the Gillam brothers, but someone else?'

'No, you haven't got anything wrong, but it's not quite as simple as you make it sound. I never ever said a word to Saul about being his girl. I promise you, Ma, I didn't. He just grew to believe I *was*. I'm not, and never intend to be. But . . . he never asked anything

73

of me and so I thought there was no reason for me to tell him he was wrong.'

'You let him go off thinking he'd left his girl back here?'

'I suppose so . . . but it didn't matter then. I hadn't met Wes.'

'So Wes *does* mean something to you?'

'Yes, but he doesn't know and I don't want him to know. Not yet.'

'Well, it's your life, my girl, but don't try to be too clever or you'll likely lose them both. I'm not at all sure that wouldn't be best for all of you. When I first met your pa I'd have followed him anywhere he wanted to take me. I'd have died on the battlefield in his place had it been possible. One thing's certain. I'd never have played him off against anyone else.'

'I think I feel the same about Wes, Ma, but things are more complicated for me. It might be different if Wes and Saul weren't brothers.'

'Well, you'll need to sort it out as soon as you can – but, if I'm not mistaken, the young man at the heart of your dilemma just passed by the window . . .'

A few moments later the door opened and Wes entered the kitchen.

'Hello, Wes. Come on in and get warm while Saranna makes you a cup of tea. You look as though you're in need of one. Would you like a drop of something in it, to warm you more quickly?'

Colour flooded to Wes's cheeks and he looked quickly at Saranna's mother, to see if there was a hidden innuendo in her question. But Nancy was busily pouring something from a bowl into the saucepan bubbling on the fire. She appeared to have nothing else on her mind but the meal she was cooking.

'I don't think I'd better have anything to drink. I'm not used to it, I suppose. If it hadn't been for Saranna I doubt if I'd have reached home safely last week.'

'At least you've enough sense to know the state you were in – and the courage to accept the cause of it. I've known grown men who'd blame everything else but the drink. Sit yourself down and I'll dish up. It's mutton stew – and I hope you're hungry. I seem to have cooked enough here for six.'

As it turned out, the stew would not be wasted. They had only just sat down at the table when there came a soft knock on the kitchen door. Nancy Vye and her daughter exchanged glances. Then, without a word, Saranna rose from the table and opened the door.

Two men slipped into the room without a word to Saranna. At the sight of them Wes's spoon halted, halfway between plate and wide open mouth.

The men were as villainous-looking as any he had ever seen. Ragged, unshaven and dirty, they were clearly 'men of the road'. Vagrants. Members of the huge army of homeless, workless men – and women too – who had ebbed and flowed the length and breadth of the British Isles since the end of the Napoleonic Wars. Discharged from the army and navy, and accompanied by many followers, tens of thousands of men had been loosed upon a country that lacked the means to support them.

For years now such vagrants, living by their wits, had been a scourge throughout the land. The already harsh laws of the country had been amended to embrace them, with the result that many had been shipped off to far lands in convict transports. Others ended their penury on the gallows. Yet thousands remained, a menacing presence in city, town and village.

The visitors to the Vye cottage typified the section of society they represented. Seeing Wes seated at the table, the smaller, and possibly dirtier, of the two, jabbed a finger in his direction. 'Who's this?'

'Don't you dare come into my house uninvited and demand to know who's sitting at my table, Silas Morgan! He's a friend of Saranna and his name's Wes. That's all you need to know.'

'I don't like strangers. You can never tell whether they're to be trusted.'

'I don't suppose such strangers care overmuch for you, either. Your appearance wouldn't inspire confidence in anyone who hadn't seen you on parade in the king's uniform, wearing the stripes of a corporal of light infantry.'

'That was a long while ago.' The vagrant who had objected to Wes rubbed his unshaven chin. 'I've long forgotten what it is to have anyone look at me with any respect.'

'I'd forgotten what a meat stew smelled like until I walked into your kitchen, just now,' said the second of the two men. 'Fair makes my mouth water, it does.'

'Then it's a good job I cooked more than the three of us could eat, Jason Courage. You're welcome to whatever I have to eat in my house.'

Turning to Wes, Nancy Vye said, 'Jason is Courage by name and courage by nature. He carried Saranna's pa from the battlefield when he was mortally wounded and others were fleeing to save their lives. It's sad to see such men harried from pillar to post by those who stayed home growing fat while others fought and died for them.'

Turning her attention to the two ex-soldiers once more, Nancy said, 'All the same, I'll not have you sitting at my table with hands like those. There's a bucket of water and a bowl outside. Go and wash your hands while I set places for you both.'

Grinning with anticipation of the meal to come, both men went outside to clean themselves.

'Do you often have visitors like them?' Wes asked the question as Nancy laid two extra places at the table.

'I've never turned away an old soldier yet – although I have no time for those who *choose* the open road as a way of life.'

'How can you tell the difference?' To Wes, one vagrant was no different from another.

'Had you followed the army for as long as I did, you wouldn't need to ask that question. There's a world of difference between an old soldier and a vagabond.'

Further explanations were brought to an end by the return of the old soldiers. The visible skin of both of them was somewhat cleaner now and Silas Morgan had made an effort to untangle his dark hair and present some semblance of tidiness.

For a few minutes all other topics of conversation were abandoned as the two men voiced their approval of the meal placed before them. They both fell upon it with an enthusiasm that Wes found fascinating, yet at the same time disturbing. They ate as a puppy in a large litter would eat, clearing their bowl as quickly as possible, as though fearful someone might take it from them at any moment.

Bowls emptied and the last drop of gravy wiped clean with a thick hunk of coarse bread, the two ex-soldiers leaned back and beamed their appreciation.

'That was a sheer delight, Nancy,' said Silas Morgan. 'I don't remember when I enjoyed a meal more – unless it was when we captured all of old Napoleon's supplies, outside of Vittoria. Wine as well we had then. Do you remember?'

'I remember. There wasn't a sober man in the British Army that night. If Napoleon's troops had decided to attack we'd have lost the war there and then, for certain. I can't offer you French wine to go with your meal, but I can treat you to a drop of good brandy. You ask Wes here, he had some of it last Sunday and hasn't been the same since.'

Both men gave Wes their full attention and Jason Courage was the first to speak.

'How did you get to know Nancy and Saranna, Wes?'

'Saranna and I both work for Widow Cake in Tolpuddle.'

'There's a bit more to it than that,' said Nancy. 'It was Wes who got the job for Saranna. Not only that, he sold her a pig for far less than she'd have needed to pay anywhere else. He's also the brother of the lad you met the last time you were here with Richard Pemble. Saul Gillam – do you remember him?'

'We remember Saul well,' declared Silas Morgan, and it seemed to Wes that the attitude of the two men changed towards him. 'We were talking to him only a couple of days ago. He's with Richard's men. They're in Hampshire right now, but heading this way. Saul's working for "Captain Swing", same as the rest of us who're on the road.'

Wes was puzzled. 'Who's "Captain Swing"?'

'Ah! Now that's a question that's being asked by landowners all up and down the country, and they'd dearly like an answer. Captain Swing is the man who's fighting battles for people like you. He writes letters to the farmers and landowners, telling them to get rid of their threshing-machines and not to lower wages any farther. If they refuse, then they get a visit from Captain Swing's men – and what needs doing is done.'

'My pa's just had his pay cut by a shilling a week.' Wes repeated the conversation he had overheard the previous week but which had not been discussed in the Gillam household since.

'Then you'll know why a man like Captain Swing is needed in the country areas. Give us the name of your father's employer. We'll make sure a letter goes to him. It might persuade him to change his mind and keep your father's wages the way they were.'

'What have you got to do with Captain Swing?' Nancy put the question. 'What happens to those who work on the land has nothing to do with either of you.'

'Quite true, Nancy. But you might as well ask why we should have been in Spain and France, fighting battles for those who wouldn't fight them for themselves? It's just the way we are, I suppose. Filled with concern for our fellow-men.'

'That might have been the way it was once, Silas, but far too much has happened to change you since then. What's your part in all this?'

'We're messengers, Nancy, that's all. Doing our duty to everyone by passing on Captain Swing's messages to farmers and landowners. Whether they take any notice of them or not is their business, not ours. Mind you, it's a foolish man who *doesn't* heed the warning. We've warmed our hands on many a farmer's hayrick or barn these past few months. There'll be a few more in these parts unless I'm very much mistaken.'

'You watch your step, Silas Morgan. Rick-burning's a hanging offence, as well you know.'

'I'm sure you're right, Nancy, and like I said, all we're doing is delivering letters. What either side do after they get 'em is no business of ours.'

'You tell that to a judge and see how much notice is taken, Silas.'

Looking to where Wes sat, wide-eyed, Nancy said, 'You'd best be getting on home now, Wes. Say nothing of what you've heard here tonight, if you value your life. What you've been listening to is hanging talk.'

Chapter 15

Silas Morgan and Jason Courage performed their errand well on behalf of the mysterious 'Captain Swing'.

During the course of the next few nights, warning letters were delivered by the nocturnal postmen to almost every landowner and farmer in the district. The letters, signed in the name of 'Captain Swing', were written in various hands, some displaying a degree of learning, others less literate.

All carried the same message: pay the farmworkers a minimum wage of at least ten shillings a week and destroy the hated threshing-machines. Most letters contained one or two of these demands and no more. Others contained blood-curdling threats, setting out the consequences to the recipients should their demands not be met.

Only those farmers who possessed no threshing-machines and who had not cut the wages of their labourers failed to receive a letter. The warnings indicated a high degree of collusion and co-operation from the farmworkers of the Tolpuddle area, a fact that was not lost upon Magistrate James Frampton.

A second note was delivered to the farmers and landowners of the area. This time it came by day and was signed by the Moreton magistrate. They were summoned to an urgent meeting on Sunday afternoon, to discuss the mutual threat posed by 'Captain Swing'.

The landowners and farmers, together with a number of the area's clergy, gathered in one of the largest rooms in Moreton House. They were assembled to discuss a threat that affected each of them equally, but the common threat did not necessitate a breakdown of the social order. Those men with considerable land-holdings were seated with the magistrates at the front of the room. Behind them, also seated, were the 'lesser' gentry, clergymen and a sprinkling of gentleman farmers. Tenant farmers stood self-conscious and perspiring at the rear of the room.

This was an occasion when James Frampton felt the importance of his office was appreciated to the full – and he made the most of it.

Each arrival had been greeted at the entrance to the house by a butler, conducted to the meeting room by a servant and offered refreshments there. James Frampton did not put in an appearance until everyone was present and the faintest air of impatience was displayed by some of the assembled men.

The magistrate strode purposefully into the room, a sheaf of papers beneath his arm. Nodding to the assembled guests who rose to their feet politely, he slapped the papers down on a small table at the front. The sound effectively silenced a group of loud-voiced farmers standing together in a corner of the room who had not noticed his entrance.

'Good morning, gentlemen, I trust my servants have taken care of you? Please accept my apologies for not being on hand to greet you in person. Unfortunately, as you are aware, we are experiencing a difficult period in our country's history. As senior magistrate for this area, I regret there are occasions when I must place common courtesy second to my duty to king and country.'

There were murmurs of understanding among James Frampton's audience and a general nodding of heads.

'Now, I realise most of you are busy men too, so I will waste as little of your time as I deem necessary.'

From the pile of documents on the table in front of him, James Frampton selected a small piece of paper. Holding it in his hand, he looked about his audience and then began to read aloud.

> Sir,
> Unless you pay your laberors ten shillings per week and destroy your threshing machenes, you will receve a visit from the undersined and his men.
> Captain Swing

Looking about the assembled farmers, landowners and clergy, Magistrate Frampton took the letter in both hands and tore it down the middle.

'There, gentlemen. I am as contemptuous of this "Captain Swing" as I am of his uneducated spelling. No doubt he cuts a fine figure with the simple labourers he claims to lead and represent. He will find Dorset gentlemen and farmers far less gullible! Here, I sincerely believe, he will meet far more than his match.'

Someone broke into applause and the sound swelled as it spread among Frampton's listeners.

'However ...' The magistrate held up a hand for silence. 'However, we must not be complacent. This contemptible band of rogues and vagabonds has caused a great deal of damage and distress throughout the southern counties of England in recent months. I sincerely believe they have been encouraged to cause such havoc by the lack of resolve of many of my fellow magistrates and the farmers in their areas. Indeed, I have seen a Home Office letter stating that certain farmers are using this unfortunate situation to their own advantage. They see it as a lever to have their own rents and tithes reduced.'

James Frampton looked beyond the seated 'gentlemen', to where the tenant farmers stood in stolid silence. 'Such an attitude can only encourage those who threaten the peace and stability of our land.'

There was a chorus of 'Hear! Hear!' from the seated gentlemen and continued silence from the standing farmers.

Acknowledging the approbation with a curt nod of his head in their direction, Magistrate Frampton then aimed a barbed smile at the tenant farmers as he added, 'Fortunately, I believe we have a more responsible breed of farmer here in Dorset. Not only will the demands of such rabble be resisted but, if we band together, we can bring them to the justice they so richly deserve.'

From his place at the front of the room, the Moreton magistrate could see uncertainty on the faces of many of the standing farmers. He directed his next words at them.

'No doubt some of you are thinking, "Why should I become involved? We've had the letters, yes, but the rick-burning and machine-wrecking is happening many miles away. It won't happen here." You are wrong, gentlemen. Very wrong indeed. The reason I have called this meeting today, at such short notice, is an urgent note despatched to me in great haste yesterday. It came from a magistrate at Blandford Forum. He informs me of a riotous gathering accompanied by arson, robbery and intimidation in the Cranborne Chase area, a scant twenty miles from here. Matters are so serious that a gallant troop of Wiltshire Yeomanry has been sent to the area. My latest information is that they have engaged the rioters with the result that there are a number of dead and wounded on both sides, and a great many arrests have been made.'

There were gasps of disbelief from the assembled men and Magistrate Frampton was well-satisfied with the effect of his words.

'I repeat, gentlemen, all this happened not in some county far removed from us, but on the borders of Wiltshire and our own Dorset. Furthermore, the note contained a warning we must take very seriously indeed. Although the Wiltshire Yeomanry defeated the rioters who were terrorising that county, they were able to apprehend only a small percentage of their number. Many are still at large – *and are reported to be heading in this direction!*'

The room erupted into a babble of sound as gentlemen, clergy and farmers expressed their consternation. James Frampton had always been regarded by those who helped him to administer the law in the district, as being a 'theatrical magistrate'. One who obtained a great deal of satisfaction from the dramas that frequently unfolded within the walls of his courtroom. He was pleased with the effect of his announcement upon his guests and allowed them to express their feelings for some minutes before finally calling them to order.

'Gentlemen! Gentlemen . . . if you please!'

When he once more had the full attention of his audience, James Frampton said, 'I have passed my colleague's note on to the commanding officer of the cavalry stationed at Dorchester, but he has a great many other commitments to meet. I feel it is our duty to make plans, here and now, to defend our own properties. I intend to appoint as many special constables as possible, and also organise those of us who possess military experience into highly mobile mounted pickets. These will scour the countryside to ascertain the whereabouts of these bands of hooligans and report back to me here. May I have a show of hands, please, for those who wish to volunteer their services?'

A forest of arms rose in the air. Included among them were the black-cloth sleeves of a number of clergymen.

'Splendid!' James Frampton beamed his pleasure. 'May I say I expected nothing less of Dorset men. Gentlemen, I will call for more drinks, then we will get down to working out the details. I am convinced that our women and children will sleep more securely in their beds because of the decision we have taken here today.'

Chapter 16

Working in the garden of Moreton House, Wes was aware of the comings-and-goings of horses and carriages along the driveway. No one had told him what was happening but he assumed there was some sort of meeting going on. Judging by the number of ministers in attendance, he thought it might have something to do with Church affairs.

His task for the day was clearing up dead leaves. It was a near-impossible feat. The gardens of Moreton extended to many acres and included numerous trees and bushes. He was clearing an area of shrubbery and doing his best to work quietly. Josephine Frampton and Fanny Warren were playing a game with racquets and a ball on a lawn nearby. He had no wish to attract the attention of the magistrate's grand-daughter.

Wes had seen Fanny arrive in a small trap with her father a couple of hours before. Many of the guests who had arrived at the same time were now leaving. No doubt she and her father would be leaving soon too. With Fanny gone he believed it was likely he would be subjected to the unwelcome attentions of Josephine, if she realised he was at Moreton.

Wes was raking leaves in the vicinity of a small summerhouse when he heard footsteps among the dried leaves. Apprehensively, he looked up, expecting to see Josephine Frampton. Much to his relief, but somewhat surprisingly, he saw it was Fanny.

'Hello, Wesley.' She smiled a greeting. 'I saw you from the lawn. Do you work here every Sunday?'

'Only for another couple of months.' Aware that Josephine might put in an appearance at any moment and report him to her grandfather for not working hard enough, Wes redoubled his efforts. 'Mr Frampton ordered me to work here every Sunday for three months as a punishment for allowing a horse to wander over his lawn.'

'That seems a swingeing punishment for something so trivial.' Fanny was indignant. 'I don't suppose you deliberately allowed the horse to go on his grass?'

'No.' Wes decided he should change the subject. He did not

want this girl repeating his conversation to Josephine. 'I thought you were playing ball with Miss Josephine?'

'I was, but Josephine's in a peculiar mood this afternoon. I've decided to keep out of her way until it's time to go home – it shouldn't be long now.'

'There's been a lot of people visiting Magistrate Frampton today. I've never seen so many.'

'It's because of all the threatening letters everyone's been getting from this "Captain Swing". Mr Frampton's called a meeting about it. I think he wants the county to raise a troop of yeomanry. My father thinks it's all a lot of nonsense. He doesn't think there *is* such a person as "Captain Swing". Do you?'

It was an unexpected question, but before Wes could reply to Fanny they both heard the voice of Josephine calling for her friend.

'I don't want her to find me . . .' Looking about her, Fanny saw the summerhouse. 'I'll hide in there. Don't tell her where I am.'

A moment later there was a crashing in the undergrowth and Josephine came into view. She looked petulant.

'Have you seen Fanny Warren?'

'No, Miss Josephine.' Raking vigorously, Wes made his reply without looking up at Josephine. He had hoped this would be sufficient to send her away to look elsewhere. Instead, she moved closer to him. He could see her feet as he raked, head down.

'Look at me when I talk to you, Wesley Gillam.'

'I have work to do.'

'*Look* at me – and stop raking or I'll tell my grandfather you've been rude to me and he'll punish you.'

Reluctantly, Wes raised his head and looked at her, slowing his work until he stopped altogether.

'That's better. Now, aren't I more attractive than your filthy village girls? Answer me!'

'You're a very pretty girl,' Wes said reluctantly. She *might* have been pretty if she did not have a permanently petulant expression.

'Do you look at me and think you'd like to kiss me?'

Decidedly uneasy, Wes said, 'I wouldn't dare have such thoughts about you.'

'Yes, you do. I can see what you're thinking when you look at me.' Moving closer, she said, 'Would you like to do more than just kiss me?' She was uncomfortably close now. 'Would you?'

Moving a pace away from her, Wes began raking furiously. 'I have to finish my work or I'll be in trouble with Mr Cull.'

'You'll be in trouble with *me* if you don't stop raking and do as *I* tell you!'

Suddenly Josephine put her foot down hard on the head of the rake. Before Wes could save it the rake fell from his hands. He stooped to pick it up, but Josephine beat him to it. Snatching it up, she threw it hard into the bushes.

'There! Now you have nothing to distract you.' The flushed cheeks of Josephine Frampton had not been caused entirely by her exertions in relieving him of the rake and Wes felt more uneasy than ever.

'Do you know how planters in the West Indies select their male slaves when they buy them?'

Totally confused, Wes shook his head.

'One of my uncles has a plantation in Jamaica. I heard him telling my grandfather what they do.' Looking speculatively at Wes, she said suddenly, 'I'll show you. Drop your trousers.'

Wes's mouth fell wide open in astonishment. He could not believe he had heard Josephine correctly. Her next words put it beyond any doubt. 'You heard me. Take your trousers down. Do it this instant!'

Gathering his wits together as best he could, Wes said bewilderedly, 'No . . . I can't do that.'

'You *will* do it. If you don't, I'll scream and get you in trouble.'

It was with the feeling that a bottomless chasm was opening beneath him that Wes shook his head and repeated, 'I can't . . .'

Josephine's scream was so loud that it startled Wes. He felt it could have been heard in Tolpuddle.

'Stop it! You'll have everyone from the house coming to see what's wrong . . .'

Josephine's answer was to scream again, this time holding the sound until her eyes bulged from her head and the veins stood out on her neck. _

By the time the scream died away Wes could hear people crashing through the undergrowth towards them.

Josephine gave Wes a triumphant look and said, malevolently, 'I warned you.'

As the first man forced his way through the nearby bushes, she crouched low to the ground and began to wail in simulated anguish.

'Over here!' A man came into view and called back over his shoulder. A few moments later Magistrate Frampton arrived on the scene, accompanied by Reverend Warren and a number of other men.

'What's going on here?' James Frampton looked from his grand-daughter to Wes, and back again. 'Josephine, what's the matter?'

Somehow, she had managed to rub dirt into her eyes and her

85

face looked a mess. Pointing an accusing finger at Wes, she said, 'It's him. He . . . touched me.'

'I did no such thing!' Wes could not contain his indignation. 'I haven't touched her.'

'Yes, he did.' Some of the dirt had got into Josephine's eyes and produced a fair imitation of tears. Turning her face up to her grandfather, she added, 'I hit a ball into the bushes. When I came looking for it he grabbed me. He . . . he lifted my dress and touched me . . . here . . .'

Josephine waved a hand vaguely in the direction of the lower half of her body then covered her face with her hands and appeared to break down and weep once more.

'The boy needs whipping to within an inch of his life,' declared one of the watching men, looking hot-eyed in the direction of a dumbfounded Wes.

'He'll have a whipping – and far more beside,' promised Magistrate Frampton. 'Lay hold of him, someone. Before he runs for it.'

Wes could not have run. He was surrounded by men who had been at James Frampton's meeting. He began to protest that he had done nothing, but he was grabbed by two men and his arms twisted cruelly up behind his back, forcing his head down towards the ground.

'We need some rope to tie him,' said one of the men holding him.

'I keep some manacles at the house,' said the magistrate. 'We'll put them on him and I'll have him conveyed to the cells in Dorchester.'

'I've done nothing,' protested Wes, speaking painfully as the pressure on his arms was increased.

'Shut up!'

The order came from one of the men holding Wes as he began propelling him towards the house.

'The boy's right. He did nothing. I had him in my view from the time Miss Josephine went into the bushes until she began screaming. He never went within an arm's length of her.'

Len Cull, the Moreton head gardener, had come upon the scene unnoticed. His quiet words brought everyone to a standstill.

'Are you saying Josephine is lying, Cull?' The look James Frampton gave his head gardener was filled with angry disbelief.

'I'm saying only what I saw, sir. The boy never went near Miss Josephine.'

'How do you know? You weren't here! You're just saying that because you don't like me. You never have. You've always been horrible to me!'

This time Josephine's tears were real, albeit prompted by rage.

'I'll deal with you later, Cull. Take the boy to the house.'

'Wesley *didn't* do anything.' A young girl's voice brought everyone to a halt once more and they all turned to where Fanny Warren was approaching from the direction of the summerhouse. 'What the gardener said is true. Wesley never went near her.'

'How do *you* know, Fanny Warren? You weren't here. I know you weren't because I was looking for you . . .'

'I was hiding from you, in the summerhouse. I saw everything that happened – and heard it, too.'

'She's lying to save him. She's sweet on him. You heard her call him "Wesley". They come from the same village.'

'Is this true? Do you know the boy?' Stern-faced, James Frampton addressed his question to Fanny.

'We both know him,' Reverend Warren replied on behalf of his daughter. 'Tolpuddle is a small village. We all know each other there.'

'I'm still not convinced. Why on earth should Josephine lie about something as serious as this?'

'Perhaps Fanny can enlighten us?' Reverend Warren turned to his daughter. 'Tell us everything that happened.'

'Why do you want to believe her and not me? *I'm* the one he attacked, not *her*.' Josephine's distress was not feigned now.

'Fanny?'

'I . . . I'd rather not say.' She was embarrassed.

'There! You see, she didn't see anything. *She's* the one who's lying.'

'Fanny, you must tell us what you saw and heard. It's very important. Not least for Wesley.'

Fanny cast a glance in Wes's direction. He was able to stand upright now, although the two men who had secured him still held his arms. It seemed the sight of him standing pinioned decided her.

'I was hiding from Josephine in the summerhouse . . .' Observing James Frampton's sudden frown, Fanny explained, 'She wasn't in a very nice mood and I didn't enjoy being with her. While I was hiding there, Josephine came through the bushes and asked Wesley if he'd seen me. When he said he hadn't, she started teasing him. When he tried to get on with his work, she snatched the rake from him and threw it in the bushes – over there.'

Fanny nodded to where the head of the rake could be seen protruding from a bush.

'Is this all you claim happened? Josephine suddenly began teasing the boy?'

'No, there was more.' Fanny looked at the ground, her cheeks

87

scarlet, until her father said gently, 'Go on, Fanny. Tell us every-thing you saw and heard.'

'She . . . Josephine, ordered Wesley to take down his trousers, but he wouldn't.'

'I don't believe a word of this!' James Frampton exploded in angry disbelief. 'Do you really expect me to believe that Josephine would tell a . . . a *garden boy* to lower his trousers? It's preposterous.'

'Josephine said she overheard an uncle from Jamaica telling you how they chose male slaves for the plantation. She was going to demonstrate it with Wesley.'

The sudden, unguarded expression upon James Frampton's face left no one watching in doubt about the truth of the story Fanny had just repeated.

'This whole incident is quite ridiculous. Gentlemen, if you will excuse me. My grand-daughter is extremely distressed. I must take her to the house.'

'What about the boy?'

The question came from one of the men who still held Wes's arm, although it was no more than a token grasp now.

The magistrate seemed to have temporarily forgotten Wes. Now he rounded on him. 'You've been nothing but trouble since I first set eyes on you. I don't want ever to see you again, you understand? And stay out of trouble. If you ever appear before me in my court, you'll suffer the maximum penalty the law will allow me to impose.'

Turning to his head gardener, James Frampton said, 'I'll have something to say to you too in the morning, Cull.'

Having issued this warning, the disgruntled magistrate set off for the house, firmly holding the hand of Josephine who was now shedding genuine tears. Fanny Warren, her father and the other men followed on behind.

Wes owed Fanny a very deep debt of thanks and he wished she would look round, but she walked beside her father, her eyes downcast.

'I told you Miss Josephine was trouble, young Wesley. You're a very lucky young man. If your vicar's daughter hadn't come for-ward and said her piece you'd be on your way to prison right now and I doubt if you'd have been a free man for many a year.'

'I realise that. I have you to thank too, although I don't think Magistrate Frampton appreciated your honesty. It could cost you your job.'

'It might,' agreed Len Cull philosophically. 'But it could prove a blessing in disguise. Lord Anderson has asked me many times to go to his estate near Weymouth as his head gardener. He asked me last only a couple of weeks ago. It's a better opportunity than I'm ever likely to have around here, 'though before today I haven't been able to make up my mind. This is just enough to tip the scales, so don't you feel sorry for me, young Wesley. Go off home now and do like Mr Frampton told you. Keep out of trouble – and forget you ever heard of Moreton House and the Frampton family.'

Chapter 17

Wes was about a mile from Moreton, on his way home, when he heard the sounds of a trotting horse and rumbling wheels coming along the lane behind him.

As it drew nearer, without looking round, he moved off the road to allow it to pass. Instead, the animal slowed to a walk and stopped beside him.

The horse was pulling a trap, inside which were the Reverend Warren and Fanny.

Giving Wes a brief but sympathetic smile the clergyman said, 'Get in, Wesley. You'll no doubt welcome a ride home. It has been a very difficult day for you.'

'It's all right, I can walk.'

Wes quite liked the Reverend Warren, but he never felt entirely at ease with him. He never felt comfortable in the company of any clergyman. It was a state of mind brought about by his father's frequently stated contempt for their way of life and lack of evangelical drive.

'I don't doubt it, but I'm offering you a chance to do something the easy way. Get in.'

Fanny opened the small door at the rear of the trap and smiled at Wes. Feeling ill-at-ease, he climbed the step and sat down on a small, leather-cushioned seat, opposite Fanny.

As her father flicked the reins and the horse set off at a smart trot, Wes began hesitantly to thank Fanny for her part in rebutting Josephine Frampton's accusations against him.

'I only told the truth,' she replied, adding indignantly, 'but it's a good thing I *was* there to hear and see what happened. I think she was unforgivably horrid to you.'

'I really can't understand why she should lie about you in such a way, Wesley. Can you throw any light on the matter?'

'I think it must just be the way she is. It was her fault I was working at Moreton in the first place . . .'

Wes told the vicar and his young daughter the story of Widow Cake's fall and his ride to Moreton to fetch the magistrate. He also related how Josephine had frightened his horse and then told her grandfather he had deliberately put it across his lawn. He added, 'I believe she's told lies about under-gardeners before today. Mr Cull, the Moreton head gardener, said she's had two of them dismissed without references by making false accusations against them.'

Turning his head to look at his daughter, Reverend Warren frowned. 'Were you aware before today of the type of girl she is, Fanny?'

'I've always known she isn't a particularly nice person. But I never thought she'd go this far to spite anyone. Especially someone she hardly knows.'

'It most certainly is not normal behaviour. I doubt very much whether you are ever likely to achieve another invitation to Moreton. Should one come, however, I feel it must be refused.'

'I'm sorry . . .'

'My dear boy, it's not your fault.' Reverend Warren waved Wes's apology aside. 'I should be thanking you. I shudder when I think that Fanny might have become embroiled in young Josephine's tangled web of deceit and unspeakable behaviour.'

Embarrassed by the memory of what Josephine had tried to do in the bushes at Moreton, Fanny changed the subject abruptly. 'How is Widow Cake now?'

'She's improving,' replied Wes. 'At least, her leg is. Her temper hasn't changed very much.'

Reverend Warren smiled. 'Her bark has always been far worse than her bite, Wesley. She is very fond of you. I know because she has told me. Do you still read the Bible to her on Sunday mornings?'

'Yes. I think she enjoys that.'

'I *know* she does. Have you ever considered trying to bring her to a Sunday service in my church, Wesley? We would all be delighted to see you both there.'

'I don't think she'll be well enough to consider that for a very long time,' said Wes quickly. He knew what his father would say if he went to the village church, even if it were only to help Widow Cake.

'Then Fanny and I will call and see her some time in the week. Please pass my kind regards on to her.'

They were approaching Tolpuddle now. No one in the small cart noticed the slim figure standing close to the hedgerow in the lane that led to the Vye house. But Saranna saw them. She returned to her own home with a heavy heart to tell her mother that Wes would not be coming for his evening meal this Sunday.

Arnold was at the Gillam cottage. He was accompanied by Mary

Riggs, the shy young girl he hoped one day to marry. As was usual when he came visiting, he was tucking into a man-sized meal.

'Hello, Wes.'

Arnold spoke around a piled forkful of potato that disappeared inside his mouth and was swallowed before he spoke again. It always seemed to Wes that Arnold ate as though he feared that at any moment someone might come along and demand to share his meal.

'I came to tell you that Farmer Hooper from Southover brought the cow for Widow Cake this morning. I saw him taking it there and helped him. Widow Cake let me stay on and get the cow settled in. She said I'd been a great help. She's promised I can come in to help you tidy the hedges around the fields for the next couple of weeks.'

Looking suddenly bashful, Arnold said, 'Mary and me will likely be wed sometime next year. I'll need to get all the work I can. To put some money by for us.'

Rachel Gillam's delighted glance shifted from Arnold to the scarlet-cheeked Mary. 'Well I never! And there's you not said a word about it before today! You're a dark horse and no mistake, Arnold Cooper. Fancy you courting young Mary and keeping it quiet all this time.'

'I told Wes,' said Arnold. 'But I never told anyone else.'

'So our Wes knew, did he?' Rachel Gillam gave her son a disapproving look. 'Why is it you never tell me anything of what's going on? If it hadn't been for Arnold telling me that Vye girl will be looking after this cow, I'd never have known she was still working for Widow Cake. I knew she'd gone there for a day or two after the fall. I had no idea she was still there.'

'I didn't think you'd be interested in knowing what Saranna was doing. I seem to remember Pa saying he didn't want to hear her name mentioned in this house ever again.'

Before his mother could comment on this statement, Wes said, 'But I can tell you one good piece of news. I won't need to go to work at Moreton House any more.' Leaving out the embarrassing details, Wes told his mother what had happened at Moreton House that afternoon.

'The evil-minded little hussy! Who'd have thought that the grand-daughter of a magistrate could tell lies like that? You're best out of that place, my lad, and no mistake. I hope you thanked young Fanny Warren for taking your part? She's a good girl that one, for all she's Church of England. When you're looking for someone to marry – 'though that won't be for many a year yet – when you do, you'd do far worse than to take that girl as a yard-stick. I only wish our Saul had found himself one like that. He might still be here, in this house, instead of off goodness knows where, doing heaven knows what.'

'I'm glad you and I'll be working together for the next week or two, Wes,' said Arnold, happily, as though he had heard nothing of the conversation that had just taken place. 'I'll ask Saranna if I can help her with the cow sometimes, too. She's a good cow, and due to have her calf any day, so Farmer Hooper told me. He said that when she does she'll give so much milk that Widow Cake could supply half of Tolpuddle, if she's a mind. It's the sort of cow I'd like Mary and me to have one day.'

Wes and his mother exchanged glances and suddenly the tension that had been building between them at the mention of Saul and Saranna evaporated. Smiling at the simple young man, Rachel Gillam said, 'You and Mary will have everything you want one day, Arnold. The pair of you are going to be very happy – and I'll be happy too when someone else is feeding you. Every time you come visiting you eat me out of house and home! Now, hurry and finish that up. I've an apple pie waiting to fill the gap I know you have left. Then you'll need to get off home. Wes's father will be home any minute with his soul filled to overflowing and an empty belly.'

Eli Gillam returned to his home only minutes after Arnold and Mary had left. As his wife had predicted, his soul was replete with the good works he had been carrying out for the Lord that day. He was also glowing with self-righteousness.

Eli had heard of the troubles that were moving closer to the Tolpuddle area and was bitterly opposed to such action. In each of the chapels he had visited that day he had launched a fierce attack on the mysterious 'Captain Swing'. He also castigated the men who followed him so blindly, blatantly disregarding the laws of the land.

Thundering out his words in the voice that usually threatened a fire and brimstone reward for unrepentant sinners, the preacher proclaimed, 'This is England, not France. In our country justice is dispensed in the courts of the land for all to see. It cannot be achieved by a rowdy mob which requires the devil's darkness to cloak its despicable activities. Any man from my congregation who plays any part in such goings on will be damned by me – and doubly damned by the Lord. When others try to lead you along false pathways, remember my words and turn your back on them, as our Lord himself turned his back on the Devil in the wilderness.'

Listening to his father speaking of his admonition from the pulpit as he sat in the kitchen tucking into a heaped supper plate,

Wes wondered how he would have interpreted the 'justice' promised him by Magistrate Frampton that day in his parting threat.

Wes wondered, but said nothing. His father had made up his mind and stated his position publicly. He would not change it now because of anything his younger son might have to say.

Chapter 18

Wes's first task when he arrived at work the following day was to inspect Widow Cake's cow and give his verdict on the animal. He had hoped Saranna would be present, but she did not come from the house.

Wes felt guilty about the previous day. After being taken to his door by Reverend Warren and Fanny he realised that Saranna would have been expecting him to call at the Vye cottage, as he usually did.

The opportunity to explain to her did not occur until time for the midday meal came around. Saranna brought tea to Wes and Arnold when they were seated in the yard, sharing the bread and cheese Wes had brought from home.

She studiously avoided Wes's eyes and he knew she had been offended by his failure to call at her house.

'That's a very nice cow Widow Cake's got. Farmer Hooper's done her proud.'

'Yes.' It was the merest concession to civility. No more.

Wes realised more was expected of him and said, 'I'm sorry I didn't call in to see you on my way back from Moreton House yesterday.'

'You don't need to apologise to me. I saw you going home early with Fanny Warren, so I didn't expect you.'

In spite of her words, Wes knew she was offended. 'Reverend Warren offered me a ride home with them. I couldn't refuse.'

'You *could* have, but why should you? A ride in a pony trap with a vicar and his daughter's far better than calling in to see a widow who'd got supper cooking for him, and *her* daughter.'

'That's a foolish thing to say, Saranna. Anyway, I couldn't refuse the offer of a ride. Fanny Warren had just saved me from going to prison for a very long time.'

His words had the desired effect upon Saranna. With Arnold listening open-mouthed to every word, Wes told her the story of his confrontation with Josephine Frampton, going into somewhat more detail than he had with his mother.

When he ended the tale, Saranna exploded with indignation.

'The lying little bitch! And there's me been feeling guilty about pushing her in the river. I should have let her drown!'

'You *pushed* her in the river that day? Deliberately? Why?'

Embarrassed by her admission, but defiant, Saranna replied, 'She'd been pretty horrible to you and the opportunity was there . . . so I took it. I'm glad now. She deserves everything that's done to her.'

'That's what Fanny says . . .'

'Does she indeed? Then if *she* says so then it must be right. Mind you, with her being a vicar's daughter I'd expect her to have a bit more Christian forgiveness for others.'

With this unexpected *volte face*, Saranna flounced back inside the house, leaving a bewildered Wes convinced he would never understand this volatile girl.

That same evening, at about eight o'clock, Wes was sitting in the kitchen of the Gillam cottage, shaping a new handle for a spade, when there came a soft knocking on the door.

At the table, Rachel Gillam was stitching elbow patches on her husband's jacket. She looked up in surprise. 'Answer that, Wes. It's probably someone for your pa. Tell 'em they'll find him down at the chapel, at a meeting. They'd best go and find him there because I doubt if it will break up much before ten o'clock.'

Putting down the unfinished handle, Wes went to the door in a slightly irritable frame of mind. He had hoped to complete the handle tonight and it had already taken longer than expected.

It was not anyone for his father. Standing outside in the darkness was Saranna. She looked agitated and before he could say anything to him said in a low whisper, 'Wes, I must speak to you . . .'

'Who is it?' his mother called from the table.

Wes realised it would be useless trying to lie to her. 'It's Saranna. Saranna Vye.'

Wes thought he heard a gasp of surprise. 'What's she doing here? Well, don't keep the girl outside with the door open, letting in the cold air. Tell her to come in. It's high time I met up with her.'

Saranna entered the kitchen uncertainly, as though in doubt about her welcome. She wore her usual too-short thin dress. The only concession she had made to the cold was a shawl belonging to her mother, flung around her shoulders.

'Lord love us, girl, you must be frozen, coming out in this weather dressed like that . . . Come on over here by the fire and warm yourself.'

Rachel Gillam took the opportunity to look the girl over. She was younger than Rachel had been led to believe. She was also painfully thin and far too scantily dressed for this time of year. Rachel was also surprised to observe that the girl had a wide-eyed, open face. There was not the faintest hint of the slyness she had for some reason expected to find there.

'It's all right, Mrs Gillam. I don't feel the cold.'

Suddenly, Rachel remembered that this girl was a friend of her eldest son. She immediately assumed her visit had something to do with him.

'What are you doing here? Have you heard from our Saul? Is he in trouble?'

'I haven't heard from him since he left Tolpuddle – and I don't expect to.'

It was the *narrow* truth, but it was the truth. If Rachel Gillam had asked if Saranna had heard any news *about* Saul a lie might have been necessary. Her glance went to Wes.

'Widow Cake thinks her cow is going to calve tonight. She'd like Wes to be there.'

'What for? Cows are calving all the time in the fields. I've never heard tell of any of them that needed a midwife to tend her.'

Saranna smiled. At the same time, in spite of her assurance that she was not cold, she shivered. It was not missed by the other woman.

'You come and have a seat by the fire. Widow Cake's cow will have been carrying that calf for nine or ten months, I dare say. Another few minutes won't do any harm. The calf will arrive when it's good and ready, with or without help from our Wes.'

Busying herself at the fire, Rachel said, 'I'm glad to have the opportunity to meet you, at long last. Our Saul would often mention you.'

'I don't know why, Mrs Gillam. We didn't meet up all that often, really. When we did he always had other village lads with him.'

'I should hope so!'

Her indignation caused Wes to smile behind his mother's back as she continued, 'Things might have changed a whole lot since I was a girl, but it's still not done for a young man and a girl to spend time together without others being around to see they don't get up to any mischief.'

The disapproving words contrasted with the hot cup of tea and bread, butter and blackberry jam in generous portions placed on the floor beside Saranna's chair.

As the girl ate, Rachel looked at her critically. 'That dress has seen better days.'

Wes opened his mouth to protest at what he considered to be

his mother's rudeness, but Saranna spoke first. 'You're quite right, Mrs Gillam. It's seen a great many better days. It's a dress my ma wore when she was with Pa in Spain. I've got another dress for best, but this will do until I can afford the material to make myself a new one. That shouldn't be too long now I'm working regularly for Widow Cake. The trouble is, Ma hasn't had too good a time over the last few years. We need lots of things that are far more important than a new dress for me.'

'You're no doubt right, girl, but I've a couple of dresses doing nothing but grow old in a box upstairs. I had them when I was a girl. I grew out of 'em years ago but they were too good to throw away.'

With a glance at her son, Rachel added, 'I kept 'em in the first place thinking they'd be fine for a daughter one day, if ever I had one. I never did, so you might as well get some wear out of them. I had a bit more flesh on me than you have, so you'll need to take them in a bit, but you'll like them, I promise you that. I did.'

'That's very kind of you, Mrs Gillam . . .'

Rachel waved the girl's thanks aside. 'Better you should have them and make some use of them than let them rot away doing nothing. I'll look them out and send them in to Widow Cake's in the morning. Now, eat up, girl. You've got a bit of filling out to do.'

Chapter 19

'I like your ma.' The observation came from Saranna as the kitchen door closed behind Wes and herself in the darkness. 'But I don't think she'd like me very much if I'd told her what I know about Saul.'

'You've heard from him? But you said . . .'

'I said I haven't heard *from* him. That's the truth. But Uncle Richard came to the cottage today. He's there now, boasting of what's going to happen to those farmers who won't get rid of their threshing-machines and pay a "living wage" to their men.'

'What's all that got to do with Saul?'

'Some of Uncle Richard's men have come to Dorset from Kent, stirring up trouble along the way. He says they're "putting backbone" into the farm labourers. Saul's with them.'

'I can't believe Saul is stupid enough to get mixed up with smashing machines and setting fire to ricks! Pemble should know better too. He won't achieve anything for farmhands by going about things in such a way.'

'I don't believe Uncle Richard is very concerned about winning anything for anyone – unless it's himself. If the farmers and landowners agree to the men's demands everyone will go happily back to work and he'll be a leader without an army. While he's seen to be having some success there'll always be desperate men eager to join him. Without discontent, Richard Pemble would be nothing.'

They walked on in silence for a while, Wes was sunk deep in troubled thought. They were heading towards the home of Widow Cake when he came to a sudden halt.

'If this is the real reason you came to see me, why are we going this way?'

'Because what I said about Widow Cake's cow was the truth too. She *does* want you to look in on it.'

The cow had no need of their presence. When they entered the cow-shed and lit a lamp they discovered she had obligingly produced not one, but two female calves.

The cottage had been in darkness when they arrived, but Saranna's excited chatter as they left the cow-shed brought a quick response from a bedroom window.

'Is that you, Saranna? Is Wesley with you? What's happening to the cow?'

'She's had two female calves, Mrs Cake.' Wes called out the good news.

'Two? Well I never! I told you she needed some attention. It's a good job you were with her.'

There was a sudden change in the widow's tone of voice and Wes knew her mind was wrestling with the profit and loss that would result from two calves instead of one.

'Two, eh! They'll drink twice the milk of one . . .'

'You can always sell one and keep the other. It will fetch you a profit and still mean you have the start of a dairy herd, if that's what you want.'

'You let *me* do the thinking for the future of my own land, Wesley Gillam. All you need do is make certain the cow and calves are all right then get off home. It's a good job you were on hand to see the calves born, but I'll not take it as an excuse for coming in late for work tomorrow morning.'

The window closed with a resounding bang and in the yard Wes shook his head in resigned disbelief. Beside him Saranna giggled uncontrollably.

Saranna and Wes walked to the Vye cottage in the darkness, their conversation alternating between the possibilities for a small dairy herd on Widow Cake's land, and the more serious subject of the troubles in which they believed Saul to be involved.

Uncle Richard Pemble was in the kitchen of the cottage with seven other men. They were seated about the kitchen table on which stood a large flagon. The room was hazy with tobacco smoke and the air carried the heady aroma of cheap brandy.

The occupants of the room fell silent when Wes and Saranna entered until Nancy Vye said quickly, 'Richard, this is Wes Gillam. The lad I've been telling you about. The brother of Saul.'

Richard Pemble relaxed visibly, although the other men about the table still stared at Wes suspiciously. Extending a hand, the self-appointed labourers' leader said, 'I'm pleased to meet you, young man. Your brother is an enthusiastic supporter of our cause. In fact, I don't know how I ever managed without him.'

Wes thought the man's manner over-effusive and he mistrusted him immediately. He shook hands coolly as Pemble spoke to his companions.

'It's all right, Saranna works with young Wesley and I've known his brother for a couple of years. Now, you all have your instructions so there's no need for me to say any more. Good luck to you all.'

The men rose from the table and filed silently out through the kitchen door without a word to either Pemble or their hostess. Wes wondered who they were and what they were doing here, in the Southover cottage. They were not local men and their presence in the district would be viewed with suspicion by any constable or magistrate. They had the appearance of vagrants and would have been immediately drummed out of most towns.

As Nancy Vye opened the kitchen windows, muttering darkly about smoke and stale air, Richard Pemble spoke again to Wes.

'Would you like to work for the betterment of the working man, the same as your brother, Wesley? I could make good use of you.'

'I'm quite happy working for Widow Cake, thank you. The reason I'm here is to try to get some news of my brother. The family's concerned for him. What's he doing?'

'He's serving his fellow men, Wesley. Persuading them to join together in an invincible association. To make a stand against those employers who are cutting wages for no other reason than to increase their own profits. To show the error of their ways to farmers who are buying those diabolical threshing-machines. Casting men and women who've worked for them for years on parish relief.'

'Do you mean that Saul is going around smashing machines and burning ricks?'

'Of course not! Whatever gave you such an idea? No, Wesley, my men don't do such things . . .'

Richard Pemble's words and accompanying smile should have been reassuring. However, for the second time that evening Wes found himself doubting this man's sincerity.

'Those who serve me need use no violence, Wesley. They usually find logical argument suffices. Oh no, young sir. Any violence that may occur surely stems from those who are frustrated in their quest for a fair wage in return for a full day's work. Men who ask only for the means to lead a dignified life. Sufficient to support a wife and children without going cap in hand to the very men who drove them to poverty in the first place. Very modest and moderate aims, surely?'

Wes could find no hole in the man's argument, but he said, 'If your aims are so reasonable, there should be no need for violence or rick-burning by anyone. Do you try to prevent it from happening?'

'My task is not to protect the farmers and landowners, Wesley.

They are more than capable of doing that for themselves. I feel it my duty to help those who work the land to improve their increasingly meagre lot in life.'

'The best way you can do that is by preventing them from breaking the law, surely? A man can't do much for his family once he's been arrested and thrown into jail – and that's what going to happen if there's trouble around here. Magistrate Frampton called a meeting of farmers and landowners at Moreton House yesterday. Afterwards, Reverend Warren told me that Frampton's appointed a lot more constables and is going to try to re-form the county yeomanry.'

'Is he, indeed? Thank you for your most interesting information, young sir. I'll follow your advice and do what I can to prevent any of my followers, or their labouring friends, from suffering arrest. Unfortunately, I doubt if I will be able to prevent all violent incidents. Men are learning by bitter, frustrating experience that unless farmers and landowners fear the consequences, they will take no notice of a labourer's just demands. It's a harsh fact of this world of ours, as I fear you will one day learn.'

'Where's Saul now? I'd like to talk to him.'

Pemble shrugged. 'I have no idea. I've been on the road for a couple of weeks. I believe he has too. If I meet up with him I'll certainly ask him to get in touch with you.'

Apparently dismissing Wes from his mind, Richard Pemble smiled up at Saranna's mother. 'Nancy, my love. Did I hear you say you had some mutton pie to spare for me? I'm famished and I still have to ride on to my lodgings in Dorchester. While I eat I'll tell you of some mutual acquaintances I met on the road recently . . .'

Wes knew he would obtain no more information from Pemble. Feeling irrationally angry with the man, he left the house.

He had not reached the gate when the door opened and shut behind him and he heard Saranna's bare feet running on the pathway. Her voice called, 'Wes . . . wait!'

Stopping at the gateway, he waited for her. 'Wes, I heard Uncle Richard and Ma talking earlier. Ma asked about Saul, same as you did. He told her that the last he heard of him Saul was with some other men at Cranborne Chase. I don't know where that is, but I thought you might.'

Wes nodded. 'I've heard of it. It's not too far away, beyond Blandford. Thanks, Saranna, but why didn't Richard Pemble tell me this?'

She shrugged. 'I don't know. Perhaps because he doesn't know you well enough to trust you yet. He's a very suspicious man. What will you do now? Will you try to find Saul?'

'I'm not sure. I believe he's most probably heading in this direction anyway. If he's not I might go looking for him and try to persuade him to return home. I don't like Richard Pemble, Saranna, and I don't trust him. I believe that if Saul stays with his men, he'll end up in serious trouble.'

'I think so too. Uncle Richard uses people and doesn't really care about them, whatever he says to the contrary.'

'If you can find out any more, let me know.'

'I will. Wes . . . if you do find Saul before we have time to meet again, ask him to come and see me, please? There's something I want to talk to him about.'

'Don't worry, I'll make certain that Saul doesn't return to the area without calling on you. But I'm sure he would anyway.'

Wes turned away abruptly and walked briskly off along the lane. He still felt angry. The anger was directed at Richard Pemble, but if he was honest with himself he knew he would have to accept that it had been re-kindled by the information that Saranna was anxious to see Saul once more.

Wes would have been surprised had he known that Saranna stood for a long while at the cottage gate in the darkness – and she was as unhappy as he was. He would have been equally surprised had he known the reason she wanted to talk to his elder brother. The knowledge would certainly have taken the edge off his anger.

Chapter 20

For the next few days Wes suffered from a troubled conscience. He could not make up his mind whether or not to tell his mother what he knew of Saul. He knew that if he did, he would need to make a great many explanations about his visits to the Vye cottage and tell her of the men he had met there. The problem was that his mother would then deem it her duty to tell his father.

The result would be a repetition of the arguments and accusations concerning Saranna. This time it would be Wes and not Saul who would be the target of his father's anger. Eli Gillam might even decide to inform Magistrate Frampton of what he knew . . .

On the other hand, if Saul returned to the Tolpuddle area and landed himself in trouble and Wes had said nothing to anyone . . .!

He thought the problem over from every possible angle without arriving at a decision. He eventually decided to keep his own counsel. He would take whatever action was necessary if, or when, the opportunity arose.

He was to witness the troubles stirred up by Richard Pemble's teachings sooner than he might have anticipated.

The following evening, shortly before he was due to finish work, Wes was in the fields with Arnold when he heard a hubbub from the track that wound over the hill behind Widow Cake's home. It was the sound of many men shouting, singing and chanting intermittently.

It had been a crisp, dry day and Wes and Arnold had been completing work on the hedges of one of the fields farthest from the house.

It was a few minutes before Wes realised that the unfamiliar noise was the sound of a mob on the move – and it was drawing nearer.

'Quick, Arnold, back to the house.'

'I haven't finished yet . . .'

Grabbing Arnold's arm, Wes propelled him in the direction of Widow Cake's cottage, silencing his protests and urging him to move faster.

104

When they were still a field's breadth from their destination, Wes looked back. Dusk was falling, but it was still light enough for him to see the vanguard of a veritable army of men coming over the hill. He was alarmed to see quite a few of them carrying either pitchforks or staves.

Wes and Arnold reached the house to find Saranna and Widow Cake in the garden. The two women had heard the noise but could not yet see the men advancing towards them.

'Get inside the house, quickly.'

'Don't you order me about in my own house, young Wesley. Not while I'm paying your wages . . .'

There was no time to argue and he said, 'Better me than have a mob of men give you orders, Mrs Cake. Go inside and bolt the doors – close all the windows too. With any luck they'll by-pass the house. There's nothing for them here, but we don't want to tempt them.'

Widow Cake would have continued to argue but Saranna said firmly, 'Come on, Mrs Cake. Wes is speaking sense. These are the men who've been terrorising the countryside for weeks. There's no telling what they might do if they learn Wes and Arnold are the only men about the place.'

Wes was not certain whether he should accept this as a compliment to his logic, or a slur on his ability to protect the two women against the advancing men.

Grumbling every limping footstep of the way, Widow Cake eventually allowed herself to be led inside the house. Wes breathed a deep sigh of relief when she had gone. There was likely to be trouble enough without having interference from the fiery widow-woman.

'What do you think the men will do when they get here, Wes?'

'I don't know, but we won't take any chances. Go and close the door of the cow's house – and shut the chickens away too.' If any of these men were of the type he had seen at the Vye house, he would put little past them.

'You don't think they'd do anything to the cow or her calves?' Arnold was aghast at the thought.

'We just don't know, Arnold, but we'd be foolish not to take precautions.'

As Arnold hurried away to carry out his instructions, Wes wondered what the mob might demand from him or Widow Cake. Their avowed targets were the farmers and landowners. The ageing widow hardly came into either category. She was, however, an easy target for anyone with mischief in mind.

Taking up position at the cottage gate, Wes waited for the arrival of the men with a mixture of fear and excitement.

The noise being made by the approaching mob became far greater as it drew nearer. He believed it must contain at least four or five hundred men and the thought made his knees go weak. Eventually the leading ranks came into view and at sight of Wes standing by the gate they set up a cheer that was echoed mindlessly by those behind them.

A few minutes later men were crowding around the gate but, as yet, no one tried to come in. In fact, they did not appear to know what they would do next.

Not until a large, bearded, ruddy-faced man pushed his way through the crowd around the gate was anything said directly to Wes.

'Hello, son. Do you work here?' The man spoke in a not unkindly way.

'I do.' Wes's reply was cautious.

'We're all farm labourers, marching for our rights. Are you with us?'

'I appreciate what you're trying to do, but I work for a crippled widow-woman. She needs me here to take care of things.'

There was a swell of sound from the mob and Wes thought as many men seemed to appreciate his position as were murmuring against him.

At that moment Arnold came around the side of the house and the men seized upon his arrival eagerly, calling for him to come with them.

'How much land does the widow-woman have?' The man who had first spoken to Wes asked the question.

'About fifteen acres.'

'It doesn't take two young men to look after a widow-woman and fifteen acres. Besides, the day's just about over as far as work is concerned.'

Pointing to Arnold, the spokesman said, 'You can come with us.'

'Me?' Arnold was delighted to have been singled out by the man, even though he knew nothing of what it was all about. Turning to Wes, he asked, 'Can I go, Wes?'

The question put him in a predicament. He could not hurt Arnold's feelings by telling the mob's spokesman that the lad was simple, yet he did not want him to go off with these men. They would not help him if trouble erupted, and Arnold was too slow-thinking to protect his own interests.

'Arnold needs to go home to take care of his grandmother. She's a widow too.'

'With so many widows around it sounds as though they have need of a few more men around here. Perhaps we should plan on staying for a while!'

The voice came from the heart of the crowd about the gate and provoked a laugh from many men near to the speaker, but the spokesman rounded on them angrily.

'That's enough of such talk. We're here to demand a wage that a man's family can live on. No more, and no less.'

To Arnold he said, 'We need every available man in the area to give us his support. It doesn't need two of you to look after a few fields. Are you with us?'

After a quick glance at the disapproving Wes, Arnold nodded eagerly. 'Yes!'

'Good man!' The spokesman swung the garden gate open. 'Come on then. We've a few farmers and a vicar or two to have words with before the night's over.'

'Arnold!' Wes's call halted the eager young man as he was closing the garden gate behind him. 'Be sensible and act responsibly. If it looks as though there's likely to be trouble, think of how upset Mary would be – and get on home.'

Arnold acknowledged Wes's warning with a nod of his head, but he was already being swept along with the human tide that filled the narrow lane and spilled over the verges.

As the mob marched by, many who had not heard the exchange between Wes and their leader jeered him, demanding that he come out and join them.

For his part, Wes was busily scanning faces, hoping to catch a glimpse of Saul. But he was not among these men. Neither was the young Tolpuddle man who had left the village with him.

Wes recognised a number of men among the crowd as farm workers from some of the outlying farms, but the vast majority were strangers. He believed most probably had little interest in the well-being of the farm labourer and his family. In common with Richard Pemble, they were probably exploiting the situation for their own ends.

These were the men responsible for the extortion and petty larcenies that had accompanied the recent progress of the mob through the counties of Southern England. It was the actions of such men, as much as the demands of the agricultural labourers, that had prompted retaliatory measures by the country's magistrates.

The tail-end of the mob comprised a motley miscellany of crippled and sick men, and women too. When they had passed by, Saranna came from the house and stood beside Wes at the gate.

'Me and Widow Cake were watching from the window. She was impressed by the way you dealt with them. For a while we thought they were going to come in through the gate and ransack the house. What did you say to stop them?'

'I didn't need to say anything. They were more interested in

107

getting me to go with them than in coming in. I told 'em I worked for a widow who needed me here. It was a pity Arnold came to the front of the house when he did. They took him off instead. The trouble is he hasn't got the sense to break away and leave them if they get up to mischief.'

'Wesley, what's going on out there? Why has Arnold gone off with that mob of ne'er-do-wells?'

'He didn't have any choice, Mrs Cake, I was just telling Saranna about it. They're going around the district gathering all the men they can to join them. Then they intend calling on the farmers and demanding that they pay a fair wage. They said they'd be calling on a vicar or two as well. They're probably wanting them to reduce their tithes.'

Amelia Cake sniffed derisively. 'They'd be better saving their breath and praying for what they want. If Our Lord came back to earth to feed the multitude with his loaves and fishes, the clergy would demand their tithes before he's be allowed to hand them around. All the same, I think you ought to go into the village and warn Reverend Warren that the mob might call on him. From the look of some of them I saw, he'd be wise to lock the doors and put up shutters at the windows.'

'If I meet up with the mob again they'll force me to join them . . .'

'You persuaded them to leave you alone once, you can do it again. Tell them you're on an errand for me and I need you back here again quickly.'

Wes thought the mob were not likely to take notice of him again, but he owed a debt to Fanny Warren and her father. If he cut across the fields he hoped he might stay clear of them.

As he went out through the gate, Saranna said anxiously, 'Take care, Wes. I recognised some of the men in the crowd. Most are wanted felons. They're as bad as you're likely to find anywhere.'

Wes acknowledged her warning then set off down the lane. He had no intention of meeting up with the mob again if it could possibly be avoided.

Chapter 21

Wes's plan for avoiding the marching agricultural workers and warning Reverend Warren of their intentions suffered an early setback. Although the marching men were not aware of the fact, news of their approach had travelled ahead of them with a messenger despatched by the magistrate of the district they had last terrorised. As a result, they found the lane into Tolpuddle blocked by a hastily summoned force of yeomanry.

There were no more than fifteen of the mounted gentlemen militia, but they carried arms and the true representatives of the agricultural labourers had no wish for such a confrontation. Like Wes, they left the road in favour of the adjacent fields. In accordance with a pre-arranged plan, they also split into a dozen smaller parties.

There were too few of the yeomanry to do the same. After a hasty consultation, they decided they would follow one of the larger parties and ensure they caused no trouble.

Unfortunately for Wes, many of the less savoury elements of the mob remained in one of the other groups. It was these men, with no thought of reasoned discussion in mind, who settled on the vicarage as their target.

It had grown dark now and Wes had no idea of what was happening in the village. As part of their preconceived plan to confuse those who sought to contain them, each group of men was making as much noise as possible.

To Wes, making his way through the fields towards the village, it seemed that the whole of Tolpuddle had erupted in noise. It was not until he had scaled the rear wall of the vicarage and made his way through the large orchard to the garden, that he realised other men were here before him.

The sound of voices made him suddenly freeze. Then there was the sound of breaking glass and a cheer rose from the throats of perhaps a dozen men as one of the windows at the rear of the vicarage was shattered.

Wes's first instinct was to flee from the garden, but his thoughts went to Fanny Warren. If for some reason she was alone in the house, she would be terrified by what was happening around her.

Suddenly, the clamour of the men at the front of the house ceased abruptly. Wes had no way of knowing what was happening there and his hopes that the men between himself and the house would go to investigate were quickly dashed. They began to enter the house through the broken window.

In fact, Reverend Warren had come out from the front of the house and confronted the noisy mob there, calling on them to make their demands known.

The cry went up immediately that they wanted money. Almost as an afterthought, one of the few farm hands who had been carried along with this particular group of demonstrators, cried out that they also wanted a reduction in the tithes demanded from farmers by the Church. The high percentage of their crops which went to the Church was one of the reasons given by the farmers themselves for being forced to cut wages.

Reverend Warren's immediate response was to call for a spokesman to come forward and discuss details with him.

From the midst of the crowd a man shouted, 'We want money, not talk.' His fellows shouted their agreement, one of them accusing the Tolpuddle vicar of 'playing for time'.

The Tolpuddle vicar was a patient man, even if those confronting him were not. 'Gentleman, I am perfectly prepared to be reasonable – but only if I am dealing with men of a similar disposition.'

The wave of anger that swept through the mob was an almost physical thing. It reached out and touched Thomas Warren and he took an involuntary step backwards, towards the door.

'Don't let him go inside!' 'Stop him!'

The knot of men about the front door of the vicarage surged forward, but at that moment there was a shout from another, larger group of men, advancing up the path to the house.

'That's quite enough of that. We'll have no violence here – or anywhere else for that matter.'

It was the authoritative voice of the man who had spoken to Wes outside Widow Cake's cottage.

'D'you hear me? Back off, or you'll be taking on considerably more than you can handle.'

The men who had been advancing on Thomas Warren shuffled back slowly and reluctantly, grumbling their displeasure. It came as a great relief to the vicar.

'Are you the men's spokesman?' He addressed the new arrival.

'We have no spokesman. No leaders. We're all equal here, sharing a common purpose. That way there's no one man can be picked upon for doing any more or any less than another.'

'Such an arrangement is quite understandable,' agreed Reverend Warren. 'However, it does create certain difficulties when it comes to discussing your demands.'

'Our demands are so simple they require very little discussion, Reverend. However, if it's your wish that I should air our grievances, I'll gladly oblige.'

'You're an erudite man, sir, and no stranger to the art of discussion. Are you a Methodist preacher?'

'What I am is of no consequence, Reverend. Neither will you hear any names mentioned among us. All we seek is an assurance that all farm labourers will be paid a wage that's sufficient to feed our families. We also ask that no machines will be used to rob us of our jobs.'

'I am in full agreement with a man being paid a wage that keeps his family and himself from being a burden on the parish. But why should I be a target for you and those with you? I employ no farm labourers.'

'In one word, Reverend, tithes. You see . . .'

At that moment the sound of a scream broke in upon the discussion. It was a woman's or a girl's voice and it seemed to come from somewhere at the rear of the house.

The farm labourer's spokesman and the Tolpuddle vicar looked at each other in silence for a brief moment only, then Thomas Warren turned and ran inside the house.

'Come with me.' The spokesman snapped the words at two of his companions, then followed the Reverend Warren into the house.

It was apparent to Wes that the men at the rear of the vicarage had smashed the window with the sole intention of gaining access to the house. One of the first men to enter opened the rear door to the remainder. A few minutes later all the men had disappeared inside.

Wes was in a quandary. He had hoped to be able to warn Reverend Warren of the approach of the mob, without being seen himself. But he was not certain the vicar was even at home. He decided the best thing would be to make his way through the shrubbery and find out what was happening at the front of the vicarage.

He had started on his way when he heard the men returning from inside the house to the rear door once more. They appeared to be leaving the house but in the faint light from the stars he could see they were carrying something between them. It was probably something they had stolen.

Wes stepped farther into the shrubbery, allowing the

undergrowth to hide him from view. He could not see what it was the men had taken from the house. They laid the object on the grass and crouched about it, hiding it from his view. They appeared to find something amusing. Suddenly, one of them cursed. 'She bit me! Give her the back of your hand, Alf. That'll stop her struggling.' At the same time there was a scream and the agonised voice of a girl begged, 'Please! Don't . . . Leave me alone. Please . . .!'

It was Fanny Warren the men had carried from the house and they had her on the grass . . .!

Without pausing to think of the possible consequences to himself, Wes broke clear of the bushes and charged across the ground between them. He was spurred on by yet another scream, this one ending in a moan that followed the sound of a blow.

Wes burst upon the group with fists and feet flailing. Initially he succeeded in scattering them, so great was the shock of his unexpected arrival.

His foot rolled on something lying on the ground and, bending down, he picked up a wooden stave, left there by one of the men. Picking it up, he wielded it to a considerable effect, striking three or four men before a voice said, 'What's the matter with you? It's only one – and he's a mere slip of a lad.'

Wes turned to face the man who had spoken, but he never even saw the man's outline. Something struck him a violent blow on the forehead and the world exploded about him in a myriad blinding lights.

Chapter 22

Thomas Warren emerged from the back door of the house at a run. It was dark here, but he could see a struggle taking place some paces away. In the midst of the mêlée he could hear the sobs of his daughter.

He ran towards the scene, but was overtaken by the man to whom he had been speaking at the front of the house, together with his companions.

Pushing him none-too-gently to one side, the man said, 'Leave this to us, Reverend.'

A moment later the three men threw themselves into the struggling group. When Fanny's attackers became aware of the strength and ferocity of the newcomers, they broke and ran, leaving one of their number unconscious on the ground.

'Fanny! What happened? Are you all right, girl?'

Even in the faint light of the stars, Reverend Warren could see that much of his daughter's clothing had been ripped from her body. A moment later she was clinging to him, trying to control her sobs.

'Can you walk to the house?'

'Yes.'

She walked beside him, pulling her torn clothing about her as they went.

At the door they were met by a male servant carrying a lantern. Thomas Warren's initial reaction was anger because he had not prevented the men outside from carrying off Fanny from the house, but one look at the man's face told the Tolpuddle vicar that the servant *had* come into conflict with the mob. His right eye, almost completely closed, was as purple as a bishop's cassock.

Averting his eyes from the near-naked Fanny Warren, the servant handed the lantern to the vicar. 'I'm sorry, sir. I was on my way to Miss Fanny's room when I met up with a number of men ... men of a most unsavoury character. They hit me with something and bundled me in a cupboard. I only managed to make my escape a few seconds ago. Take the lantern, sir. I'll go and find Miss Fanny's maid to come and help her.'

113

Thomas Warren took the lantern and glanced at Fanny. He immediately placed himself between the light from the lantern and his daughter. In that brief glance he saw more of her than he had since the day she was born.

'Come, dear. We'll get you to your room. When your maid's tended you we'll have a talk. These men will pay for what they've done, I promise you that.'

'Father! Wesley's out there somewhere. Wesley Gillam.'

'Is he, by God! Then he'll suffer for this too . . .'

'*No!* You don't understand. He tried to help me. When the men were . . . attacking me, he suddenly came in among them, fighting them. If it hadn't been for him . . .'

She left unsaid what would have happened had it not been for Wes's intervention. 'One of the men hit him with something. I fear they might have killed him. He's probably still lying outside in the back garden.'

'I'll go and find him, just as soon as we have a maid to help you.'

Reverend Warren put a hand to his forehead. 'I wish your mother were here right now and not in London. She'd be more use to you than I. On the other hand, if she had been, she would most probably have been a victim of the mob too. I really don't know what England is coming to, Fanny. I thought such things could only happen in France . . .'

Thomas Warren returned downstairs, after passing his daughter into the care of a maidservant who was herself in a state of some distress. Below he met the mob's spokesman, who had come to the rescue of Fanny.

'My deepest apologies for the distress caused to your family, Reverend Warren. This was not the work of any of the agricultural labourers who marched to Tolpuddle tonight. The men who attacked your daughter have probably never put in a day's work on the land – or anywhere else. They are vagrants. Vagabonds of the worst kind, although the one we picked up unconscious seems to be no more than a lad. He's better dressed than most of them too.'

'When you march in defiance of the laws of the land you must expect to attract those to whom the law means nothing. You are as guilty of what happened tonight as the men who attacked my daughter. But where is this lad you found unconscious? Fanny said one of the villagers tried to rescue her and was knocked unconscious by her attackers.'

'My men have taken him to the front of the house. They were going to tie him up and leave him for the constables when they arrive, as they surely will any minute. I don't want to be here

114

when they do. Magistrate Frampton's brand of justice doesn't appeal to me.'

'Take me to this lad before you go. I don't agree with you about Magistrate Frampton, but I fear if the constables once have Wesley Gillam in their hands there will be little chance of righting a wrong.'

When Wes regained consciousness he became immediately aware of his painful, throbbing head. He also realised he was in an unfamiliar room. It was high-ceilinged and there was an elaborate chandelier hanging almost immediately above him.

'Ah! I'm pleased to see you've come back to us, Wesley. I was beginning to think I'd need to send for a doctor to bring you round.'

The voice was that of Reverend Warren, but when Wes turned his head to look at him it produced such pain in his head that he winced.

'You've suffered a very nasty blow to your forehead. I *should* send for a doctor, but we'll wait to see how your head feels when your mother arrives. I've sent a servant to fetch her.'

'How's Fanny?' Memories of the moments before he was knocked unconscious flooded back to Wes. He remembered her lying on the ground, surrounded by some of the worst elements of the mob.

'She's in her room, recovering from her ordeal. It would have been far, far worse had it not been for your intervention, young man. Fanny and I are deeply in your debt. The only thing I can't understand is what you were doing here in the first place. I refuse to believe that a young man of your intelligence would throw in his lot with a mindless mob.'

'They came over the hill behind Widow Cake's cottage and tried to force Arnold Cooper and me to go with them. They took Arnold, but let me stay behind at the house to take care of Widow Cake. While I was talking with them they said they were going to call on a couple of vicars. We guessed you'd be one of them and Widow Cake sent me to warn you. I cut across the fields to try to beat them here, but I arrived too late.'

'You arrived in the nick of time, young man – thank God! I must find some way of rewarding you.'

As they were speaking, a doorbell jangled somewhere in the house.

'That will no doubt be your mother, Wesley. I'll go to meet her, if you'll excuse me.'

A couple of minutes later, Wes heard footsteps in the passage-way outside the room. Then the door opened and his mother came in. She was accompanied by Reverend Warren – and Saranna.

'Well! You look a right mess and no mistake! What's all this Reverend Warren's been telling me about you getting involved in fights and rescuing young Miss Fanny? I don't know, there's me thinking you're safely at work at Widow Cake's and away from all the trouble. The next minute this young lady's on my doorstep asking if you'd returned home safely.' She indicated Saranna.

'Widow Cake was worried when you didn't return, Wes. I said I'd come and see if you'd gone on home.' Saranna did not add that the suggestion of coming to look for him was entirely her own.

Now she and Wes's mother had located him, Saranna was extremely relieved. On the way through the village they had met a local man hurrying to his home. He reported that Magistrate Frampton and his constables were riding the countryside, arresting anyone who was abroad without a satisfactory reason.

Nevertheless, she was distressed to see Wes's injury. There was a serious cut in addition to the lump and the bruising and one of his eyes was beginning to close. Had the blow landed a couple of inches lower he would have lost the sight of his eye. As it was, she feared he would always carry a scar on his forehead to remind him of this evening's happenings.

All the talking going on about him was causing Wes's head to ache more than ever. But he had been lying here long enough.

'I think I should go home now.'

He pushed himself up slowly from the couch on which he had been placed. The pain in his head made him feel physically sick, but he persisted.

'Are you quite certain you're all right, Wesley?' Reverend Warren asked anxiously as he saw the pain on Wes's face. 'You are quite welcome to remain here for as long as you wish. Until morning, if need be.'

'I'll be all right.'

Despite his assurance, Wes felt the room suddenly tilt away from him. Saranna realised what was happening to him and moved swiftly. She supported him with her shoulder beneath his armpit and an arm about his waist until he ceased swaying.

'Don't worry, Reverend. We'll have him home in no time. Thank you for taking care of him.' Rachel Gillam spoke to the vicar as she followed Saranna and the slow-moving Wes from the room.

'My dear lady! It is I and Fanny who owe a debt of gratitude to your son. I would like to call on you in the morning, to satisfy myself he is on the road to recovery. I also wish to discuss something with you that I will need to think about tonight.'

Helping Wes from the room, Saranna heard the conversation between Thomas Warren and Rachel Gillam and felt uneasy. It was a very similar feeling to the one she had when she saw Wes riding from Moreton House with the vicar of Tolpuddle and his daughter. She had accepted the feeling as simple jealousy then. Now she was not so certain.

Saranna had learned never to ignore her intuition. It was telling her now that Reverend Thomas Warren and his well-bred young daughter had the ability to come between Wes and herself.

Chapter 23

Preacher Eli Gillam returned home late that evening having suffered a great many indignities. He was in no mood to listen to the part his son had played in rescuing the daughter of a Church of England clergyman. He had suffered, albeit indirectly, as a result of the march of the men who claimed to represent farm labourers such as himself.

James Frampton was the cause of his indignation. The Moreton magistrate had succeeded in routing the demonstrators, but he had not restricted his actions to the roads and lanes around Tolpuddle.

The vicar of the nearby village of Affpuddle had been subjected to similar demands as his Tolpuddle colleague. Fearing for his safety, the clergyman had parted with three guineas.

However, no sooner had the jubilant demonstrators departed from Affpuddle than the vicar rode off to complain to the Moreton magistrate.

Magistrate James Frampton was already abroad with his constables, fired with enthusiasm for his mission against all who disturbed the king's peace. Upon receipt of the vicar's complaint he set off to find those guilty of this latest outrage. By their action in extorting money from the rector and threatening him with violence, they had committed a capital offence.

Honest farm labourers and not-so-honest vagrants had all forsaken the lanes and roads, taking to fields and woods to evade the zealous magistrate's men. Frustrated at finding no one to arrest, Magistrate Frampton decided he would extend his search.

A prayer meeting was under way in the Tolpuddle chapel, in defiance of the mayhem outside in the village street. Suddenly, the doors burst open and Frampton and his constable entered the place of Methodist worship. In stentorian tones that carried above their rising protests, Frampton ordered everyone in the room to remain seated.

To add insult to injury, Frampton had brought the Church of England vicar of Affpuddle with him. It was to him the magistrate now turned.

'Can you recognise any of the men who took your money among those here?'

'I protest most strongly.' Eli Gillam tried to control his rage, knowing the Moreton magistrate was quite likely to turn it against him. 'This is a prayer meeting of men and women going peacefully about the Lord's business.'

'And I am a magistrate, going about the king's business,' retorted Frampton. 'There have been a series of serious disorders in the Tolpuddle district tonight. I have questioned a number of arrested malefactors. Most belong to Wesley's church. Have any men entered this building during the past hour?'

'Every man and woman here holds a Methodist ticket, signed by me. Each is known to me personally and they have been here all evening. No one has left, and no one has entered since then. We have held our meeting despite the noise of galloping horses outside and the shouting of your constables.'

While the two men were holding their stiff and acrimonious conversation, the Affpuddle vicar had been walking up and down the aisles, peering closely at the seated Methodists.

The magistrate turned to him now. 'Do you see anyone here you recognise, Vicar?'

He stopped at one line of seated members and peered closely at a pale, dark-haired youth. Straightening up, he said, 'This looks very like one of them.'

The accusation provoked an unexpected wave of mirth from the others in the chapel. The Moreton magistrate looked about him in puzzled annoyance before returning his attention to the youth.

Before Frampton could say anything, Eli said to the youth, 'Stand up, Simon.'

'I . . . can't, Mr . . . Gillam. You . . . you know . . . that.'

The young man spoke with difficulty, his words indistinct.

'Why not?' Enraged by the increasing merriment about him, Frampton snapped the question at Eli.

'Simon has been unable to stand unaided since the day he was born. He was carried into our church this evening, as he is for every meeting. He can talk only with great difficulty. Now, sir, you are interrupting our meeting . . .'

'I'll interrupt it for a while longer,' said the tight-lipped magistrate. 'We'll not be leaving until my constables have taken the names of every man, woman and child here.'

An hour and a half later, when Eli arrived home, he was still incensed by the manner in which his prayer meeting had been disrupted by the magistrate from Moreton and the Affpuddle vicar, and in no mood to sympathise with his son who had been injured in support of the family of a Church of England clergyman.

'The boy was a fool for getting mixed up in something that was none of his business. He might well have ended up in prison. Frampton interrupted my meeting tonight. He would have arrested young Simon Todd had it not been proved to him that the poor lad couldn't even stand by himself.'

'So he hurt your pride! Where's the blood or a bruise? Perhaps you have a bump somewhere because of it?'

Eli glared angrily at his wife for a moment or two before the impact of her words went home.

'Is Wesley badly hurt?'

'He has a nasty cut and bruise on his forehead. It will probably leave him marked for life.'

'Where is he now?'

'He went to bed as soon as we got him home . . .' Rachel bit back the information that Saranna had helped get him back to the cottage. Now was not the occasion to bring her name into the conversation. 'His head hurt so much he could hardly see straight. I think he must have gone off to sleep immediately.'

'He was lucky it wasn't far worse. I'll speak to him tomorrow and tell him to keep well clear of all these troubles. Frampton has made it clear more than once that he detests Methodism, and those who practise it. Nothing would delight him more than to put as many of us as possible in prison or, better still, pack us off to Botany Bay.'

'It's a good thing our Wesley was there to rescue the poor Warren girl. Goodness knows what those men would have done to her if it hadn't been for him.'

'I still say it's nothing to do with us. Men who organise such mobs should be called to account for their actions, but there are faults on both sides and I don't want any member of this family getting involved. Now I'm off to bed. The meeting tonight went on much later than I'd intended thanks to Magistrate Frampton. I need to be up early in the morning. The mob has been visiting farmers as well as clergymen tonight. I'll need to check they haven't done any mischief to Tom Priddy's land or buildings.'

'I thought you were strong against involving yourself in anything the mob is up to? None of our business, you just said.'

'Looking after Priddy's business is looking after *our* interests too. He pays my wages . . . such as they are. It's entirely different.'

'Yes, it would be.'

Eli looked at his wife uncertainly. 'You're sharp-tongued tonight, Rachel. It's not like you at all.'

'Perhaps I am. It's been a difficult night. I've been worried sick about our Wesley, yet all you can talk about is the interruption to your meeting and not getting involved. There was a time when you'd have been upstairs the minute I mentioned Wes's being hurt, to see for yourself he was all right. As it is, I doubt if it's even crossed your mind.'

'He's had you tending him, Rachel. What more can I do? I'll look in and see him now, on my way to bed.'

'Don't bother yourself. He's already asleep and shouldn't be disturbed. Besides, it's the thought that counts, not necessarily the deed.'

Eli went to bed believing the whole world was against him that night. He did look at his son, but there was little light and he could not see the extent of his injury. Nevertheless, Wes was breathing heavily and steadily, so the Methodist minister was able to go to bed without being too concerned about the well-being of his youngest son.

Lying awake in the bedroom before Rachel came to bed, Eli was deeply troubled. It seemed his whole comfortable and predictable world was crumbling about him. Saul had left home after a foolish argument for which Eli admitted to himself he had been largely to blame. His safe, undemanding work was being threatened by the introduction of machinery. Men in authority, like the magistrate from Moreton and the Affpuddle vicar had treated a prayer meeting at the chapel with callous contempt yet he had been able to do nothing in defence of everything in which he believed. The country was in turmoil. His younger son was lying upstairs with a cut head, victim of a mob – and now his own wife seemed to be turning against him.

Eli was bewildered by it all. The only answer he had was prayer. Kneeling beside the bed in his room, he prayed for the patience and humility to understand what was happening about him and the wisdom and courage to deal with events beyond the scope of his uncomplicated mind.

He prayed fervently, as he always did, trying not to be distracted by the weight of the problems that were weighing heavily upon Tolpuddle, and his own family in particular.

Chapter 24

The next morning, Eli left the cottage before dawn. Wes was still sleeping and his father did not attempt to wake him.

Still annoyed with her husband, Rachel said little to him over breakfast. Eli went to work in the same unhappy frame of mind that had been his at bedtime the night before.

Rachel left waking Wes until it could be put off no longer if he was to go to work. She left eggs and two slices of bread frying in the skillet and went upstairs.

Wes's breathing was as deep and regular as it had been the night before and there was no break in it when she spoke to him.

'Come on now, our Wesley. I've got breakfast cooking for you downstairs.'

When Wes failed to respond, his mother shook him gently by the shoulder. After a momentary pause he continued breathing as heavily as though he had not been disturbed.

'Wesley, wake up now. I hope you're not playing one of your silly games. I've got breakfast cooking for you downstairs.'

But Wes was not playing any sort of game. He was as deeply unconscious as he had been immediately after the blow to his head.

After shaking him progressively more violently, Rachel became deeply concerned. She did not know what to do. The situation was outside her very limited knowledge of medical matters, but there was no doctor closer than Dorchester. This was a case for Rosie Amos.

Rosie lived in chaotic squalor in a tiny, two-roomed cob and thatch hovel behind the water mill. Grumbling, she opened the door in response to Rachel Gillam's insistent knocking. Two black cats promptly fled out through the doorway, pausing only to exchange blows with a tabby that successfully evaded Rosie Amos's kick and disappeared inside.

'Damn that animal! It belongs over at the mill, but it'd rather come in here thieving than catch mice over there. Help me catch it, will you?'

'I'm over here about my Wesley. He's lying in bed at home . . .'

'We'll talk about your Wesley when that cat's out of here, and not before. There he is, up on the table already. Get him and throw him out. You can move faster than me ...'

The tabby cat had its head in a half-filled basin of dripping. It could have chosen from any one of a couple of dozen unwashed dishes that were also on the table, many of them containing scraps of food, some of it green with mould.

Rachel grabbed the cat, shifting her grip to a one-handed hold on the scruff of its neck when it scratched her. In response to Rosie Amos's command she heaved the cat out through the door which was promptly slammed shut by the aged occupier.

With the door closed, the smell inside the tiny cottage was overpowering. Rachel silently cursed the animal that had forced her to enter the cottage, instead of conducting her business on the doorstep.

'Now, what's the matter with your Wesley? Been up on the common with the same gipsy girl as the other two young lads I've been treating, has he? If he has then you'd best mix him up a solution of mercury and tell him to keep away from the village girls until he's cured.'

'Wesley's been up to nothing like that,' said Rachel indignantly. 'He's had a good Christian upbringing. No, he took a nasty blow on the head from one of those troublemakers who terrorised the village last night. He was unconscious for a while, but when he came round I got him home and into bed. This morning I can't wake him.'

'Whereabouts was he hit? Front or back of the head?'

'On the front. About here.' Rachel raised a hand to her forehead.

'How's his breathing. Deep and even, or irregular?'

'Deep and even, as though he's fast asleep.'

Rosie Amos nodded her head. 'There'll be a nasty bump on his forehead too, I've no doubt?'

'It's come up like a hen's egg.'

'You'll need to put something on it to be sure the bruise is brought out.'

Reaching up to an over-crowded mantelshelf, she brought down a small, dark glass bottle, wiped the dust from it with her sleeve and held it out to the other woman. 'There's a little opium solution here. Put it on with a piece of muslin and tie it into place. As the bruise comes out he'll get better. That'll be a shilling.'

'But ... aren't you even coming to the house to see him for yourself?'

'What for? I know exactly what it'll be. Concussion's what a doctor would call it. Young Marion Brine had the same, when she was trampled by Farmer Hooper's old bull. Lay without moving or speaking for nigh on seven weeks, she did. Now look at her, she's as right as a summer's day.'

'Right as . . .? Marion Brine's as simple as a one year old!'

'Some folk might call her that, but she can do a full day's work almost as well as anyone. Like I say, that'll be a shilling, if you don't mind.'

'A whole shilling for a spoonful of opium liniment and for saying Wesley's likely to be like Marion Brine?'

'No, a shilling for assuring you he *will* recover and for putting your mind at rest. I know it's worth that to you, Rachel Gillam. You're not like that Kathleen Bullen. Meanest woman I've ever met, she was. I treated her father, same as I'm treating your Wesley, in the way I know is best. She wouldn't pay me what she owed.'

'But her father died!'

'That's right. And all for the sake of a shilling, it was.'

Rachel was grateful to escape into the chilly grey morning outside Rosie Amos's cottage. Clutching the small bottle, she hurried home to apply the opium solution to Wes's injured head. She knew she should be at work now, especially as there was no way of knowing for how long they would have to do without Wes's wages. Yet she could not leave her son lying unconscious, alone in the house. She hoped her employer might understand.

Saranna came to the house soon after nine o'clock and expressed her concern when Rachel told her of Wes's condition.

'I feared something like this might happen, Mrs Gillam. I knew Wes weren't right when we brought him home last night. When I tried to speak to him he'd suddenly start talking about something entirely different, as though he hadn't heard what I'd said. I lay awake worrying about him. Do you think you ought to get a doctor? I don't mind walking to Dorchester to find one.'

'You seem very concerned about him, young lady. Did it worry you just as much when our Saul went off to goodness knows where?'

'I'm still worried about Saul – as a friend.'

'Saul led us to believe there was something more than *friendship* between you, Saranna.'

'So everyone keeps telling me. Whatever he may have told other people, he said nothing to me. He's a very nice friend to have, but he's *only* a friend as far as I'm concerned.'

Rachel looked at her speculatively. 'And what about our Wesley? Is he a friend too?'

Saranna met Rachel's eyes almost defiantly for a moment or

two, then she dropped her gaze. 'I like him a lot, Mrs Gillam.'

Rachel sighed. 'Oh, well, you're still very young yet. You've both a lot of growing up to do.' Suddenly brisk, she said, 'Shouldn't you be at work? It won't do for us all to lose our jobs over Wesley.'

'I've already been to Widow Cake's. When neither Wes nor Arnold turned up for work, she sent me to find out what was going on.'

'Arnold isn't in? He's probably overslept. Didn't you tell me he was gathered up by the mob last night?'

'That's right. I'll call at his house on my way back to Widow Cake's, if you tell me where he lives.'

Rachel hesitated for only a moment. 'I'll go along there and see what's happening. I need to call in at East Farm to tell them why I'm not at work this morning. You stay here until I come back. I've put Rosie Amos's opium liniment on Wesley's head, like she said. I don't like to leave him alone, in case he should come round while I'm away.'

'I'll stay with him, Mrs Gillam.' Saranna could hardly contain her delight at being left in the house with Wes, albeit an unconscious Wes. 'If he comes round I'll make him a cup of tea or something.'

'I won't be gone that long.' Rachel was beginning to doubt the wisdom of leaving Saranna in the house, but she would be back before they could possibly get up to any mischief. 'You just sit down here. Wesley's at the top of the stairs. You'll hear him if he wakes.'

For some time after Rachel Gillam had left the house, Saranna sat close to the fire. She rose once to open the door at the foot of the stairs. It was ill-fitting enough for her to hear any movement from upstairs, but she wanted to be certain.

After she had opened the door, she kept glancing towards the stairs. Mrs Gillam had been gone for quite a while already. She would probably be back soon and Saranna would go back to work without even having seen Wes.

She rose to her feet twice, only to sit down again. When she stood up for the third time she had made up her mind. She would go up to take a peek at Wes. It could not hurt.

The bed was so close to the top of the stairs that Saranna could see him even before she had reached the top. He was not lying on his back, as she had expected, but on his side, and there was a linen bandage about his head holding a pad of cloth in place on his forehead.

He looked very pale and there was a discoloured swelling about one of his eyes. Saranna felt a wave of affection and sympathy surge through her as she stood beside his narrow bed. Reaching out, she almost touched the bandage, but pulled her hand back just short of Wes's head.

'Poor Wes! I wonder if you'd have risked your life had it been me the men were attacking?'

Replying to her own question in the same breath, she said, 'Yes, I think you would.'

Bending low over him, she kissed him on the cheek before turning and starting quietly down the stairs.

'That was nice!'

Startled, Saranna swung around. Wes wore the expression of a man who was having difficulty waking, but his eyes were open and he was looking at her.

'Wesley Gillam! You're supposed to be lying unconscious. How long have you been awake?'

'I didn't know I was – until you kissed me.' Suddenly his eyes shifted to the familiar things about him. Frowning, he said, 'How did I get home – and what are you doing here?'

'Your ma and me brought you home last night from the vicarage. I came to see how you were this morning and your ma asked me to stay while she went to Arnold's house, to see if he's overslept.'

'Arnold . . .? What time is it? I should be at work now.'

He moved as though to sit up but groaned and dropped his head to the pillow once more, wincing in sudden pain.

'You're not fit for work just yet. Lie there and I'll go downstairs and make you a cup of tea. It'll be a wonderful surprise for your ma when she comes back.'

As Saranna started down the stairs once more, Wes asked, 'Did Ma really ask you to stay in the house with me while she went off?'

'Yes. You were unconscious when she went so she knew we couldn't do anything wrong.'

'She obviously didn't know you were going to creep up to my bedroom and kiss me!'

When Saranna made no reply, Wes added hopefully, 'You could carry on feeling sorry for me and do it again, if you wanted to.'

'There's not much wrong with you if you're having thoughts like that, Wesley Gillam.' Saranna smiled happily, relieved that Wes had regained consciousness and pleased by what he had said. 'I'll make you a nice, sweet cup of tea and you can have that instead.'

Saranna was pouring the boiling water on the tea leaves in the cup when Wes's mother returned to the house. She was immediately given the good news of Wes's first step to recovery.

'Glory be!' Rachel clasped her hands together in an attitude of prayer. 'At least there's some good news to be had this morning.'

It took a moment for the meaning of Rachel's words to sink in. 'Why, what's happened? Is something wrong with Arnold too?'

'Very wrong. I spoke to his grandmother. Arnold didn't come home last night. She was more angry than upset. He'd told her he intends marrying Mary and she thought he must have spent the night with her.'

'But you don't think he did?'

'I *know* he didn't. I met Constable Hammer on my way back from East Farm. He's puffed up with his own importance because of what he and the rest of Magistrate Frampton's men got up to last night. He told me they'd arrested twenty-eight men as a result of the disturbances. Arnold's one of them.'

Chapter 25

Reverend Warren called at the Gillam house shortly before noon. It was the first time a Church of England clergyman had ever come to the door of the staunch Methodist preacher's home and Rachel felt ill at ease. However, the Tolpuddle vicar appeared not to notice and accepted her nervous invitation to enter the cottage.

Ducking his head to avoid the low beam above the door, he asked, 'How is Wesley this morning?'

'I was very worried about him first thing. I couldn't wake him. I think he must have been unconscious. That's why I'm home from work today. Rosie Amos gave me something to put on his head and he came round later on. I hope he might be fit enough to get out of bed later on today.'

'What would the village do without Rose Amos? I only wish she might do something for Fanny, but I fear Rosie could do nothing to help her recover from the terror to which she was subjected. However, my immediate concern is Wesley. Should he lapse into unconsciousness again you must let me know immediately. I'll have a doctor brought from Dorchester to look at him.'

'Thank you, sir. That's most kind of you. I think he'll probably be all right now, but I gather from what you've said that Miss Fanny isn't at all well?'

'I confess I am very worried about her – as you are about Wesley, of course. She was in her room weeping when I left the vicarage and did not wish to see me. I've told the servants to stay in close attendance, but I will be very, very glad when her mother returns from London. I sent for her this morning but I fear it will be a few days before her return.'

'Poor Miss Fanny. It was a dreadful experience for her. If there's anything I or Wesley can do . . .?'

'It would have been far worse had Wesley not been on hand – and that is why I am here, Mrs Gillam. I would like to do something to reward him.'

'That isn't necessary, sir. I'm quite sure Wesley wasn't looking for any reward.'

'Of course not, but had he not come to warn me about the mob

128

and fought off the men who were attacking Fanny, he would not have received his injury. Now, may I tell you what I have in mind before I speak to Wesley?'

'I have felt for many years that your son is a very bright boy. Quite exceptional. It is sad to see talent of any description wasted, so I would like to pay for him to go away and improve his education. I have a friend who takes in boarders at a school in Dorchester. That is not too far away, I am sure you will agree? Many of his pupils go on to the University of Oxford. With a year or two's extra tuition, there is no reason at all why Wesley could not go there too.'

The thought of Wes going to a university was more than Rachel could immediately take in. 'Why . . . it's a wonderful offer, sir. Wonderful. But I would have to speak to Mr Gillam.'

'Of course. Speak to him tonight and let me know his views. But it *is* a wonderful opportunity for Wesley. I am confident he will be a great credit to us all. Now, may I see him?'

Upstairs, at the top of the stairs, the Tolpuddle vicar took in the frugal surroundings without comment. It was, after all, no different to most other cottages in Tolpuddle – and a great deal cleaner than many.

Wes was lying in his bed, his eyes open, and the vicar smiled at him. 'Good morning, Wesley. You're quite the wounded soldier with a bandage about your head. But I believe you're on the mend?'

'I'm fine,' lied Wes valiantly. 'How's Fanny?'

'In a very similar state to yourself. Suffering as a result of the mayhem that took place last night. She and I have you to thank that it didn't turn out to be far worse. I've already spoken to your mother about rewarding you. As I remember, you told Fanny and me recently that you would like to have more learning. I have discussed the matter with your mother. If it is your wish, I would like to pay for you to attend a school in Dorchester and perhaps go on to a university.'

Wes looked from the vicar to his mother in incredulous delight.

'Of course, it would need to be with your father's approval.'

The light died in Wes's eyes. 'He would never give his permission.'

'I can't imagine that he would stand in your way, Wesley. Any man would surely be overjoyed to have his son receive a first-class education?'

Wes looked at the vicar silently for a few moments, then he said, 'Even he if *does* agree, we couldn't afford for me to stop working. Pa's pay has just been cut, like most farm workers'. It's hard for them to manage. That's why so many of them were on the march last night.'

'There are other ways in which they can air their grievances. Violence will solve nothing. However, this is neither the time nor the place to discuss such matters. I can see your problem, Wesley, but I trust your mother and father can come to some arrangement on the matter. If not . . . well, perhaps I can offer you some tuition at the vicarage. I'll speak to Widow Cake about it. No doubt Arnold Cooper could take on some of your work for a couple of hours each day . . .'

Reverend Warren saw the expression on Rachel's face and asked, 'Is something the matter, Mrs Gillam?'

'Yes. I'd almost forgotten, but your mention of Arnold reminded me. He's been arrested and taken to prison in Dorchester. Constable Hammer told me.'

'Good gracious me! This is difficult to believe. Arnold is not the type of young man to involve himself in anything for which he might be arrested.'

'Why has he been arrested?' The question came from Wes.

'The constable said he was with a group of men who met up with a Dorchester magistrate and a number of constables a couple of miles west of Tolpuddle. They were coming from a farm where some threshing machines had been damaged. I believe there was a scuffle when he and the others were arrested.

'Why should they want to arrest Arnold in the first place? He wasn't one of the men who was causing all the trouble. They *made* him go with them. Took him from Widow Cake's cottage. They would have taken both of us if I hadn't persuaded them that Widow Cake couldn't cope for herself and needed someone to stay at the cottage.'

Wes's angry indignation was causing his head to ache, but he appealed to his mother.

'I must do something to help him, Ma. You know Arnold. He would never do harm to anyone, but he'll be confused and frightened if they've locked him up in a cell.'

Wes started from his bed, but unbearable pain pressed down upon his head like a great weight. Groaning, he sank back to the pillow.

'I'll see what I can do to help Arnold,' said Reverend Warren. 'But I won't be able to leave Tolpuddle until Mrs Warren comes home. I daren't leave Fanny. . . .'

'Of course not. I'll speak to Widow Cake about Arnold. She might have some ideas.' Rachel expressed her sympathy. 'You must go back to Miss Fanny now, sir. She might have come to her senses and be calling for you this very minute.'

'Yes, I fear you might be right, Mrs Gillam. You will speak to your husband about Wesley? He is a very bright lad, you know.

130

He deserves to be given an opportunity to better himself.'

'I'll do what I can – and thank you very much, sir. I appreciate your calling to see him. Wesley does too, but I fear his head is troubling him at this moment.'

'I can see that, Mrs Gillam. Take good care of him. In the meantime I'll see what I can find out about Arnold. If need be I will write to the magistrate who arrested him. Arnold is not the type to involve himself with the men we saw in Tolpuddle last night. A mistake has been made. Once the facts have been explained, I don't doubt that he will be released from custody. Good day to you, Wesley – and good day to you too, Mrs Gillam.'

Chapter 26

After Reverend Warren had left the Gillam cottage, Wes lay in his bed thinking of all that had been said during the Tolpuddle vicar's visit. There was much to consider. Arnold's arrest was a matter of great concern, but Wes believed it was a mistake that would be quickly rectified. He was far more excited about the possibility of schooling in Dorchester and how it might open up his future. It would mean an awesome change in his way of life. In the life of the whole family.

The thought of his father gave Wes pause in his flight of fancy. Eli would never agree to his going away to school, fees paid by a Church of England clergyman. Wes's elation quickly turned to gloom.

He thought about the matter from every angle for more than an hour. His head ached more and more until, eventually, he fell into a deep sleep that verged on unconsciousness.

When he awoke the room was in darkness and he knew something had roused him. Then he heard the sound of his father's voice raised in anger in the room below.

Wes knew immediately that it had to do with him, and Reverend Warren's generous offer to finance his education.

'You shouldn't have allowed Warren to step over the doorstep, Rachel. I'll not have an Anglican clergyman coming here and disrupting my household. Splitting son from father – and trying to divide husband and wife!'

'Don't over-react, Eli. Reverend Warren came here to thank Wesley for saving his only daughter from those men. To show his gratitude, he's offered to give our son – *our* son – the sort of learning that's usually given only to the sons of gentlemen. It's such a wonderful opportunity for the boy, Eli. Think about it. It's the sort of chance in life that poor people like us can only dream about.'

'An opportunity to do what? How would he use such learning? Will it be for the good of the Methodist Church? Will he become a minister? If I thought the answer would be yes, I'd let him go. No sacrifice would be too great to achieve such an end. But

Reverend Warren wouldn't send him if he thought his money would pay to educate a *Methodist* minister. Anyway, Wesley has no enthusiasm for the wonderful teachings of his namesake. Indeed, his lack of interest in the Church, and that of his brother, has been the subject of much sad comment within our society. It causes me much personal pain.'

'Eli, as I have said very many times, life – real life – doesn't begin and end at the chapel door. We should accept the opportunity that's being offered to our Wesley with gratitude. With learning he'll be able to put his God-given talents to a much more worthwhile use than spending his days working for Widow Cake here in Tolpuddle.'

'What's waiting for him in the next life is of far more importance to the boy than what he does in this one, Rachel ...'

'Stop being so pompous and hypocritically self-righteous, Eli Gillam. I'm sick of it!'

Rachel's sudden unprecedented outburst took her husband by surprise. He looked at her in open-mouthed disbelief, but Rachel was not done yet.

'Does the Methodist Church ban men because they have money in this life? No. Does it tell wealthy farmers and landowners they are not welcome because they are not suffering in this life? Of course not. They are welcomed with open arms, even though they flaunt money and lands that have been passed on to them. I've not met one of them who has earned anything he owns. God has seen fit to give Wesley a good brain, Eli. It's *his* gift to our son. Would you dare to say it shouldn't be appreciated to the full? Would you dare say that?'

'Rachel, I'll not have you speak like that in this house. I can understand the strength of your feeling on the matter. After all, Wesley is the child of your body, your youngest child, but that gives you no right to talk to me in such a manner. I am your husband. Think about it sensibly. What would people say if I allowed a Church of England vicar to pay for my son to go away to school? I would never be able to hold up my head in chapel again.'

Rachel looked at her husband in silence for so long that he began to feel uncomfortable and said, defensively, 'I've said all there is to say on the matter. We'll speak no more about it.'

'Oh yes we will, Eli. I never thought I'd see the day when my husband would put his own pride before the future of one of his children – and that's what's involved here. It doesn't seem to matter to you what would be best for Wesley. That he's been offered a wonderful opportunity to become something more than a farm worker. A chance to break free from this miserable existence that you and I are forced to endure. But your *pride* won't allow it! It was your pride that drove our Saul from home. Your pride that wouldn't allow you to apologise for being wrong about him. Are you going to drive Wesley out in the same way, Eli? Well then, since pride is so important to you, where was it when Thomas Priddy said he was docking a shilling from your wages? But I'm forgetting, he's a good Methodist – even though he can afford that shilling a week he's stopped from your wages far more than we can.'

'That's enough, Rachel!' Eli thundered out the words in his best chapel fire-and-brimstone voice, but she refused to be intimidated.

'There's a proverb which says: "The devil wipes his tail on a poor man's pride", Eli. Remember that when you're telling others of their vices.'

'I'll not be spoken to like this in my own house . . .'

'Since all this argument seems to be about me, can *I* say something?'

Wes had come down the stairs unnoticed. He stood now in the corner of the room, pale and bandaged, looking from one to another of his warring parents.

'Wesley! You shouldn't be down here. You might have come over giddy coming down the stairs.'

Rachel hurried across the room to her son and Eli fell silent at sight of Wesley standing none too steadily with a bandage about his forehead. Beneath the bandage a bruise extended beyond his left eye which was closed and surrounded by swollen and discoloured flesh.

Eli spoke almost defiantly to his son, uncomfortably aware that Rachel had swung around to face him when he began to speak. 'I've just told your ma, I don't doubt that Reverend Warren's offer to you is well-intentioned, but we don't need to accept charity from the vicar of Tolpuddle just yet.'

'It's my life you're talking about, Pa. My future. Don't I have anything to say about it?'

'You're too young to know your own mind . . .'

'No, Pa.' It was not usual for Wes to interrupt his father, but he did it firmly now, looking straight at him. 'I'm old enough to bring money into the house – and it's because of the need to bring in money that I can't go away to school.'

Eli glanced triumphantly at his wife. 'There! Wesley knows himself that it wouldn't be right.'

'I didn't say it wouldn't be right. If things were different for us it would be all I could wish for in life. But things are bad and likely to get worse. We need my money coming in.'

'You mustn't let such thoughts lose you this chance to do some-thing with your life, Wesley,' his mother pleaded. 'We'll manage, I promise you.'

'I know you'd try, Ma, but it would be too much for you – and for me too. If I went away to school I'd need clothes and . . . oh, all sorts of things we couldn't afford. Things that I couldn't ask Reverend Warren to give me. It just wouldn't work.'

'You've put a lot of selfless thought into this matter, Wesley. I'm proud of you.'

'Yes, Pa. I *have* put a lot of thought into it. But, although I can't possibly go away to school, I'm going to accept the vicar's offer of schooling in the evenings, after work – and one or two afternoons in the week too, if Widow Cake will let me go.'

'You'll do no such thing!'

It was an automatic reaction from Eli and everyone in the room knew it.

Rachel expressed her views immediately. 'You can't praise Wesley in one breath for thinking things out and in the next tell him he's wrong.'

'I will if I believe all his thinking has resulted in the wrong answer.'

'What you mean is you won't agree if it's not the answer *you* want.' Hands on hips, Rachel glared at her husband.

'There's no need for you and Pa to argue about me, Ma.'

Returning his attention to his father, Wes said, 'I *have* thought about it, Pa, and I've made up my mind. Doing things this way, I'll get extra learning and still be able to bring money into the house – that's if you still want me to stay at home?'

'Of course you'll stay at home! Whatever next?!'

Rachel Gillam was not a large woman, yet, standing in the centre of the room, arms akimbo, she dominated the room and gave her husband an ultimatum.

'He *will* stay, Eli – and he'll take his lessons in the evenings too. You drive him out of this house, the same as you did Saul, and I'll go too. We'd see then how your pride would cope with *that*!'

Eli looked from wife to son in utter bewilderment. He was unused to having either of them disregard his wishes. Yet here were both of them standing together against him. It was more than he could cope with without the Lord's help.

'What's the world coming to when a man is no longer master in his own house? I'm defied by my son – both my sons – and now my wife too! This is a sad day and no mistake. A very sad day. I'm going out, to the chapel.'

Taking his coat down from a peg behind the door, Eli shrugged it on as he left the house.

When the door had closed behind him, Wes said unhappily, 'I'm sorry, Ma. I didn't mean for you and Pa to quarrel like that over me.'

'Don't think it was entirely over you, Wesley, although it might seem that way. Much of what I said has been festering inside me since before our Saul went away. It'll be better for everyone now it's out.'

'But . . . what about Pa? What do you think he'll do?'

'I know exactly what he'll do. He'll go to chapel, get down on his knees, pray a lot and think a lot. He'll come to realise that we're right in what we've said and in what you've decided. Don't expect any apologies from him, but he'll accept in his heart that he's being unreasonable. He's a good man, Wesley, for all that he's stubborn and prideful. You'll get your schooling and when you've made something of your life your pa will be as proud of you as though it was all his own idea in the first place. You'll see.'

Chapter 27

Wes went to work the following morning. His forehead pained him, but he no longer had the skull-crushing headache from which he had suffered for the previous twenty-four hours.

The first thing he did upon his arrival was to look in through the kitchen door, hoping to see Saranna. She was not here, although the fire was lit and a kettle was singing quietly on the hob. Noticing that the log pile was very low, he began carrying logs from the wood-shed to the kitchen.

As he made his second trip, Saranna came into the yard with a broom to sweep the slate flagstones. Greeting him with a warm smile, she said, 'Neither Widow Cake nor I expected to see you back at work for a few days. How are you feeling?'

'I've enjoyed better days, but I'll survive.'

'I came to your house to see how you were last night.'

Wes stopped with his load of logs and frowned. 'No one told me you'd called.'

'That's because I only came as far as the kitchen door. I never knocked or anything. I could hear your father inside. He sounded angry, so I went away again.'

'He was angry . . .' Wes told Saranna of the family argument and of its cause.

She listened to his explanation and it was impossible to deduce from her expression what thoughts were running through her mind. 'Will you be going away to school?'

'No, but I intend having lessons at the vicarage on as many evenings a week as Reverend Warren will give me. Perhaps I'll be able to go for an afternoon too if Widow Cake will let me off.'

Brushing the flagstones slowly and thoughtfully, Saranna asked, 'What do you intend doing with yourself after you've got all this learning? Become a preacher, like your pa?'

'No!'

It came out with such vehemence that Wes felt it necessary to give Saranna an explanation. 'Every preacher I've ever met always believes he's right about whatever he happens to be talking about, and never really hears what anyone else says to him. I don't want to be like that.'

'So what *are* you going to do then?'

'I don't know, Saranna. I only know I don't want to spend the rest of my life working for Widow Cake, or someone just like her, for a shilling a day.'

'You carry on chatting outside in the yard and you'll lose your shilling a day from me, Wesley Gillam. Get on with what you have to do and stop holding Saranna up. She's got work to do too.'

Wes glanced up to see Amelia Cake looking at him from an open bedroom window. He moved off towards the kitchen door, but her voice brought him to a halt once more. 'Have you heard anything of Arnold?'

'Not since Ma got news of his arrest from Constable Hammer.'

'I was hoping he'd be back at work by today. If you hear anything about him, you let me know straightaway, you hear?'

There was plenty of work to be done in the vicinity of the house and Wes worked steadily until noon when he stopped for his midday meal. He was eating in the wood-shed when Saranna came out with a cup of tea for him.

Seating herself on the logs, she suddenly said, 'Was Miss Fanny with the vicar when he called on you yesterday?'

'No, he said she's taking a long time to get over all that happened that night. It seems she hasn't left her room since.'

Saranna made a noise in her throat that might possibly have expressed sympathy. 'I expect you'll be seeing a lot of her when you begin taking lessons at the vicarage?'

'I might, but I doubt it. She'll have her own things to do and I'll be working hard to make the most of my time there. Anyway, does it matter whether I do or not?'

'Not to me, it doesn't. I just think she's sweet on you, that's all.'

'That's a stupid thing to say, Saranna. Fanny mixes with folk like the Framptons. People with money and large houses. I'm just a village boy – and from a Methodist family too. If you're saying that just because she and her father have always spoken whenever they see me, then you might as well say she's sweet on every boy in the village!'

Wes felt he had been forced on the defensive and the knowledge irritated him. Taking only a mouthful of tea, he stood up. 'I'm going back to work. I've got that ditch behind the house to clear. Unless it's done it will take only one good storm for the cottage to be flooded out. It's taking me a lot longer without Arnold to help me. He's a good, strong worker and I miss him.'

Not at all contrite about the effect of her questioning on Wes, Saranna said, 'Poor Arnold. I wonder when they're going to set him free.'

'The sooner the better. I need help with that ditch.'

He was leaving the shed when Saranna said suddenly, 'Saul's back in the Tolpuddle area.'

Wes spun around to face her. 'How do you know? Where is he? Have you seen him?'

'I haven't – but my ma has. He called in to see her on the night of all the troubles, just before the riot began in Tolpuddle.'

'I hope he didn't get mixed up in it. You don't suppose he's in Dorchester gaol right now too!'

'No, he was heading south towards Crossways when he left our place.'

'Why didn't he call in to see our ma – or me?'

Saranna shrugged. 'I don't know. You'll need to ask Saul when you see him. He's bound to come back, sooner or later.'

After Wes went out to carry on with his work, Saranna made her way to the barn which held the cow and its two calves. She had thought it better not to tell Wes all she knew. During the night when Saul had said he would be in the vicinity of Crossways there were no fewer than seven rick fires in the area. All the ricks belonged to farmers who had cut the wages of their workers by a shilling a week.

Halfway through the afternoon, Wes straightened up from the ditch he was clearing and saw Mary Riggs hurrying towards Widow Cake's cottage. She worked at the vicarage and he thought she might be coming to find him. He waved to her, but she appeared not to see him and entered the cottage. Wes decided her visit had nothing to do with him after all. She had probably come with some message for his employer from the vicar.

Only a few minutes later, Wes heard his name being called and looked up to see Saranna standing in the cottage garden.

'Wes! Wes – come quickly!'

Throwing down the spade he had been using, Wes hurried to the cottage. Entering the kitchen he saw Mary. Sitting in an armchair across the fireplace from Widow Cake, she was crying bitterly.

Saranna explained, 'She's been to Dorchester to see Arnold. He came up in the magistrates' court today and Mary expected he'd be set free and sent back home. Instead he was charged with some other men with destroying a machine on one of the farms along the Dorchester road. They've committed him to prison and he's to be tried by a court of special something-or-others, who are being sent from London.'

'They didn't even let me go down to the cells to speak to him,' wailed Mary. 'All I could do was sit in court and listen to all the lies they said about him. I sat behind him the whole time, but he didn't even know I was there . . .'

As Mary's tears flowed ever more freely, Widow Cake snapped, 'The government has appointed Special Commissioners to try the cases of those who've been involved in the riots. I've heard all about them. By all accounts they're no better than Judge Jeffreys was – and when he came to Dorchester he sent nigh on a hundred men to the gallows.'

The widow's words caused Mary to wail louder than ever. 'I'll never see him again, I know I won't . . . and we were to be married.'

'Hush, girl. We'll see about this.' Turning to Saranna, Amelia Cake said, 'Give Mary something to eat and drink – and quieten her down, for goodness' sake. It doesn't help Arnold and it makes me bad-tempered. Wesley . . . go and find Reverend Warren. Tell him I want him here – and quickly. He and I have things to do.'

Chapter 28

When Wes was shown in to the vicarage by a servant, he found Reverend Warren in almost as distraught a state as Mary Riggs. The Tolpuddle vicar seemed relieved to see him.

'Have you come to call on Fanny? She'll be very pleased to see you, I'm sure. Perhaps talking to someone of her own age might snap her out of her dreadful melancholy mood. I really don't know what to do with her. It wasn't until this morning I learned from a servant that she hasn't eaten since the evening she was attacked by those scoundrels. It's quite abominable that such men can roam the countryside putting decent, law-abiding citizens in fear of their lives.'

'I'm very sorry to hear about Miss Fanny, sir, but that isn't really why I'm here. I've been sent by Widow Cake. She wants to see you urgently.'

'Dear, dear, dear! It seems that it never rains but it pours. Do you know what it's all about?'

'Yes, sir. It's about Arnold Cooper. He appeared in the Dorchester magistrates' court this morning. Mary Riggs went to see him, expecting he would return home with her. Instead, she said he was charged with helping some other men to destroy a threshing-machine. He's due to appear before a court of Special Commissioners.'

'Arnold charged with destroying a threshing-machine? That's quite preposterous! Why should he do such a thing? His livelihood isn't being threatened by them!'

'We all know that, but Widow Cake says something needs to be done urgently. She wants to speak to you about it.'

'Why me?'

'I don't know, sir, but she sent me here to fetch you.'

'Oh dear, oh dear! Why does the good Lord have to send so many things to try me. I do my very best, but I fear I shall be found sadly wanting when Judgement Day comes. Wesley, please pay a call on Fanny while you're here. Try to cheer her up a little. She won't talk to me, but she might to you.'

Escorted by a maid whom he had often seen about the village,

141

Wes went upstairs to Fanny's room with considerable trepidation. He found the whole house awe-inspiring. It had many rooms, some of them larger than the Gillam cottage, wide, high-ceilinged corridors and carpeted stairs. There was luxury here such as he had never seen before.

When they reached a white-painted door on the first floor, the maid knocked briefly before turning the handle. Stepping inside the room, Wes's first impression was of airy lightness. The room had light walls, light curtains, and crisp, light bedclothes. There was also a mirrored dressing-table in the room upon which was an assortment of brushes and bottles of many shapes and sizes.

Propped up at the foot of the bed was a beautifully carved wooden doll with lifelike glass eyes and dressed in the very height of fashion.

'I've brought a visitor to see you, Miss Fanny,' said the maid.

'I don't want to see a visitor. I don't want to see anyone.' There was a brief pause before she said hesitantly, 'Who is it?'

'It's Master Wesley Gillam, Miss. Him from the village.'

Wes thought the body beneath the bedclothes tensed and Fanny's voice said, 'I don't want to speak to him – or to anyone.'

'Well, miss, seeing as how he's here now, I really think you should talk to him. While you're making up your mind I'll go down to the kitchen and get Cook to make a cup of tea for him.'

Without waiting for a reply, the maid walked out of the room, leaving Wes peering at the back of Fanny's head, that being all he could see of her. He felt decidedly uncomfortable and out of place.

'I'm sorry you're still not feeling very well, Miss Fanny, but it's hardly surprising. It was a frightening business for you. I spent most of yesterday in bed too. Not that I remember much about it. I was out for the count for most of the time.'

'Does your head hurt now?'

Wes found Fanny's question encouraging. At least she was talking to him. Reverend Warren had given him the impression she was speaking to no one.

'It hurts a bit and I can't see out of one eye, but it looks worse than it is. Were you hurt anywhere?'

There was no reply to his question and Wes fidgeted through a long silence until he broke it by saying, 'Do you know Arnold Cooper? He works with me at Widow Cake's sometimes. He's a little bit simple, really. When the mob came by they made him go with them and he's got himself arrested. It sounds as though he might be in serious trouble. Your father has gone to see Widow Cake about it now.'

'I hope they arrested the men who attacked me!' Fanny spoke vehemently.

'I hope so too. Would you recognise any of them again?'

Now she had begun to speak to him, Wes tried to keep her talking.

Fanny shuddered beneath the bedclothes. 'I could never forget the face of the man who came into my room and . . . and grabbed me. There were others behind him, but I didn't see them. Then . . . then they dragged me out into the garden . . .'

Fanny's voice broke and she began weeping softly.

'I'm sorry, Miss Fanny.' Wes felt ill-at-ease in a bedroom with this girl whom he really did not know very well, and whose background was so far removed from his own. Everything in the room breathed gentility. 'I'll leave you alone now.'

'No! Please don't go yet, Wesley. Please?'

Her plea came as the maid entered the room carrying a tea tray. The maid's eyebrows rose questioningly, but the glance she cast in Wes's direction was one of approval.

'I've brought you some tea, Master Wesley. I'll pour it for you, then I'll just pop down to help Cook in the kitchen for a few minutes.'

The statement of intent was accompanied by a conspiratorial wink in Wes's direction. 'I know it's not proper to leave a young man alone with a young lady in her bedroom, so I won't be too long. But, after all, you did save her life.'

Wes was not quite sure what saving her life had to do with being left with Fanny in her bedroom, but he made no comment. Fanny too remained silent until the servant had left the room. Then she said, 'That eye looks as though it's very painful.'

Wes was startled. Fanny was lying with her back to him with the bedclothes pulled up to her neck. All he could see of her was the back of her head. How could she know what his eye looked like?

His glance went to the mirror on the dressing-table and his eyes met Fanny's. She must have been watching him in the mirror from the time he first arrived in the room. The thought made him feel more ill-at-ease than ever. He wondered what revealing expressions he had allowed her to see.

'My eye and my head are uncomfortable now, that's all. But what about you? Your father said you haven't left your room since that night. He's very upset because you won't speak to him. He's very concerned about you, Miss Fanny, and worried that you won't tell him what's wrong.'

'I *can't* tell him. I *can't*!'

'So something *is* wrong? Can you tell me?'

'No!'

This time she seemed less emphatic and Wes thought he could detect indecision on the face reflected in the mirror.

Suddenly, Fanny turned over in her bed and looked directly up at him. He could see clearly now that there was deep unhappiness, almost fear, in her eyes. 'Wesley ... can I trust you? *Really* trust you. I mean, never to say anything of what I tell you to *anyone*?'

'You can trust me ... but perhaps it's something you ought to tell someone else. Your mother, perhaps?'

'I certainly couldn't say anything to *her* – but I must speak to someone. You're the only one I feel I can trust, Wesley. It's about ... that night.'

She looked away from him quickly before continuing, 'How long were those men ... attacking me? Before you drove them off?'

Wes frowned in concentration. He realised the question was somehow very important to her. 'I don't know, really. Not long, I don't think.'

'Please, Wesley, try to remember. It's very important to me.'

Wes tried hard to remember the confused events of that night. He had seen the men carrying Fanny from the house and laying her on the grass, although he had not known it was her at the time. He recalled the men crowding about her and her sudden cry: 'Please don't! Leave me alone. Please ...'

Remembering now, he went suddenly cold. 'It couldn't have been more than a few minutes.' Then, hesitantly, he asked, 'They didn't ...?' He did not know how to ask the question, but it was unnecessary.

'I don't *know*. That's the whole trouble, I really don't know. They did all sorts of horrible things to me. Things that hurt, but I don't know if they did *that* ...'

Fanny's face screwed up in anguish. Burying her face in her pillow, she began sobbing. Her shoulders heaved and the one hand he could see clutched the bedclothes so tightly her knuckles showed as white as the sheet.

Fanny was so desperately unhappy he felt he wanted to reach out and comfort her. For a moment he held back, fearful she might scream, or something.

'Please don't cry.'

Hesitantly he put out a hand and rested it on her shoulder, avoiding touching the part where her night-shift had slipped away to reveal her pale skin. 'Please don't cry any more. I'm sure they couldn't have done anything to you before I got to them. It all happened far too quickly. I didn't realise it was you they were carrying from the house until I heard your voice. Then I was in among them. There wasn't time for them to do anything.'

It was not strictly true. The man had Fanny on the ground for some minutes before Wes realised what was happening. Besides, the only knowledge he had of the time necessary to perform such an act came from listening to his ma and pa in the darkness of the night. It had always seemed to be a very brief happening then.

Fortunately, his lack of practical knowledge seemed not to matter. His reply had the desired effect.

Fanny turned a tearful face up to him and said, 'Do you really think so, Wesley? Honestly?'

'Honest.'

Wes felt certain God would understand and forgive him.

'Oh, Wesley ... thank you.' Clasping the hand that was still resting upon her shoulder, Fanny carried it to her damp face.

Tearfully, she said, 'You don't know how much I've worried abut everything. About ... perhaps having that awful man's baby. I couldn't face it. I wouldn't want to live.'

Her words alarmed Wes. It was a possibility that had not occurred to him. What if she *were* to have a child?

'You aren't having his baby, so you can forget all about it and hurry and get well.'

'I think I will be able to now, Wesley. Thank you so much. I owe you a lot, don't I?'

'It isn't all one-sided, Miss Fanny. Remember what happened over at Moreton House? If you hadn't spoken up for me then I'd have been in very serious trouble.'

'I only spoke up about what I'd heard. I didn't have to risk my life as you did that night – and please stop calling me "Miss" Fanny. I'd much rather you just used my name.'

There was a knock at the door. A moment later it opened and the maid came in.

'You haven't drunk your tea, Master Wesley,' she said disapprovingly.

'No.' With a maid in the room, Wes was very aware of Fanny's tear-damp cheeks and puffy red eyes. He knew the maid had seen them too. 'I really must return to Widow Cake's now. She'll be expecting me back at work.'

'Will I see you again soon, Wesley?' asked Fanny.

'Yes, your father has offered to give me some schooling. I hope to be coming here one or two evenings a week.'

'That's good.' Fanny looked pleased. 'And thank you again, Wesley. I really do feel much better now.'

Turning to the maid, she said, 'You can leave me too. I think I'll dress and come downstairs.'

Outside the bedroom the maid felt there was no need to keep up the formality required when in the presence of a member of the Reverend Wheeler's family. Giving Wes a cheeky look, she said, 'I don't know how it was you managed to cheer her up like

that, Wesley Gillam, but I'll call for you when I'm feeling down.
You can give me some of the same!'

Chapter 29

There was much activity centred upon Widow Cake's cottage during the next few weeks as moves to prove Arnold's innocence gathered momentum.

The cottage was chosen rather than the larger and more convenient vicarage because it was felt many would come here who might be reluctant to go to the home of the Church of England clergyman.

Nevertheless, Reverend Warren was a regular visitor and one day brought with him the solicitor he had instructed to act for Arnold. The solicitor took a detailed statement from Wes and interviewed a number of others in the village. Many had been gathered in by the mob and had witnessed the arrest of Arnold.

Unfortunately, these men, although eager to help Arnold, were ruled out as prospective witnesses by the solicitor. He pointed out that by giving evidence they would be forced to admit their own involvement and in so doing they would lay themselves open to a similar charge.

The Reverend Warren was, however, able to offer some hope for the imprisoned young man. A number of threshing-machines had been destroyed in the riots, but it was being suggested that the farmers whose machines had been destroyed actually encouraged the mob in their attacks. It was suggested they thought they might secure a reduction in the tithes claimed by the Church if they could point to the damaged machines and claim they would need to pay to employ additional labour instead.

The solicitor also thought that Wes's evidence of the manner in which Arnold had been recruited by the mob would stand the young man in good stead when the case came before the Special Commissioners appointed by the government.

Early in 1831, some weeks after Arnold's arrest, Wes was working in one of the fields well away from the cottage when he saw Constable Hammer come along the lane and call in at the cottage. The parish law-enforcer did not stay for long and he was still in sight when Saranna came out to the back yard and called loudly for Wes.

He found Widow Cake on her feet and leaning heavily on the stick she always carried nowadays. He was hardly through the kitchen door before she said, 'We're going to Dorchester. The Commission is meeting tomorrow to try Arnold and the others. Run home and tell your ma that you won't be home tonight. On your way back call in on Farmer Priddy and tell him I want to borrow his horse and cart, right away. We'll be staying in Dorchester tonight.'

'But what about the animals? The cow, calves . . . and the pigs?'

'You just do as I tell you – and ask Farmer Priddy if his daughter will come and tend the animals tonight. Tomorrow night too, if we're not home. He'll know all about it, we've already discussed what was likely to happen.'

'What about Mary? Shouldn't she be told that Arnold goes on trial tomorrow?'

'Saranna will tell her. Mary can come with us to Dorchester if she's a mind to.'

Thinking of the simple nature of Arnold's intended bride, Wes asked, 'Is that wise? Taking Mary to the trial, I mean?'

'No, but can you think of anyone with more right to be there?'

Wes had to concede that Widow Cake was right. Hurrying away he first called in at his own home and told his mother what was happening. He left again after snatching up a few items of clothing, hardly giving her time to protest about the fact he would be away from home for one or possibly two nights.

Leaving his mother still expressing her doubts about the whole thing, Wes made his way to the farm of Thomas Priddy. On the way he met Saranna returning to the Cake cottage with Mary. Arnold's fiancée looked pale and worried and Wes paused to reassure her.

'You'll be all right, Mary. Saranna and Widow Cake will take good care of you.'

'I'm not worried about me, Wes.' Mary turned a tear-stained face in his direction. 'It's poor Arnold. How must he be feeling tonight, knowing what's to happen tomorrow?'

'You're a good girl, Mary, but you mustn't worry about Arnold. Widow Cake and Reverend Warren are doing all they can for him. He'll be back with you come tomorrow night, you just wait and see.'

The quartet from Tolpuddle were not the only ones making their way to Dorchester that day. The roads into the town were extremely busy. As dusk fell Wes drove the farmer's horse and cart past Cornhill, and they saw a fair in full swing in the market place there. A whole troupe of entertainers was taking full advantage of the crowds in Dorchester to attend the trials.

The influx of men and women from the rural areas had already filled the town's inns and hostelries. Dorchester was busier than on a market day. After being turned away from three inns, Widow Cake made a stand at the Royal Oak.

The news that there was no room was given to Wes by a surly ostler engaged on saddling up a horse in the hostelry yard.

When Wes returned to the cart and passed on the news to the others, Widow Cake's lips pursed in a tight line that Wes knew from experience meant trouble for someone.

He was about to lead the horse on, to go in search of lodgings elsewhere, when Widow Cake said unexpectedly, 'Take us into the inn yard.'

Holding the bridle, Wes said, 'But the ostler told me . . .'

'I know very well what he told you. Now do as I say. Take us in to the yard.'

Wes was bewildered by the order, but he knew better than to argue with his employer when she had made her mind up about something. Turning the horse in as tight a circle as was possible in the road, he took the horse and cart through an archway into the inn yard.

'Hey! Where do you think you're going with that? I told you there's no lodgings left. Now back that lot out. You're blocking the yard.'

'Are you talking to me, young man? If you are then you'd better watch your manners, or you'll be looking for work elsewhere.'

'Who . . .?' The ostler would have argued further, but the expression on Widow Cake's face caused him to falter. He did not know her and she might be a friend of his employer. Work was hard to find.

'I only said . . .'

'I heard very well what you said, and I found the manner in which you said it offensive. Go and fetch the landlord, if you please.'

'Yes, ma'am, but he's a busy man . . .'

'Go and fetch him this instant!'

As the ostler scuttled away to carry out Widow Cake's orders, Wes looked at the widow-woman with undisguised admiration – but not for long.

'Don't stand there gawking at me as though you're a simpleton! Move the cart farther into the yard. Over there, where it will block the stable doors.'

Wes had just manoeuvred the horse and cart into a position that satisfied Widow Cake when the ostler emerged from the

149

inn. He was accompanied by a heavily perspiring man wearing a stained leather apron.

'What do you think you're doing?' As had the ostler before him, the inn-keeper addressed himself to Wes.

'*I'm* the one you should be speaking to, not my employee. I told him to position the cart here – and it won't be moved until a room can be found for us.'

Standing by the head of the cart-horse, Wes was aware that two men had ridden into the yard, but he was too engrossed with the altercation between Widow Cake and the inn landlord to take much notice of them.

'Don't be foolish, woman. If you'd wanted rooms you should have come to town earlier. Now, move that cart. You're blocking the entrance to my stables and inconveniencing my customers.'

'Don't you *dare* tell me not to be foolish – and who is it has taken all your rooms? Local folk? Or court officials and Commissioners who have come here to try our Dorset men?'

A number of men had followed the landlord from the inn and they were being joined by many more as news of the altercation in the yard spread. Wes realised that Widow Cake's oratory was intended to include them.

'Well, landlord, are you going to answer me? When you do, think on it that I, and others like me, will still be living here – as will you – when all the men from London have returned home and put Dorchester out of their minds. We'll remember that you gave rooms only to those who came to send our young men to prison – men for the most part whose only crime is to appeal to farmers and landlords for a living wage. Who want to support their wives and children without charity from the parish. Are you turning away all those like me – a crippled widow-woman who's had an uncomfortable ride all the way to Dorchester? Who's here to speak on behalf of a poor, simple young man who was caught up in a crowd and is lying in prison as a result?

'Answer me, landlord, and make it loud, so that all your customers can hear what you have to say. Hear – and remember.'

There was a great murmur of sympathy from the crowd standing behind the landlord and he looked around quickly, aware of the loud mutterings of: 'Yes, tell us where your sympathies lie, landlord,' and, 'Give the widow-woman a room.'

'My support is for our Dorset men, of course.' The landlord was perspiring even more freely now, although the night air was cool. 'But there isn't a room to be had, not here nor anywhere else in Dorchester tonight – and you're blocking the way to the stables.'

'We'll not budge an inch until I'm offered a room. I'll not see young Arnold Cooper go to prison because you're greedy for a hangman's money.'

The inn's customers were vociferous in their support for Widow Cake now. Wes thought they were likely to get out of hand, but at that moment one of the two men sitting their horses beneath the inn archway came to the inn-keeper's rescue.

'Landlord, you have two rooms reserved for my companion and me. We'll be happy to share one.'

Bringing his horse alongside the cart, the man smiled down at Widow Cake. 'Take the room with my compliments, ma'am. I trust your eloquence in court will prove equally successful and secure the release of your young friend.'

Before Widow Cake could so much as thank the man, he had dismounted. Handing the reins to the ostler, he shouldered his saddle-bags and pushed his way through the crowd to the inn.

'There! I knew we'd find a room if we were insistent enough. It will be crowded with the two girls and myself in there, but I have no doubt we'll manage. You'll need to find somewhere for Wesley, too, of course.'

There was a triumphant glint in Widow Cake's eyes as she said to Wesley, 'Make certain the cart is put somewhere safe – and take care of the horse yourself. I don't trust an inn where they can't find a room for a widow-woman when the fate of a poor country lad is at stake.'

Returning her attention to the landlord, Amelia Cake said, 'I would like you to thank the gentleman who gave me his room, on my behalf.'

The customers from the inn had begun to return inside, disappointed that the argument between the indignant widow and the landlord had been settled so swiftly, and without any violence – from either party.

'You and the two girls will be sleeping in one of the largest and best rooms in the place. All I can offer the lad is a bed of hay in the loft, over the stable. He can think himself lucky to have that. It's a better bed than many will have tonight, including the one you've been talking about. Him who's locked up in the city gaol.'

'Wesley will sleep well enough in a bed of hay and you needn't concern yourself about Arnold. We'll have him out of prison and back in Tolpuddle by tomorrow night.'

'Don't you be too certain of that, missus.' There was more than a hint of malice in the landlord's voice as he added, 'The man you've just turned out of his room is Sir William Kennedy. He's the man who'll be prosecuting the lad you've come to help.'

Chapter 30

With the unexpected assistance of the ostler, the cart was tucked in a corner of the inn yard and a stall found for the horse. The ostler spoke of Widow Cake with considerable awe. He told Wes the landlord was a hard-drinking, hard-swearing man, and he'd never expected the day to come when he would meet a woman who could get the better of him.

'Mind you,' added the ostler, shaking his head, 'I don't think I'd care to work for her meself.'

Wes grinned. 'Oh, Widow Cake's all right – just as long as she's on your side.'

When he had seen the horse stabled for the night, he made his way to the roomy hay-loft above the stables. It was immediately apparent this was not the first occasion someone had been obliged to sleep here. There were even a couple of clean blankets folded over the rack which held hay-forks.

Wes had chosen his corner and laid his blankets out when he heard steps on the wooden ladder leading to the loft. He thought it was probably the ostler returning, but to his surprise Saranna climbed into the loft.

Peering through the gloom, lit only by a flickering candle standing in a saucer-shaped pewter holder, she said, 'Hm! You should be quite comfortable here – but that's not the way to make a bed. You'll need far more hay than that beneath the blankets if you don't want to be lying on bare boards by the morning.'

As she talked Saranna took up the blankets and stuffed armfuls of hay in the corner before replacing the coverings once more.

'There, that's the way it needs to be. You'll sleep better than Mary or me. We've only got a blanket each between us and the floor of our room. I've a good mind to come and sleep here myself!'

A long, uncomfortable silence greeted Saranna's quip and Wes thought she probably wished she had chosen her words with more care.

'How does Widow Cake like the room?'

'She's perfectly happy with it, but is feeling tired. She's having a meal sent up to the room and Mary is staying with her. I said I wanted to walk around Dorchester and perhaps look at the fair that's here. I expect it'll be busy there tonight. One of the chamber-maids said crowds of people have come in because it's expected there'll be a hanging or two when the trials are over.'

Saranna and Wes both looked at each other and Wes knew she too had suddenly thought of Arnold. She added lamely, 'Widow Cake says I'm not to go to the fair on my own. She said I was to find you and ask you to go with me.'

'It's no use me going to a fair. I've got no money. I haven't even been able to buy anything to eat for myself tonight.'

'I've got money.' Unselfconsciously, Saranna reached beneath her dress and pulled out a small purse. Opening it, she revealed a guinea. It was one of those given to her by Magistrate Frampton for 'saving' his grand-daughter.

'I've been keeping this to buy dress material. My ma says she'll help me make it, but she's not very good.'

'My ma is. She'll help you.'

'Do you think so? Well, let's go and see if they're selling some pretty cloth on any of the stalls around the fair. We should still have plenty of money left to enjoy ourselves.'

Saranna pulled a second coin from the small purse. 'Here's a shilling too. You can borrow this until Widow Cake pays you tomorrow.'

Saranna saw his uncertainty and knew he was weighing an evening's enjoyment against his family's need for money. 'You probably won't need to spend it, but I thought you might like to have it just in case you saw something you wanted to buy.'

'Thanks.' Wes pocketed the money. 'What I'd really like to do is get into the gaol and see Arnold, but I suppose if I did I ought to take Mary.'

'I shouldn't do that, Wes. Go and see Arnold, but don't take her with you. She would only upset him. What he'd probably really like is something nice to eat. To make him feel better when he stands up in court tomorrow. Perhaps we could buy him a pie, or some bread and cheese.'

They bought Arnold a hot pie from a stall at the edge of the market, almost within sight of the grim, grey walls of the prison. The fair itself was lively and noisy and packed with young men and women enjoying themselves. The atmosphere was contagious, but as Wes and Saranna left the noise and bustle behind and approached the forbidding prison, they both fell silent.

'I don't suppose they'll let us in at this time of the evening,' said Saranna.

She half-hoped her supposition would prove right. The fact

153

they had made the effort to visit the unfortunate Arnold might satisfy Wes. She immediately felt guilty at having had such a thought.

'Probably not, but I intend to try.'

There was a very large iron ring hanging from the gate of the prison and when Wes used it as a knocker he could hear the sound it made echoing inside the grim building.

After a long time they heard the jangling of keys from the other side of the gate, then a small grille opened and a face peered out at them.

'What d'you want? If it's visiting, you're too late. We don't allow visitors in after dark. Come back tomorrow.'

'We've only just arrived in Dorchester from the country and the friend we want to see will go on trial tomorrow.'

'Then you can see him in the courtroom.'

'We've brought something for him to eat. I don't suppose he's eaten very well since he was arrested.'

'I don't suppose he has, but they don't come in here to grow fat.'

'Please!' Saranna spoke for the first time. 'We realise it's putting you to a lot of trouble, but would a shilling make it worthwhile?'

There was a brief pause before the gaoler said, 'It might, 'though two would be better.'

'We haven't got two,' replied Saranna. 'That's more than a day's wages where we come from.'

'This prisoner you want to see. Is he one of the farm workers who's coming up before the Commissioners?'

'That's right. His name's Arnold. Arnold Cooper.'

'All right then, a shilling it is. But it will have to be a brief visit. You'll need to leave before the night men come on duty.'

Wes and Saranna stepped in through the small gate and it slammed shut behind them. The prison looked even more forbidding from inside, with only an occasional oil lamp casting a yellow light from a smoke-blackened niche in the stone walls. Saranna placed a shilling in the outstretched hand of the gaoler, then took a tight grip on Wes's arm.

The gaoler led them along a series of narrow, ill-lit corridors, past stout, closed doors which had only a palm-sized grille to let in light and air. There were a number of unlit cage-like cells alongside the corridor. From these came rustlings from the straw-covered floor and they heard an occasional moan, as though someone was in pain. Worst of all was the smell that pervaded the whole prison. It offended Wes's nostrils and made his stomach heave.

The gaoler eventually halted at one of the cages. Holding the lantern he carried high against the bars, he called, 'Arnold Cooper, are you in there?'

The gaoler needed to call three times before there was movement at the back of the cage. Eventually, a figure moved cautiously towards them from the deep shadows of the communal cell.

'What is it? Who wants me?'

As Arnold came within range of the lantern, Wes gave a gasp that expressed both alarm and shock. The young Tolpuddle man had never been exceptionally smartly dressed, but he had always appeared clean and reasonably tidy. This was not the same Arnold Cooper. Dirty, unkempt, and apparently unshaven since the night of his arrest, he could easily have been taken for one of the many vagrants who were whipped through town when they put in an appearance.

'It's Wes, Arnold. I've brought Saranna with me. We've brought a pie for you.'

'A pie! Where?'

'Here.' It was snatched from Wes's hand and crammed into Arnold's mouth. The young Tolpuddle man ate like an animal, constantly looking to right and to left, as though fearing someone was about to steal the pie from him.

As Arnold ate, Wes scrutinised him as much as was possible in the uncertain yellow light from the lantern. It pained Wes to see the condition of his friend. He realised that it mattered nothing to Arnold at this moment that he and Saranna had come to visit him. The simple young man's whole being was centred upon the food that was being crammed into his mouth with unbelievable speed.

'Are they treating you all right, Arnold?'

He gulped down the last of the pie before replying. Looking about him furtively, he said, 'No. Some of these are bad men. They are bullies and do bad things.'

He looked about him once more in a manner that seemed to have become a habit with him. 'They don't bother me too much now, I'm too strong for them,' Looking at Wes proudly, he said, 'I'm as strong as any three men in here.'

Arnold pointed to a small figure lying on the straw at the back of the prison cage and Wes realised a young boy was sharing the cell with the others. 'He's the one who suffers most. He was here before I came, but he's got me to look after him now.'

Suddenly Arnold peered at Wes through the bars. 'You've hurt your face. What happened?'

'Some of the mob broke into Reverend Warren's house and attacked Miss Fanny. When I tried to rescue her I was hit on the head. It's almost better now.'

Arnold pointed to two men who sat together in a corner of the open-barred prison cell. 'They were there. They boast of raiding houses and said what they did to a vicar's daughter. Shall I drag them over here for you to look at? I can. I fought one of 'em yesterday.'

This was a different Arnold from the simple, gentle young man who had been Wes's friend for so many years. He looked towards the two men seated on the floor at the far side of the dark cage. Seeing them close to would be a waste of time. It had been dark at the time of the attack. He would not be able to recognise any of the men who had attacked either Fanny or himself.

'No, Arnold, you just stay out of trouble before you appear in court tomorrow. Try to clean yourself up and shave before then. Not only for the Commissioners, but for Mary too. She'll be in court to see you. She's here in Dorchester right now, with Widow Cake. We'll all be in court ready to take you home with us.'

Arnold's expression had suddenly cleared at mention of Mary and he said eagerly, 'How is she? I wish I could see her.'

'You'll see her tomorrow, Arnold. We thought it would upset her too much if we brought her here.'

Arnold was silent for a minute or two, then he said, 'What's going to happen to me, Wes?'

'It's time you went now. The night shift will be here soon,' the gaoler broke in on their conversation.

Nodding acknowledgement of the gaoler's words, Wes replied to Arnold's question, 'We're going to tell the Commissioners tomorrow how you came to be mixed up with the mob. If all goes well you'll be returning to Tolpuddle with Mary and the rest of us tomorrow.'

'I wish I could come with you now,' Arnold pleaded plaintively.

'You must go now if you don't want to be locked in all night,' the gaoler insisted. The thought of such a possibility alarmed Saranna. She took Wes's arm and spoke to Arnold.

'We'll see you in court tomorrow, Arnold. I'll tell Mary you send your love to her. That will make her very happy.'

Wes looked back as they passed through the door from that section of the gaol. He could just make out Arnold, still clinging to the bars of the prison cage, gazing after them.

Chapter 31

The slamming of the heavy gate echoed behind them as Wes and Saranna walked away from the prison. Wes was disturbed and upset at what they had both seen. He felt he had somehow failed Arnold by leaving him behind in such company as was in the communal cell.

Saranna was more philosophical. 'Everything that can possibly be done for Arnold is being done, Wes. Tomorrow he'll be out and the whole of Tolpuddle will want to speak to him and hear of his experiences. Arnold will be the hero of the village for weeks.'

She squeezed Wes's arm reassuringly. 'Come on, let's go and enjoy the fair. I doubt if we'll ever have another chance to do this together.'

Before long, Saranna's liveliness had succeeded in cheering Wes. For a while he was able to enjoy much of what the fair had to offer. It was surprisingly large, one of the most impressive ever seen at Dorchester. The fair had been on its way from Bristol to Portsmouth when it heard of the imminent trial of the Dorset men. It had immediately changed its plans, rightly assuming there would be a huge influx of people to Dorchester to witness the trials and their outcome.

One of the highlights of the fair was a tent containing wax effigies of many of the crowned heads of the world, together with many other personalities. Wes protested at having to pay an entrance fee of sixpence for the exhibition, but admitted that the figures inside were eerily realistic.

He particularly enjoyed Saranna's scream when she saw the wax head of the late Marie Antoinette, Queen of France. The eyes of the decapitated queen stared up at her from a basket placed beneath a guillotine which was liberally daubed with red paint.

There were many other entertainments at the fair in addition to the waxworks exhibition. Dancing bears, a tight-rope acrobat, a troupe of juggling dwarfs, glass-blowers, and a variety of puppet-shows. Each was advertised with a vociferous enthusiasm that added greatly to the excitement.

They had almost exhausted all the fair had to offer when they found themselves near a growing crowd at the very edge of the entertainments. They needed to push their way towards the front of the gathering before they realised it was a speaker addressing the crowd on the advantages of a Trade Association encompassing agricultural workers.

Tugging at Wes's sleeve, Saranna said, 'Let's go, Wes, I don't want to hear any of this.'

'All right . . . No, wait! That's Ebenezer Jack speaking. He's one of the preachers on the same circuit as my pa.'

Reluctantly, Saranna stayed by Wes's side as the advocate of Trade Associations thundered out his words in his best preaching voice.

'. . . Things are going from bad to worse for the agricultural workers of this country. We cannot rely on the government or anyone else to do something for us. We must help each other and help ourselves by joining with others for a common purpose. United we are strong. But we must not misuse that strength in violent acts. That will unite those who employ agricultural workers and they will have the weight of government behind them. Yes, and ordinary law-abiding people will take their side too. We do not want to lose sympathy for a cause that is just – and I can think of no cause that deserves justice more.'

'He's right you know,' said Wes, fired with the man's enthusiasm.

'It's all just hot air. No one who's listening here will do anything about it – especially him. He's a preacher, and they just like to hear themselves talking.'

'All the same, what he's saying makes a lot of sense . . .'

Suddenly the crowd around them erupted into sound and began to move unexpectedly. For a moment no one seemed to know the cause of the agitation, then two words began to be repeated. 'Magistrate . . . constables . . .'

'Stay where you are. They can do nothing.' The voice of the preacher rose above the din. 'We have a right of free speech. We're doing nothing wrong . . .'

The preacher may have believed in what he was saying, but most of the crowd were aware that they were in Dorchester because the trial was about to begin of men who had gathered together in pursuit of such a 'just cause'.

They began to move away from the constables. A few moments later they were given an added incentive to leave. Acting on the magistrate's orders, the constables moved in on the crowd and began dragging men and women from it.

They were moving faster now, and Wes and Saranna were moving with them. They were swept along beside a wall for some minutes before Wes spotted the deeper shadow of an alleyway. He pulled Saranna inside it.

'Quick, down here!' Still holding hands they moved farther into the shadows until they left the noisy, protesting crowd behind. When they reached another alleyway, crossing the first, it was Saranna who pulled Wes on. They were heading away from the crowd now and both began to relax.

Suddenly, Saranna stopped. 'Do you know where we are, Wes?'

'No, do you?'

'Yes, we're in the alleyway behind the Antelope Inn.'

In spite of the excitement of the past minutes, Wes managed a grin. 'Oh! What are we doing here? Don't tell me your conscience has been bothering you all this time about the price you paid for Widow Cake's piglet?'

'What would you do if I said yes? Would you make me pay the price I once offered?'

'What do you think?' It was a flippant reply and when she made no response he thought he might have offended her. 'It wouldn't make any difference. You said afterwards that you wouldn't have anyway.'

'No, I didn't. I told you I wouldn't lift my skirt for a man in daylight. It's dark now.'

'Does that mean . . . you would? You want to . . .?' He had difficulty in recognising his own voice.

'If *you* want to.'

He still thought she must be bluffing, but then she moved closer. Reaching up, she placed her arms about him and kissed him, at the same time pressing hard against him. Suddenly he realised this was no bluff and his arms went about her.

After a few minutes he was touching her as he had once before in Tolpuddle. Then she had pushed him away and left him. Now she suddenly said, 'Not here, Wes. Let's go to the hay-loft, above the stable.'

'All right.' Wes's mouth felt so dry he had difficulty in getting the words out.

They walked along the alleyway and down the road in silence. His hand was still holding hers, reciprocating the squeeze she occasionally gave his fingers. Once she looked up at him and the expression on her face made him feel at least a head and shoulders taller.

There was a lamp burning low in the stable, but the hay-loft was in darkness. Wes climbed the ladder ahead of Saranna and felt sure she must be able to hear the rapid beating of his heart. He had never made love to a girl before and felt a great deal of uncertainty, but knew that was not going to stop him.

159

At the top of the ladder he stood and waited for her. Briefly, they held hands once more. Then they walked to the corner where his blankets were, and here they kissed again. With their bodies pressed against each other his hand began a voyage of discovery through her dress and she did nothing at all to stop him.

When his hand slipped inside the dress there was a gasp from Saranna but she pushed herself forward and his hand cupped her naked breast.

'Please, Wes . . . let's lie down.' She gasped the words, her lips against his cheeks.

They went down together, lying on the hay, and he half-turned on his side to undo his trousers. As he did so his elbow hit something solid behind him. Something that moved . . .

''Ere, what the bleedin' 'ell do you think you're doing? You want a bed, you find another corner to sleep in. I got 'ere first. Bleedin' cheek. Who are you? Where's that tinder box and me candle.'

The voice was that of a man, and he sounded annoyed. Wes could hear the man groping for his tinder box. The next moment Saranna had slipped from his arms and he heard her feet on the ladder. Then there was the sound of the stable door opening and closing . . . and she was gone.

Later that night, nursing his frustration in the corner farthest away from the stranger who had appropriated his bed, Wesley wondered whether they would ever have such a chance again.

He thought about Saranna until the moment he fell asleep, but his final thought was a rather disturbing one. He wondered how she had known in the darkness that they were in the notorious alley behind the Antelope Inn?

Chapter 32

Wes was awakened by the sound of voices, the clink of harness and the blowing of horses from the stables beneath his make-shift bedroom. No light was showing at the loft's dirty and cobweb-adorned window, but he knew that Dorchester was waking.

He lay in the hay for a few minutes, thinking of what had almost happened between himself and Saranna the previous evening. He remembered how it had felt holding Saranna to him. The feel of her slight body . . . It gave him a warm yet vaguely embarrassed feeling.

Remembering, he sat up and looked to the far corner of the hay loft. There was just enough light from the stable for him to see a dark form still sleeping on the blankets he had placed there.

He would have lain back again, but his memories were taken over by darker pictures, of Arnold as he had seen him in the grim prison cell inside Dorchester gaol. Wes thought of the day that lay ahead for all of them. It was not a pleasant thought. He would gladly have forgone what the day offered had it not been so important for the simple young Tolpuddle man.

Wes rose from his bed of hay and went down through the stable. There was a pump outside in the inn yard and he used it to splash a couple of handfuls of water on his face, shivering as he dried himself on his kerchief.

The sky was lightening by the time he made his way into the inn. He found Widow Cake at breakfast with Saranna and Mary. He had wondered how Saranna would greet him after the fiasco of the previous night. He need not have been concerned. Her smile was both bold and conspiratorial.

Beside her, Mary seemed to be merely picking at her food but across the table from the two girls, Widow Cake scowled.

'What time do you call this, Wesley? Do you need to have your mother around you in order to rise early?'

'I've been up a long time, Mrs Cake. I've fed and tended the horse, checked the cart, and made arrangements with the ostler for them to remain here until we're ready to return to Tolpuddle.'

'Ha! I've only got your word for that. You know very well I

161

can't go and check for myself. But as you're here you'd better sit yourself down and have some breakfast.'

A waitress had headed for the kitchen when she saw Wes enter the dining-room. She returned now and, as he sat down, set a well-filled plate in front of him.

Wes was still eating when Widow Cake pushed her plate from her. 'I'm sitting in a draught here. Mary, go to the room, find my shawl and bring it down to me.'

When the girl had gone, Amelia Cake looked across the table at Wes. 'Saranna told me you went to see Arnold last night. She wouldn't say more because Mary was in the room. How is he?'

'He doesn't seem to be coping with prison very well. He looked ill, bewildered, and dirty. If he doesn't clean himself up and have a shave this morning, he'll go into court looking like a vagrant.'

'If he gives that impression to the Commissioners they'll sentence him as though he were one. Did you tell him to clean himself up?'

'Yes, but I doubt whether prisoners are given the wherewithal to make themselves tidy. No one seems to care very much for them in there.'

'I've heard the poorhouse isn't very much better – and that's where Arnold's grandmother is going to end her days if we don't get him released today. Here's Mary coming back now. Hurry up and finish breakfast and we'll make our way to the courtroom. There'll be a great many people trying to cram in there today. We don't want to risk being shut out and unable to give our evidence on Arnold's behalf.'

As Widow Cake had anticipated, the street in front of the court was packed with men and women. All were eager to gain seats to witness the trials. Most knew at least one of the men accused of various offences connected with the 'Captain Swing' disturbances, as the riots were being called.

Widow Cake's authoritative personality, loud voice and the indiscriminate use of her heavy walking-stick meant the small party soon made its way to the front of the crowd.

Once here they came to a halt. A large, red-faced tipstaff, aware of his own authority, proved impervious to Widow Cake's methods of persuasion. He declared pompously that only officials of the court were being allowed inside. Not until Mr Fielding, the counsel briefed by Reverend Warren for Arnold's defence, put in an appearance were they allowed in. Explaining they were essential witnesses for one of the defendants, the counsel led them through to the courtroom.

The court was much smaller than Wes had imagined it would

be. It was so small that, even though no members of the public were yet there, it appeared crowded. Much of the space in the room seemed to be taken up by open-top cubicles set not only at floor level, but at various heights around the walls. These were entered by means of separate stairways. The whole of the small room was painted a depressing dark brown and cream.

Widow Cake and her party were seated in the small area set aside for the public. The front few rows were designated for witnesses and separated from the public gallery by a low wooden partition. Steeply tiered, this section was situated behind a small, high-sided dock. From the dock a ladder-steep, enclosed staircase wound down to the cells beneath the courtroom.

Widow Cake grumbled loudly about having to climb a high step to reach the seats pointed out by a court usher. Eventually she and the others were allowed to take their seats in the front row, at floor level.

Wes sat next to Saranna and both were fascinated by the court officials in the well of the court: dark-gowned counsel, uniformed ushers and constables all seemed busy. As more officials and witnesses entered the courtroom it seemed to Wes there would soon be no room for anyone else.

Eventually the public were allowed to enter the courtroom through another door. They came in noisily, squabbling and jostling for places behind the witnesses. They were soon jammed shoulder to shoulder on the hard benches behind Wes and the small party from Tolpuddle.

When it seemed the court could not hold another soul a number of be-wigged barristers entered the room. Among them Wes recognised Arnold's counsel. He was accompanied by Reverend Warren and both men seemed very agitated. They looked around the courtroom and, spotting Widow Cake and the others, came across the crowded court to speak to them.

Red-faced and angry, Reverend Warren said, 'We have just received some most alarming news. Arnold is not being tried for the same offences as the others. He is being separately charged with an assault that is alleged to have taken place during a riot that occurred near Athelhampton.'

Athelhampton was a village a couple of miles to the west of Tolpuddle.

'What sort of nonsense is this?' Amelia Cake's voice could be heard above the hubbub of the courtroom. 'Arnold Cooper has never assaulted anyone in his life – nor would he. Someone must be lying. Who is he supposed to have assaulted?'

'Charles Fisher, a curate here in Dorchester. Unfortunately, he also happens to be a magistrate, which makes the whole matter a great deal more serious for Arnold. I am waiting to see Fisher when he comes to court.'

'I should think so too. What are you doing about it?' The widow's question was directed at Arnold's counsel.

'I will do all I can. Unfortunately, I knew nothing about the charge until I came to court today. It is most unsatisfactory. I have been given no time at all to prepare a proper defence. I intend asking the Commissioners to put the case back, but I doubt if they will agree to my request. I understand they are anxious to deal with everyone as swiftly as possible. Mr Justice Alderson needs to return to London.'

'If Arnold's case is put back, does that mean I have wasted my time and money by coming to Dorchester and spending the night here?'

'This a most serious matter, Mrs Cake. It is not only young Arnold's freedom that is at stake now but his very life. An assault occurring during the course of a riotous assemble is a felony – punishable by death.'

A wail from Mary caused every head in the court to turn towards her before Saranna moved to comfort her.

Giving Amelia Cake a frosty glance, Arnold's counsel said, 'Be sure I will acquaint the Commissioners of your inconvenience when I approach him, madam.'

'I should think so too!' Amelia Cake was not at all discomfited by Mr Fielding's disapproval. 'Although I doubt if a high-and-mighty Commissioner will take any notice of the inconvenience caused to a poor, invalid widow-woman.'

At that moment, Reverend Warren said, 'There's Charles Fisher now. I'll go and speak with him.' Unexpectedly, he added, 'You come with me, Wesley. Will you speak with him too, Mr Fielding?' he asked the counsel.

The lawyer shook his head vigorously. 'I dare not approach a prosecution witness before the hearing – but I wish you luck, sir.'

With Wes following behind, Reverend Warren pushed his way across the courtroom to where his fellow-clergyman stood dabbing his forehead with a handkerchief. When he saw Reverend Warren, the magisterial clergyman beamed as though the two were old friends and extended a hand to him. 'How nice to see you, Thomas. But what are you doing here, today?'

'I'm here to give evidence of good character on behalf of a rather simple young parishioner of mine. He was unwittingly caught up in this unruly mob. I thought it was all going to be quite straightforward. Much to my dismay, I have just learned he is now being tried for an attack upon *you*! I find it hard to believe. He is a most gentle lad. The whole village loves him and we were all

164

overjoyed when he recently announced he is to wed a young village girl. Mary is, like poor Arnold, somewhat simple, yet she too is most generous and kind.'

Reverend Fisher looked pained, and mildly embarrassed. 'I am sorry, Thomas, but I regret it was indeed an assault. Fortunately he did not hit me, but he struck my horse with a pick-handle.'

'Where did Arnold get hold of a pick-handle?' asked Wes. 'When the men forced him to go with them he was unarmed.'

Charles Fisher seemed indignant at Wes's interruption and Reverend Watson hastened to explain his presence. 'Wesley saved my own daughter from the mob. He works with Arnold and was present when the unfortunate young man was forced to accompany the rioters.'

'Your young friend wrested the handle from one of my constables – possibly, as I must admit, in self-defence. I was forced to remonstrate with the constables about their over-enthusiastic use of the weapons they carried.'

'You actually *saw* Arnold attack your horse with the pick-handle?' Wes persisted.

The Dorchester curate hesitated. 'No – but I felt my horse jump when it was hit. It was one of my constables who said the blow had been aimed at me.'

'Did Arnold just leap from the crowd and hit out at you?'

'Really, young man, such questions should come from His Majesty's Commissioners, not from you.' The curate's indignation at Wes's persistent questioning could be contained no longer.

'That, of course, is quite true, Charles, but the whole thing is so out of character for Arnold. I too would like to know the answer.'

Charles Fisher seemed suddenly ill-at-ease. 'Well, no, he did not exactly leap at me from the crowd. It seems he was pinned against a wall by my horse at the time – but there can be no doubting his action. He was recognised by the constable whose pick-handle he seized.'

'So Arnold might very well have struck your horse to prevent himself from being crushed against the wall?' This time Thomas Warren was the inquisitor.

Again there was hesitation on the part of the Dorchester curate. 'In any other circumstance I might say that was quite likely. However, this was a very serious riot . . .'

'Charles, this young man was part of that riotous mob *against his will*! He was forced to accompany them. He suddenly found himself being attacked by your men and crushed by your horse. You are a man of God, like myself, Charles. Can you honestly stand up in this court and say Arnold *attacked* you? We are discussing a capital offence. Are you certain enough of his guilt to have Arnold's execution on your conscience for the rest of your life?'

'I am a magistrate too, Thomas.'

'You are a clergyman, Charles. A man of the cloth. I don't doubt it means every bit as much to you as it does to me. I beg you, don't throw away this young man's life . . . this *decent* young man's life . . . without searching your conscience very, very thoroughly.'

The clerical magistrate was saved from further embarrassment by a court usher.

'Gentlemen, do you mind taking your seats? Their Honours the Commissioners are about to come into court.'

Chapter 33

Wes and Reverend Warren had only just returned to Widow Cake and the others when an usher shouted for the court to 'be upstanding'.

Everyone in the courtroom rose to their feet, creating a great deal of noise. Wes turned around in time to see the three Commissioners, who were actually three High Court Judges, enter the courtroom. The robed and bewigged men walked towards three high-backed seats behind the Bench.

Inclining their heads to the officers of the court, they took their places. Counsel and the officers of the court responded with much deeper bows before the officials in the courtroom sat down.

The court was called to order and, flanked by his two colleagues, Mr Justice Alderson addressed the Grand Jury. The men who had the task of establishing the innocence or guilt of the accused sat in two rows in the small courtroom.

The judge's address was long – and biased. Noting that a number of those appearing before him were charged with damaging threshing-machines, he discoursed on the economics of machinery. This done, he commented on the duties of the gentry. Not their duties to their fellow men, but in discouraging lawlessness and prosecuting those who broke the law. The learned judge then went on to discuss poverty. He indicated that the poverty of the working man, and the misery it brought upon him, could be greatly mitigated if he practised prudence and understood more fully his civil, moral and religious duties.

Finally, Mr Justice Alderson pointed out to the Grand Jury that the Commissioners had not come to Dorchester to inquire into grievances, adding that they were here only to decide the law.

Satisfied that the Grand Jury knew where their duty lay, the Commissioners called for the first defendants to be brought into court.

While everyone in the well of the court was chatting to each other about the words of the learned judge, six men were led up the steep stairs from the cells beneath the courtroom. Three of the men Wes recognised immediately as being farm labourers from the Tolpuddle area. The other three were strangers.

The men were charged with being part of a riotous assembly and the evidence given was brief. A magistrate told how he was appraised of a marching mob of men who were, apparently, demanding that their weekly wages be increased to ten shillings. The magistrate confronted them, and when they refused to disperse, read the Riot Act. Shortly afterwards, the arrests began.

None of the men argued with the magistrate although more than one protested that they had set out to harm no one but were merely calling on the farmers of the area.

After the judge pointed out to the Grand Jury that the offence was sufficiently proven by the failure of the six to disperse after the reading of the Riot Act, the men were found guilty.

Two of the unfortunate prisoners had previous convictions for poaching offences. These were sentenced to be transported for life. The other four were transported for a period of fourteen years, the judge claiming he was being 'merciful'. He pointed out they might well have paid for their crime on a scaffold.

This first case set a pattern for the day. Men – and women too – were brought up from the cells and charged with either riotous assembly or the destruction of threshing-machines. A fortunate few, chosen by the apparent whim of the judges, were sentenced to terms of imprisonment in their native land. Most were banished to the penal colonies of Van Diemen's land or Botany Bay for periods of seven, fourteen years – or for life.

The period of the sentence of transportation was no more than a judicial nicety. Very few of those who left the shores of England would ever return. They knew it and so too did their wretched dependants, whose punishment was almost as severe as those who stood in the dock. Parted from their loved ones, almost certainly for ever, they were doomed to a bleak future in a parish poorhouse.

When the court recessed for lunch, Reverend Thomas Warren went off to find his fellow-clergyman from Dorchester. He was more determined than ever to persuade the curate to withdraw the charges he had laid against Arnold.

Leaving Widow Cake and a thoroughly dejected Mary sitting in the courtroom, Wes and Saranna went off in search of food for the small party.

'Do you think Reverend Warren will be able to persuade his friend not to prosecute Arnold?'

Saranna broached the subject that was uppermost in both their minds. They had left the overcrowded court behind and were making their way along the street towards the bakery.

'I hope so,' declared Wes fervently. 'If he doesn't I doubt very much whether Mary and Arnold will ever see each other again.'

'It isn't fair!' cried Saranna. 'It isn't fair on Mary and Arnold, and it wasn't fair on those men who've been transported by that judge – or Commissioner, or whatever he wants to be called. Most of those who came before him were the same as Arnold. They *had* to go along with the mob and that was *all* they did. They didn't harm anyone.'

'Perhaps you should blame men like your Uncle Richard Pemble, for putting such ideas in their heads? If he hadn't done that they wouldn't have ended up in court and being transported.'

'You don't believe that any more than I do, Wes. The men were marching because they're desperate. They can't support their families with the money they're being paid. It's all very well for that old judge to tell men as well off as himself that the poor must practice "prudence". He and the other judges will be sitting down now to a meal that will cost each of them more than any farm worker has ever been paid for a week's work. What do they know of either poverty or prudence?'

'Keep your voice down, Saranna. Everyone's jittery in town today. If a magistrate or constable hears you, you're likely to end up in front of the judge with Arnold and the others.'

Wes had made his remark jokingly, but Saranna took it seriously. 'Yes, I am – and do you think that's right? That judge in court can say whatever he thinks about *us*, the poor people, no matter how stupid or thoughtless it is. Everybody just nods their head and agrees with him. If one of us says what we think about *them*, we're likely to be arrested and charged with inciting a riot. I don't like Uncle Richard very much, but the things he says make a lot of sense to me.'

Saranna and Wes were among people who had just left the courtroom. Many had heard Saranna's loudly spoken words and were nodding agreement with her sentiments. Wes thought it was time he silenced her before they both got into serious trouble. Taking her by the elbow, he steered her into a nearby narrow alleyway, away from the crowds on the main street.

'Wesley Gillam, what do you think you're doing?'

As Saranna protested, Wes suddenly remembered all that had occurred the previous evening. Acting on a sudden impulse, he kissed her.

When he broke off the kiss, she looked up at him, startled. 'Why did you do that?'

'Because it suddenly came over me that was what I wanted to do more than anything else.'

'If you really mean that, Wes, then I'd like you to do it again, please.'

This time she responded to him as she had the previous evening and they did not break away from each other until they heard some children shouting as they came along the alleyway towards the main street of the town.

Back on the street, Saranna took his arm. Looking up at him almost shyly, she said, 'I won't mind if you always do that when you want to make me be quiet, Wes.'

He grinned, feeling strangely content with himself. 'I'll remember, but I doubt if Widow Cake would understand if it happened too often at her cottage.'

Chapter 34

Arnold's case was the first to be heard after the lunchtime recess. When he climbed into view from the stairs to the small dock, Wes heard Widow Cake draw in her breath abruptly. The simple young man had washed and shaved and made an effort to tidy himself, but he looked pale and gaunt. When he stood facing the judge, Wes saw that Arnold's hands held behind his back were shaking uncontrollably.

Before anyone else could speak, the counsel briefed by Reverend Warren rose to his feet. 'If it pleases M'Lord, I have been briefed by Mr Cooper's vicar to represent the prisoner. Unfortunately, I was not informed until this morning of the exact nature of the charge against him. I am therefore totally unprepared to present a defence on his behalf. I therefore request My Lords that, in the interests of Justice, this particular case be put back until the next Assizes.'

Mr Justice Alderson, seated between his two colleagues, briefly consulted first one and then the other. Then he said, 'We do not consider Justice would best be served by postponing this trial. It is, as I understand, a perfectly straightforward matter. The trial will proceed.'

As the three stern-faced judges sat facing the terrified young prisoner, the charge was read out to him.

'Arnold Cooper, you are charged that on the evening of fourth December, eighteen hundred and thirty, during a riotous assembly, you made an assault upon the person of Reverend Charles Fisher, a curate and magistrate of this town. How do you plead, "Guilty", or "Not Guilty"?'

His hands shaking more than ever, Arnold opened his mouth a couple of times before any words came out. 'I didn't do nothing to no one, sir. I was squashed up against a wall by the gentleman's horse and . . .'

'Save your explanations for later, if you please, Cooper.' Nodding to his clerk, Mr Justice Alderson said, 'A plea of "Not Guilty" will be entered.'

The prosecuting counsel rose to his feet. As he began to present the case for the Crown, Wesley recognised him as Sir William Kennedy, the man who had given up his room at the inn to Widow Cake. It was the first case he had presented to the court that day. Prisoners brought before the court earlier had been prosecuted by the county's own barrister.

When he whispered the news via Saranna, Amelia Cake nodded, tight-lipped. 'I recognised him as soon as he stood up.' As she spoke, Wes observed that she had Mary's hand firmly grasped in her own. It was the only comfort the young girl would receive in the courtroom that day.

Sir William said the court had already heard of the riots that had taken place, and the fear in which the populace had been placed. He went on to detail the felony with which Arnold was charged. He stated that after the Riot Act had been read by the magistrate, the rioters were ordered to disperse. It was now, he declared, that the prisoner made a determined attack upon Reverend Fisher.

Arnold had been trying to follow what prosecuting counsel was saying and now said loudly, 'I didn't attack no one. I was just trying to shift that old horse off me. It was squashing me up against the wall.'

'Be quiet!' snapped Mr Justice Alderson. 'Your turn to speak will come later.'

'Well . . . why's he telling lies about me? I didn't attack no one . . .'

'Silence!' This from the clerk to the court. 'If you interrupt any more you'll be sent back to the cells and the case will be heard without you.'

'I'm sorry, sir. Don't send me back to that cell. I'll be quiet.'

From behind the dock, Wes saw Arnold begin to shake once more. However, the young prisoner remained quiet and prosecuting counsel completed his summary of the assault Arnold was alleged to have committed.

The first witness to be called was Reverend Charles Fisher. As he entered the witness-box, he cast a swift glance across the courtroom in Arnold's direction.

'Reverend Fisher, will you tell the court what happened on the night when you so courageously faced a hostile mob and read the Riot Act to them?' Prosecuting counsel smiled up at the Dorchester curate.

Licking his lips nervously, Reverend Fisher looked apologetically at the red-robed judges seated behind the bench. 'My Lords, after giving this matter a great deal of thought, I realise that, in fact, I witnessed nothing. Nothing at all. If it pleases Your Lordships, I would like to withdraw my complaint.'

'Fortunately, Reverend Fisher, it is not within your power to withdraw the charge made against this prisoner. He is being prosecuted by the Crown. I am disappointed that you, a magistrate of this county, will not stand up and give evidence on behalf of law and order, but it will not affect the outcome one iota. You *did* read the Riot Act to this man and his fellows?'

'Yes.'

'Thank you. That will be all.'

'My Lord, may I examine this witness?' The request was made by Arnold's counsel who had risen to his feet.

'About what, pray? He has informed us he read the Riot Act – a matter about which there is no dispute. For the rest . . . you heard him tell this court he witnessed nothing. The witness may step down.'

The next witness in the prosecution's case was the special constable whose pick-handle weapon had been seized by Arnold. He told with great gusto how he and his fellow constables had charged into the crowd of rioters and driven them back along the village street. He spoke of driving a small section of the crowd back against a wall. It was here, he declared, that the pick-handle he was wielding was wrested from him by Arnold. A few moments later Magistrate Fisher rode up, having been temporarily halted by a stone which hit him on the cheek, drawing blood. It was then that the constable saw Arnold strike his blows at the magistrate.

When the constable's evidence came to an end, Arnold's counsel rose to his feet to question him. 'Constable, it was a dark night and a large crowd of men were milling about. Everyone was excited – and understandably so. Yet you have stated quite categorically that the blows from the prisoner were aimed at Reverend Fisher. I put it to you that what you saw was merely an attempt by my client to prevent himself from being crushed against a wall by Reverend Fisher's horse?'

'They were aimed at the magistrate, sir. I'm as certain of it as I am of standing here.'

'Yet you have admitted the prisoner was against the wall and the horse was between him and you. I repeat, in all the confusion and the darkness, you could not have seen what occurred.'

For a moment the special constable looked perplexed. He was rescued by Mr Justice Alderson. Speaking to Arnold's counsel, he said, 'I feel you are wasting the court's time Mr Fielding. Evidence has been given that the prisoner wrested a weapon from the hands of this constable. It is surely reasonable to assume that a certain amount of violence was employed in such an act. We also have undisputed evidence that Magistrate Fisher was injured by a stone during the rioting. There seems to be a mistaken assumption that unless the attack on an individual is made with some deadly weapon, those so concerned are not liable to be called to full account for their actions. It should be known by all persons that if the same injury be inflicted by the blow of a stone, all and every person forming part of a riotous assembly is equally guilty as he who may have thrown the stone. Furthermore, all alike are liable to be put to death for the actions of that one. I think this witness has said all that is necessary on this point. He may stand down.'

Arnold's counsel looked for a moment as though he was prepared to argue. Instead, he made a helpless gesture and sat down.

'Are there any more witnesses for the prosecution?' Alderson asked the prosecuting counsel.

'I could call others, M'Lord, but they would merely repeat what has already been said quite adequately by the last witness. I feel the prosecution is able to rest its case.'

'Quite so, Sir William. Mr Fielding, do you have any witnesses for the defence?'

'As I explained to Your Lordship at the opening of this case, I was not aware of the seriousness of the charge until this morning. I have had no time to prepare what I consider to be an adequate defence. However, I do have three witnesses. The first is my client's employer who will tell the court of his exemplary character. The second is the vicar of his parish who will say that my client is recognised by all as being a somewhat "simple" soul. My third witness works with my client and will tell the court how Mr Cooper was forced to go with the other farm workers against his will. He was not connected with the men who are responsible for the many regrettable acts which took place on the night in question.'

'Mr Fielding, this is a court of law, specially commissioned by His Majesty's government. We are here to bring to justice those who have offended against the laws of this land by riotous behaviour and irresponsible disregard for persons and property. I have listened very carefully to what has been said during this trial. It has not been denied that the prisoner was part of a riotous assembly. It has not been denied that his actions were violent, in the very least. It has not been denied that he obtained a weapon by an act of violence. It *cannot* be denied that during the course of this riotous assembly a magistrate sustained an injury inflicted by a member of that unlawful assembly. Unless you can produce a single witness to dispute the facts that have already been presented, I must consider this case on the evidence we have been given.'

'My Lords, I have been given inadequate time to prepare the defence for a client who stands before you charged with a capital offence. That in itself I consider to be inexcusable. Now I seek to prove that the character of the prisoner is such that the acts he is alleged to have committed are totally out of character. You deny me even this small concession. My Lords, it is justice we are here to dispense today. The justice of an *English* court of law, not the questionable justice of a Spanish inquisition, or a revolutionary French tribunal. I repeat, a man's life is at stake. For this reason alone I demand that I be allowed to present such witnesses as are available to me.'

'I find your remarks offensive, Mr Fielding. We have heard, with complete impartiality, of the events of the unfortunate night in question. I believe we should now leave the question of the prisoner's guilt to a jury of twelve honest men. They too have heard the evidence. I trust they will judge the case on the facts presented to them and not shirk their patent duty.'

The jury were absent for no more than fifteen minutes. When they returned to their seats not one of them looked in Arnold's direction and Wes's hopes sank.

'Gentlemen, have you reached a verdict on which you are all agreed?'

'We have, M'Lord.' The reply was given by the jury foreman.

'And how do you find the prisoner?'

For a moment it seemed every man and woman in the court-room held their breath.

'Guilty, M'Lord, but the members of the jury request that this court may show the prisoner mercy when passing sentence.'

There was a gasp of horror from the spectators, then a scream from Mary that turned every head, including Arnold's. The tortured expression on his face was something that Wes would remember for as long as he lived.

'Arnold Cooper, you have been found guilty of an assault, committed whilst you were part of a riotous assembly. Is there anything you would like to say before sentence is passed upon you?'

'I ... only ...' Arnold struggled to find words. 'Don't send me back to that cell downstairs, M'Lord. Please ... I ... I want to go home ... with Mary.'

As though Arnold had not spoken, Mr Justice Alderson said, 'Arnold Cooper, I pass upon you the only sentence I can possibly pass for a crime such as this. A crime that strikes at the very heart of law and order in this country of ours. You will be taken from here to a place of execution and there, on a date to be fixed, you will be hung by the neck until dead – and may the Lord have mercy on your soul.'

175

The passing of the death sentence upon Arnold Cooper brought uproar from those in the public gallery. While the ushers were sent among them to quieten them down, Mary sat sobbing, her head bowed to her knees. Suddenly, Amelia Cake struggled unexpectedly to her feet.

Shouting in her exceptionally loud voice, she advanced unsteadily upon the Bench. 'You call that *justice*? You sentence a simple and honest young lad to death and in the same breath have the audacity to speak of the law and order of England? I've seen the law of Napoleon Bonaparte at work – and I tell you, it was fairer than yours, for all he was a Frenchman.'

Advancing upon the Bench, stick waving in the air, she said, 'You've sentenced an innocent lad to death on little or no evidence for striking a magistrate. Very well, let's see how you sentence me for striking a *judge* with my stick.'

Amelia Cake did not carry out her stated intention. She reached the Bench and raised her stick to strike Mr Justice Alderson. But, even as the judge cowered and raised an arm to protect himself, Widow Cake suddenly faltered. Fighting for breath, she fell to the floor.

Belatedly, two of the ushers dashed to the spot where the widow lay gasping. Looking up at Mr Justice Alderson, one of them said, 'Shall we arrest her and take her to the cells, M'Lord?'

'No, Usher. It would appear justice has been delivered from above. Let her friends take her from here. Should she survive perhaps she may ponder upon the mercy of the judiciary she seems to hold in such low esteem.'

Chapter 35

It was a sombre party that travelled back to Tolpuddle during the evening when the trial was over. Widow Cake lay in the back of the cart on a bed of hay, with Saranna and Mary beside her.

The widow had been carried semi-conscious from the Dorchester courtroom. At Reverend Warren's insistence she had been taken to the home of a nearby doctor with whom he was acquainted.

She had recovered consciousness by the time they arrived at the doctor's and the examination took place under protest.

The doctor declared the widow to have suffered an attack of 'apoplexy'. It was a diagnosis scornfully dismissed by Amelia Cake.

She was still muttering acidly about it now, from the back of the cart.

'Apoplexy, indeed. That doctor is no different to any of the others I've met with. They're all charlatans. They spit out a long word, knowing full well that most of those they're treating won't know what they're taking about. Then they demand a fat fee, just for thinking up long words and making wild guesses. You're supposed to be a bright lad, young Wesley. When you've finished taking lessons from Reverend Warren you use your learning to find long words, then you too can become a doctor. You'll make a fortune out of poor people like me.'

'If it wasn't apoplexy, why do you think you collapsed in the courtroom, Mrs Cake?'

Wes asked the question as he peered ahead in the darkness, trying to discern where the narrow road ended and the verge began.

'The same reason as I sometimes faint at home. If I stand up too quickly it sends a rush of blood from my head to my legs and I come over giddy. The same thing used to happen to my grandmother when I was a girl. She knew what it was, and so do I. It's only a fool doctor who needs to put a fancy name to it so as folk will think they're getting something for their money.'

'Do you think they really will hang Arnold?'

177

Mary's plaintive question cut across the discussion on the merits and demerits of doctors. It was doubtful if she had heard any part of it.

'He'll not hang if I, Arnold's counsel, or the Reverend Warren have anything to do with it. Mr Fielding says he's sending a plea for mercy to Lord Melbourne, the Home Secretary. Reverend Warren intends doing the same, once he's collected signatures from everyone in Tolpuddle on a petition.'

'I know that whatever happens I'll never see him again, but I don't want him to be hanged. Arnold has done nothing to deserve that.'

Mary began to cry, as she had on and off since they left Dorchester.

'Hush, girl. Arnold wouldn't want to know you were behaving like this. He knows he's done nothing wrong and he'll make his peace with the Lord, whatever that judge has decided to do with him.'

'I'm getting down to lead the horse,' said Wes gruffly. 'I can't see well enough to let him make his own way.'

He was both angry and upset at the outcome of the court case and found Mary's deep and noisy sorrow too harrowing to take at close range.

Leaving aside the injustice of the convictions against the men involved in the many disturbances throughout the country, the punishment meted out by the Commissioners was extremely harsh. Furthermore, it would affect a great many innocent women and children in addition to the men who had been convicted in court.

The Commissioners could not have been unaware of the widespread results of their sentencing. One man, sentenced to be transported for seven years – the maximum penalty allowed by law for damaging a threshing-machine – had made an emotional plea to the court. He begged to be allowed to take his eight-month-old baby son with him into exile. He told the court the child's mother had died of typhus a month before and there was no relative to bring him up.

During the hearing it had never been suggested that this particular man had taken an active part in attacking the threshing-machine. Yet the Commissioner's response to his plea was merciless. He told the man he should have thought about the future of his motherless son before 'allowing' himself to become part of the mob that caused the damage.

Wes remembered with considerable bitterness that Mr Justice Alderson had boasted that England's judicial system was the envy of the civilised world. Walking along the quiet English country lane, leading the horse through the darkness, Wes thought bitterly about Arnold's savage sentence. He wondered just what there was in such a system to be envied by anyone.

Suddenly and unexpectedly, Saranna was walking beside him. Her hand found his and his fingers were squeezed affectionately.

'Is Widow Cake all right?'

He asked the question as much to hide the absurd pleasure he felt at having her walking hand-in-hand with him as for any other reason.

'I think she might be asleep.'

'And Mary?'

'She's almost cried herself to sleep, too.'

They walked in silence for a while before Saranna asked quietly, 'Do you think poor Arnold really will hang?'

'I'd like to be able to say no, but I just don't know any more.'

'Poor Arnold. Poor Mary too. She'll never really get over this.'

They walked on in silence once more for a while longer and then Wes asked, 'What about us, Saranna? How do you see our future?'

For a long while Saranna seemed to be thinking about her reply, then she said, 'How would you like to see it?'

Wes was plucking up the courage to tell her he wanted them to have the future together when a peevish voice from the cart called, 'Saranna? Where are you, girl? What are you up to?'

'I'm here, Mrs Cake. Talking to Wes.'

'Are you indeed! No wonder he's taking his time. Come back here and let him liven the pace up a bit. At this rate it will be dawn before we reach home.'

There was the sound of the widow moving in the hay and then she called out once more, 'Wesley? Where are we?'

'No more than half-a-mile from Tolpuddle. Ten more minutes and you'll be in your own home getting ready for bed.'

'I should hope so, too. Saranna! Come back here and help me to sit up. I'll need to get up gradually if I'm not to collapse again.'

Saranna gave Wes's hand an extra hard squeeze and made her way back to Widow Cake.

Wes felt very happy, but his happiness brought guilt with it too. Arnold was under sentence of death. Mary was breaking her heart as a result, and Widow Cake was barely able to walk. Yet he felt able to entertain the hope of a whole new life with Saranna.

When they reached Amelia Cake's Tolpuddle home, the widow said, 'Saranna, when you've helped me up the stairs to my bedroom, you can go and take a message to Mary's mother for me. Tell her Mary will be staying here with me tonight. The girl will

179

get little sympathy if she goes home and I need company. I might have another of those attacks of "apoplexy" that man who calls himself a doctor was talking about.'

As Wes held the horse's head so it would not move while Saranna and Mary were helping the widow from the cart, Amelia Cake called out again, 'Wesley! You take the horse and cart straight back to Farmer Priddy. Make certain he knows you've returned them – and no dallying along the way, you hear? I'll not have him charging me for keeping the cart for another day, saying he didn't know it had been returned.'

Wes shook his head in amused disbelief at Widow Cake's words. She, at least, could be relied on to remain the same, no matter what was going on in the world about her.

He was leading the horse and cart away from the cottage when Saranna came running along the lane after him.

'Wes, will you be meeting me later tonight?'

'I'd like to, Saranna, but I think I ought to go straight home and tell Ma what's happened to Arnold. Then I want to go to the chapel and tell Pa. Hopefully he'll be able to get everyone at his Bible class to sign a petition for Arnold's release. When I've got it I'll take it and give it to Reverend Warren. I doubt if any of them would sign if the vicar asked them himself. It's important that we get as many names on the list as we can.'

'Of course.' Saranna tried hard to hide her disappointment. 'I'll speak to Ma too, when I reach home. There are quite a few farmers in Southover who will know Arnold. Anyone who's ever met him will sign, I'm sure.'

'I'm sure they will. I don't think Arnold ever did anything in his whole life to hurt anyone.'

They were standing close to each other and neither wanted to be the first to go. Wes tried to find the words that were in his mind. Hesitantly, he said, 'Saranna . . . , if things had been different . . . If I hadn't been so concerned for Arnold, this would have been a wonderful couple of days. Being with you, I mean.'

'I'm glad, Wes. Very glad. That's how it's been for me too.'

Saranna kissed him then and it lasted for a long time. But this was different to the last time they had kissed in the darkness of the Dorchester inn's hayloft. There was nothing demanding or challenging for either of them. It was a kiss between two young people who were both aware they were on the threshold of something extraordinary and new for both of them.

So engrossed were they in their thoughts and with each other that neither was aware of a figure standing in the shadows of the lane, not very far away.

After watching their outlines become one against the background light of the window of Widow Cake's cottage, the shadowy figure moved swiftly and silently away to merge with the darkness of the night.

Chapter 36

Saranna was very disappointed that she would not be seeing Wes again that night. She *wanted* to see him. To be with him. Their relationship had just entered an exciting, albeit dangerous phase. Every girl in the land was aware of the consequences of pregnancy outside marriage.

The bastardy laws were harsh and relentless. But Saranna knew they would not deter her when the opportunity occurred to make love with Wes. Indeed, she intended making such an opportunity. She wanted Wes and, if she did become pregnant, she believed he would marry her.

Thoughts of marriage brought her back to all that had happened at Dorchester to destroy the hopes and happiness of others.

It had been a distressing day. Poor Mary was heartbroken by the plight of Arnold. No amount of reassurance given to her by Saranna and Amelia Cake could ever console her. She knew Arnold would never be able to marry her now, even if by some miracle his life was saved. With tearful honesty she had faced up to the fact that now she could not marry Arnold it was unlikely she would ever find a husband.

Saranna was thinking of Mary and Arnold as she turned into the lane that led to the Vye cottage. Suddenly, a figure detached itself from the shadows of the hedgerow. There was just enough light for her to see that it was a man sporting a dark beard.

She started back, thoughts of what had happened to Fanny Warren suddenly foremost in her mind.

'Since when have you flinched from me, Saranna Vye?' It was a voice she recognised immediately.

'Saul! You're the last person I expected to meet tonight. I wasn't flinching, but in these troubled times any girl needs to be wary of men who leap at them from out of hedgerows.'

'Why should you fear an attack? There's not a man on the road between here and London would do anything to harm you or your ma.'

'There was a time when any girl would be safe, but not any

more. Not since the mob who came to Tolpuddle dragged Fanny Warren from her own home and attacked her.'

'They did that? Well, she has always been far too prim and proper. It probably did her some good. But why are we talking about her? You haven't seen me for weeks. Don't I get a kiss, at least?'

'Why should you? You never got one when you left. At least, not from me, you didn't, and you're not going to get one now.'

'That's not the sort of welcome I've been looking forward to from my girl.'

'I'm not *your* girl, Saul Gillam. I never have been. I'm glad I've met you tonight – but only so I can put that straight, once and for all. I suggest you go home and tell everyone there what I've just said too. They seem to have the wrong idea about us.'

'You've been talking to my family? Who? It certainly won't be Pa . . . Or perhaps it's Ma? No . . . Then it must be our Wes. That's it, isn't it? You've fallen for our Wes. Is this why you're not interested in me any more? It won't last, you know. It's only because he's here, in Tolpuddle, and I'm away.'

'Can't you get it into that thick head of yours that I've *never* been interested in you? Not in that way. I like you, yes, but as a friend – and that's all.'

'What about our Wes . . . is he a friend too?'

Saranna did not like the manner in which Saul was pursuing the matter. He had changed during the weeks he had been away. Had grown harder. She no longer felt entirely comfortable in his company.

She also remembered the question her mother had once put to her. Asking whether Saul looked upon her as 'no more than a friend'. She thought it would probably be as well not to disclose the depths of her feeling for Wes.

'Me and Wes both work for Widow Cake now. We see each other every day. I like him, yes, same as I like you and a lot of other people. I like your ma too.'

'You're sure you're not sweet on our Wes?'

'I've already answered that. I've said all I'm going to about it. Who I might or might not be sweet on is none of your damned business! Now, are you coming back to the cottage for something to eat, or going home to visit your ma? If you're going home, I suggest you shave that beard off first. It frightened me when I saw you tonight and it would upset your ma.'

'The beard stays. As for going home, I don't think I'll take the chance in case Pa's there. We'd only get into an argument again, same as before.'

'What you mean is he'll want to know what you're doing. Are you ashamed of telling him?'

'Why should I be ashamed? One day Pa, and all those who think like him, will come to realise that we're fighting battles that they should be fighting for themselves.'

'You sound just like Uncle Richard. The only difference between you is that you probably believe it to be true.'

'What's that supposed to mean?'

'You work it out for yourself. Anyway, your pa won't be home, as you should know. This is one of the nights when he takes a Bible class.'

'You *do* know a great deal about what goes on in the Gillam household, don't you? All right, I'll go and see Ma and Wes but first I'll come inside with you and have something to eat. That will give Pa plenty of time to get out of the house and go off to his precious chapel.'

Wes was in the shed at the back of the Gillam cottage, chopping kindling wood by candlelight. He had told his mother about Arnold's trial and she had shed a tear for the simple young man. Talking about his friend had depressed Wes. After paying a visit to the chapel he decided to go out to the shed and work. Suddenly, from the back door his mother called excitedly, 'Wesley! Come in quickly . . . our Saul's come home. Hurry!'

Pausing only to snuff out the candle, Wes ran from the shed.

Saul stood in the kitchen, not entirely at his ease, but grinning broadly from beneath an unfamiliar black beard.

'Saul! It's wonderful to see you. We've all been worried about you . . .'

Wes hugged his brother warmly, then stood back for a more detailed appraisal. 'You've lost weight . . . and that beard! If I'd come face to face with you in some back lane, I'd have run a mile!'

'That's what I told him. Look at my face. I try to kiss my son and it looks as though I've stuck my head in a blackberry bush.' The mild complaint was contradicted by the happiness evident in Rachel Gillam's expression at having her son under her roof once more.

'Yours isn't exactly a face I'd want to come up against unexpectedly, young brother. You look as though you've taken a beating from someone. How did it happen?'

Saul heard Wes's and his mother's account of what had occurred when the mob marched on Tolpuddle, and of Arnold's arrest and trial. Such talk brought an atmosphere of gloom to the room, until Rachel said, 'It's wonderful to see you, Saul, are you home for good?'

Observing his sudden change of expression, she said hastily, 'But you'll be staying for a while, of course?'

'No, Ma. I can't even stay the night. The only reason I'm here is that I was asked to deliver something to someone on the coast near here. I'm on my way to see someone in Wiltshire now, then I'll be heading back to Kent. That's where I'm living at the moment. I'm keeping busy, you see.'

'You're leaving again at this time of night? What sort of work is it that has you travelling the roads after dark? It's not safe for decent folk to be abroad with all that's going on. But why are we wasting time talking about you leaving? You'll wait and see your pa before you go?'

'No, Ma, I don't want to see him. He and I have nothing to say to each other – not unless it's to disagree. You know that.'

His words brought hot tears welling up in Rachel Gillam's eyes, but she did her best to blink them back. Her eldest son had come home to see her. He would be with her for a much shorter time than she would have wished, but it was a brief interlude to savour. It must not be wasted with tears of recrimination.

The evening passed all too quickly for Wes and his mother. Saul was brought up-to-date on all the local news. He, in turn, told them some of the many things he had seen since leaving Tolpuddle. Despite this, neither Wes or Rachel Gillam was quite certain what Saul had actually been doing while he was away from Tolpuddle.

All too soon, it seemed, he said, 'I must be going now if I'm to reach Wiltshire by dawn.'

'You'll come back and see us again soon, and stay longer?' It hurt Wes to hear his mother pleading in such a heartfelt way.

'As soon as I can. That's a promise.'

'I'll walk with you to the edge of the village,' said Wes, reaching down his coat from behind the door.

The parting between mother and son was a tearful one and, when Wes looked back, he saw his mother still framed in the cottage door.

'You've made our ma very happy tonight, Saul, even though she's in tears because you're going away again.' Wes made his observation as they walked side by side along the Tolpuddle street. It was cold and he hunched down inside his coat.

'How about you? Are you pleased to see me too?'

'Of course I am. I never wanted you to go in the first place.'

'I know you didn't – and I haven't forgotten the money you gave me. I'll pay you back one day. When I'm able to put a little money by.'

'You won't earn much by rick-burning, Saul.'

'Who said I'm rick-burning? Saranna?'

'She didn't need to say anything. I'm not a fool, Saul, I know you're one of Richard Pemble's men.'

'It has to be Saranna who's told you. Repeating stories like that is dangerous for everyone concerned, Wes.'

'Well, we often speak about you. You do know we're both working for Widow Cake now?'

'Of course, Saranna told me.'

'You've seen her? Tonight?'

'Of course I have. After all, she *is* my girl. I went to see her before I came home. She was even more upset than Ma because I couldn't stay with her for any longer.'

After Wes had remained silent for many minutes, Saul said, 'Do you and Saranna get along all right?'

'Yes.' It was a clipped, tight-voiced reply.

'I'm pleased about that. Keep an eye on her for me will you, Wes? Make certain no one tries to steal my girl from me while I'm away.'

'If that's what you really want.' Wes found great difficulty in making the promise.

'Of course it's what I want. One day I expect to come back and marry her. It won't be for a while, but she's promised to wait for me.'

After they had walked on in silence for a while longer, Saul said, 'You'd better not come any further, our Wes. There might be constables about. They don't seem too fussy about who they arrest these nights. Poor old Arnold. He didn't stand a chance, did he?'

'No.' Wes removed his right hand from his pocket and extended it towards his brother. 'Take care of yourself, Saul – and come back again as soon as you can. Ma misses you. She misses you a lot.'

'It seems it's my lot in life to be fatally attractive to women.' Wes saw the glint of Saul's white teeth in the darkness of his beard. 'Take care of both of them for me, Wes, and don't make a habit of rescuing too many women. It's a dangerous habit.'

As Saul set off cheerfully into the darkness, Wes went home in a thoroughly despondent mood. He had intended broaching the subject of his brother's relationship with Saranna. It seemed it had been on Saul's mind too, but he had not said what Wes had been hoping to hear.

Wes had been expecting Saul to say there was nothing between himself and Saranna. Perhaps give his blessing to both of them. Instead, he had made it very clear that his own relationship with Saranna was a serious one. He had even asked Wes to ensure she stayed faithful to him.

Wes's joy at the romance that had sprung up with Saranna had turned sour. It had become a painful and impossible situation.

Chapter 37

'Have I done something to offend you, Wes?'

He had known it was Saranna entering the wood-shed even though he had his back to the door. Outside the snow lay a foot deep as far as could be seen across the countryside. There was nothing Wes could do in the fields but he was avoiding carrying out any work inside Widow Cake's cottage.

'No, why?'

Wes was glad the door had closed behind Saranna when he turned around to face her. The snow blocked out much of the grey light coming through the shed's small window.

He did not want Saranna to realise the torment and hurt he felt. They were emotions he found difficult to hide when she was standing so close to him.

Wes was particularly hurt about the manner in which she had led him on. Made him believe she felt the same way about him as he did about her, when all the time she had remained Saul's girl.

Her deceit was painful enough for him to bear. How much more so would it be for Saul if he were to learn she was playing such games with his own brother?

'I thought ... after Dorchester, you'd want to see me, to be alone with me again, some time?'

'I'm with you now. We work in the same place. We can't help seeing each other.'

'That isn't what I mean, Wes, as you well know. *Have* I done something to upset you? If I have, I'm sorry. I never meant to, I promise.'

She sounded genuinely upset. For a moment Wes was on the verge of blurting out his feelings and telling her why he felt this way. He checked himself in time. If Saranna was one day to be his brother's wife she must never know how deeply *he* felt about her.

'Why should you have done something to upset me? I've been far too busy to be upset about anything. What with my lessons, and the petition calling for a pardon for Arnold, I've had no time for anything else.'

Wes turned back to his chopping, but she did not go away.

188

'Do you see much of Fanny Warren when you're having your lessons?'

'She has lessons with me.'

'Oh!' Saranna waited until he split another log before asking, 'Are you sweet on her?'

'What . . . if I am? That shouldn't . . . trouble you in any way.' Wes spoke between swings of the axe.

'No? No, I suppose it shouldn't, really.' Saranna sounded suddenly small and defeated, but Wes resisted the urge to turn around and look at her.

He had split another log into four before she spoke again. 'I came with a message from Widow Cake. She wants you to go to Mary's home and collect her belongings. Mary is to live here from today.'

This news did cause Wes to turn around, but the door was already closing behind Saranna. Wes felt guilty about the way he had spoken to her, but he told himself it was she who should be feeling guilty. She had led him on. Led him to believe she was growing fond of him. More than fond.

He split another couple of logs and the last angry swing of the axe left it embedded in the chopping block.

Wes put his head around the kitchen door somewhat apprehensively, but Saranna was not here. Mary was standing at the kitchen table kneading dough, closely supervised by Widow Cake who sat in a rocking chair beside the fireplace.

'Is Mary coming with me to collect her things?' He put the question to the widow.

'It won't need two of you to carry whatever belongings she has. Now, either come in or go out, but don't let all the heat out of this kitchen. You'll spoil the dough, and the Lord alone knows I've had to work hard enough to get it this far.'

Wes stepped into the kitchen. Once inside he asked the question that had been uppermost in his mind since Saranna told him what was happening. 'Is Mary going to take over the work of the house from Saranna?'

'I'll decide who's going to do what in my house. Why? Is there some reason why she should?'

'No . . . I just wondered, that's all.'

'Then stop wondering and get on with doing what you're told, or it will be *you* who'll find there's someone here taking your place.'

Mary had been listening to the conversation with some interest. Amelia Cake turned to her. 'Mary, go outside to the dairy and bring me in a fresh jug of milk. Saranna should have started milking the cow by now.'

Waiting until the kitchen door had closed behind the girl, Amelia Cake asked Wes, 'Is everything all right between you and Saranna?'

'There's no reason why it shouldn't be.'

'That doesn't answer my question. I thought you were both as thick as thieves when we were in Dorchester – and on the way home too. Since then I haven't seen you speak a word to each other and she's moping around like a cow that's just lost its calf. I can't put up with having two girls in the house with long faces. It's depressing.'

Wes said nothing and after waiting a few moments, Amelia Cake said, 'Whatever it is that's wrong, you sort it out – and quickly, do you hear?'

Resentful of her interference, Wes nodded. Then, as she shooed him away, he made his way from the house.

The mother of Mary Riggs was only slightly less simple than her daughter. However, whereas Mary's nature was as warm and generous as that of the man she had hoped to marry, Eliza Riggs had been soured by life.

Mary's belongings were tied up in a pathetically small bundle in the passageway of the small house. Eliza pointed it out and allowed Wes in to collect it.

'Take it, and I hope Mary's happier with Widow Cake than she is here. I'm well rid of her, the way she's been lately, though I can't for the life of me see what Amelia Cake wants to take her in for. Mary's neither good for man nor beast at the moment. I don't know why she ever got mixed up with that Cooper boy in the first place. I always told her he'd never amount to anything – and now she knows I was right. Him never having regular work, what sort of a life would it have been for her with him?'

'He's a good man, Mrs Riggs, and he loves Mary very much.'

'Love? Love would put babies into Mary's belly – but precious little food! Love, indeed. Wives and families have needs and love doesn't bring money into the house. You'll find that out for yourself one day, Wesley Gillam.'

Wes tucked the bundle beneath his arm and was just leaving the house when Eliza Riggs called him back. 'There's a letter here for Mary, although why she should get a letter I don't know. She can't read and there's no one she knows well enough who'd want to write to her.'

She handed Wes an envelope which was sealed with a small blob of candle wax.

The envelope was addressed in a neat hand to 'Mary Riggs, Tolpuddle'. Slipping the letter into a pocket, Wes asked, 'Did the man who brought it say who it's from?'

'He didn't even say where *he'd* come from. All he said was that he was in a hurry to get home again before the snow became too thick for anyone to travel. I hope he didn't come from far, whoever he was. Half an hour after he'd gone the snow was falling thick and fast.'

When Wes went into Widow Cake's kitchen after carefully and noisily stamping his boots free of snow on the step outside, Saranna, Mary and Amelia Cake were all inside.

Placing the bundle on the floor, Wes produced the letter. 'Your ma said this came last night for you, Mary.'

'A letter for me?' She looked at him, slack-mouthed. Echoing her mother's words, she said, 'No one writes to me. I can't read.'

'Would you like me to read it to you?'

Mary nodded, still stunned by the novelty of having a letter addressed to her.

Breaking the seal on the envelope, Wes opened the letter with a reverence that matched the uniqueness of the occasion. In common with Mary, he had never had a letter actually addressed to him.

Opening out a single piece of paper, Wes looked at the signature first, and started. 'It's from Arnold!'

The excitement of his announcement gripped everyone in the room, until Mary said, 'But . . . Arnold can't write.'

Wes was not listening. Scanning the contents, he suddenly exclaimed, 'Arnold's been . . . reprieved.' He found difficulty with the unfamiliar word, but added quickly, 'He's not to die!'

There were shrieks of joy from both girls and even Widow Cake appeared happier than Wes had ever seen her.

'When is Arnold coming home?'

Mary's over-simplification of the situation sobered Wes, but before he could reply, Amelia Cake said, 'Stop selecting tit-bits for us, Wesley. Read the whole letter.'

Holding the letter up in front of him, Wes read:

Dear Mary,
    I have just been given the wonderful news that I have been granted a reprieve. I am not to die after all. Instead, I am to be transported to New South Wales, for life . . .

This revelation brought a wail of despair from Mary, but she was quickly hushed by Amelia Cake, who added, 'Let Wesley finish, Mary. There might be something more of importance.'

    . . . It means I will never see these shores again, but the

191

padre has told me that if, as will probably be the case, I am settled on a farm I should be able to send for you. When you arrive there we can marry and settle down to a good life in a new country.

I hope it will be soon because I miss you and I don't like it here, in prison.

Your ever faithful,
Arnold

Added to the bottom of the letter were the words: 'This letter written on behalf of the above Arnold Cooper, by Joseph Peake, sentenced to die on the morning of February 1st for forgery.'

This last paragraph brought a sharp intake of breath from Amelia Cake. 'The first of February? That's today!' Crossing herself quickly, she said, 'May the good Lord have mercy on him and take the writing of this letter for Arnold into account when He passes judgement.'

Looking across the room at Mary, who seemed uncertain whether to smile or burst into tears, Amelia Cake said, 'This is wonderful news for you, Mary. All you need now is patience.'

'How long must I wait, Mrs Cake?'

'Lord help us, girl, don't start counting the days yet or you'll surely go mad. The great news is that Arnold is to live. He won't forget his promise, you need never concern yourself on that count.'

'I don't suppose Reverend Warren knows yet,' said Wes. 'If he'd heard he would have come along to tell us about it straightaway.'

'So he would. Go along and tell him right away, Wesley. You're not earning your keep here while we have all this snow about.'

Wes left the house, aware of Saranna's eyes following him as he went.

Chapter 38

Snow held the Dorset countryside fast in its grip for ten days. When it had cleared sufficiently to make road travel less of a hazard, Reverend Warren took Mary and Wes to Dorchester. They were hoping to be able to visit Arnold before he set off on the long journey to Van Diemen's Land.

They arrived at the prison too late. All those farm labourers sentenced to transportation by the Special Commissioners had been conveyed two days before to the prison hulks moored at Portsmouth.

However, the disappointed trio from Tolpuddle were in time to witness another group of men leaving Dorchester gaol bound for the hulks. Among them were two men known to the Tolpuddle vicar. Sentenced by a regular court, they were being transported for destroying a threshing-machine.

Reverend Warren was able to speak to the two men. If Arnold was still on his hulk they would pass on Mary's promise to wait for his summons, however long it took.

In return, Reverend Warren would convey a final message of forlorn hope to the families of the two men. He also promised to do what he could for them, even though one of the men was a staunch Methodist.

As they were returning to Tolpuddle, Reverend Warren said, 'It is very sad when young men who are not criminals, in a real sense, are subjected to the fullest rigours of the law. However, perhaps they have only themselves to blame. Becoming involved with the type of men who go around attacking young women in their own homes and putting fear into innocent men and women will not help their cause.'

'I'm sure you're right, Reverend Warren. But I think vagrants attached themselves to what began as a peaceable rally and they were the cause of much of the trouble.'

'The farm labourers set out to bully others into submission through fear. They should have expected unruly elements to attach themselves to such a cause.'

'Possibly, but farm workers with large families are becoming desperate. How else can they get people to realise they just can't feed their families if wages are cut? It seems to me there are too many greedy people in this world. To the farmer, a shilling cut from a worker's wage means an extra shilling profit in his pocket. To the worker it's a shilling's worth of food taken from the mouths of children who are already going short.'

Tight-faced, the Tolpuddle vicar said, 'Rioting is not the way to solve anything, Wesley. Indeed, now the farm workers have been defeated by the forces of law and order, I have no doubt at all they will suffer even more. At a recent meeting presided over by Mr Frampton of Moreton it was agreed that a further shilling cut in wages is inevitable.'

'But . . . they can't do it! It means my father will bring home eight shillings a week – that's after a lifetime spent working for the same farmer. Even then, he's better off than most. You know Tom Cross? He has six young children and everyone says his wife is dying. How can he possibly manage on eight shillings a week?'

'The case of Tom Cross is a sad one indeed, Wesley. It does you credit to care about such people, but I can assure you the parish will not allow them to starve.'

Reverend Warren spoke with the smug satisfaction of a man convinced of the rightness of the small world in which he played an important role. In that moment Wes realised *why* riots and disturbances were taking place throughout the country.

The vicar of Tolpuddle was kindly disposed towards the agricultural workers. It was more than could be said for the many of his fellow-clergymen, land-owners and the wealthier farmers. If *he* did not understand that a working man found it humiliating to accept charity from the parish, what hope was there for peace in the land?

While Wes pondered on this, the vicar said, 'You've gone very quiet, Wesley. Are you having some deep thoughts on the subject of agricultural wages?'

He was about to reply with the argument that an employer should pay a fair wage in return for the work being done by his workers, but changed his mind.

For very many years Reverend Warren had lived in a village where most men were farm workers. If he was not already aware of the pride that lived deep within every one of them, no argument Wes could put forward would convince him.

'I was wondering about Arnold.'

This remark brought Mary into the conversation and for much of the remainder of the journey Wes was able to think his own thoughts without interruption while Mary chattered to the Tolpuddle vicar.

194

When they reached Widow Cake's cottage, Reverend Warren said, 'Wes, take the pony and trap on to the vicarage for me. Pass it over to the stable lad to do whatever is necessary. Tell Mrs Warren that after I've had a chat with Mrs Cake, I must go and call on Arnold's grandmother. She'll need to be placed in the poorhouse, I'm afraid. That will be a very difficult meeting, but once it's over I shall be straight home. Mrs Warren does worry about me, especially since she has been unwell.'

Mrs Warren had been 'unwell' for as long as anyone in the village had known her. But, if indeed she *was* unwell, she was an example, as Widow Cake was fond of saying, of 'creaking gates lasting longest'.

After passing the pony and trap over to the stable lad and giving the vicar's message to one of the servants, Wes turned to leave the vicarage. As he went down the path he heard his name being called. Looking up, he saw Fanny waving to him from an upstairs window.

'Wesley! Wesley! Wait there. I have a couple of books for you.'

He stood on the pathway, stamping his feet to keep the cold at bay. He wondered why Fanny particularly wanted to give him the books today? It could have waited until he came for a lesson the following day.

Fanny came from the house and handed him two books. She was not wearing a coat and Wes suggested she should go straight back inside.

'It's all right. Did you see Arnold?'

'No, he'd already been taken to the prison hulks at Portsmouth.'

'Poor Arnold.' Suddenly, and fiercely, she added, 'I hope the men who attacked me are among those who have been sent there.'

Wes remembered Arnold's revelation that a cell-mate in Dorchester gaol had been bragging of what he had done to 'a vicar's daughter'. He said nothing. It was seldom possible to meet with Fanny these days without some remark being passed about her frightening experience at the hands of the Tolpuddle mob.

He chose a safer topic by thanking her for the loan of the books.

'You'll like them, I know. There's a book of poems by Byron. It was given to me only a week ago. The other is a translation of Greek mythology I thought you might find of interest.'

Fanny suddenly shivered. 'It *is* cold. Come inside for a few minutes.'

Wes hesitated. He was aware that Mrs Warren approved

neither of her husband giving lessons to him, nor of Fanny becoming too friendly with a 'village boy'.

'Where's your mother? I gave a message to the groom for her.'

'Oh, you don't need to worry about her. She didn't feel well after lunch and went to her room. She'll be there until tea-time.'

Somewhat reluctantly, Wes followed Fanny around the house to the front door and then into the hall. There was a fire burning here and Fanny made for it immediately, spreading her hands in front of it to warm them.

Wes waited, wondering what it was Fanny wanted to speak to him about. The answer was not long in coming.

'Josephine Frampton was here yesterday.'

'Oh? I'm glad you are friends again. I didn't like to feel I'd caused you to fall out with anyone.'

'She's not a friend. Well . . . not a *real* one. Her grandfather brought her. He said it was high time we resolved our foolish quarrel. What he really came here for was to tell Father the farmers are lowering their wages once more. He told Father he must stand firm against any bid to make him cut tithes.'

'Your father told me on the way home today about the wages cut. It's going to make things very hard for everyone.'

'Yes, Father told Mr Frampton so.'

Fanny said nothing for a few moments and Wes had an uncomfortable feeling they were approaching the *real* reason why she had wanted to see him.

'I don't like Josephine very much, but I've been hoping for some weeks that I might see her. She knows so much more than I do about . . . things, and I needed to talk to someone.'

'What sort of "things"?'

'The sort of thing that I believe might have happened to me when I was attacked by those men.'

Wes's heart sank. It had been a frightening experience for Fanny, but it should have been receding from her memory by now. Instead, it was becoming an obsession with her.

'I don't doubt that Josephine knows far more about *that* than you do. Even so, I wouldn't say she's the right person to give you good advice.'

'But I have to talk to someone about it, Wesley, don't you see? I've told you how I feel, but you don't know enough to tell me what I want to know. Josephine does.'

'What did you ask her?'

'I asked her how I would know if I was pregnant.'

'You don't think you are?' Wes was aghast at the thought of such an eventuality. 'No, of course you don't. Anyway, it's far too early to tell.'

'Well, that's the sort of thing I want to find out. How will I *know*?'

'Was Josephine able to tell you?'

'Not everything. But she told me one or two things that I didn't know about.'

'I wouldn't trust everything Josephine says, Fanny. She won't have forgiven you for taking my side over at Moreton. She might say things just to make you worry. Why don't you speak to your mother about it? She'll be able to give you better advice than Josephine.'

'I couldn't do *that*! Besides, she's not very well. It would only worry her. Father says we mustn't do that.'

'Well, I don't think you're pregnant. I believe that in a few weeks' time you'll be laughing at yourself for ever worrying about such a thing.'

'I'd like to think so, Wesley, but Josephine says I should know for certain very soon.'

Feeling this conversation had gone far enough, Wes said, 'I must get back to Widow Cake's now. If I take too long she's likely to reduce my wages. We'll need every penny if my pa's pay is cut. Thank you for the books. I'll bring them back as soon as I've read them – and I'll see you tomorrow. I have another lesson then.'

Wes headed for the door, but Fanny called to him once again. 'Wes, I asked Josephine a lot of questions, but I never told her about the attack by the men.'

'You're very wise. Had you done so she would tell everyone she knows.'

'Probably ... but it might have been better than what she believes now.'

'What's that?'

'She believes that you and I ... That if I'm having a baby, *you* are the father.'

Chapter 39

'What's the matter with you, girl? I swear you've sighed at least a dozen times while you've been peeling that one bowl of potatoes. Do you find the task so boring?'

'It has nothing to do with the potatoes.'

'There's a surprise! Well, if it's not the potatoes then it must be young Wes Gillam. What's he done to upset you now?'

The exchange between Saranna and her mother was taking place in the kitchen of the Southover cottage. It was a Sunday. Saranna had not been to work and Nancy Vye had completed her Sunday chores at the Tolpuddle vicarage.

'It's more what he *hasn't* done than anything else. When we went to Dorchester for Arnold's trial I felt we had somehow become ... close. I know it was an awful time for everybody, what with Arnold's trial and him being sentenced to death and everything, but I felt happy inside. I thought Wes had realised he felt the same about me as I feel about him. It was all right the evening we came back. Yet the next day everything seemed to change. Ever since then he's seemed to be trying to avoid me.'

'What happened between you and Wes at Dorchester? You didn't do anything I should know about? You're not likely to find yourself in trouble?'

'No, of course not. Perhaps we *should* have done something. He might be behaving differently if he thought he needed to marry me.'

'I'll have none of that talk from you, my girl. We can do without that sort of trouble. Anyway, perhaps you've made it too obvious how you feel about him. No young man likes to feel he's being pursued by a girl. Any girl.'

'It wasn't a case of either of us pursuing the other. It was ... we both found we thought the same of each other. At least, I thought it was *both* of us.'

Saranna shrugged. 'It's not just that. Everything seems to have changed since Mary Riggs came to live at Widow Cake's. She's a nice enough girl, but she just seems to mope about the place, bemoaning the loss of "her Arnold".'

'A bit like you with young Gillam, you mean?'

Saranna glared at her mother, then gave her a brief, lop-sided grin. 'Perhaps. But the real trouble is that there's not enough work for two girls in the cottage. I know it and Widow Cake must know it too. Every day I think perhaps this is going to be the day she'll tell me I'm no longer needed there.'

'Would that bother you very much, Saranna? *Really* upset you, I mean?'

Something in the way her mother asked the question made Saranna look up at her. 'Why do you ask that?'

Nancy picked up a knife and moved to stand beside her daughter. Picking up a potato she began to peel it carefully, paring the thinnest of skins from it. 'You're not the only one to have a man on your mind – or the only one to be thinking of the future. You know your Uncle Richard was here last week?'

Saranna replied with a nod of her head, waiting for her mother to continue.

'We've known each other for a great many years. He was a good friend to your father and I knew his late wife. We've both been alone for a great many years – and we both know what loneliness is.'

Saranna put down the knife and the potato she was holding. Looking at her mother in disbelief, she said, 'Are you telling me that Uncle Richard has asked you to marry him?'

'That's right.'

'What have you said?'

'I've told him I'll think about it and give him an answer when I've spoken to you.'

'Have you thought about it?' Saranna resumed peeling the potato she was holding, but at a very slow speed.

'Yes. I think I shall marry him, Saranna. It won't be for the same reasons I married your pa. I could never love another man as I loved him. Richard knows that. But I'm not getting any younger and one day you'll go off with your own man – either Wesley Gillam or someone else. It's a marriage that will give me security, Saranna. That and company too. You and I get along better than most mothers and daughters, but I do miss having a man about the place sometimes.'

'You wouldn't have Uncle Richard about too often. He spends most of his time travelling the country – stirring up trouble.'

'We talked about that. He said the time isn't far off when there'll be no need for him to travel as much as he does now. He'll be organising an Association of Farm Workers, with others doing the travelling for him. He'll be an important man then, Saranna.'

'Where will you live?'

'Richard owns his own house in Kent. We'll live there.'

'It sounds as though everything has already been worked out. Am I included in these plans you both have?'

'Of course you are! You're my daughter – and very important to me. I'm not *deserting* you, Saranna. I'm merely planning a new future. You'll be included in it, if it's what you want. If not, I'm sure Widow Cake will be able to put you up, in spite of what you say about her having Mary Riggs there.'

'No.' Saranna made a vicious attack on a potato with the knife she held. Nancy winced as half the vegetable fell into the wooden bucket with the peel. It could just as easily have been the tip of her daughter's thumb. 'No, Ma. There's nothing to keep me here any more. If you go to Kent with Uncle Richard, I'll come with you.'

At the time when Saranna and her mother were discussing their futures, an equally serious discussion was taking place in the Gillam cottage at Tolpuddle.

'It's a bitter pill for a man to swallow, Rachel. At a single stroke the farm workers have had their wages cut to eight shillings a week. It's not a question of one farmer falling on hard times and asking his men to work for less. The farmers must have already met and decided on the cut, regardless of the need for it or the hardship it's likely to cause. It's immoral.'

'You won't find me arguing with *that*, Eli. The farmers have caught the landowners' disease. They're out to make a profit for themselves as quickly as possible. It doesn't seem to matter any more who they trample underfoot in the scramble.

'That's funny! You're both beginning to sound just like our Saul. But when he used to say things like that, you would both argue with him. Tell him he didn't know what he was talking about.'

Wes was sitting at a table in the corner of the room, a book open in the small ring of light cast by a candle lamp. He was working out some sums that Reverend Warren had set for him.

'His arguments always went too far,' declared his father. 'He would decry Methodist principles – and I won't have that in my house.'

'Oh? Have Methodist principles stopped Thomas Priddy knocking a shilling off your wages? No, he's making money with the rest of the farmers. It's just the way our Saul said it would be. When it's a choice between principles and profit, a Methodist farmer is no different to any other sort.'

'That's enough, you two. I sat here night after night listening to one son arguing with his father. He's gone now because of it. I don't want to lose my other son the same way.' Rachel was alarmed at the vehemence of Wes's words.

'It's all right, Rachel. It's a sad admission to have to make, but there's truth in what Wesley says. Methodists like Thomas Priddy are behaving no better than anyone else. I have a sermon to write tonight. I'll use that as my theme. "Is there a price that can be placed upon a man's soul? If so, is it as low as a shilling a week . . ." I'll go off to the chapel and make a start on it now, before the others arrive for our meeting, and before it slips from my mind.'

Eli Gillam went off muttering to himself about farmers who were prepared to sell their souls for the sake of a shilling a week.

When he had gone, Rachel cast a glance in Wes's direction. 'When did you start thinking along such lines as you used in argument with your father, Wesley? For a few minutes it might have been our Saul in the room arguing with him.'

'No, Ma. Saul would get so heated when he argued that he'd forget the facts. By doing that he'd allow Pa to prove him wrong. I don't do that. I prefer to let the facts speak for me. That way I can't lose – and Pa knows it.'

'I must say, I've never heard your father admit he's wrong – about anything. But where have these ideas of yours come from? I can't imagine Reverend Warren's teaching you about such things. Are you picking them up from the same place our Saul did? I hear some very unsavoury characters find their way to the Vye house at Southover.'

'I wouldn't know. I haven't been there for some weeks.'

'I won't say I'm sorry to hear it. One thing your pa and I *do* agree on is that Saul never started arguing about such things as "the rights of the workers" until he began spending time over there. Mind you, I still think there's a lot of promise in that young Vye girl. What's her name again?'

'Saranna.'

'That's right, Saranna. Do you still see anything of her – outside of work?'

'No.' Wes bent his head over his work once more. 'Do you mind if we stop talking now, Ma? Reverend Warren will expect me to return these sums to him tomorrow and I'm not halfway through them yet.'

Rachel said nothing in reply, but it did not stop her from thinking. Wes's reply had been a not very subtle means of making her drop the subject of Saranna. She wondered why. She felt it was time she paid another visit to Widow Cake, to see how the ageing widow was keeping.

Chapter 40

That night, sixteen corn ricks were fired in the countryside around Tolpuddle. Among the first to burst into flames were two on the farm of Thomas Priddy, the employer of Eli Gillam.

The flames from his ricks sent a flickering cry for help through the window panes of many Tolpuddle cottages. The occupants proved uncharacteristically reluctant to respond to the call.

When Eli Gillam and Wes arrived at the scene of the fire on the Priddy farm no other employees were there. The near-frantic Thomas Priddy and his bucket-wielding family were by now ready to give up the hopeless battle. The ricks were burning so fiercely it was impossible to stand within efficient dousing distance. There would be little work for a threshing-machine on the Priddy farm this winter.

'Who would have done such a thing to me?'

Thomas Priddy bewailed the fate of the ricks as he, his family and the two Gillams stood in the yard of his farm. Crackling merrily across the yard, the fruits of a year's toil sparked heavenwards in a fiery sacrifice.

'You're not suffering alone, Thomas.' Eli pointed southwards. Beyond Southover there were more fires. Shrunk in size by distance, they twinkled like beacons in the darkness.

'It would seem that Captain Swing and his followers are expressing their displeasure with the farmers of Dorset,' Eli commented to his employer.

'But I can't afford to take a loss like this! I'm not a wealthy landowner like Magistrate Frampton and many of his farming friends.'

'No, Thomas, you're an independent farmer – as you're so fond of telling everyone. Yet, when Magistrate Frampton and the others cut a shilling from the wages of their workers, you wasted no time in following suit, saying you couldn't afford to stand aside. No doubt this "Captain Swing" fails to appreciate the difference between you and the other farmers who've done the same.'

'You're not telling me you approve of the actions of Captain Swing and his revolutionaries?'

'I side with no law-breakers, Thomas, as well you know. I've preached against them from the pulpit more often than any other man but, unless I'm mistaken, the other ricks we can see burning belong to James Haddy and Cuthbert Pring. Like yourself, both were swift to reduce wages for their men.'

'You don't understand, Eli. Times are difficult for farmers.'

'Are they any easier for widow-women? Has Widow Cake cut your wages, Wesley?'

'Not once. I'm now paid one-and-six a day. Nine shillings a week.'

'There you are, Thomas. A boy of seventeen and he's taking home more than his father who's worked for the same farmer for all his life. A man who preaches in the same chapel and reads from the same Bible.'

'Widow Cake doesn't employ the number of men and women I do, you know that.'

'She's employing more than she was a few months ago. I suspect some of them are kept on more from compassion than the need to employ them. She may be Church of England, but there's many could take an example from her.'

When Thomas Priddy made no reply, Eli said, 'There's nothing more we can do here, Wesley. We'll go on home. I'll be here at the usual time in the morning to help clear up, Thomas. At least the livestock is safe. By the look of the blaze over at Cuthbert Pring's farm it's taken hold of at least one of his barns. His loss is likely to be greater than yours – if that's any consolation to you.'

Walking home from Priddy's farm, Wes said to his father, 'Listening to you talking to Thomas Priddy reminded me of our Saul. Yet when he would say the same sort of things to you, you'd argue with him.'

'There's a time for things to be said, and a time to remain silent. Saul could never work out the difference. All the same, I too could hear Saul's words when I was speaking to Thomas. Perhaps we'll be able to talk things over without anger when he comes back from wherever he is right now.'

The rick-burnings were the subject of conversation for everyone in Tolpuddle the following day. All agreed that whoever carried out the arson attacks was familiar not only with the area, but also with those who lived there. Someone who possessed knowledge of those farmers who had dropped the wages of their farm workers. It was these farms only which had suffered attack.

However, that evening, when Wes went to the vicarage for his usual lesson, he found Fanny bursting to tell him other news. She tried twice to whisper to him while her father was in the room with them. Forced to lapse into impatient silence once more she restrained herself with difficulty.

Then Reverend Warren was called to the front door. One of the village women had given birth to a son. The proud father was at the door to arrange a christening.

'I'll be as quick as I can,' said the Tolpuddle vicar. 'In the meantime carry on with the work I've given you. It should keep you occupied for longer than I shall be.'

The door had hardly closed behind her father when Fanny leaned across the table she and Wes were sharing, 'Have you heard of the happenings at Moreton last night?'

'The rick-burnings? They didn't only happen at Moreton . . .'

'*No!*' Fanny was more animated than he had seen her at any time since before the attack on her. 'It's far more exciting than a rick being burned. Josephine's run away from home!'

Wes looked at Fanny in disbelief. 'Why would she do that? She's so pampered at Moreton she'd have to be quite mad to want to leave.'

'She *was* pampered, but not any more. Her grandfather's finally found her out. My maid's sister works at Moreton and she called here this afternoon with the news. It seems that for some weeks there's been a lot of talk at Moreton about Josephine carrying on with a new groom. Mr Frampton must have heard the rumours. He went to the groom's room behind the stables at lunchtime yesterday and found Josephine and the groom in bed together! There was a terrible argument. Mr Moreton thrashed the groom and dismissed him on the spot. Many of the servants saw Josephine running off to the house half-naked and clutching her clothes to her.'

'So she's managed to get someone else into trouble?' remarked Wes bitterly. 'Well, at least Magistrate Frampton can't doubt the evidence of his own eyes.'

'I think he knew before yesterday – but that wasn't the end of it. The maid from Moreton said there was a dreadful row that went on most of the afternoon and into the evening. Mr Frampton blamed her mother for much of Josephine's behaviour. He said she'd paid far too much attention to her own wants and not enough to Josephine's upbringing. He asked her what his son would have thought had he lived to see her behaving in such a selfish manner? She began to cry, but it had no effect on him. He said he wanted her out of the house. He promised to support them both, for the sake of his poor, dead son, but he also has his reputation as a magistrate to think about. He would support them only on his own terms. He owns a house in Devon, somewhere in the heart of Dartmoor. He told her they could go there to live. There were no neighbours to corrupt Josephine any more, and only an ageing couple who cared for the house and garden.'

'That wouldn't suit Josephine,' said Wes. He was secretly pleased that the magistrate's wayward grand-daughter had finally been exposed for what she was.

'It didn't,' agreed Fanny. 'Josephine said she wouldn't go there to live. Mr Frampton said he had already anticipated such an attitude and it mattered little as Josephine would spend only short holidays there. For the remainder of the year she would be a pupil in a dame school somewhere in Wiltshire, in a spot almost as remote as Dartmoor! The Moreton maid said what with Josephine's mother weeping and Josephine throwing a tantrum, she'd never heard such goings on at Moreton. But Mr Frampton was unmoved. He'd made up his mind and nothing would change it.'

Now he had been given time to digest the news, Wes felt a sense of relief. He had been very worried that Josephine would use the knowledge she thought she had about him and Fanny to cause some mischief.

'Josephine has got exactly what she deserves. I doubt if the idea of going to his bed came from the groom.'

'I'm quite sure you're right, Wesley – but that isn't the end of the story ...' Fanny had great difficulty in controlling her excitement. 'Last night, while the house was in turmoil, with everyone coming and going after the fire-raisers, Josephine ran away from Moreton. They say she's gone off with the groom. Her grandfather's put out a hue-and-cry for her.'

'I feel sorry for the groom. When they catch up with him, Josephine will put all the blame on him, whether he's guilty or not. Magistrate Frampton will make certain he's put away for a very long time.'

Fanny had exhausted the excitement generated by the story she had to tell Wes. She began sliding into her usual morose character once more. 'Of course, now Josephine's gone I have no one I can talk to about all the things that are worrying me.'

She looked up at him and he was dismayed to see tears glistening in her eyes, 'You're the only one I can tell things to, Wesley. I speak to you about things I never thought I would be able to tell anyone, man or woman, boy or girl.'

Fanny gave him a look that was filled with all the misery and self-pity she felt. 'You're very important to me, Wesley. If I didn't have you, I don't know what I would have done by now.'

Chapter 41

At about the time Eli was talking to Wes about Saul, the subject of their conversation was no more than three miles from Tolpuddle.

Sheltering on the lee side of a corn-rick, Saul was trying to breathe life into the contents of a tinder-box held in the unsteady hands of his companion.

'Hold it still, can't you? If you don't we'll still be crouching here trying to get a flame when dawn comes.'

'I can't hold it any steadier. My hands are freezing cold. Let's go and try somewhere else . . .'

'No! We'll light this one.'

A few minutes later Saul's determination gained its reward and the small flame was swiftly transferred to the corn-rick. Growing rapidly, the flames climbed the side of the rick. Greedily and with increasing noise they swiftly devoured straw, husk and seed.

'You can warm your hands now – but not for long. This is one of Magistrate Frampton's ricks. He has men out patrolling his land at night.'

The need for self-preservation proved stronger than Jonathan Galton's desire to warm his hands. Soon the two men were climbing a nearby gate into the lane that ran alongside the field.

Jumping from the gate, Saul became aware of a horse and rider standing before them. He would have run had the rider not spoken at that moment.

'I saw what you did.' The accusing but refined voice was that of a young girl. It was most unusual to find a young girl – a *genteel* young girl – out riding at this time of night.

'What are you going to do about it?'

'That depends on you. I don't care about the rick being fired. It serves him right as far as I'm concerned, but I should think you'll want to get away from here as quickly as possible.'

'What's that got to do with you?'

'I want to get away too and I'd like to have someone with me.'

'Where are you heading?'

'Anywhere, as long as it's away from here.'

'Saul, let's get going quickly! That rick's burning well now. It will be seen for miles around.' Jonathan's urgent voice came back to him from the darkness farther along the lane.

'If you go along that way you'll walk straight into the men who are guarding the track to Crossways. They're on the road to the west of the village, too.'

'How do you know so much?' Saul demanded.

'Do you want to stay here chatting until someone comes along and catches you, or are you at least going to try to make your escape?' The horse dropped its head to crop at the grass verge of the lane and she jerked it up petulantly. 'I certainly am.'

'Which way do you suggest we should go?'

'Back through the fields. There are a couple of bridges across the river, then on to the forest. You can go in any direction you want then.'

'You seem to know a lot about the area and what's going on here. Who are you?'

'My name's Josephine. That's all you need to know.' She thought it wise not to disclose that her surname was Frampton.

'That's fair enough. Come on, Jonathan, we're going back into the field, past the rick.'

As the trio passed through the field gate, Saul said, 'Make certain you keep that horse of yours quiet if you're riding with us for a while.'

'I'll only ride her until morning, then I'll turn her loose. A girl on a horse will be far too conspicuous.'

'Does that mean someone will be looking for you?'

'Probably. Not that it matters, they'll not find me. I'll make quite certain of *that*.'

They walked on in silence for a while, then Jonathan, who was walking some distance ahead, called softly that he'd found the river. He wanted to know in which direction they would find the bridge.

'Try off to the right. I'm sure it should be along that way somewhere.'

The bridge was found a few minutes later. Once the horse had been coaxed over, Saul asked, 'Where do we go now?'

'That depends on you. Which way are you heading?'

After a momentary hesitation, he replied, 'We're travelling eastwards.'

'That's really not a great help. Eastwards towards Bournemouth, Blandford . . . or where?'

'We'll make for London first of all.'

'Oh, good! I like London. There's always something exciting going on there.'

'I doubt if the London you're likely to see with us will be the London *you're* used to. In the place we're going all our friends are of the sort that would make you move to the other side of the road if you met them. Although the people on the other side of that road would be exactly the same!'

In a rare moment of compassion, Saul suddenly said, 'Why don't you forget about running away or whatever it is you think you're doing, and just go home? You won't enjoy the sort of life Jonathan and I are leading.'

'I have no home to go back to now. I thought I had, but they're going to send me away. Anyway, you don't need to concern yourself about me. If you don't want me to travel with you, I can probably find someone else who does.'

Her suggestion did not meet with Saul's approval at all. This girl knew them by their first names at least. She had also seen their faces in the light from the burning rick. She would be able to identify them. He would rather she remained with them, at least until her story of being a runaway had been verified or disproved.

'You can stay with us, but as I said before, you'll need to get rid of that horse. It can't hide in a ditch or under a hedgerow, as we'll have to more than once.'

'I'll get rid of it in the morning. I'm not used to walking long distances so we'll travel farther if I keep it until then.'

Her reply made sense and Saul agreed. But the night's drama was by no means over just yet.

After a couple of hours had passed they were in a forest and no longer in countryside with which Josephine was familiar. Saul thought they should travel on the roads once more if they were not to become lost. However, whenever they left the shelter of the forest they found the roads busier than they ought to have been at this time of night. There seemed to be parties of men riding in every direction. When the moon showed itself from behind the high clouds it was also possible to see that the horsemen were heavily armed.

Saul felt happier when they reached the edge of the forest and had fields ahead of them. It made for faster travelling.

'Are we going to travel all night?'

Josephine put the somewhat petulant question to Saul. It must have been past midnight and they had been travelling for some hours.

'We've a way to go yet before I feel we can relax. Anyway, you've nothing to complain about. You've been riding your horse for most of the time.'

'Saul, can you smell smoke?' The question came from Jonathan. He added, 'I've smelled it for some minutes but it seems much stronger now.'

'Does it matter?' Josephine was smarting from Saul's brusque reply. Had they been back at Moreton House this man would have been one of the servants or gardeners. She would have been putting *him* in his place. 'It's nothing to do with us.'

'It *will* be if someone's been burning ricks. We'd be hard put to explain what we're doing here.'

Standing up in her saddle, Josephine called out, 'I can see a glow over there. Flames too . . . It seems to be far more than just a rick. I'd say it was a barn at least. It might even be a farmhouse.'

'Damn!' the expletive came from Saul.

'Perhaps it's an accidental fire?' said Jonathan hopefully.

'I doubt it,' replied Saul. 'It's probably been set by some of the local men. That means that magistrates, constables and gentry will be buzzing around the countryside like wasps around a burned nest, looking for someone to sting. We'd better try to find a road leading away from the fire and get as far away as we can.'

The small party was already too late. Wages had been dropped in this district too and there had been a spontaneous rising of the farm workers. Smashing threshing-machines, burning ricks and calling *en masse* upon the local farmers, the labourers had demanded that their pay be restored.

The magistrates hereabouts were more prepared for trouble than they had been at Tolpuddle. Old yeomanry units had been reformed and given orders to stamp out violence – no matter what the cost. When Saul, Jonathan and Josephine reached a crossroads they found it guarded by yeomanry.

Saul heard the voices in the darkness before they reached the crossroads – but the part-time soldiers had also heard *them*.

'Halt! Who's there? Advance and be identified.'

'It's that damned horse of yours that they've heard.' Saul hissed the words to Josephine. 'Turn it around, dismount and give it a sharp slap on the rump. Let them chase after it if they want to. By the time they catch up with it we'll be well on our way.'

'But . . . my clothes?'

'It's your clothes or our lives! Grab what you can and do as you're told. Quickly!'

Josephine slipped from the horse's back. She just had time to grab the saddle-bags before Saul gave the horse a resounding smack on its rump.

The startled horse bolted back the way they had come. Saul dragged Josephine into the shelter of the hedgerow as the yeomanry went past in hot pursuit.

'We'll go this way.' Backing through the hedgerow, he forced a narrow space through which the others could pass.

It was rising ground beyond the hedge and Josephine was soon floundering in the wake of the others.

'One of you help me with these bags. They're heavy . . .'

It was more in the nature of an order than a request, and Saul reacted true to character.

'You've no servants here, girl. If that's what you want you'd better turn around and go home. Stay with us and you'll need to learn that you carry everything you want for yourself.'

Josephine struggled along behind the others until, unexpectedly, Jonathan came back to help her. 'Let me take them. I'll manage.'

He slung the bags over a shoulder and took her arm, hurrying her along after Saul.

On the far side of the field they moved into forest once more. Jonathan had just said, 'We should be all right now . . .' when a voice called from in front of them.

'Here's some of them, over here!'

Before the trio could turn back a shot rang out and Jonathan let out a cry of pain. 'Saul . . . I've been hit. It's bad . . . Saul, help me!'

Saul grabbed Josephine's arm and dragged her though the trees, away from the increasing din behind them.

Pulling back against him, Josephine said, 'He's been shot. Aren't you going to help him?'

'Don't be a fool. Jonathan knows what will happen to any of us if we're caught. You too, probably. We'd be hung. Just shut up and run – and hope they don't catch up with us.'

Josephine struggled against his grip for a moment only, then she too was running with him, trying to ignore the branches that struck her face and caught at her clothes.

They were still hurrying when dawn broke, but by now Josephine was so exhausted she could no longer think straight. When they finally reached a small clearing with a stream trickling through it, Saul said, 'I don't think there's any fear of them finding us now. We should be safely out of their reach here.'

'Thank God! But what about . . . Jonathan?'

'The shot probably killed him. We must hope so. If it didn't, and they got him to talk, then I'll be a wanted man now.'

Josephine had dropped face-down beside the stream and was drinking from it. When she had drunk her fill she turned to look at Saul. Lacking the energy to rise from the ground, she lay on her back, breast heaving.

To her surprise, Saul grinned and she said, 'What is it? What are you smiling at?'

'You. I wish there was a mirror. You're scratched, bruised and muddy. Much better than I suspect you looked when you met up with us last night. You look as though you're one of us now. That's the way you'll be expected to look.'

Dropping to his knees, Saul also took a drink from the stream. When he had finished he sat back on his heels and looked down at her. 'If you're going to travel with me there's something else that'll be expected of you – and this is as good a time and place as any other to learn what it is . . .'

Chapter 42

It took twelve days for Saul and Josephine to reach London. They were days – and nights – during which Josephine was forced to make radical changes to the way in which she had been taught to think and to behave.

She had gained a certain amount of sexual experience with a number of men. Without exception, they had all been men of a similar station in life to Saul. Servants, garden boys and stable lads in the main. All had been in the employ of her grandfather. Consequently, she had always been in charge of situations that had been largely of her own making.

Saul was different. He took her when *he* felt like it. He used her as though making love to her was his right, ignoring the infrequent occasions when she objected to either the time or place of his choosing.

Despite this indignity, Josephine took a fierce pleasure in Saul's love-making. On most occasions she was as demanding as he.

She also took to their hard life on the road surprisingly well. They fed most of the time on rabbits, chickens and the occasional game bird which Saul either poached or stole.

Occasionally they would buy something at a village or market place, especially if they happened upon a fair or market day. Such luxuries were invariably purchased with Josephine's money. She had brought a considerable sum with her, although she never told Saul how much, nor did she ever give him money to make purchases for them.

Saul seemed not to resent her reticence on the matter. He took what she provided as matter-of-factly as he took her.

When they eventually reached London, it proved to be as much of an eye-opener for her as Saul had predicted it would be. They stayed with friends of his who lived on the east side of London. The small house seemed to bulge at the seams with men – and women too – who came and went as they chose. There were always empty mattresses on the floor on which they could sleep and no one laid claim to any particular mattress or room. It was a case of the first one who went to bed had the choice of both room and bed. Only twice did Josephine and Saul have the same mattress on consecutive nights.

The total lack of privacy did nothing to deter the couples from regular love-making. Josephine was fairly certain that many of the girls shared more than one bed during the course of each night.

Before retiring to the squalid rooms, most of the occupants of the house would spend their evenings in a dingy, back-street ale-house. Here, much of the talk was of the impending 'revolution' and the war that was to be waged against the country's gentry.

For the first few nights such talk alarmed Josephine. She wondered whether the authorities should be alerted about the aims of her companions. Then she realised it was only talk. Although many of those in the room had undoubtedly fired ricks and smashed threshing-machines, they were totally lacking the organisational skills necessary to overthrow authority at even the lowest level. Their 'revolution' would never progress beyond talk and petty crime.

It was here that news of the death of Jonathan Galton was brought by Richard Pemble. He announced the death to the room at large. For a few minutes at least it had a sobering effect on the customers.

'How long did Jonathan live after being shot?' Saul called out the question across the crowded room.

After a swift and frowning glance at Josephine, Pemble replied, 'I understand he lingered for two days. Why do you ask?'

'I wonder how much he had to say to those who took him,' said Saul, non-committally.

'He said nothing. He would not even tell the magistrate his name, or from whence he had come. They suspected he had a number of companions with him when he was shot, but they found no one and gave up looking long before Jonathan died.'

The Association organiser gave Josephine another puzzled glance before adding: 'In my humble opinion he was going about his innocent business when he was slain. Jonathan is yet another martyr to the cause of all agricultural workers. He will be sadly missed by all those who are seeking association with their fellows.'

'He was a true friend,' declared Saul, with melancholy hypocrisy. 'When I'm next in Tolpuddle I'll tell his family he met with a sad accident. It would grieve them to know the truth.'

'True. True.' Richard Pemble still seemed to find it difficult to take his eyes from Josephine. Seating himself at their table, he sat facing her and Saul.

Without taking his eyes from the girl, he spoke to Saul, 'Who's this?'

'She's from Dorset too. She was with Jonathan and me when he was shot.'

Pemble's frown deepened. 'Then she'll know more about you than is good for anyone. What's her name?'

'I can understand perfectly well what you're saying, even though your English isn't of the best,' Josephine flared up angrily. 'I can also speak and answer questions for myself. My name is Josephine. As Saul has already said, we met in Dorset. Now you're as wise as he is. Perhaps you'll be courteous enough to introduce yourself – although courtesy does not seem to come naturally to you.'

Startled by her abrasive and forthright manner, Pemble seemed to be struggling with a variety of emotions. Suddenly, he smiled. 'You've put me firmly in my place, young lady – and you're quite right. It can prove dangerous to bandy names about unnecessarily. Josephine it is. If we expect you to respect our ways without question, we must respect your reasons for secrecy too. My name is Richard – that too will suffice. You'll pardon my manner, but ... No matter, you're a friend of Saul and you're very welcome. We'll speak again, I have no doubt.'

Richard Pemble beamed at her then rose from his seat and moved on to the next table. During the course of the evening he moved from one table to another, frequently in deep discussion with many of the customers in the ale-house. Yet every so often his gaze returned to Josephine and the thoughtful expression would return for a moment or two.

She had been in the ale-house for a couple of hours and was beginning to become bored when two men and a girl entered. The girl was older than Josephine by a couple of years, and evidently well-known here.

A roar of greeting went up as she came through the doorway. She immediately went around the room kissing all the men. Occasionally she would also fondle them in a manner that was so grossly obscene even Josephine was shocked.

On the first occasion it happened it was done with such open casualness that Josephine thought she must have been mistaken. Then the girl did the same thing to the next man she kissed and it brought shouts of approval and crude suggestions from the drinkers in the room.

When the girl reached Richard Pemble, she treated him with more restraint. Pemble kept her talking for many minutes and at one time both he and the girl looked across the room to the table where Josephine sat.

When the girl left Pemble she came straight across the room

and greeted Saul by name, treating him in the same manner as she had the others in the room.

Then she turned her attention to Josephine. 'Hello, luv. I'm Meg. I believe your name's Josephine? Pleased to meet you.'

Without waiting for an invitation, Meg sat down on the stool beside her. 'There's usually a few of the girls in here when this lot are in London. You'd like 'em, they're a lively lot, but it seems it's only you and me tonight. Never mind, I can keep 'em amused, how about you?'

Josephine shrugged. 'I haven't really thought about amusing anyone. Saul came here and I came with him. When he leaves, I'll leave too.'

To Josephine's surprise, Meg looked at her admiringly. 'Cor! You're posh, ain't you, and only young too? Where'd you learn to speak like that?'

When Josephine made no reply, Meg leaned closer to her and in a conspiratorial tone of voice, said, 'I know a few generous gentlemen who'd pay well over the odds to have a dollymop who spoke posh like you. When you gets tired of Saul, or he gets tired of you, come along and find me. I'll see you're all right. You 'ave my word on it.'

Standing up, Meg paused before moving away from the table to add quietly, 'Don't forget, luv. Whenever you need a few extra shillings in your purse, you just come along and see Meg. I might even get you to teach me to talk posh, like you do.'

Chapter 43

Wes watched surreptitiously as Saranna made her way from Widow Cake's cottage across the fields to where he was working. He was cutting up an elm tree, brought down in a storm months before. Saranna walked slowly, almost as though she was reluctant to reach him.

Wes watched her progress as he swung an axe through the air, striking the tree with more enthusiasm than accuracy. He thought she probably had some message for him from their employer. No doubt Widow Cake had some task for him closer to the house, where she could watch him and ensure he was not slacking.

Wes had avoided speaking to Saranna in recent weeks. He felt embarrassed that he would need to speak to her now. He had tried his best to keep out of her way because he was still very hurt by the deceitful way she had behaved towards him. He knew he was in love with her and had come to believe she felt the same way about him.

He observed that Saranna was not walking with the usual spring in her step. She seemed unhappy. He wondered whether it was because she too was embarrassed at having to come and talk to him, or whether something had happened inside the cottage to upset her.

He thought it probably had something to do with Mary. Arnold's sweetheart was slow-moving and slow-witted. At times this made far more work for Saranna than there had been before. Mary's arrival at the Cake cottage to 'help' with the house and dairy had not been an altogether unqualified success.

Despite Wes's resolve to appear to be too busy to notice her approach, his shoulders ached from his over-zealousness. He was obliged to stop and rest his muscles when she had almost reached him.

'Hello!'

He spoke first. As he did so he recognised the material from which the dress she wore had been made. It was the cloth she had bought from Dorchester market, the evening before Arnold's trial . . .

Recalling that night caused him more pain than his aching muscles. He still believed she was the most wonderful girl he had ever known.

Stopping a few paces from him, she said quietly, 'I've come to say goodbye to you, Wes.'

'Goodbye?' he repeated stupidly. 'Where are you going? Has Widow Cake sent you on an errand somewhere? She usually sends me. If it's a long way, I'll go instead. This old tree will wait to be cut up. I'll go up to the cottage and speak to her . . .'

'I'm not off on an errand, Wes. I'm leaving here. Leaving my work with Widow Cake, and leaving Southover too.'

Her announcement took him completely by surprise. His dismay was so clear to see that it should have given Saranna some satisfaction. Instead, she felt nothing but a deep, dull unhappiness.

'Why are you leaving? Have you fallen out with Widow Cake? It's easy to do, I know, but she doesn't really mean anything by her ways. You should know that by now . . .'

Wes floundered as he tried to think of a logical reason why she should be going away.

'It's nothing to do with Widow Cake, Wes. I like her, I really do. She's said nothing to me, even though we all know there's not really enough work for two girls in the cottage.'

'Not right now, maybe, but there'll be plenty of work in the spring. Widow Cake will probably be getting another cow, perhaps a couple more calves too. We'll need extra help then. Someone in the dairy for much of the time. Mary can't do it all.'

'She'll have to. I'll be moving right away from Southover. Ma and me are going to Kent.'

'Oh!' Now Wes thought he understood and he felt foolish about trying to persuade Saranna to stay here. 'Have you heard from Saul?'

'No. Why should I? Anyway, what's that got to do with anything? We're moving to Kent because Ma is going to marry Uncle Richard. She said I could stay here if I wanted to, but there isn't anything here for me any more, is there?'

Saranna looked directly at Wes as she added the question to her explanation.

Wes wanted to tell her that if she was not his brother's girl there would be every reason for her to stay. To tell her that he did not want her to go to Kent – or anywhere else. But she *was* Saul's girl and Saul was no longer in Tolpuddle. He was in Kent.

'No, I suppose not,' he replied unhappily.

Saranna looked unhappy too. Defeated. 'Well then, I'll say goodbye.'

'When are you going? You're not leaving right away, surely?'

'We're leaving in the morning. It's a bit sudden, but Uncle Richard isn't one to waste time when a decision's been made about something. Now that Ma's agreed to marry him, he wants the wedding to be as soon as possible. He sent a cart to pick up our things. It arrived today. Will you be coming to Southover to say goodbye to my ma?'

'No . . . yes! I don't know. I'll try.'

'I'll give Ma your answer. Perhaps she can make more sense out of it than me.'

It was a weak attempt at a joke, but there was no response from him.

'Goodbye, Wes.'

'Goodbye, Saranna.'

Wes felt empty and desperately unhappy. Saying goodbye to Saranna was even worse than the day that Saul had left home.

Saranna lingered a moment or two longer, then she turned and began to walk away.

There was something about the way she carried herself as she went that presented a picture of utter dejection and brought a lump to Wes's throat.

'Saranna!'

She turned immediately.

'Yes?'

'I just want . . . . to wish you good luck. I'll miss you.'

Her face contorted strangely. 'I'll miss you too, Wes. Lots.'

She turned, and suddenly she was running towards the cottage. Running as though afraid he might come after her and speak to her once more.

Behind her, Wes picked up the axe and began chopping at the tree as though his life depended upon it.

Amelia Cake and Mary were in the kitchen when Saranna entered the cottage through the back door. She would have passed through, but the widow's voice brought her to a halt. She had not missed Saranna's red eyes and flushed face.

'Where do you think you're going, girl?'

'I thought I'd make sure everything was all right upstairs . . .'

'No, you won't, you'll stay right here and make a cup of tea for us. Mary . . . go outside and milk the cow, then settle her and the calves down for the night.'

'But . . . it's only early afternoon!'

'If you want to stay working for me you'll learn to do as you're told, without argument. Off you go, and don't come back inside until everything's been done just the way I'd want it to be.'

When Mary had left the kitchen, still shaking her head at

having to carry out the evening work in the afternoon, Amelia Cake returned her attention to Saranna once more.

'When you've made that tea, you can sit down here and tell me what this is all about.'

'What is there to tell? My ma is getting married and going to live in Kent. She wants me to go with her.'

'It's a funny sort of marriage when the bride-to-be wants another woman living in the house with her and her new husband – and that's what you are, young lady. You're not a girl any more. You're a woman.'

Saranna poured two cups of tea and handed one to her employer, trying not to meet her eyes.

'You've taken me by surprise, I'll tell you that.'

'You've got Mary, Mrs Cake. She may not be the brightest girl in the world, but she's willing to work and she's kind-hearted.'

'Kind-hearted she may be, but I don't pay her to go around being nice to people. I pay her to do the work here – and she'll not do that unless I'm behind her every minute of the day. Even then she'll not do it at half the speed you do.'

'I'm quite sure she'll do her best . . .'

'Do you know *why* I took her on in the first place, Saranna?'

'Because she was unhappy at home, I thought. That and what had happened to Arnold.'

'If that's what you believe, then you think wrong. I took Mary Riggs on because I'd watched you and young Wesley together more than once. I saw the way you both looked at each other. It's a look I've seen many times before – and don't tell me I'm wrong, because I know I'm not. I thought to myself that before long there'd either be a churching for the pair of you, or else you'd have a baby on the way. Whichever it was, I'd be left without anyone to work in the house for me. Mind you, I was hoping you and Wesley would wed. That way I knew I could get you back in the house to work again. It would have been nice to have a husband and wife working for me. I'd have kept Mary on too, of course. By then there would have been enough dairy work for her. With me to keep an eye on her, she'd have been able to cope with that.'

While Widow Cake was talking, Saranna had kept her gaze firmly on the cottage floor.

Suddenly, the widow leaned forward and gripped Saranna's arm affectionately for a few moments. When she released it, she said quietly, 'What's gone wrong, Saranna? What's happened between you and Wes to change everything?'

'I wish I knew, Mrs Cake. I really wish I knew.' The uncharacteristically warm gesture from the widow had touched Saranna

219

deeply. She found difficulty in holding back the hot tears that burned her eyes. 'While we were at Dorchester I thought . . . I thought that Wes loved me, the same as I love him. But then . . . he changed, all of a sudden. He tried to avoid me . . . didn't want to talk to me. I don't know what I've done wrong.'

'Did you ask him?'

'I tried, but he just didn't want to talk to me. Yet . . . when I told him I was going, just a little while ago, I . . . I had the feeling that he still thinks the same way about me. But . . .' She blinked the tears away angrily. 'If he does, if he *really* does, then he's a funny way of showing it, that's all I can say!'

'Men are a bit like that, Saranna. Your ma would tell you the same. They don't like showing us the way they feel. I've no doubt both she and I have seen men going into battle, knowing full well they were probably going to die. They'd laugh and joke as though they were going to take part in the greatest game in the world. Yet, deep inside, they were as frightened as a baby left alone in the dark. I don't know why it is, girl, but they feel they mustn't show their real feelings, same as we do.'

'Well, it's too late now. Ma and me will be gone in the morning. I'll never see Wes again.'

'I don't believe that, Saranna, and I hope you don't, either. What's meant to be, will be – and I believe you and Wesley are meant for each other. I'll try to find out what strange idea he's suddenly got in his head. It may take time, but if I find out that he thinks the way I believe he does, I'll find some way to send him after you. Remember that, girl – and never lose hope. I won't. You're a soldier's daughter and I'm a soldier's widow. We're two of a kind, you and I – and I make a habit of getting what I want.'

Chapter 44

For some days after Saranna had moved to Kent, Wes found it difficult to put heart and soul into his work for Widow Cake.

There had been a great deal of emotional tension between Saranna and him during the past few weeks. Yet, in a strange way, he had been happy in the knowledge that she was still close. It always gave him a thrill when he caught a glimpse of her. There was even a painful pleasure in needing to speak when they met face-to-face, or when they were in the kitchen in Widow Cake's presence.

While Saranna remained at Southover he could hope that a miracle might occur to make things the way they had been. Or the way Wes believed they had been, before Saul's last visit to his home village.

Now the hope had gone – and so had Saranna.

There was more work for Wes to do now. Mary was a willing enough worker, but she was irritatingly slow. Most days Wes had to take on some extra task in the dairy or cow-shed. If he had not, it would never have been done. He began to realise how much work Saranna had taken on, much of it to help him.

The remaining bright spot in Wes's life was the tuition given to him by Reverend Warren. Twice a week Widow Cake allowed him to take an afternoon off and he would spend four hours at the vicarage. When he came away, Wes would have enough work to keep him occupied at home during the lengthening evenings.

Nevertheless, Amelia Cake did not intend that Wes should educate himself at her expense. On the afternoons that Wes attended lessons he had to return to her small-holding and put in a couple more hours' work before going home.

One afternoon, Wes was in the classroom at the vicarage with Fanny and her father. He was gnawing at his lip as he tried to work out one of the sums set by Reverend Warren when Fanny unexpectedly said, 'Father, as you can't take me to Ardval Manor this evening, couldn't Wesley come with me?'

'I . . . I really don't know.' Her father looked from one to the other uncertainly.

'Oh, please, Father! If I can't go this evening, when *can* I go?'

Wes was bewildered. 'I don't know what this is about, but I can't go anywhere this evening. When I leave here I have to go back to Widow Cake and make up the time I've lost.'

'Then tonight is out of the question anyway,' said Reverend Warren. 'But I think we should explain to Wesley.'

Pouting, Fanny said, 'Father has promised to buy me a puppy. At church on Sunday someone mentioned that Lady Killian has some beautiful Maltese poodle puppies at Ardval Manor. In a weak moment Father said I could go and look at them and buy one if I really liked it. Now he's having second thoughts about it. It's thoroughly mean of you, Father.'

'I'm doing no such thing, Fanny,' protested Reverend Warren. 'But you heard what Wesley said. He is unable to go with you.'

'I could go tomorrow night,' said Wes, trying to be helpful. 'I finish work at Widow Cake's at about six o'clock.'

Reverend Warren still looked dubious, but by now Fanny was close to tears. 'If I *don't* go to see them soon all the puppies will be gone. *Please*, Father.'

'I . . . I don't know. You and Wesley . . . People will talk so. However, Wesley *is* my pupil . . . Fanny, go along to my study and fetch my diary, will you, please?'

When his daughter had left the room, the Tolpuddle vicar said to Wes, 'I really am very, very concerned about Fanny. How do you think she is, Wesley? You're close to her own age. Perhaps she talks more to you than she will to either me or her mother?'

Wes knew he needed to phrase his reply carefully if he were not to be questioned further. He wished Fanny had never confided her fears to him, 'I don't think she's fully recovered from the attack on her. It upset her far more than anyone realised.'

'You're probably quite right, Wesley. She took it far more to heart than I believed would be the case. She's certainly not her old self yet. She is ready to burst into tears if someone so much as says "Boo!" to her. That's partly why I have agreed she may have a dog – a small one, of course. I hope it will finally take her mind off what happened. Give her an interest in life. But this business of taking her to choose one is posing all sorts of unexpected problems. The trouble is, of course, that her mother is away at the moment. If she were here everything would be all right.'

Wes failed to respond to this observation. Mrs Warren was known to be away from the Tolpuddle vicarage far more often than she was at home.

Mrs Warren was a city woman, born and brought up in London. The villagers said maliciously that her heart was not in the country but in the city where she had been born. They declared that the pull of city life was stronger than the love she bore for either her husband or daughter.

'I'd be happy to go with her to Ardval Manor, if you'd like me to.'

'I know you would, Wesley. It's a very kind offer. Very kind indeed. But I'll need to see . . . Ah! There you are, my dear.'

The vicar broke off his conversation with Wes as Fanny returned to the room carrying a leather-bound book which she handed to him.

Thumbing through the pages, Reverend Warren murmured, 'Now, let me see . . . Where are we?'

Pausing at a page he perused it closely before turning the next few pages more slowly. Then he muttered, 'Oh dear! Oh dear! I really am even busier than I realised. I had completely forgotten about the bishop's conference! I am going to have to cancel something. No, my dear, I can't possibly accompany you . . .'

'But you *promised*!'

Fanny's wail of disappointment would have melted the heart of a much harder man than the Reverend Thomas Warren.

'All right, Fanny. All right, my dear. Since Wesley has very kindly offered to accompany you I will accept his offer. It will certainly be frowned upon. Young women of good breeding should never be accompanied only by a young man, on *any* occasion, but . . . well, Wesley *is* my pupil, after all. As such he occupies a special position in our household . . . Is that all right with you, Wesley?'

'Of course.'

Wes knew the vicar's reluctance was due not so much to the fact he was a young man accompanying the vicar's daughter to the house of a titled lady. It was apprehension that Fanny should be seen in the company of a farm labourer, and the son of a Methodist lay preacher.

'When I finish work tomorrow I'll go home and change and then call here for Miss Fanny.'

'Thank you, Wesley. Thank you very much.'

For a moment Wes thought the excited girl might hug him. But Fanny had seen the doubt on her father's face at her enthusiasm. Running to him, she gave *him* a big hug, instead. 'Thank you too, Father. You've made me very happy. Happier than I have been for a very long time.'

It was enough. Over the head of his daughter, Reverend Warren beamed at Wes. He would risk the censure of the county's gentry if it meant his daughter would be taking a step closer to normality.

Chapter 45

It was three miles to the home of the dowager Lady Thomasine Killian. Reverend Wheeler had taken the pony and trap with him so Wes and Fanny walked all the way. Fanny was bubbling with excitement at the thought of seeing the puppies and having one for herself. Yet she still looked quite ill. Her face was pale and drawn and she had large dark smudges beneath each eye.

Wes felt concern for her and twice asked her whether she felt well enough to carry on or, if she would like to rest for a while.

'You *are* an old fuss-pot, Wesley Gillam, but it is nice to have you concerned for me.' In a moment of sheer, uncomplicated affection she linked her arm through his and hugged it to her. Embarrassed, he remembered it as a gesture that Saranna would often make. He did not like to take his arm away.

'I'm perfectly all right. Besides, I would never forgive myself if we took a rest and arrived at Lady Killian's only to learn she had given the last puppy away just minutes before.

'You don't know how happy I am to be having a dog at last, Wesley. It's something I've wanted for as long as I can remember. Mother's never wanted me to have one. That's why I was so relieved when you said you'd come with me to Ardval Manor. If we'd waited until she returned from London, I know very well she would have said I couldn't have it. You've been very kind to me, Wesley. I really don't know what I would have done without you these past few months. They've been horrible.'

Embarrassed by her expression when she turned her face to him, Wes said, 'It's me who should be thanking you. You and your father. I'm learning a lot from him – and you too.'

'Is that all it is, Wesley? Gratitude because you're having lessons with my father?'

She was teasing him, but he was uncertain how to reply to her half-serious accusation.

'Of course not. I like you both a lot.'

She released his arm and from being a happy, excited girl she reverted to the way she so often was these days. Pale and drawn and with the expression that her father found so worrying.

Suddenly, Wes realised what the expression was. It was fear. Fanny was suppressing a great fear, and he knew it had its roots in the evening when the mob had come to Tolpuddle.

Coming to a halt, Wes turned her to face him. Not knowing quite what to expect, she looked at him, startled.

'Fanny, why are you still so frightened? I realise that what happened to you was a terrifying experience, but you should have put it behind you long before this. It's something that will never happen to you again.'

'It doesn't have to happen *again*, Wesley – and it isn't over yet.' Choking on her words, she repeated, 'Oh no, it's not over yet, not by a long way. My ordeal is only just beginning.'

'I'm sorry, Fanny, I'm afraid I don't understand. Are we talking about the same thing, or has something else happened to make you so unhappy?' He looked at her uncertainly. 'You're surely not still worried about . . . what you told Josephine?'

'Yes, I am – and I wish to God I weren't. I've prayed every night that I would wake up in the morning and realise it was all just a bad dream. A nightmare.'

Suddenly she began shaking, almost as though she were about to have a fit, and he put a hand out to steady her. Grabbing his hand as though it had become a lifeline, she looked at him with eyes filled with tragedy. 'I think . . . I'm almost certain now that I'm pregnant, Wes. I'm carrying the baby of one of the men who attacked me.'

He looked at her in bewildered disbelief. 'I don't believe it, Fanny. You *can't* be. I told you when we spoke about it before, there just wasn't time for anything to happen that would make you pregnant. You agreed with me then. What's happened to make you change your mind? There must be *something.*'

'Nothing definite, but Josephine said . . .'

'*Josephine said!* Fanny, you can't believe anything she said to you. You should have known that in the first place. She would say anything if she believed it would make someone unhappy. Anything that was likely to cause trouble. Not only that, she'll never forgive you for siding with me and opening her grandfather's eyes to what a liar she is. Besides, you were attacked months ago. Think about it, Fanny. Think of all those women you know who've had babies. By the time they are as many months pregnant as you think you are, they are so big that everyone knows about it. You're as slim as you were a year ago.'

'It doesn't always show. Rebecca, my maid, was telling me the other day of a friend of hers. She had her baby in a field last year, when she was hay-making. She never even knew she was pregnant. She never noticed any change in her shape or anything.'

'You should know better than to listen to such stories. They're just servants' tales.'

Still trembling, Fanny said, 'I wish ... I could believe you, Wesley. I really do.'

'You *must* believe me, Fanny. If you don't you're going to get yourself in such a state you'll make yourself really ill – and there's no need, I promise you.'

He put his other hand up to hold her in a bid to bring her trembling to a halt and suddenly she was leaning against him. Looking up, she kissed him and then she stood back.

Wes looked around quickly, concerned that someone might have seen them. But it was a quiet country lane and there was no one in sight.

'Thank you for wanting to help me, Wesley. Thank you for everything.' Becoming aware of his embarrassment, she said, 'That's the first time I've ever kissed a man other than my father. I won't do it again, I promise. At least, not until you want me to.'

Lady Killian met them in the hallway of Ardval Manor. In her arms she held a silky-haired Maltese dog that stared at the intruders indignantly and 'wuffed' its disapproval. Wes was immediately struck by the similarity between the expressions on the faces of dog and mistress. For a moment he wondered who had stolen the expression from the other.

'Who is this?' Lady Killian pointed a bony finger in Wes's direction and he thought he was about to be relegated to the kitchen.

'Wesley is a pupil of my father. He has come to help me chose a puppy.'

'Has he, indeed. No doubt he's a Methodist with a name like Wesley. I am surprised at your father entertaining such young men in his house. Oh, well, since he's here he'd better come in with you.'

Her glance took in his cheap shirt and trousers disapprovingly. They were his Sunday best and put on especially for the occasion. Yet Wes had an uncomfortable feeling neither measured up to her standards.

Leading the way, cradling the dog in her arms, Lady Killian took them to an elegant study. Along the way she spoke continuously to the dog, telling it that Fanny and the 'Methodist young man' had come to have a look at her puppies.

They were curled up together in a basket placed beside what was apparently Lady Killian's armchair. Fanny made a sound of delight and dropped to her knees beside the basket. As she did so, one of the pups awoke and tried to climb up the side of the basket towards her.

226

Picking it up, Fanny held it close against her cheek and it immediately began licking her face. While Fanny cuddled it, Lady Killian said to Wes, 'What are you going to do with all this learning Thomas Warren's giving you?'

'I haven't thought very much about it yet. There's so much to learn. I just want to know as much as possible about everything.'

'Huh! Learning is dangerous for those who don't know what to do with it. It makes ordinary men and women dissatisfied with their lot. Just you remember that. I blame the clerics for much of the trouble this country's in today. They place far too much importance on learning. It would be better if they spent more time bringing their parishioners closer to God.'

Turning her attention to Fanny who was still cuddling the dog to her cheek, Lady Killian said, 'Is that the one you would like?'

'Oh, yes, please. It's absolutely *delightful.*'

'Well, as he chose you, I suppose there's no more to be said. Dogs have far more sense than humans. They know what they want immediately. As you and the puppy have made up your minds, you'd better take him with you. He's not likely to take to anyone else.'

'Can I? Can I really?'

Fanny's face was so radiant it brought a smile to Wesley. He was convinced the pup would lay the ghost of that violent October night.

'Tell your father to come and see me about payment whenever he's passing by. There's no hurry.'

As Wes and Fanny were leaving the house, Lady Killian spoke to him once more. 'The law is a good career, young man. There's always a place in a lawyer's office for a bright young lad with learning. You seem well-mannered and quite presentable. I still don't hold with learning for the working classes, but I have even less time for wasted effort. When Thomas Warren has taught you all he knows, you come and see me. I have a nephew who is senior partner in a solicitor's office in Dorchester. He'll take you on if I say so. You, girl. Take care of your pup and bring him to see me sometimes. I want to be sure you're looking after him properly'

Lady Killian remained in the doorway of her home and when they were almost out of speaking range, called, 'And don't get calling the pup Wesley or any such Methodist name. I'll not have any pup of mine named after a non-conformist!'

Chapter 46

'Mary! MARY! Where *is* the girl? If she doesn't begin preparing my supper soon, I won't be eating until midnight.'

Leaning on her stick in the kitchen doorway of her cottage, Amelia Cake called the errant girl. Complaining to Wes who was stripped to the waist and washing in a tub in the back yard, she added, 'I swear I use up more energy chasing that girl than ever I did when I was doing all my own work. Have you seen her?'

'You sent her with milk for Miss Brine and Widow Bullen.' The two women were among Tolpuddle's oldest inhabitants. 'She's not back yet. I expect she stopped to do some chores for them, same as she always does.'

'She went off *hours* ago. She's been gone long enough to clean both their houses from top to bottom,' the widow grumbled with grand exaggeration. 'Any servant girl worth her salt would have the work done while Mary was still wondering where she should make a start. I dread to think what their home would have been like had she and Arnold married.'

'It would have been a very happy home, Mrs Cake. One we'd both have been pleased to visit.'

Amelia Cake gave Wes a tight-lipped glare. 'Is all that learning you're getting teaching you to contradict a poor widow-woman who's only trying to get some supper for herself?'

Wes had completed his work for the day and was about to go home, but he had nothing special to do when he arrived there. Hesitantly, aware he might be making a grave error, he said, 'You tell me what needs doing, Mrs Cake, and I'll do it for you. I expect Mary will be back before many more minutes have passed.'

Amelia Cake snorted derisively, 'I wouldn't be too sure about that, but if my supper doesn't get started before long I'll go hungry. Mary put some ham on to boil, but all the water steamed away. I've had to drag the pot on to the hob. It needs boiling water added to it, but the kettle's far too heavy for me. I'd have scalded myself, likely as not.'

'That's all right, I'll do it.'

'Then there's potatoes need peeling – and carrots scraped and put on to boil. That'll do for a start.'

The heavy kettle was steaming away, half on the fire and half on the hob. It was the work of only a minute to add boiling water to the pot containing the ham and set it back on the fire. Wes's peeling of the potatoes proved equally successful, despite Widow Cake's protest that he was cutting most of the potato off with the peel. As Wes felt he was peeling little more than the colour off the outside of the vegetable he did not take her too seriously.

It was the same story with the carrots, but when Wes failed to react to her chiding, Amelia Cake grumbled ungratefully, 'I suppose that will have to do. The worst day's work I ever did was allowing Saranna to leave me. I still don't understand why she wanted to leave Southover and go all that way, do you?'

'She had no choice, Mrs Cake. Her ma was getting married and moving away.'

'So? When I was her age I ran away to marry a soldier. I thought she might have wanted to stay here, to be near you.'

'I'd once hoped she might too, but I had no right to ask anything of her. She's my brother's girl, not mine.'

'What are you talking about . . . your brother's girl? Who told you that?'

'Saul himself. He was home the night we got back from Dorchester.'

'That's a different story to the one Saranna told me. She was as disappointed as I am that you didn't ask her to stay here.'

Widow Cake's words distracted Wes. He wasn't watching what he was doing and the knife cut his finger. Fortunately, it was not a serious cut. The cold water would soon cause it to stop bleeding. 'You must have misunderstood her. She *is* Saul's girl . . . but here's Mary now. She can carry on preparing your supper.'

Walking away from Widow Cake's cottage, Wes thought of what had been said. She *must* have misunderstood Saranna. Saul had been so adamant that Saranna was his girl. That he wanted Wes to warn others off . . .

Wes was still thinking about it when he reached the village and met one of the village girls who worked at the vicarage as a day-maid.

Smiling at her, as they were about to pass each other, he said, 'Hello, Kathy, how is Miss Fanny's pup?'

To Wes's surprise, the girl stopped and her words brought him to a halt too. 'Well may you ask! There have been ructions at the vicarage. Mrs Warren came home today. She wasn't at all happy about Fanny having a dog in the house – not that you can call such a tiny creature a "dog". It might have passed off had the poor little beast not been naughty right outside the door of Mrs Warren's bedroom. Poor little thing, you'd have thought it was one of they great elephant things, the fuss she made. Said she wasn't going to have the filthy creature in the house. She made the gardener take it outside and put it in that old shed, along by the orchard. Reduced Miss Fanny to tears, it did. When I came away from the house the poor girl was out in the shed with the pup. I wouldn't be surprised if she doesn't stay there all night.'

'Where's Reverend Warren? He won't let her stay out there all night.'

'He's in Sherborne for some conference with the bishop. It would never have happened at all had he been here. He may well be weak, and under his wife's thumb, but he wouldn't have allowed her to upset poor Fanny the way she did.'

Leaning closer to Wes, the vicarage maid said conspiratorially, 'I shouldn't say it, seeing as I work at the vicarage an' all, but she's got no heart that Mrs Warren. No heart at all. I wouldn't like to have her for my mother, that's for certain.'

The vicarage maidservant went on her way fairly bristling with indignation.

Wes was already late for his supper and he was hungry. Yet he was also deeply concerned for Fanny. The Maltese puppy had brought a degree of normality back into her life, although she was still tortured to the point of obsession by the events of the October night. The pup had helped blur the memory – no more. If she suffered another setback now the outcome could be catastrophic for her.

He decided he should pay her a visit before it became fully dark.

There was a dim light burning in the shed where the maid had told him Fanny was keeping the pup company. He opened the door carefully so as not to blow out the candle and saw her kneeling on the floor, cradling the little dog in her arms.

Aware of the door opening, Fanny turned a tear-streaked face towards him. 'Wesley! Mother says I can't have Hector in the house. She had him put out here. He was crying pitifully when I came out to him.'

Wes assumed that Hector was the name Fanny had given to the pup. It was one among many others she had mentioned on the way back from Lady Killian's house.

'He would probably have cried all night had he stayed in your room. He's not used to being away from his mother and the other pups yet. He'll be missing them.'

'I know. All the more reason why he should stay in the house with me. He'll be dreadfully lonely.'

'It'll probably only be for tonight, Fanny. Your father will be home tomorrow. He'll sort it all out.'

'I doubt it. Mother can be very determined when she makes up her mind. Besides, she doesn't like any sort of animal. She never has.'

'It's going to be all right, I promise you.'

Wes had looked more closely at Fanny and was extremely concerned. She was very worked up about her new pet, and was agitated and wild-eyed. Kneeling beside her he stroked Hector. The dog stared at him from Fanny's arms.

Suddenly, Fanny rested her head against Wes for a couple of moments. 'Hector is a wonderful pet, Wesley, and I *do* love him. But ... why are you here? Father isn't home to give you a lesson ...'

'I met Kathy, your maid, when I was on my way home from Widow Cake's. She told me what had happened. She said you were here and feeling unhappy. I thought I'd come and see if I could do anything.'

'You're very kind, Wesley.' They were kneeling close together and now she leaned against him. 'But I don't think anyone can do anything to help me now. My life seems to become more unbearable with every day that passes. These last few months have been the unhappiest of my life. Nothing seems to go right for me. Nothing at all.'

Alarmed at her air of defeat, Wes said, 'You mustn't talk like that. You're going through an unhappy time at the moment, that's all.'

He put a comforting arm about her. 'Look at Hector. He's a beautiful little dog – and he's *yours*. It may make you unhappy because he has to stay out here tonight, but tomorrow I'm sure everything will be all right again. Your mother's probably tired after her long journey from London. Tomorrow she'll be feeling better and you'll have your father here too, He'll make things all right again.'

Fanny was crying again now, but through her tears she said, 'Do you really think so, Wesley?'

'I do. Just stop crying now.'

Instead, she buried her head farther into his shoulder as she said, 'I don't know what I would have done without you, Wesley. I really don't ...'

At that moment the door opened and Mrs Warren was standing there. She seemed to swell with rage before Wes's eyes. As he released Fanny, she shouted, 'Fanny! What on *earth* do you think you are doing? I come here thinking I may have been hard on you and your new pet – and what do I find? You and a ... a *village* boy! Go to your room – THIS INSTANT!'

'I can explain, Mrs Warren...' Appalled at the situation in which he found himself, Wes climbed hurriedly to his feet.

'I need no explanations. The evidence of my own eyes is quite enough for me. Nothing can explain that away. Go – and quickly, before I have you put under lock and key and send for the magistrate.'

'It isn't what you think, Mother. I was...'

'I don't want to hear another word from you, my girl. Go to your room before I thrash you – and that animal will go tomorrow, too, with its filthy, disgusting habits. Though it's no doubt a suitable companion for a girl who chooses the company of village boys.'

'Please, Mrs Warren, allow me to explain...'

'I have said all I intend saying on the matter. Fanny, go to your room. Boy... leave this house immediately – and I never want to see you here again.'

Pushing a protesting Fanny ahead of her, Mrs Warren stalked back towards the house, leaving Wes standing at the entrance to the shed, while the pup began to whimper at being left without attention once more.

Turning back to the pup, Wes said, 'I'm sorry, Hector. I'd take you home with me for the night, but in the mood she's in at the moment, Mrs Warren would have me arrested for stealing you. Don't worry, we'll have everything sorted out tomorrow.'

Chapter 47

'You're very quiet this morning, young Wesley. Are you still feeling tired? I do hope you're not sickening for anything. They were saying in the village yesterday that there's an outbreak of cholera in Dorchester again. With all these vagrants travelling the roads it could spread across the whole county in no time. Have any of them come begging up at Widow Cake's?'

'There have been no vagrants, Ma, and I haven't got cholera – or anything else. I'm feeling all right.'

Wes had arrived home late from the vicarage the previous evening and had not wanted to give his mother explanations. He had told her he was feeling tired and went straight to bed without his supper.

He had been kept awake for much of the night by the complaining of his empty stomach, but told himself he would not have slept anyway. He was too worried about what Mrs Warren would tell her husband when he returned from his meeting with the bishop.

'No, Widow Cake wouldn't tolerate beggars, for all that she's so good to you. You're lucky to be employed by a widow who doesn't feel she needs to do the same as every other employer. There's talk going around that the farmers are going to lower wages yet again. It would be the last straw for those of us who work on the land. How can a man respect himself when he needs to go cap in hand to the parish and beg for help to feed his family? It's not right,' Eli protested.

'It may not be right,' retorted Rachel, 'but you won't find many farm workers willing to risk transportation by trying to do something about it. Not any more. The farmers and landowners know they've broken the will of the workers to put up any resistance again them. That's why they feel able to lower wages yet again.'

Rachel spoke with feeling as she transferred pieces of fat bacon from a hot skillet to the plates of her husband and son.

'What you say is only partly true, Rachel. I think the time has arrived for those of us who have never supported violence to demonstrate that our way is the right way. To show we can

233

achieve our ends by peaceful means. I believe that in this, as in our Church, strength is built on unity. I am suggesting we should write to Richard Pemble, the man who is advocating the formation of a Farm Workers' Association . . .'

Eli was talking in what Rachel referred to as his 'chapel voice'. As was her habit on such occasions, she had simply stopped listening. Instead she was watching Wes tucking into his breakfast with enthusiasm.

'Well, you can't be too bad, young man, not if your appetite's anything to judge by. You're putting it away faster than I can cook it this morning.'

'I've told you, Ma, I'm fine.'

Back at the range, Rachel raked grey ash from the seat of the fire. Straightening up, she glanced through the window and stiffened abruptly.

'The vicar's out early today . . .'

It was still twenty minutes short of six o'clock and there was a heavy drizzle in the air.

'He's coming here!'

Turning to look to where Wes sat frozen in fear, a forkful of egg poised halfway between plate and mouth, she demanded, 'Have you been up to anything you shouldn't have?'

The look he gave his mother brought a tortured plea to her lips. 'Oh God! What have you done, Wesley?'

Before he could reply there was a prolonged and urgent knocking on the door and a rattling of the latch.

While Rachel dithered, Eli rose from his seat and crossed the room to the door.

The bolt still secured the door. It was a necessary precaution in these times, with so many vagabonds roaming the countryside.

Drawing back the bolt, Eli lifted the latch. Reverend Warren almost fell inside the room as the door opened, so great was his haste.

With no eyes for anyone in the room except Wesley, he demanded, breathlessly, 'Wesley, do you have any idea where Fanny might be?'

'Isn't she at home?' Wes realised it was a stupid question as soon as it had been asked. If Fanny had been at home her father would not be here asking about her.

'Her maid looked into her room to see if she wanted an early morning cup of tea about a half-hour ago. She was not there. Her bed has not been slept in. Mrs Warren told me how she found you both together in the shed last night . . .'

The Tolpuddle vicar held up a hand to silence Rachel who was about to demand an explanation from her son. 'We can discuss that matter later. Right now I am very anxious to find Fanny. Very anxious indeed. The Frampton girl has disappeared without trace and I have no intention of losing Fanny in a similar fashion.'

'Is Hector . . . her puppy, still in the shed?'

'No. He too has gone. You don't think . . .? Mrs Warren told me there had been a misunderstanding about the dog. She was cross because it had been dirty or some such thing, I believe. Surely that would not have been sufficient reason for Fanny to run away?'

'The last thing Mrs Warren said about it was that she would get rid of the pup today.'

'It must have been said in the heat of the moment. Fanny is familiar with her mother's ways. She would have known that, I am quite certain.'

'If Fanny had been her usual self, perhaps, but she was very, very upset. The pup had already been ordered out of the house. It . . . it was very important to her, sir. That's why I was trying to comfort her when Mrs Warren came to the shed and found us. That's all I was trying to do, sir, I swear it.'

'But . . . she would surely not leave home because of a silly misunderstanding?' Reverend Warren believed there must be something that Wes had not told him. 'Is there something else that's upsetting her, Wesley? Something you haven't told me? Perhaps something between the two of you? This is important, Wesley, so I would like the truth, if you please. I want to find Fanny – and find her quickly.'

'There will be nothing between your daughter and my son, Reverend Warren.' Eli spoke stiffly and pompously. 'He's been brought up to respect girls and to lead a decent life.'

Rachel had been watching her son closely and now she said, 'There *is* something, Wesley. I think you had better tell us.'

There was a lengthy silence while Wes fought a losing battle with his conscience. He had been taken into Fanny's confidence and she would never again trust him if he broke that confidence. But if she had run away she might be in very real danger. Fanny's safety was of more importance than her opinion of him.

'Yes, there is something more. I'm only involved because Fanny desperately needed someone to talk to . . .'

Wes took a deep breath and looked around at each of their faces before he spoke to Reverend Warren. 'She . . . Fanny thought she was having a baby.'

Both Reverend Warren and Wes's mother gasped and now it was the vicar's turn vehemently to deny his daughter's apparent promiscuity. 'Never! Fanny would never shame me in such a manner. I don't believe you. Besides, who could possibly be the father? You're the only one . . .'

Suddenly running out of words, Reverend Warren stared at Wes accusingly.

'It wouldn't have been her fault if she *had* been pregnant. It was because of what happened that night when the mob attacked your house. She believed they did something to her before I went to help her.'

'But that's nonsense! It all happened so many months ago. Evidence of her pregnancy would be quite apparent to everyone by now.'

'That's what I told her, but she came back at me with a story told to her by one of the servants. It was about a girl who didn't know she was pregnant until she gave birth in a field during hay-making.'

'You were there that night, Wesley. You saw what was happening. Surely you would know?'

'I *told* her nothing had happened to her. I told her she was all right, but she seemed obsessed with the idea that she was having a baby. It got worse instead of better just lately. That's why Hector – the pup – was so important to her. For the first time for months she had something to take her mind off what had happened. I think she knew how important it was too. That's why she was so upset when Mrs Warren had Hector put out in the shed. I tried to explain this to Mrs Warren last night when she said Hector had to go. She wouldn't listen . . . or perhaps I didn't try hard enough. I don't know.'

Reverend Warren had been watching Wes as he talked. Now he sat with bowed head for a long while. When he raised it, on his face was an expression that displayed all the deep grief he felt. 'You have shared this burden with Fanny for all this time and said nothing?'

'How could I? It would have betrayed her trust – and she desperately needed someone to trust. I tried to help her . . .' Wes made a faint gesture with his hands. 'I'm afraid I've failed miserably.'

'Poor Fanny. I feel we have all failed her. Thank you for telling me this, Wesley. And thank you for the support you have given to her. It makes it even more important that we find her quickly.'

'Do you have any idea where Fanny might have gone, Wesley?' Eli spoke for the first time. 'Is there any special place where she might go?'

He shook his head. 'She only ever shared the one secret with me. Nothing more.'

Eli took command. 'It's still early. None of the farm workers will have gone to work yet. Wesley, you take the village to the east. I'll take the west end. Find everyone you can. Tell them to meet on the green. Every man, woman and child who can walk. We'll organise search parties. Reverend Warren, ask your friends who have horses to scour the lanes farther afield. We'll find her. You'll see.'

Fanny Warren *was* found, late in the morning, but no one had any cause for rejoicing. Wes found Hector first, hopelessly tangled in the lower brambles of a blackberry bush, beside the ominously named 'Devil's Brook', close to where it flowed into the river.

Wes was attracted to the pup by its whimpering. Cold and wet, it was apparent the little dog had been here for a long time. It was a grim band of villagers who now concentrated their search along the river bank.

Eli first saw Fanny's body, held by a bed of rushes more than a half-mile from where Wes had found Hector. With two other men he waded into the mud of the river and brought the body ashore where it was quickly surrounded by silent and respectful villagers, many of them in tears.

There was insufficient evidence to prove beyond all doubt how Fanny had met her death. The inquest jury was told only that there had been a comparatively minor argument between Fanny and her mother about the future of Hector – now returned to Lady Killian.

A verdict of 'Accidental Death' was recorded. The coroner suggested she had probably strayed into the river by mistake during the hours of darkness, while she was wandering with her dog, upset by the events of the evening.

The funeral in the small Tolpuddle churchyard was a quiet affair attended by her family and a few local gentry. Magistrate Frampton was among them. The villagers watched from a respectful distance. Only the Reverend Warren knew that the small bunch of violets adorning the coffin as it was lowered into the narrow grave had been picked from the hedgerows than morning by Wes.

Chapter 48

The London to which Josephine had been taken by Saul was not the exciting city of her memories. Indeed, it was dirtier and more squalid than any place she had ever seen. The streets and alleyways were cluttered with stinking filth and household debris of every description. The noise of crying babies, barking dogs and quarrelling men and women went on day and night.

The houses were small and overcrowded. The children numerous, quarrelsome, and even dirtier than the homes in which they proliferated.

Saul and Josephine would occupy their mattress until late in the morning when hunger or the demands of nature drove them from the house. Once awake, the remainder of the day might be spent squatting, back against a wall on some street corner, in the company of others like themselves.

If it rained, or someone could produce a coin or two, they would adjourn to a cheap and crowded ale-house until it was time to return to the grubby mattress in the lodging-house.

Josephine began to find such a monotonous way of life irksome. She complained to Saul, but he brushed her complaint aside brusquely, saying, 'It was you who were so eager to come to London while we were in the country. Now I've brought you here, you're still not happy.'

'*This* is not London. At least, it's not the London I knew. When I came here there was always something happening, things to do. Interesting people to talk with.'

'I'm sorry I can't organise a carriage with liveried coachmen and a grand ball attended by royalty, Miss Josephine. I'm afraid the alleyways around here are too narrow to take a coach and horses. But I can offer you plenty of people to talk to in a common ale-house.'

Their conversation was overheard by a number of the customers around them and provoked sniggers.

Angered by his sarcasm, Josephine retorted, 'And just what am I supposed to talk to them about? How you're going to change the world when you and half-a-dozen friends have toppled the government of England? Or shall I join in a three-hour discussion about whether ricks burn better in Dorset or Sussex? Assuming, of course, that someone here has the faintest idea of where they were when they fired them.'

Josephine turned to walk away but Saul reached out for her. Taking a painful grip on her arm, he wrenched her around to face him.

'You'll take care what you say about such things. *We're* nct playing the sort of games most of your friends enjoy. Men have died for what we believe in. Men who've sat with us in this very room. Some would still be alive today if others had learned to keep their tongues still.'

Wrenching her arm free from his grip, Josephine said, 'People with such secrets to keep should not discuss them in cheap ale-houses and gin-shops. But there's Meg just come in. I'm going to speak to her. She has more to say than any of your friends here.'

Meg saw Josephine pushing her way across the overcrowded room and waved a hand high in animated greeting.

When Josephine reached her side, the other girl said, 'I'm surprised to find you still here. I thought you and Saul would have moved on.'

'I wish we had, I'm bored stiff. Saul's idea of a good time is talking to his friends, either on a street corner or in here. As far as he's concerned, the rest of London doesn't exist.'

'You *do* sound fed up. Tell you what, if it's a change of scenery you want, why don't you come back to my place? I've got a bottle of gin tucked away there. We can sit and drink in a bit more comfort than we have here. It's quieter, too.'

Josephine looked across the room. Saul was deep in conversation with some of his more militant friends. Although he looked up in their direction once or twice, they would be putting the affairs of the country to rights until the early hours of the next morning. If she stayed in their company for even a quarter of that time she would end up screaming.

'All right.'

The two girls pushed their way against the tide of men and women coming in through the doorway. While Josephine ignored the various lewd offers made by some of the men, Meg responded with obscenities that brought roars of drunken approval from her listeners.

Outside in the narrow alleyway, shadowed by houses overhanging on either side, Meg paused. 'Hark at them in there! To listen to 'em you'd think they was having the time of their lives. Yet all that most of 'em are doing is spending their money on cheap drink that'd poison a dog. At the end of it they'll throw up in the street and, as likely as not, fall down in the gutter and have their pockets picked. When they wake up they'll swear off drinking for at least four or five hours. Come evening they'll be back in there again. Drinking the same rot-gut, with the same so-called friends, and they'll tell each other what a wonderful time they had the night before.'

'You sound as though you don't like them very much.'

'Men are fools – but we're as bad for letting 'em run our lives the way they do.'

Meg sniffed deprecatingly. 'The only thing I can say for 'em is that I've never paid for my own drinks in there. I hope you're the same.'

Josephine had paid for most of Saul's drinks and for many of those downed by his friends. She said, 'Saul doesn't have a lot of money.'

'He never will have while he spends so much time in places like that.'

While they were talking Meg was leading the way through a veritable maze of alleyways. She stopped now, produced a key and opened a door in what appeared to be a blind alleyway.

The door led directly to a steep flight of stairs. At the head of the stairs another locked door was opened. Much to Josephine's surprise they then passed into a small but neat and tidy room.

'This is nice,' she said with genuine appreciation. 'In fact, compared with the place where I'm staying with Saul, it's a veritable palace.'

Meg looked at her admiringly. 'I wish I could talk like you, Jo. Believe me, I had more years than I like to think about living in places like the one where you're staying. I was born in one. Then one day some bloke I went with took me back to his place for the night. Sparkling clean it was. Sheets on the bed, pictures – and it smelled nice. It was like nothing I'd ever seen before. The bloke himself gave me a hard time, but that night gave me a purpose in life. Something to work for. I was determined that one day I'd have a place just like it. Well, here it is. There's a bedroom through that door and a scullery through the other one. Downstairs there's a tailor's shop, and there's a privy out the back that I don't share with more than a dozen others. It's heaven. But let me find the gin I promised you, then I'll show you around.'

Meg pulled a stoneware flagon from a cupboard beside the window. 'Here we are. It's none of that cheap stuff you've been drinking in the ale-house. It's real "Hollands", brought in 'specially for me by a friend who's captain of a barge. He sails from London to Amsterdam. He took me with him once. I enjoyed it, but they all talk a different language over there.'

Another symbol of gracious living possessed by Meg was a couple of glasses. She mixed sugar and gin in one and handed it to Josephine.

As Josephine sipped her drink, Meg looked critically at her guest's clothes. 'That's a nice dress you're wearing, Jo, but it's as dirty as a tinker's apron. Take it off while you're here and I'll wash it for you. We'll hang it to dry in front of the fire and it'll be ready for ironing by this evening. You can have an all-over wash too if you'd like. There's a tub in the scullery.'

'That would be a real luxury, Meg. It's the only thing I've missed while Saul and I have been on the road. But what will I wear while my dress is drying?'

'You can wear one of mine. It might be a bit small for you, but that won't matter, there's only you and me here to see it.'

The dress was washed, and then Josephine had her all-over wash using water boiled on the fire and carried in at frequent intervals by Meg. When she had finished she sat in front of the fire, head towards the grate, hair hanging down like a curtain in front of her face to dry.

As she sat eating bread and cheese and drinking sugared gin, Josephine felt a warm glow flooding over her. She had no idea of time passing as she and Meg talked.

It must have been quite some time because when Meg was clearing away the remains of the bread and cheese, she said, 'That dress has dried more quickly than I thought. It's ready to iron already.'

'I'll do it,' said Josephine, brightly.

Meg laughed. 'That I'd like to see! Have you ever ironed anything for yourself before?'

'No.'

'That's what I thought. Help yourself to another gin while I put an iron on the fire. It'll be a real pleasure to press something of quality. While I'm doing it you can tell me something about your life.'

It was said casually, but suddenly Josephine remembered Richard Pemble. When they had met in the ale-house he had thought he knew her. She remembered how, when he was talking to Meg, they kept looking in her direction.

'What do you want to know?'

'How about the sort of home you were brought up in? Your mother and father . . . Things like that. The sort of life I've never known, I expect.'

'I was brought up in the country. My father died many years ago and so we went to live with my grandfather. But when he put me and my mother out, I left home. That's really all there is to tell.'

As she was speaking, Josephine found she did not want to think about life at Moreton.

'What sort of house did your grandfather have? I bet it was bigger than this one.'

Josephine smiled. 'Yes, just a bit larger.'

'Is your grandfather an important man?'

'He thinks so.'

'You don't want to talk about it very much, do you?'

'No.'

Meg shrugged. 'That's all right with me. After all, it's your life.'

Meg was using a cloth to hold the hot iron handle, lifting it gingerly from the fire. Keeping a cloth between the dirty iron and Josephine's clean dress, she ironed as the steam rose.

'Have you thought any more about what we were talking about the other day?'

Josephine frowned. 'I can't remember what that was. Remind me.'

'Going with the man I told you about? The one who fancies a posh dolly-mop.'

'I've never done anything like that.'

'It's no different to going with your own bloke. Sometimes it can be better. Not only that, you can make a nice little bit of money at the same time.'

'How much money?'

'That depends. Catch him when he's had a few drinks and feeling randy and it could be pounds. He's got plenty of money, I know that for certain.'

For a minute or two the only sound in the room was steam hissing from beneath the iron. Suddenly and unexpectedly, Josephine said, 'All right.'

Meg looked at her, not certain she had heard aright. 'What do you mean: "All right"?'

'I mean, all right, I'll go with him. When?'

Meg grinned at Josephine. 'As soon as I finish ironing this dress. We'll go before you have time to think too much about it and change your mind.'

Chapter 49

When Josephine's dress had been ironed to Meg's satisfaction, she hung it over the back of a chair in front of the fire. Then she brushed and groomed Josephine's long hair. When it was done, she said, 'I have to go out for a few minutes. Pour yourself another gin and get dressed. We'll go out soon after I come back.'

Left alone, Josephine thought of what the evening and night ahead held for her. She had a succession of mixed feelings. A sense of excited anticipation, apprehension – and misgivings she could not analyse. She was not concerned about the actual act she would perform with a stranger. She did not lack experience of this.

By the time Meg returned Josephine was ready and Meg expressed her satisfaction with the way she looked.

'How are we going to get to where we're going?' Josephine asked the question as they left the house together.

'It's really no more than walking distance,' replied Meg, 'but tonight I think we'll catch a carriage as soon as we get on the City Road. It'll be better if you arrive fresh. We want to make as much money from your first customer as we can get.'

The carriage dropped them off in Piccadilly and the two girls turned into St James's Street to within sight of Brooks's Club.

Here they waited. As they stood together in the busy street, Josephine found herself caught up in the excitement of the bustle about them. Here were people from all walks of life. Buskers, beggars, vendors, and men and women of quality, some in carriages, others walking along the wide pavements.

This was the London she remembered. The place she had expected to be taken by Saul. Josephine gave a wry smile at the thought. She should have known better. Saul would have been like a tadpole among goldfish here. He was a country boy. A Tolpuddle boy. Whatever he did, he would never be anything more.

Beside her, Meg said, 'There's a lot more life here than where we live.'

'Yes. This is the London I remember.'

'Is it now? Is there anyone here who might recognise you?'

It was a possibility Josephine had not thought about. She did so now and shook her head. 'No one who knows my grandfather would expect to see me here.'

'I hope not or we might be in trouble ... Hang on! Here's the geezer coming out of his club now. You stay right here, I'll bring him to you. Remember, go along with whatever I say.'

A man was standing somewhat unsteadily at the top of the steps outside the famous gambling club. He was older than Josephine had imagined he would be. At least forty.

After negotiating the half-dozen steps down to the pavement, he was met by Meg, but did not appear to be overjoyed to see her. As they spoke he shook his head a couple of times. Then Meg pointed in Josephine's direction and beckoned to her.

Uncertainly at first, puzzled by the man's behaviour, Josephine moved out of the shadows where she had been standing. She stopped when she reached the circle of yellow light cast by a lantern affixed to railings outside the club.

Seemingly more interested now, the man walked towards her and looked at Josephine more closely. 'Hm! She's cleaner than most.'

His accent was not that of a gentleman. For all his expensive clothes, Josephine thought he probably came from Lancashire or Yorkshire. He had probably made his money in industry there.

Peering even more closely into her face, the man asked, 'What's your name, girl? Where are you from, eh?'

There was a strong smell of whisky on his breath. Avoiding an urge to recoil from him, she replied, 'Josephine – and I'm in London now. That's all I think you need to know.'

'You're certainly well-spoken, and spirited too.'

Turning to Meg, he asked, 'You say the girl's a virgin? How much is she going to cost me?'

'More than you've got most likely, especially if you've been in there losing your money.' She jerked her head in the direction of the club he had just left.

Brooks's Club was notorious as a place where fortunes were lost and – less frequently – won.

'As a matter of fact, I won tonight. Won handsomely. So, as I'm feeling particularly generous, I'll pay you ten guineas.'

'For a girl of her class – and this her first time too? I could ask twenty in Whitechapel.'

'You could ask for the moon, but you wouldn't get it. Fifteen guineas – and that's my final offer.'

'I don't want to go to bed with someone who's too mean to pay my worth.' Josephine spoke up unexpectedly. 'Let's go to Whitechapel.'

'No, wait.' The man seemed startled by her interruption. 'All right. Twenty it is – but you'd better be worth it, my girl. I'm not a man to throw that sort of money away.'

'She'll be worth every penny. But treat her well. She's not one of the back-alley girls you're used to having around here.'

'Where are we to spend the night? It needs to be somewhere discreet. I'm a well-known and respected businessman, used to my comfort.'

'I've made arrangements at a place that should suit you. It's not two minutes' walk from here. They'll want cash in advance, mind. It's five shillings, so I'll take that and the twenty guineas now.'

'Oh no you won't! Here's ten guineas. She'll get the other ten when I leave – and you can take the five shillings out of what you have.'

The man extracted the money from a heavy bag of coins that weighed down his overcoat pocket. He handed it to Meg, saying, 'Now let's get away from here, before someone sees me with you.'

The room to which Meg took them was in a lodging-house in a run-down but reasonably respectable street near Leicester Square. The front door was standing open and there was no one to challenge them when Meg led the way upstairs.

She had a key and used it to unlock a door on the first floor. Inside, a lamp was lit on a side table and a small fire burned in the grate. There was a large bed in the room which was otherwise sparsely furnished, but it was clean and tidy.

'I'll have the key, if you don't mind. I'll not have this young lady sneaking out on me until I'm satisfied I've had my money's worth.'

As Meg handed over the key, Josephine had a moment of panic. 'Where will you be, Meg? How will I find my way back?'

'Don't worry. I'll be downstairs when you're through . . .' Lowering her voice, Meg added, 'And don't worry about *him*. He's all puff and very little wind. Five minutes in bed and it'll all be over.'

Meg was not far out in her reckoning. When he finished gasping and wheezing and rolled his not inconsiderable weight off her, Josephine felt great relief. She also felt cheated. She had expected to get something from the experience, even if it was no more than a sense of shame. This too had been conspicuously absent.

Lying beside her, the man said, 'You all right, girl?'

'Yes.'

'Good. I expected more from you, but it is your first time. We'll have a little rest and do it again. You've some things to learn, but I'm just the man to teach you.'

The lamp had been extinguished and the only light in the room came from the fire, the random flames teasing the shadows on the walls. When her companion began snoring gently, Josephine watched one particular shadow, at the same time thinking about the course her life had taken in recent weeks. She wondered what the reaction of her mother and grandfather would be if they knew she way lying in bed with a man of very little breeding whose name she did not know and who had paid to make love to her.

Magistrate Frampton would be deeply shocked. She was not so certain about her mother. She too would claim to be horrified, yet Josephine suspected she would not be averse to going to bed with a man herself if the reward were high enough.

Josephine was still thinking along these lines when there was a sound from the door. It sounded as though a key was being stealthily turned in the lock. She thought she must have imagined it – until she saw the door handle turning.

The door opened slowly and a man entered the room. She was about to cry out when, to her horror, she recognised him.

'Saul!' So astonished was she that his name came out before she could stop it.

Her first thought was that he had somehow found out what she was doing and had come to make trouble.

'Saul, I . . .'

He held a finger to his lips and advanced towards the bed until he reached the chair upon which her companion had carefully folded his clothes. Only now, when Saul began to search through the pockets of the coat, did she realise the truth of why he was here.

As she watched in stunned amazement, Saul looked in her direction. 'Get up and get dressed,' he hissed, adding maliciously, 'Unless you want to try to explain things to him when he wakes up.'

Josephine moved gingerly away from the man lying beside her until she was able to swing her feet to the floor. She hoped the man would remain asleep but, to her consternation, he suddenly sat upright in the bed.

'Wha—what's going on? Josephine . . .' He suddenly saw Saul. 'Who are you? What are you doing with my clothes . . . HELP! THIEF!'

As Josephine struggled into her dress, the man leaped from the bed and lunged at Saul. He went sprawling to the floor when Saul stepped to one side but was on his feet again in an instant. Looking flabby and slightly comical in his nudity, he leaped at Saul once again.

This time his weight was sufficient to knock Saul off balance, the heavy money bag he was holding falling to the floor.

The man went after it on hands and knees as Saul struggled to his feet within inches of the fire. He rose with a brass poker in his hand and Josephine screamed.

Whether it was a warning to the man, or an attempt to stop Saul, she did not know herself. Neither aim succeeded. As the man turned his head the poker crashed down and he fell to the floor.

Saul did not cease his beating even when the man lay still on the carpet, blood seeping from one ear. Not until Josephine ran to take hold of his arm did he stop.

'What are you doing, Saul. You've killed him . . .'

'He attacked me first, you saw that.' Snatching up the money bag, Saul looked quickly about the room. 'Make sure you leave nothing behind that can be traced to you. Come on, let's get out of here.'

Without waiting for her, he ran from the room. With one last horrified glance at the man who had paid with his life and his evening's winnings for making love to her, Josephine hurried after Saul.

There were a couple of women in the passageway and one demanded, 'What's happening? I heard someone shouting for help.'

Pointing to the room she had just left, Josephine said, 'In there. A man needs help.' Then she was fleeing after Saul.

Neither he nor Meg was in the hall, but they were waiting with increasing agitation in the dark street outside. As Josephine reached them they heard a woman's hysterical screaming from the house they had just left.

'Run!' cried Saul, and matched word with deed.

Meg and Josephine followed suit, but they did not catch up with him until they had left the lodging-house far behind and the chance of successful pursuit was over.

Chapter 50

The villagers of Tolpuddle remained in a state of shock for some weeks following the tragic death of Fanny Warren. The festivities usually held to celebrate the first day of May were cancelled and for two months Reverend Warren was not seen in the village. Services continued to be held in the Tolpuddle church each Sunday, but they were conducted by a young curate who travelled to the village from Dorchester.

Wes no longer went to the vicarage for lessons. Nothing had been said, but he realised he would no longer be welcome there, even if Reverend Warren were to be at home. His lessons had been an acknowledgement of the part he had played in rescuing Fanny from the mob.

It seemed an empty victory now. She had died as an indirect result of what had taken place on that night. Wes thought that Reverend Warren might now actually blame him for contributing to her death.

He was constantly torturing himself with the thought that Fanny's life might have been saved had he told the vicar earlier of his daughter's anguish.

Although his lessons had come to an end, Wes continued with his studies as best he could in his own home. However, he had other matters with which to occupy his time now.

For the first time in Wes's lifetime, Eli Gillam was taking an interest in something not connected with the Methodist Church. The plight of the farm labourer had become a matter of grave concern in the Tolpuddle area. More and more farm workers were being forced to turn to the parish council for relief.

Wages had dropped to a level where a loaf of bread took two-thirds of a full day's pay. Life was no easier for those with large families who had been in the habit of baking bread at home. A stone of flour meant parting with more than two days' pay. Tea, at five shillings a pound, was beyond the average family's means, and shoes at four shillings a pair took half a man's weekly wage. Of necessity, a farm worker's wife and children now went barefooted.

Some families had no wages coming in at all. The threshing-machines had taken work from many during the winter. Now that spring had arrived, it seemed there was far more labour available than there was work.

Men could not manage on the wages they were being offered, yet most were prepared to undercut their neighbours. So desperate were they not to end up in the workhouse that they were prepared to go to any lengths in order to retain what freedom they possessed.

Those who failed were faced with the heartless rigours imposed upon them by a poorhouse overseer. Arnold Cooper's grandmother was already in the village poorhouse and she was being joined there by many of those who had felt sorry for her plight.

The cottage where she had lived for more than sixty years belonged to the manor, but the ownership had recently passed to a clergyman who lived elsewhere. A letter sent from the cleric's solicitor gave her three weeks in which to pack up the chattels of a lifetime and leave.

The reason, as given by the solicitor, was that the new Lord of Tolpuddle would not have the dependant of a convicted felon housed in a manorial property.

Wes and his father had both tried hard to find a new home for the aged woman, already bewildered by the loss of her grandson, but to no avail. Most of Tolpuddle was manorial property. No one would risk incurring the wrath of their landlord. The poorhouse became her new 'home'.

'It's a cold, heartbreaking sort of place,' declared Eli, when he returned from a Sunday visit to the old woman. 'I couldn't even give her the comfort of a short service. The overseer there says it's a Church of England workhouse and he'll have no nonconformists spreading discontent among the inmates.'

'He'll soon be too busy to worry about non-conformists,' said Rachel, bitterly. 'I went to see Tom Cross's wife today. She's a very sick woman and her husband has had his wages cut, same as everyone else. She says they're so short of money, they can't pay the rent. Their cottage belongs to the manor, same as Granny Cooper's did. I can't see them getting any more sympathy and understanding than she did.'

'I think there might be someone at the manor this week,' said Wes. 'I saw two carriages turn in there when I was on my way home tonight.'

'I'll go and speak to the Lord tomorrow night,' said Eli. 'Perhaps if I tell him of Tom Cross's plight and plead for a reduction in rent for the family he might listen to me. Reverend St John and I may not worship in the same Church, but he's a man of God as well as being Lord of the Manor. He will surely show some compassion towards his fellow-men. Will you come with me, Wesley?'

Flattered that his father wanted his company on such an errand, Wes readily agreed. His father rarely asked for his company. On the way to the manor, Wes learned the reason.

'The Reverend St John is a Church of England clergyman who dislikes Methodists. He might refuse to speak to me. You, on the other hand, took lessons with Thomas Warren in the vicarage. We might need to mention that . . .'

As it happened, Eli Gillam's guile was to no avail. The carriages seen by Wes arriving at the manor had brought the Reverend St John's brother to the great house. He came as a tenant to occupy the manor house with the intention of farming some of the manorial lands.

After introducing himself and Wes, Eli stated his business. The new tenant listened to his plea with growing impatience.

'I'm here to farm, Mr Gillam, not to distribute largesse among the families of my brother's tenants.'

'I'm not suggesting you give Tom Cross and his family money, sir. Only that you show a little Christian forbearance.'

'Can I presume from the name you have given your son that you are a Methodist, Mr Gillam?'

'I am, sir.'

'And this Cross? He's a Methodist too, no doubt?'

'He was baptised into our Church, but we've seen little of him since his wife became ill.'

'Nevertheless, he *has* turned his back on the established Church and all it stands for. Yet you have the cheek to come here begging for that Church's support. That comes under the heading of hypocrisy, surely, Mr Gillam?'

'I came here to beg for nothing, sir. Only to ask that you help relieve the heavy burden on Tom Cross by telling him his home, at least, is secure.'

'I am sorry to disappoint you, Mr Gillam. I have not come to Tolpuddle to set myself up as a public benefactor. I am a working farmer. I need to pay rent to my brother and I have my own family to support. Regrettable though the present circumstances of this man Cross may be, I have no doubt that much of his troubles stem from his own lack of thrift during better days. He will also, I am quite sure, have contributed to Methodist funds? I suggest you ask your minister to help alleviate any distress this man's family may be suffering.'

Eli stood his ground and would have made one last plea for Tom Cross and his family. Seeing his father standing before the new occupant of the manor, hat held nervously in his work-calloused hands, Wes felt keenly the humiliation of the other man's scorn.

'Come on, Pa. You're wasting your breath and Mr St John's time. It seems Tolpuddle has lost its Lord of the Manor and gained yet another seven-shillings-a-week-farmer.'

'I have every intention of bringing wages down to *six* shillings a week as soon as is practical,' was the unruffled comment of Cuthbert St John. 'I trust your own employment is secure, young man. Your insolence will not soon be forgotten.'

As father and son walked away from the manor, Eli said, 'You shouldn't have angered him, Wes. No good can come of it.'

'No good came of your patience,' retorted Wes. 'He was treating you with utter contempt. Mr St John may be in Tolpuddle to farm, but he's living in the manor and it seems to me he intends behaving as though he *is* the Lord. I don't think the village is going to enjoy having him live here.'

They walked on in silence for a while before Wes asked, 'What will you do now, Pa, give up?'

'I can't do that, Wesley. I am reluctant to take on authority. The man who does so never comes out as a personal winner. However, I think something needs to be done, for the sake of my fellow-men.'

Wes's spirits took a dive. His father had slipped back into his pompous preacher's manner of talking. He expected him to utter a quotation from the Bible that would mean he need do nothing except amplify that quotation for use in his next chapel sermon.

Instead, Eli said, 'I intend doing something our Saul advocated a long time ago, Wesley. Perhaps I should have listened more to him. I am going to speak to George Loveless tonight. He has a brother in London who has written to him about the advantages of joining a Trades Association, a union of men with a common purpose. I think it is time all farm workers joined together and spoke with a loud voice. If we do not, our cries will be lost in the darkness that seems to be enveloping this fair land of ours.'

251

Chapter 51

For very many years there had been a deep division in the Tolpuddle community. On one side were those who worshipped in the ancient parish church dedicated to St John. On the other, an increasing number of men and women who chose to worship in the chapel. The two factions went their separate ways, with no intermarrying and a minimum of social contact. Each was convinced the road taken by the other led not to heaven but to damnation.

The twelfth-century church had borne witness to christenings, confirmations, marriages and funerals, not to mention the early non-conformist protests of countless generations of Tolpuddle residents. To those who remained in the established Church it represented an unchanging pattern of life, in which each could follow his or her own particular course.

The Church offered reassurance without demanding uncomfortable commitment, or fuelling exhausting ambition.

In sharp contrast to such an easy-going faith, the Methodist Church marched its members along a narrow, well-defined path from which they strayed at the risk of their eternal souls.

Not for them the indolence of those who took the easy road to heaven. Methodists advanced towards the same goal as their fellow-villagers with banners flying and bugles sounding, scarcely pausing as they thrashed the devil along the way. Theirs was the vibrance of a young Church.

Each Church was disdainful of the other, an attitude encouraged by those who led them. Each was convinced they had little in common with the other. Yet the greed of the farmers and landowners succeeded in bridging the gap the Churches had created over the years.

On a soft, summer night, every agricultural labourer who lived in the village and surrounding area gathered on the sloping Tolpuddle Green. With them were a sprinkling of women and a great many children, the latter treating the occasion as an opportunity to play games of tag.

The men assembled in self-conscious, yet defiant groups. For a while, Church of England denominations remained with their fellows and Methodists with theirs. Then, finally, sheer numbers drove them together in one large, murmuring crowd.

The men were addressed by a number of speakers. Standing beneath a giant sycamore tree at the edge of the green, each told of the cuts they had been forced to take in their wages. They enumerated the hardships borne by the families of workers and spoke bitterly of the uncaring attitude of the men they had served, some for upwards of fifty years.

Many of the speakers were lay preachers belonging to the Methodist Church. Among these were George Loveless and Eli Gillam from Tolpuddle.

'We have heard this evening stories of the desperation kindled among us by the concerted actions of our employers,' declared Eli when it was his turn to speak. 'Every man here has a similar tale to tell – and many of the more pitiful stories have yet to be heard. Tales of whole families who have not tasted meat for many months. Who will not be able to afford *bread* unless something is done immediately to ease their plight.'

Eli was in his best fire-and-brimstone manner this evening. 'Yet knowing the hardships the wage cuts are causing is one thing. Doing something positive is another. Can anyone offer any suggestions?'

'Burn their ricks,' shouted a voice in the crowd, and the suggestion met with noisy approval from some sections of his audience.

'There will be none of that talk here,' shouted Eli sharply. 'Neither will there be any violent behaviour. We all know what the consequences were when such a protest disturbed the peace in Tolpuddle late last year. We are being sadly wronged by those who employ us, but we will not do the same.'

'After stirring up a mob in such a manner, how do you propose preventing it from breaking the law, Gillam? By making fine speeches?'

Unseen by the speaker and the majority of those listening to him, Reverend Thomas Warren had joined the crowd on the edge of the village green. Now, having made his presence known, he pushed his way forward until he was standing in the small cleared space before Eli.

It was the first time the vicar had been seen abroad since the tragic death of Fanny. To Wes, standing in the forefront of the crowd, it seemed he looked strained and tired.

'There was a fine speaker at the front door of the vicarage on the night you have already mentioned. He assured me that the men with him meant no harm to anyone. He was telling me this at the very moment that other men were at the rear of the house, attacking my poor daughter – and your son, Gillam.'

Reverend Warren turned to face the farm workers. 'Men, women – yes, and children too lose their lives at the hands of mobs. The actions of many farmers are causing hardship, I cannot dispute that. Yet men and women are not dying as a result of such difficulties – as they surely will if we see mobs set loose on our countryside once more. Think, I beg you, before you take such irresponsible action.'

'I could not – and would not – make light of your grief, Reverend Warren,' Eli addressed the Tolpuddle vicar respectfully in reply. 'I hope you may draw some comfort from the knowledge that every man in Tolpuddle, whatever his denomination, shares your grief. But children are lying awake at night in the houses of the farm labourers. They are crying with hunger because of what the farmers are doing in their greed. The children of these same farmers and landowners will not go hungry if their fathers pay out an extra shilling per man in wages. The farmers will not faint as they walk their fields because they haven't had a proper meal for days – or even weeks in some cases. Look around you on a market day, Reverend. It's easy enough to distinguish the wives and daughters of farmers from those of the labourers. They are the ones who wear shoes. A farm worker can no longer afford to buy any for his own family.'

His words brought a rising tide of agreement from the listening crowd. As the noise grew it drowned the shouts of Mary Riggs who had run all the way to the green, arriving hot and wild-eyed. Scanning the crowd to find Wes, she saw him near the front, close to the speakers.

Pushing her way towards him, red-cheeked and shaking with agitation, she seemed oblivious to those about her as she called to him.

Only when the loud murmur of the crowd began to die away could her voice be heard.

'Wes! Wes! You must come quick. Widow Cake sent me to fetch you. Something terrible's happened. Terrible!'

Wes pushed his way to meet her. The crowd, their attention suddenly diverted from Eli and the other speakers, parted to allow Mary and him through.

Mary was shaking almost uncontrollably by the time he reached her. Wes took her by the upper arms in a bid to steady her. 'It's all right, Mary. You've found me now. Take a deep breath and tell me what's happened.'

She did exactly as she was told, and the words tumbled out. 'Widow Cake sent me up to Tom Cross's house with some eggs and milk for his poor wife and family.'

Shaking violently once more, she took another breath, 'I got no answer when I knocked, so I went in.' Suddenly she burst into tears. 'It was horrible, Wes. I never see'd anything like it in my life . . .'

Wes put a comforting arm about her heaving shoulders. 'It's all right, Mary. Just tell me what you found.'

Turning a tearful face up to him, she said in a hoarse whisper, 'They was all dead. Every one of 'em. Poor Tom had killed his wife and children, then himself. I found him hanging from a bacon hook in the kitchen . . .'

Ironically, the violent deaths of Tom Cross, his wife and the whole of their young family so shocked the community that this news succeeded where demonstrations and demands had failed.

By the time representatives of the farm labourers met with their employers a few days later, resistance to their demands was no more than a token. The deaths of the Cross family would weigh heavily upon the consciences of the farmers for many months to come.

It was agreed the farm labourers of the Tolpuddle area would receive the same wages as their fellow workers in neighbouring areas.

The troubles of the farm workers of Tolpuddle were over – or so it was believed. Unfortunately, like the inexorable tide that ebbed and flowed not many miles away on the Dorset coast, the troubles had merely receded for a while.

They would gather strength and return to batter the resolve and dignity of the men of Tolpuddle. By so doing they were to change the lives of Wes and his family for ever.

BOOK TWO

Chapter 1

For a long while after the tragic deaths of the Cross family, life in Tolpuddle returned to its familiar pattern for those who lived there. It seemed that things were as they had always been. Most wanted them to remain that way and few of the villagers were sorry to see the eventful year of 1831 come to an end.

When the next year passed uneventfully, they began to relax. Life was once more the way it had been before Napoleon Bonaparte turned Europe into a battlefield on which so many Englishmen were sacrificed.

Despite the return to normality of Tolpuddle village life, momentous events were taking place in the world beyond Dorset's borders. The long-overdue reform of Parliament had taken place; in the factories of the industrial Midlands, the working hours for children had been reduced to twelve a day; a new London bridge had been opened over the River Thames, and railways were beginning to trace a fragmented pattern on the maps of England. Elsewhere ricks were still being fired by discontented agricultural workers.

But none of these things affected Tolpuddle directly. Most of those who lived here knew little about such worldly happenings.

For Wes, it was a lonely time. He had expected the emptiness he felt so keenly when Saranna left her work at Widow Cake's cottage and moved to Kent, to grow less. It did not. It seemed there was something at Widow Cake's to remind him of her every single day.

He sometimes wondered whether she and Saul had married by now. He thought they probably had, but there had been no more news of his brother than there had been of Saranna.

Wes would often cease work for a few minutes when a party of vagrants passed along the lane beside Widow Cake's land. He hoped he might one day recognise one or more of the men who had been in the habit of calling at the Vye cottage when Saranna and her mother lived at Southover.

Thoughts of Saranna and of Saul were passing through Wes's

mind as he cut and split logs in the back yard, with which to stock the wood-shed there. Widow Cake always liked to have the shed filled with logs before winter set in.

She was fond of telling Wes of a time in her childhood when thick snow covered the land for two weeks. During this time no one had been able to leave the vicinity of the house to gather wood. Widow Cake made the repeated assertion every year that she did not intend she should be without wood were such snows to occur again.

Thinking as he worked, Wes remembered that the logs he was splitting now came from the same elm tree he had been working on when Saranna told him her mother was marrying Richard Pemble and they were to leave Southover.

The Association leader had not been to the Tolpuddle area since. Wes realised his frequent visits to Southover had owed more to the presence of Nancy Vye than dedication to his cause.

He had just split a log when he heard the back door open. The next moment Mary called, 'Wes, come into the house. Quickly!'

Dropping the axe to the ground, Wes hurried into the kitchen, 'What is it, Mary. Is something the matter with Widow Cake?'

'There's nothing wrong with me, young man. What has that silly girl been saying to you? All this fuss just because a letter's been delivered to the house for her. It's probably from that mother of hers asking for money, that's all.'

Mary's mother had left Tolpuddle the year before, to share a house in Bristol with her widowed sister. The sister's late husband had owned a small cobbler's shop. When he died he left his widow enough money to ensure she would not end her days in a poor-house, but she was not generous with it.

'It is about Ma, I'm sure it is. She must be ill, or something.' Mary stood in the centre of the kitchen with the letter in her hand, trembling with trepidation.

'Put the girl out of her misery, Wesley. Open the letter and read it to us.'

The letter was creased and stained and there was a tear on one edge of the envelope. Wes thought it looked as though it had come from much farther away than Bristol.

Tearing the envelope open carefully, he smoothed out the two sheets of paper before turning to the second page to glance at the signature. He gave a start of surprise and said, 'It's from Arnold. The letter's come all the way from Australia.'

Mary gave a squeal of delight, 'What's it say, Wes? Read it to me.'

260

Dear Mary,

I am writing to tell you I have reached Australia safely, after a voyage that was surely as close to hell as anyone will find in this life. I was very lucky when I got here to be assigned to Mr Arthur Trevail. He is a Methodist and farms about thirty miles from Sydney. He has treated me with great kindness and says that if I behave well I shall be a free man in seven years, or perhaps before.

There is much talk here that all agricultural workers transported because of the riots in England are to be pardoned.

Lastly, I am sorry for all the distress I have caused you, dear Mary, but Mr Trevail says that if you are of a mind to come out here, we can marry and he will have a little house built for us on his farm.

Please come, Mary. I miss you so much and I know we can find happiness here. I hope Wes and Widow Cake are well. I am sorry for the trouble I have caused you all.

Your loving Arnold.

'He's alive and well . . . and he wants me to go there and marry him!'

Mary sat on the kitchen chair, her hands clasped before her, tears streaming down her face. 'I haven't lost him, Mrs Cake. He still wants me. I . . . I'm so happy.'

'There's more to the letter, Mary, written by Mr Trevail. He says he wrote the letter at Arnold's request and hopes you will come out there. He says he has a lot of land and is very pleased with Arnold's work. He says you and Arnold will have a good life on his farm. He ends with instructions on what to do and who to ask for when you land at Sydney.'

'Well now, fancy that! Whoever thought Arnold would find his feet in such a way after coming as close as he did to being hung.' Amelia Cake shook her head disbelievingly.

'I don't want to think about such things, Mrs Cake. Not today. I just want to be happy knowing that Arnold still loves me and wants me to marry him. I'm just . . . so happy!'

The tears rolling down Mary's plump cheeks belied her statement, but both Amelia Cake and Wes understood.

'What will you do, Mary? Will you go to Australia and marry Arnold?'

Wes put the question to the tearfully happy girl, but it was Amelia Cake who replied for her. 'What sort of foolish question is that, Wesley Gillam? Of course she'll go to Australia to be with him, even though it will mean leaving me in Tolpuddle with no one to look after me. But we won't speak about such things today

– and I can see there'll be no work done in the house that won't need doing all over again. Off you go, girl. Go up to the poor-house first and tell Arnold's grandmother about the letter – not that she'll understand much. Her mind's gone, so I'm told. Then you can let the village know that Arnold has written to you. There hasn't been much to celebrate this last year or two, but this should please folk.'

Mary needed no urging. Stripping off her apron as she went, she hurried from the room.

'That was a very kind thing to do, Mrs Cake. Is there anything I can do to help while Mary's away?'

'I'm not helpless, Wesley. I can get about and do things in my own house, although perhaps not as quickly as I would like. Even so, I expect I'll be as fast as Mary ever was. Lord alone knows how I'll get her to work after this. All she'll be able to think of will be Arnold, Australia, and getting married. The girl will be impossible.'

Wes smiled. He had worked for Widow Cake for long enough to know she was as happy as he was with the knowledge that Arnold was well. It sounded too as though he had the prospect of leading a reasonably settled life in Australia. 'You've got to admit it's good news though, Mrs Cake?'

'I haven't *got* to admit to any such thing, young Wesley! All I know is that if Mary goes off to Australia – and she surely will if she has any sense in her head – I'll be left on my own here. A poor widow-woman, hardly able to stand and with no one around to look after me properly. So what's good about it for me, I'd like to know?'

'I expect my ma will be able to come in and help, if you'd like her to? She's not doing very much at East Farm at the moment. One of the sons there has married and his wife helps about the house.'

'You're not one to miss an opportunity, are you, Wesley?'

'Not if it means more money coming into the Gillam house, I'm not.'

'Well, I've no doubt you're going to need it. I had someone from Southover Farm call on me last week. Her sister lives in Dorchester. She's heard the farmers have begun cutting wages for farm labourers everywhere. You'd have thought the farmers around Tolpuddle had learned their lesson, but I don't suppose they ever will. Yes, Wesley, it'll be all right for your mother to help me out when Mary goes. Mind you, if you'd had sense enough to marry Saranna when you had the chance, there'd be no need to go looking for anyone else. She was a good girl, that one. She'll make someone a very good wife.'

Wes did not feel like reminding Widow Cake of the claim she had made when Saranna left. She had said then that Mary had been taken on only because, if he *had* married Saranna, there would have been children and Saranna would not have been able to work for her.

The thought that Saranna might now have children – Saul's children – took the sharp edge off the pleasure Wes felt over Arnold's letter.

Chapter 2

Only four days after Arnold's letter arrived from Australia, Wes received news of Saranna. Unfortunately, it was accompanied by such a startling revelation that all else was completely over-shadowed.

It occurred late on a Sunday morning. Wes was walking back home from his usual visit to read the Bible to Widow Cake when he saw a man sitting on the grass verge at the side of the lane. The man was a vagrant, and Wes did not take too much notice at first. There were still a great many such wandering about the countryside.

As he drew nearer, Wes thought the man looked familiar. A few steps farther on he became certain. This was one of the men who had once been entertained by Nancy Vye at the Southover cottage.

Delving into his memory, Wes was almost level with the man before he remembered his name. Stopping by the vagrant, he said, 'It's Silas Morgan, isn't it? Ex-Corporal Silas Morgan?'

The man was eating a hunk of bread, upon which was balanced a large slab of cheese. He paused momentarily, then took a large bite before asking indistinctly, 'Who wants to know?'

'Wes Gillam. We met at Nancy and Saranna Vye's house, over at Southover. It must be two years ago now.'

The vagrant stopped eating for a moment to peer more closely at Wes. 'That's right, I recognise you now. I was with Nancy not four weeks since. We were talking about the times when I'd come visiting her at Southover.'

'You've seen her that recently? Saranna too? How is she?'

'She's grown into a fine woman. Takes after her mother. If I was a young man I'd give up the open road and marry her myself.'

'She's not married then . . . Saranna?' Wes spoke hopefully.

'Not yet, though I heard a rumour when I was there that something in the wind was blowing her in that direction.'

'Oh! Who is it that she might be marrying? Is it Saul?'

'You talking of the Saul that came from here? Went off about two years ago . . . before I met up with you at the Vye cottage?'

'That's him. He's my brother.'

'Of course! I remember now. You mean . . . you haven't heard?' Silas Morgan swallowed the cheese in his mouth and promptly began coughing, staring at Wes with watering eyes.

'Heard what? We've had no news of Saul since Arnold Cooper was transported.'

Wiping his eyes and mouth with the back of a grubby hand, Silas Morgan said, 'Well, young sir, I'm sorry that I'm the one to bring you such bad news, but no one else could have done it 'cos they don't know – and they won't hear of it from me. If Saul follows Arnold Cooper to Australia he can consider himself to be a lucky man! Very lucky indeed. If it's Saul that Saranna was planning to wed, I hope she hasn't done anything about it yet. If she has she'll be a widow before she's many months older!'

'What are you talking about?' Wes was thoroughly alarmed. 'What's Saul supposed to have done – and where is he now?'

'There's no "supposed" about it. He was caught firing some-one's rick. As to *where* he is . . . Last I heard he was in gaol in Marlborough and not planning to move very far.'

'How long ago was this?'

'Couple of weeks. Why, you planning on going to see him?'

Wes nodded, bemused by the news of Saul's arrest.

'I hope you get there in time. If you do, tell him Silas Morgan says we'll have a party when we both meet up again in hell.'

Wes wandered the lanes around Tolpuddle for an hour and a half in an attempt to think out what he should do for the best. In so doing he missed the midday meal at home, but he knew his mother would assume Widow Cake had found some work for him to do. It was a situation that occurred frequently.

He also knew his father would have been at Tolpuddle chapel that morning. After eating at home he would set off to walk to Dewlish where he was due to preach that afternoon. From there he would go on to another chapel even farther away to preach in the evening. He would not arrive home until after dark. There would be no time then for Wes to speak about what was on his mind.

Despondent, he sat on the grass verge at the side of a lane outside Tolpuddle and waited for his father. He hoped there would not be any of his chapel-going friends accompanying him.

It was a long wait. Just when Wes was thinking there might have been a change to his father's plans, he heard him coming along the lane, quietly singing a hymn to himself. He was alone.

Seeing his son seated on the grass verge, Eli frowned. 'What are you doing here, Wesley? We waited for half an hour before we ate, thinking you'd be home any minute. Your mother thought you must be working.'

'That's what I wanted her to think. I had to see you alone. I need to talk to you. I've had news this morning that our Saul's in trouble in Marlborough.'

'What sort of trouble?' asked Eli sharply.

'He's been arrested. I don't really know much more than that, but I think I ought to go and find out.'

'If he's got himself into some scrape then he must sort it out for himself. We've not had a word from him since . . .'

'Pa! I think this is much more than a scrape. He's probably in deep trouble.'

'How have you heard about this?' Eli was bewildered. 'Did someone come looking for you at Widow Cake's house?'

'It's a long story, Pa. I met someone who knows Saul when I was on my way home. He's a vagrant. He told me.'

'Saul is associating with vagrants? Small wonder that he's ended up in trouble. If he had stayed home and tried to settle down, as you have, we'd have had none of this.'

'There isn't time to go into all that now. I need to find out what's happening to him, but I wanted to think of something to tell Ma. There's also work that needs doing each day at Widow Cake's. Do you think you could go there for a couple of hours each evening when you finish work for Thomas Priddy? It should only be for a few days – a week, at most.'

Eli rubbed his chin uncertainly. He was not given to making instant decisions. He liked time to think things out carefully before making a move in any particular direction.

'I have a lot of chapel commitments . . .'

'Pa, our Saul is in trouble!' Wes spoke in exasperation. 'He needs help.'

'You're right, Wes. I'll do whatever needs doing up at Widow Cake's place. What do you suggest we tell your ma?'

'We'll say what you just suggested, that he's in some sort of a "scrape". We'll decide if there's anything more she needs to know when I come back.'

'When do you intend leaving?'

'As soon as I've been back to speak to Widow Cake and said goodbye to Ma.'

'You'll find a couple of guineas in a jar by my bedside. It's kept there for anything that might come up. It's not much but take it anyway.'

'I don't need it, Pa. I have seven pounds I've saved up myself. That should see me through.'

Suddenly and unexpectedly, Eli embraced his son. 'You're a

good boy, Wesley. Take care of yourself.'

Wes had gone some distance along the lane when his father called to him.

'Wesley!'

Wes turned.

'I will pray that you succeed in helping Saul. Tell him . . . Tell him to come home. It's time.'

Amelia Cake was more inquisitive than his father had been. She was also far shrewder. Wes told her no more than he had told his father, but her gaze never left his face while he was talking.

When he had given her his explanation, she said, 'Saul's in serious trouble, isn't he?'

'It's possible, Mrs Cake.'

'I think it's more than a possibility – and so do you. How are you going to get to Marlborough?'

'Walk, I suppose. I can't afford to travel by coach.'

'Farmer Hooper from Southover was here to see me last week about putting his cows to graze on my land again. He claimed that times are hard and said he can't afford to pay much. He suggested I take a pony and trap as payment. Said it'd help me get out and about a bit more. I told him I don't intend going anywhere, but you can go across there now and tell him I've changed my mind – but only if he throws in a saddle and tack. You can leave the trap here and take the pony.'

'That's very kind of you, Mrs Cake . . .'

'Kindness has nothing to do with it. I've been thinking about it. With a pony and trap perhaps I *could* get out and about a bit more. Anyway, it'll mean that you're back here working much quicker than if you have to walk everywhere. I don't want that father of yours spending time trying to convert me to his Methodist ideas. It's work I need here, not religion. Off you go now – and hurry back, you hear?'

Chapter 3

It was about seventy miles from Tolpuddle to Marlborough. Wes arrived late in the evening of the Monday, having walked the last five miles leading the weary and ageing pony.

He had set out from Tolpuddle the day before after having had some difficulty persuading his mother she should not come with him. He had told her no more than he felt she should know, deliberately playing down the seriousness of the matter.

He had spent the previous night at a small inn on the outskirts of Salisbury. He felt able to do this, having had a ten-pound loan forced upon him by the practical Widow Cake who pointed out that he had no idea how long he would be away. His seven pounds would not go far if he needed to find many nights' accommodation for himself and her newly acquired pony.

Marlborough was little more than a single main street – but what a main street it was! Wes had never seen anything quite as wide – or quite as busy. The town was on the main road that linked Bristol, the West Country, and Wales, with London. It seemed to Wes that carriages were almost as plentiful here as people. It was also one of the places where the horses were changed on the long-distance coaches. Coachmen announced their imminent arrival with long blasts on a horn, a differing combination of notes letting the waiting attendants know which coach was coming. The change was accomplished at great speed and accompanied by a maximum of noise. It gave the market town a vibrant, busy air.

Wes found a reasonably cheap inn, the Angel, situated on the wide main street. He put the pony into the care of the inn's ostler who proved to be extremely talkative.

'Good evening, sir. Have you travelled far?'

'From Dorchester.'

'Really, sir? We don't get many here from that way. Most of our gentlemen are travelling between London and the West. Have you come here for the hanging?'

'What hanging would that be?' Wes was tired and really not in the mood for making conversation.

'Why, there's no less than four felons being hung in the morning. It's the most anyone here can ever recall being given "the drop" at the same time. If you take a walk a little way from here you'll see the scaffold. There'll be a fair-sized crowd outside the gaol, you can be certain of that.'

Wes wanted nothing to do with such a macabre occasion but he realised it might affect the visit he proposed making to the prison.

'What is it they're being hung for?'

'Two for murder. One's a highwayman – and the other was caught setting fire to ricks. The country will be well rid of 'em, if you asks me.'

Suddenly all Wes's tiredness was forgotten. The vagrant at Tolpuddle had said Saul was due to stand trial for firing ricks.

'What's the name of the man who fired ricks?'

'I couldn't tell you that, sir. I'm not a great one for names, even if I'd heard it. Tell you what, though. The town's gaoler is inside – drowning his conscience, I'd say.'

Wes hurriedly settled arrangements with the ostler then went inside the inn. In answer to his question, the landlord pointed out a small, bearded man with a dour expression seated on his own in a corner of the taproom.

Carrying a drink to the table where the man sat, Wes said politely, 'Do you mind if I sit here?'

The bearded man looked at him morosely. 'It's an inn. You can sit where you want, I reckon.'

'Thank you.' Wes took a swig from his tankard without taking his gaze from the other man. 'I believe you're the town gaoler?'

'That's right.'

'Was the man who's being hung tomorrow in your care? The one convicted of burning ricks?'

'I had all four of 'em at one time or another.'

'The one who's being hung for burning ricks. Would his name be . . . Gillam? Saul Gillam?'

The gaoler looked at Wes from red-rimmed, watery eyes. 'You're asking a lot of questions of a man who's sitting here with a near empty tankard.'

'Of course, I'm sorry.' Wes caught the eye of one of the serving-girls and signalled. A few moments later she arrived at the table with two full tankards of ale.

Taking a deep draught and belching appreciatively, the gaoler wiped his mouth with the cuff of one sleeve.

'That's better. No, the rick-burner didn't go by that name.'

Wes breathed a deep sigh of relief, but it was short-lived.

'His first name was Saul, that I do know. But his surname was a Methodist one . . . Wesley. That's it. Saul Wesley. Mind you, I

269

doubt if that's his real name. Half of those who are hung give false names. It's so they don't bring disgrace on their families, I suppose.'

The more Wes thought about it, the more he realised that what the gaoler had said was likely to be true of Saul. He would not give his real name – and 'Wesley' was a probable choice of alias. But the gaoler was talking again.

'If you want to know more about him, why don't you try to find that girl of his?'

'She's here? Saranna's in Marlborough?'

'Don't know her name. Matter of fact, I don't think I've ever heard it, but she's his girl all right.' The gaoler looked at Wes slyly. 'Another pint would probably help me remember where she's staying.'

'I don't want to know where she's staying but, here, you can have my drink. I haven't touched it.'

The full tankard was moved to the other side of the table before West finished making the offer.

'What I really want is to get in and see Saul. Can that be arranged?'

'Well now, that might not be so easy, seeing as how he's to be executed in the morning. They like a man to spend his last night on earth making peace with the Lord.'

'Saul could best make his peace by speaking to me.'

'I don't know . . .'

'How much?' Wes tried to hide his contempt for the man whose greed showed upon his face.

'Well, as one of the night gaolers is a cousin of mine, I might be able to persuade him for, say . . . five guineas?'

'Done! Take me to him.'

'And a guinea for me.'

Wes took a coin from his pocket and slid it across the table to the avaricious gaoler. 'There you are. Now take me to the gaol. It's late already.'

The inside of Marlborough gaol reminded Wes of his visit to Dorchester with Saranna when they went to see Arnold. There were the same smells, the same vague moans and noises in the night – and the same, chilling feeling of lurking evil that pervaded the place. He wondered if Saranna had visited Saul here and shared the same memories?

'Here you are, young sir. I can't let you in the cell with him. I'm risking my job as it is, allowing you to come and see him.'

The night gaoler was a not unkindly man, his manner contrasting with that of his grasping cousin. 'As it's his last night, he's been put in a cell on his own, with clean straw, and I saw to it that he had a good meal tonight. There's a lady in the town who always sends in a good dinner for any poor soul who's facing execution.'

Unlike Dorchester gaol, Wes had been brought to a door which was of solid wood heavily reinforced with iron. In the door was a small grille measuring no more than a foot square, hinged and padlocked. This was how food was passed through to recalcitrant prisoners. It was also as close as Wes would come to Saul – if, indeed, the condemned man was his brother. It was the moment of truth.

'Saul! Saul, can you hear me.'

'Who is it?' The voice told Wes nothing. It was thick with emotion. The voice of a man aware of his fate and who had been given too much time to dwell upon it. At that moment, the gaoler with Wes held up his lantern. The pale yellow light cut through the grille and touched upon the man seated inside on a plank cot.

For a moment Wes's hopes rose once more. The indistinct figure in the cell was heavily bearded. Then the condemned man rose to his feet and all hope died as he exclaimed, 'Wes! What are you doing here? How did you know?'

It *was* Saul.

The next moment he was clasping Wes's hand through the narrow space between two of the bars. 'How did you know I was here?' he repeated.

'Silas Morgan was passing through Tolpuddle. He told me. I'd met him once before . . . at Saranna's cottage.' It brought Wes to another question he wanted to ask. But now was not the right time.

'Saul, how were you brought to this? Why?'

'Someone informed on me.' Saul spoke bitterly. Suddenly his fingers tightened on Wes's hand. 'Wes, does Ma know about me being here . . . and Pa too?'

'They both know you're in some sort of trouble and have been arrested. Neither of them know quite how serious it is.'

'They mustn't know, Wes. Never. Promise me you won't tell them.'

'It's not going to be easy.' He choked on his words. 'To . . . to keep a thing like this to myself.'

'Promise me, Wes? I beg you! I've done all I can. I'll even go to the scaffold bearing a false name.'

'Don't Saul. Don't speak of it.'

'Wes, you must promise! It's my dying wish.'

Wes nodded, fighting back the tears that stung his eyes at his brother's words. 'All right, Saul. They won't know, I promise you.'

'Thank you, Wes. Thank you, little brother.'

The fingers tightened on Wes's hand once more. 'But you're not so little now. Taller than me by the look of it. Tell me, how are Ma and Pa?'

For some minutes the two brothers spoke of family and friends. Then Wes felt he could finally broach the subject he had been avoiding since he first ascertained the condemned man was his brother.

'Has Saranna been in here to see you?'

'Saranna? Why should she come here? Is she in Marlborough too?'

Saul's reply confused Wes. 'I thought she'd come to the area to be with you? The gaoler said you had a girl in town with you.'

'Fine one she turned out to be.' Saul spoke bitterly. 'She's the one who reported me to the authorities, after we'd had a quarrel. The bitch! She should hang too. She would if I could find someone who'd believe me and if it didn't involve others.'

Suddenly, Saul gave a short, unpleasant laugh. 'You thought it was Saranna? What gave you that idea?'

Wes was bemused. 'You said ... The last time we met, when you paid a visit to Tolpuddle, you asked me to keep an eye on Saranna because she was your girl.'

'Did I? Oh, yes, I remember. I lied, Wes. I only said it because I was jealous of you. You seemed to have made a much greater impression on her than I ever had. I didn't mean anything by it.'

Wes was so dismayed by what Saul had just said that he could not take it all in immediately. His whole life had been changed by what Saul had told him two years before, and now he was saying he had meant nothing by it!

'But ... what ... who is the girl who told the authorities about you?'

'Her name's Josephine. Josephine Frampton. I met her when I was at Tolpuddle – the time you were just talking about. She'd run away from home or something.'

'Josephine Frampton ... grand-daughter to the magistrate at Moreton?'

'I knew she was related in some way. I didn't know she was his grand-daughter. Have you met her?'

'She almost had me thrown into prison once because of something she falsely accused me of. She's been your girl since then?' A sudden thought came to Wes. 'Does she know who *you* are? If she does, I have no chance of keeping all this a secret. She'll make trouble just to spite me.'

'I've never told her my name – and few of those I've travelled with know it. But ...' Saul was thinking quickly. Suddenly he asked, 'Where's the gaoler?'

Wes looked around. The man was talking to another prisoner through the bars of a communal cage some way along the corridor. Wes told Saul so.

Lowering his voice, Saul said, 'Listen carefully, Wes. If Josephine ever tries to make trouble for you, tell her you'll inform the magistrates in London that she was a party to the murder of a man in Piccadilly two years ago. She lured him to a lodging house where he was robbed and killed.' As briefly as he could, Saul told his brother of the robbery and murder not dwelling on his own part in the crime.

'Josephine Frampton was involved in something like that?' Wes expressed disbelief.

'Yes, and so was I. You let her know that you know about it and she'll never cause trouble for you again, Wes, I promise you. She's a hard girl – as hard as anyone I know – but she still has nightmares about the Bow Street Runners catching up with her for what happened there.'

Wes was still trying to assimilate what he had just been told when the night warder came back to the cell door and said, 'I'm afraid you're going to have to leave now. I have my rounds to do and I can't leave you here.'

'Can't we have just a few more minutes? Tomorrow ...' Wes could not complete the sentence.

'I'm sorry, but I shouldn't really have allowed you in here tonight.'

'I understand – and I'm grateful.'

Wes turned back to the cell door where Saul still had a grip on his hand. 'I have to go now, Saul. I'll pray for you tonight – and I thought you'd like to know, Pa told me to tell you he's praying for you too.'

'Then I shall be all right. Pa's a powerful man when it comes to praying.' Saul tried desperately hard to sound cheerful, but he failed.

'We must go now, young sir.'

'I know. Goodbye, Saul.'

'Goodbye, young brother.' After a painful last grip of Wes's hand, Saul released it.

Too choked to say more, Wes was walking away when Saul called after him, 'Wes!'

Wes turned back and heard the chinking of coins inside the cell. Through the grille, Saul passed out a few coins that gleamed in the poor light, 'It's the money you lent me when I went away ... well, *most* of it. I said I'd pay you back one day.'

Emotions choked Wes, until his brother said, 'Will you be there ... in the morning?'

273

'Do you want me to be?'

'I'd like to feel there was someone who cared near me.'

'Then I'll be there. God bless you, Saul.'

'Thank you, Wes. That's what Ma always used to say, when she tucked us up in bed. Do you remember?'

Chapter 4

The following morning proved to be a nightmare Wes wished he had never been forced to experience. He was up very early, a precaution strongly suggested by the inn's ostler. There was a huge crowd in the town for the hanging. The stableman had suggested that if Wes wished to be in the front ranks of the spectators he would need to be there early.

It was, in fact, the very last thing he *wanted*, but he had made a promise to Saul.

The mere thought of the fate his only brother was to suffer was enough to bring a lump to Wes's throat and affect his ability to see clearly.

He arrived at the scaffold in front of the gaol soon after dawn, yet there were at least forty or fifty spectators there ahead of him. Among them was a party of countrywomen who spent the time before the execution laughing and chattering merrily among themselves.

Wes found their jocularity offensive. Then he heard from a bystander that one of their village friends had been raped and murdered. Two of the men who had committed the crime were among the four due to hang this morning.

'It's just nerves with them,' said the well-informed stranger who told Wes about the countrywomen. 'They behaved in the same way outside the court while they waited to give evidence against those who are due to hang for the murder.'

By the time the hour of execution neared, the crowd had grown to immense proportions. Half a dozen soldiers had been guarding the scaffold throughout the night. Now the prison gate opened and another twenty soldiers came from inside. Each was carrying a rifle to which a long bayonet was affixed.

The hangman emerged from the prison with them. While the soldiers took up position about the scaffold he climbed the steps to the wooden platform and opened the wooden case he carried.

The crowd gasped as the executioner drew four greased and stretched ropes from the case. Affixing them to a stout cross bar, he left four elliptical nooses hanging in a neat line.

This done, the man whose grim duty they had all come to witness tested the trap-door through which the men would drop. Three times he pulled the handle of his deadly machine. Three times the clatter of the falling trap brought a gasp of approbation from the watching crowd.

For Wes, the deadly practice only increased the chill that gripped his stomach. More than once he wished he was back home in Tolpuddle. That he might never have known of what was about to happen.

Finally, the moment Wes had been dreading arrived. The prison gate opened once more and now two lines of soldiers marched out. The four condemned men walked between them, their hands firmly secured behind their backs.

The whole party advanced to the wooden platform. Here the corporal of the guard ordered the prisoners to mount the short flight of wooden steps that led to the place where they would meet their violent end.

Saul was the second of the four men and stumbled on the steep steps. Instead of helping him, the corporal of the guard barked an order to him to: 'Get up on your feet!'

The incident aroused a fierce anger in Wes, directed at the corporal. Saul climbed to his feet awkwardly but he mounted the steps on the second attempt with no further mishap. His face above the dark beard looked deathly pale and he seemed to be terrified of what was to happen to him.

When Saul was lined up with his fellow condemned men he looked out over the crowd, searching the sea of faces. His gaze stopped somewhere to the left and rear of where Wes was standing. When he glanced quickly in that direction he caught a glimpse of a woman's face.

He could not be certain but he believed her to be Josephine Frampton. She was older and dirtier than the girl he had last seen at Moreton, but he remembered her too well ever to forget her.

Wes returned his glance to the scaffold as Saul looked in his direction. Saul's eyes rested on him and Wes raised an arm in hesitant salute.

He would never know for sure whether Saul saw him because, at that moment, the hangman stepped between them. He had put a hood over the head of one man and now he did the same to Saul. Moments later a noose had also been slipped over Saul's head, the knot eased down the greased rope to a point close to where his left ear was hidden beneath the hood.

Before another two minutes had passed all four men were hooded and ready to take their brief journey to eternity.

Suddenly, one of the four began struggling against his fate. As the crowd's noise swelled in recognition of his futile attempt to stay the inevitable, the prison chaplain murmured unheard, meaningless words of false comfort. Neither stayed the firm hand of justice.

Unnoticed by the vast majority of the crowd, the hangman tugged on the well-greased lever. The four men immediately dropped from the unsympathetic world they had known, to the uncertain mercy of the next.

Wes had not intended watching this moment, but it happened so quickly he was unable to look away in time.

He let out an agonised cry, as though he had suffered a physical blow. The sound was lost as the women who had been witnesses in the trial of the convicted rapists and murderers broke into applause. Distraught, Wes looked angrily in their direction. Then a small group of Quakers dropped to their knees in front of Wes and began praying.

He did the same, welcoming an opportunity to do the only thing that could be done for Saul now.

How long he remained on his knees he did not know. When he rose the crowd was dispersing, chattering excitedly.

He saw Josephine again – and now he was in no doubt. It *was* her. She was talking to one of the soldiers – an officer – who had been guarding the scaffold. There was nothing in her bearing to indicate distress at the execution of the man whose mistress she had been for the past two years.

On his way home to Tolpuddle, Wes had time to compose himself. To prepare himself for the lies he would tell to his father and, even more difficult, his mother.

He had been brought up to tell the truth no matter what the circumstances. Lying to his mother was deceitful, but he knew that on this occasion the truth would be far more distressing than any lie he might ever tell.

He also had ample time to dwell upon Saul's revelation that Saranna was not, and never had been, his girl. The more he thought about it, the more Wes realised how much his actions had been influenced by the belief that Saranna belonged to Saul. Because of this he had unjustly accused her of deceiving him.

He thought of all the things he had said and done to hurt her. If all that had happened between them at Dorchester and afterwards had *not* been a lie, then he must have hurt her very much indeed.

Chapter 5

Wes's first act when he reached Tolpuddle was to take the pony to Widow Cake's to feed and stable it. He did not call at the cottage first, but his arrival had not passed unnoticed. The widow had seen him. She came to the back door to call him in, wanting to know all that had happened at Marlborough.

The last thing Wes wanted at this time was to have to face Widow Cake. She was extremely shrewd and more perceptive than any other person, male or female, that he knew.

Looking at her as she sat on her favourite chair, close to the kitchen fire, he realised it would be impossible to fool her but, much to his initial relief, her first concern was for the pony.

'I hope you've brought it back in good condition, Wesley Gillam?'

'The pony's as fit as it's ever likely to be,' he replied.

'And what's that supposed to mean, may I ask?'

'She's an old mare, with not too many years left in her.'

'So am I, but I'll do whatever needs doing while I'm here. Will the pony?'

'As long as the demands on her aren't too great. I had to walk the last five miles into Marlborough. But I realised when I set out that she wasn't as fit as she might be. Despite all that, I'm sure she'll do everything you want of her.'

'Good. Now, how about that brother of yours? Did you find him?'

'Yes.'

Amelia Cake waited for amplification of his one-word reply, but none came.

'Wesley, you've taken three days off work, borrowed a pony which I probably wouldn't have bought had I not believed it to be an emergency, and all you can say to justify it is, "Yes". I think you owe me more than a single word!'

'I'm sorry. It's just . . . He *was* in trouble. It's over now.'

At least this was the truth. All Saul's troubles were at an end.

'Wesley, sit down!'

The order snapped out by Widow Cake startled him, but he did as he was told

'I probably have a reputation in the village as being something of a harridan. Isn't that so? No, Wesley, don't try to evade my question. I know it's so, and so do you. I don't mind that. In fact it pleases me. It means people don't come to me with their troubles, and I'm not expected to waste my time, or theirs, gossiping with them. I'm not particularly interested in the business of others – and I don't tell them mine, or anybody else's. I also believe I know you better than anyone else. Perhaps even better than your mother on occasions. You are not fooling me when you say your brother is all right. If your intention is to put your mother's mind at ease you're not going to succeed there either. Now, what is it you're trying to hide – and failing so miserably to do?'

'I . . . I can't tell you, Mrs Cake.'

'You can, and you will. You need help if you've something that needs keeping secret from your family. Did you find Saul in deep trouble? Has he gone to prison? Been transported, even? Why was he arrested? What did they say he'd done?'

For some minutes Wes remained silent while he thought over the whole, desperately unhappy situation. The secret he was keeping threatened to tear him apart. He desperately needed to share the burden with someone.

He had known Widow Cake for many years now. What she had just said to him was perfectly true. She was not a gossip and he had never known her set out to cause trouble for anyone. She kept things to herself and always had. She was also a very shrewd woman and beneath her sharp manner was as kind as anyone Wes knew. He reached a decision.

'He was arrested for rick-burning. Ma must never know that.'

'Rick-burning? That's a hanging offence!'

'Yes.'

As the memory of Saul on the gallows flooded back, Wes was unable to look at his employer, but she was watching him closely.

'You mean . . . he *has* been hung?' There was horror in Amelia Cake's voice.

Wes nodded his head silently.

'Glory be, boy! No wonder you're in such a state. To set off to help your brother, only to find he's been hung . . .'

'He hadn't been hung when I got there. I was able to speak to him. He was hung the next morning . . . with three others. I was there.'

The statement visibly shook the widow but she recovered quickly and her practical nature came to the fore 'Before Mary went to the village she made a pot of tea for me. It's on the hob.

It'll be a bit strong by now, but that's all to the good. Pour both of us one and we'll talk of what you're to do and say about this.'

As Wes put out the tea cups, Amelia Cake said, 'One thing is certain, you were right to rush off from here as you did on Sunday. Witnessing a thing like that will have left a scar on your memory that will never disappear, yet you'd never have forgiven yourself if you hadn't. Your being there must have brought some comfort to Saul at the end. Giving succour to a dying man will count heavily in your favour when it's your turn to meet the good Lord.'

Taking the tea cup from him, she mused. 'Now, what are we going to tell your ma? You're no good at telling out-and-out lies, young Wesley. It will need to be something that's half-truthful, at least – and it needs to be convincing.'

Leaning forward in her chair towards him, she said, 'This deceit is the kindest thing you'll ever do for your mother. Telling her the truth would be the cruellest. Remember that when your conscience is bothering you. On the days when she says, "I wonder what our Saul is doing now," learn to say, "He'll be doing all right, Ma." There'll be no lie, that. He's in a better world than this one that's certain.'

She tasted her tea and pulled a face. 'Pass me some more sugar before we talk any more. We'll need to have it all settled in your mind before Mary comes back – whenever that might be. When I sent Saranna on an errand to the village it would take her half an hour at the most. With Mary it's more likely to be half a day!'

They settled down to talk over what Wes would say to his mother. During the course of their conversation he told her what Saul had said about Saranna. Wes admitted he had made a grave mistake in allowing her to leave Tolpuddle.

Amelia Cake agreed with him. Nevertheless, she kept to herself her opinion of a brother who would tell lies about something of such importance.

By the time Wes left Widow Cake's cottage he knew exactly what he had to do. He also had a fair idea of the best way to go about it. Sharing the burden he carried about his brother had helped. The soldier's widow was worldly-wise and he knew her advice had been sound.

Now it was up to him to put her advice to the test and convince his mother that Saul was all right.

Chapter 6

After all Wes's soul-searching and fear of what he would say to his mother about Saul, the reality was an unexpected anti-climax. Nevertheless, Rachel Gillam's initial reaction upon her younger son's return was much as he had anticipated.

'Did you see Saul? What's it all about? How is he?' She was in the kitchen, stitching a large patch of new material on the seat of Wes's second-best pair of trousers.

'Saul's fine, Ma. He sends his love to you – and to Pa. It was all a mistake. There was a rick fire near Marlborough. He was a stranger who happened to be in the area, so they arrested him. It all ended well when they caught the right person.'

'I knew there must have been some mistake. Our Saul's a bit wild, but he's not a criminal. Did he say anything about coming home?'

'It's not in his plans for the near future. In fact, he's on his way to work even farther away. Somewhere near Scotland.'

Wes might as well have said Saul was going to work on the moon for all that talk of Scotland meant to his mother. But it satisfied her.

'That's a pity, but the main thing is that Saul's all right. You're a good boy for going all that way to see him when you thought he was in trouble. While you were away your pa put in some work for Widow Cake and I went up there too and showed Mary what she ought to be doing in the dairy.'

Biting off a short piece of thread, Rachel frowned in concentration as she began to re-thread her needle. 'I don't know how you've stayed working for that woman all this time, Wesley. She's got a tongue like a knife-edge and wants to be knowing exactly what everyone's doing all of the time. That poor Mary! If it wasn't that she was so simple to start with, she'd be a nervous wreck by now with all the tongue-lashings she gets.'

Wes smiled thinly. He was extremely relieved there had been none of the searching questions he had been anticipating. 'Widow Cake's all right, Ma, and Mary has to be chased up. I swear she's able to sleep on her feet for half the day.'

Changing the subject, he said, 'Where's Pa? He's usually home from work by now.'

'He's at a meeting on the green with all the others from the farms hereabouts. In spite of all the promises the men were given, they've had their pay cut again.'

His mother's reply gave Wes an opportunity to escape the possibility of any further questioning. 'I'll go down there and see what's going on.'

'Don't you want something to eat? I can get it for you as soon as I've finished this. It won't be more than a few minutes.'

'I'll have something when I come home with Pa.'

'Well, don't get involved with anything the farm workers are doing. You work with Widow Cake and, whatever faults she may have, she's never docked your money just because the others are doing it. Besides, as I told your pa, the farmers wouldn't have done this unless they were pretty certain they were likely to get away with it.'

The meeting was breaking up when Wes reached the village green. He found his father deep in conversation with a number of others. All were lay preachers in the Methodist Church and they were discussing the question of the farm labourer's wages with all the passion usually reserved for chapel matters.

'Eight shillings a week some of us are down to now,' said one man. 'And when I complained about it was I told that I should make the most of it because it was likely to go down to seven before the year's end.'

'They won't be satisfied until they've driven us to the despair that poor Tim Cross suffered.'

'Perhaps that's what they want,' said another bitterly. 'With our families murdered and us committing suicide, they'd have less money to pay out.'

'It isn't a question of what *they* want,' said Eli. 'It's what we're going to do to get back the decent wage they promised us that's at issue here.'

'I'm for an Association,' said George Loveless. He was one of the men who had been prominent in the discussions a couple of years earlier, when the farmers had agreed to maintain wages. 'But it seems the men aren't ready for it yet. I say we should follow your suggestion, Eli. Get all the men in and about Tolpuddle to sign a letter expressing their dissatisfaction with wages and take it along to Magistrate Pitt. See what he says about it.'

Magistrate William Pitt lived locally. His family had once occupied the Tolpuddle manor. He was well past the age when he should have retired, but he still sat on the bench of local magistrates. It was felt he might be more sympathetic to their cause then some other justices.

There seemed to be general assent to the suggestion and Eli said, 'Once we've agreed on what we'll say in the letter, I'll get our Wesley to write it. He has a neat hand and the learning. We want to be certain there's no misunderstanding in this.'

Once again the group of preachers concurred and when Wes agreed to write the letter the meeting broke up.

'Did you find Saul?'

Eli put the question to Wes as the other preachers began to walk away.

'Yes. He's fine. It was all a misunderstanding.'

The lie to his father came easier because Eli was preoccupied with the matters that had been discussed at the meeting on Tolpuddle Green.

'I thought it might be. Tell your mother I'll be late home tonight. A few of us are holding a meeting at the chapel. We have a lot to talk about.'

Eli patted his son on the shoulder absent-mindedly, his gaze upon his fellow preachers who walked along in deep debate.

A few evenings later, Wes saw Mary coming down the hill from the direction of Widow Cake's cottage. When she saw Wes she waved and began to hurry.

'Hello, Wes. I'm on my way to see you. Widow Cake said I could come.' Mary was so excited she could hardly stand still. Reaching out and grasping his arm, she said, 'I want you to write to Arnold for me, Wes. I want you to tell him I'm going to come out to Australia to marry him.'

'Well! That's a momentous decision to make, I must say. But I'm pleased, both for you and for Arnold. You deserve some happiness. Come on to the house, Mary. I have writing things there. You can tell me what you want to say and I'll write it down for you. I'll even write your name and let you copy it on the bottom of the letter. Once you've signed it yourself Arnold will know there can be no doubt about what it says.'

As they walked along, Wes looked at Mary. There was so much happiness inside her that it bubbled over and touched him. He smiled and took her hand in a naturally affectionate gesture that would not have been possible with any other girl he knew.

'When do you intend going?'

'Widow Cake says I should leave it for a couple of months to give time for the letter to get there and so Arnold can have some things ready for me. But ... I'm not sure I'll be able to wait so long, Wes. Now I've made up my mind to go, I can remember all the things about Arnold I haven't dared think about since he was sent away.'

'Widow Cake is talking a lot of sense, Mary, as she usually does.'

They had reached the Gillam house now and Wes said, 'Come on, let's go inside and tell my ma what it is you're planning to do. She'll be pleased. She's very fond of Arnold too.'

Rachel Gillam was every bit as impressed as Wes had been.

'Fancy you travelling all that way to be with Arnold! I think it's very, very brave of you, Mary.'

'I won't mind the voyage, Mrs Gillam. Well . . . not much, anyway. Arnold wants me to be there with him, that's the main thing. Besides, what will I do if I stay here in Tolpuddle? Widow Cake's getting old and I won't be able to work for her for ever. What will I do when she's gone? I'd finish up in the poorhouse if I didn't have anywhere else to work. I'd sooner go to Australia, especially if I can marry Arnold and be with him. Things won't be easy there, I don't suppose, but we'll be together and we'll be happy, I know we will.'

Rachel gave Mary a warm hug. 'You've got the right attitude, my girl. I admire your courage. You deserve a little happiness and so does Arnold. He's a good boy. But how are you going to get there?'

Mary looked shyly at Wes who had found paper, quill and ink in readiness for her letter. 'Widow Cake says we'll need to discuss the details with Wes and ask him to arrange a passage to Australia for me.'

He was taken aback at the suggestion. 'How am I supposed to do that?'

'I don't know, Wes, but Widow Cake says she'll give you all the time off you need for it and she's going to pay for me to have a berth on board a ship. I expect she'll let you use her pony again, too.'

Wes would have protested that he had no experience in arranging voyages to Australia, but he could not bring himself to prick Mary's bubble of happiness.

'No doubt we'll be able to fix something up for you . . .'

He broke off as Mary hugged him happily and gave him a noisy kiss on the cheek.

Embarrassed as much by his mother's amused smile as by the incident, Wes extricated himself and said gruffly, 'Let's get this letter written, or you'll likely be in Australia before Arnold knows you're on your way.'

284

Chapter 7

Eli Gillam threw himself into the farm workers' campaign for a living wage with the same enthusiasm with which he embraced Methodism. Characteristically, he expected those who helped him to possess similar dedication.

Each evening for the next couple of weeks Wes was kept busy writing letters and petitions on behalf of the farm workers of Tolpuddle and the surrounding district. Wes grumbled that his father came up with ideas faster than they could be written down. It was a task that burned many inches of candle in the Gillam cottage.

There were also letters to be sent to the local farmers. They were coupled with a plea to Magistrate Pitt, asking him to use his standing in the community to force the farmers to abide by the agreement reached two years before.

Wes had also written another letter. This one had been composed by Eli and the other leaders of the farm workers during many secret meetings held in the Methodist chapel. The letter was addressed to Richard Pemble. He was believed to be trying to form an association in London which would consolidate the many infant Trades Unions throughout the country.

In their letter the Tolpuddle men asked his advice on forming their own Association or Union. The letter would not be sent immediately. The farm workers of Tolpuddle needed more time to think about the consequences that might follow such a step.

Trades Unions were no longer illegal in England – but their presence was barely tolerated by the employers. Those workers who joined or supported such Unions were victimised openly by their employers, often being dismissed for no other reason.

The men who sought to organise the Tolpuddle farm workers thought it wise not to show their hand until they knew more about the amount of support they could expect from other parts of the county. Even with maximum support they would have to rely upon the Tolpuddle labourers to take concerted action should the need arise.

The reply from Magistrate Pitt was prompt and courteous, but it contained little optimism for the success of their campaign. However, after consultation with his colleagues, Pitt had arranged a meeting with James Frampton, the most senior of the local magistrates.

The meeting would be held in Dorchester, but the town authorities had no wish to be invaded by hundreds of disgruntled farm labourers. Only three would be accepted as a representative delegation.

The three chosen were George Loveless, Eli Gillam and a relative of Loveless, by the name of Albert Brine. Wes was also going to Dorchester on the same day. There was a market in the town and Amelia Cake thought it a good opportunity to try out the pony and trap. Mary was coming to take care of her needs and Wes would drive them.

'I don't like the sound of this meeting,' said Rachel as she carefully ironed the clothes for both her men on the evening before they set off for the county town. 'If there's any future trouble involving the farm workers it'll be the three of you the constable will be after because of it.'

'Of course it won't,' said Eli, confidently. 'We're only calling on the magistrate to use his position on our behalf. To ask the farmers to keep their word and not reduce wages any more.'

'What makes you think Frampton will do anything to help you, Pa? He's a landowner and a farmer too.' Wes was working in a corner of the kitchen, making up accounts for Widow Cake. She wanted an accurate record of expenditure and profit for her expanding ventures.

'Frampton is a magistrate, appointed by the king to uphold justice – and justice is on our side.'

'I doubt if he sees it that way,' retorted Wes.

'Oh, well, perhaps you'll find him in a good mood. His grand-daughter's returned home after being given up for lost these past two years.' Rachel Gillam spat on the base of the iron to check whether it was still hot enough, unaware of her son's shock at the unexpected news.

'Josephine Frampton's come home? When?' Wes asked, all thought of Widow Cake's accounts suddenly forgotten.

Rachel looked up at him. 'She came back sometime in the past few days, I believe. I'm surprised you haven't heard. Mrs Pipe in the village does the washing for Moreton House and she says the servant girls up there are full of it. Everyone thought she'd run off with one of her grandfather's grooms because of some scandal. Magistrate Frampton even had a warrant out for his arrest. It's just as well they didn't catch him. They'd probably have hung him, thinking he'd done away with the girl and hidden the body. It seems she wasn't with him at all. She ran off because she didn't want to go to live in Devon with her mother. She found herself work as a governess to a family in Sussex, or some such place. She'd be with 'em now, she said, if they hadn't gone off to live in India. Seems that with them gone she started thinking of her mother and her grandad at Moreton and decided it was time to come home.'

'Don't tell me that Magistrate Frampton believed all that nonsense?'

'I suppose he believes what he wants to believe, same as most men do. Why, do you have some reason to doubt the girl's story?'

'Not really.' Wes was careful how he replied. He did not want his mother asking him too many questions about Josephine. 'But the girl is such a liar I'd doubt anything she said.'

In truth, Wes was thoroughly alarmed at Josephine's unexpected return to Moreton. He believed Saul had managed to keep his true identity from her. He hoped so. If Josephine had any inkling of the truth she would ensure it became known somehow.

'Seeing as how it's none of our concern, it won't matter to anyone very much. Still, as I said in the first place, it might help to sweeten Magistrate Frampton's temper when he meets up with your pa and the others.'

'I don't know why I decided to come to Dorchester in the first place. It always was overcrowded. Wesley, help me down, and then you can find a place to put up the pony for a few hours. Make certain the trap is somewhere safe too. Don't leave it anywhere where a careless wagon driver can bump into it. It won't stand a lot of rough handling. I shall have words with Farmer Hooper about it. It's no stronger than a sewing-box and I was frightened the pony was going to drop dead in the shafts before we reached Dorchester . . .'

Wes left the pony and trap at the inn where he, Saranna and Widow Cake had stayed during Arnold's brief trial.

There was so much about Dorchester that reminded him of Saranna. It seemed that every turn he took reminded him of something they had done together. He had been thinking much of her lately and wondered whether she ever thought of him . . .

He was leaving the stable, still deep in thought, when two riders came into the cobble-stone yard. Wes did not even look up until a soft voice said, 'It *is* Wesley Gillam, isn't it?'

Startled, Wes looked up and saw the girl he had hoped he would not have to face for a very long time. Josephine Frampton was seated on a horse and looking down at him with an expression he found highly embarrassing.

Glancing about him quickly, he saw another figure he recognised. Magistrate Frampton was off his horse and giving some instructions to the hotel ostler.

'I want to speak to you, Wesley Gillam.'

'Josephine, the ostler is waiting to take your horse,' James Frampton called back to her with the irritation in his voice that Wesley remembered. But Wes was relieved that the magistrate apparently did not remember him.

'You go ahead, Grandfather. It's someone who used to work for a friend. I'm just catching up on the news.'

'Don't be more than a few minutes. I'll go inside and order lunch. You'll doubtless want to tidy yourself before we eat.'

Handing over his horse, the magistrate from Moreton strode off towards the door of the inn and quickly disappeared inside.

'Help me down.' It was an order, not a request. Josephine was riding side-saddle and slipped quickly to the ground with Wes's help. Standing very close to him, she said, 'You're not a bad-looking man, Gillam, now you've grown and filled out a bit.'

Wes remembered what his brother had said about this girl. Tight-lipped, he said, 'You mentioned there was something you wanted to say to me?'

'That's right.' She plucked an imaginary loose thread from his collar and said, 'I know something you certainly wouldn't want anyone else to know about. If you don't want it to go any further, I think you had better be especially nice to me when I want something from you.'

Wes's heart sank. This was what he had been dreading. Josephine *did* know who Saul was. She was threatening to make it public. He had to prevent her at all costs.

'What is it you want?'

'All in good time. Are you married yet?'

'No . . . but what has that to do with anything?'

'Not very much, I was just making polite conversation.'

'I have no time for polite conversation with you.'

'Then I suggest you *make time* – and you will,' Josephine snapped back at him.

'All right, what is it you want to say?'

'This is neither the time nor the place.'

'Where then – and when?'

'Well now . . .' Josephine smiled at him maliciously. 'That's for me to decide. All I *will* say to you, Wesley Gillam, is that when I send word that I want you, you had better come running if you don't want me to tell the whole world what it is I know.'

Turning her back on him abruptly, Josephine handed the reins of her horse to the ostler who was waiting a respectful distance away. Without another word she walked away and followed her grandfather inside the inn.

Chapter 8

The return of his grand-daughter had done nothing to moderate James Frampton's abhorrence of anything that smacked of 'Union' between employees of any calling. It had always been his passionately held belief that for workers to have Trade Associations, Unions, or whatever else they might be called, was to give them a power they would not know how to control.

It was a power that could be manipulated by unscrupulous men. It had happened in France less than forty years before. The disorders had been accompanied by the shedding of blood on a scale that still made moderate men shudder.

The thought of such bloodshed affected James Frampton more than most. He had been in France during the early days of the revolution. What he had seen there had made him a passionate and unreasoning opponent of peasant emancipation, no matter what form it took.

He believed that the demands being put forward by all who advocated the union of tradesmen or labourers had been inspired by the French uprising, and were being promulgated with the sole intention of stirring up revolution.

The very idea of working men joining together to challenge the authority of their employers and the gentry was anathema to James Frampton.

This was the man who was to hear the complaints of the Tolpuddle agricultural labourers against the lowering of their wages.

The meeting was held in the Dorchester Magistrates' Court. Ominously, James Frampton sat in the high-backed magistrate's chair, flanked by Magistrate Pitt and another of his magisterial colleagues.

Also in the courtrooms were about a dozen farmers; some Dorchester landowners; Reverend Warren; and one of the Dorchester clergymen.

'It's almost as though we're facing trial,' whispered Eli, as he and the other two Tolpuddle farm labourers settled in their seats in the well of the court.

'I think that's how they want us to feel,' replied George Loveless quietly. 'I had my doubts about coming to Dorchester as soon as I heard Magistrate Pitt had taken our grievances to Frampton. We'll see little justice here today.'

George Loveless's words were prophetic, as the opening address of James Frampton quickly proved.

Looking over the heads of the Tolpuddle labourers, he addressed himself to the farmers, 'Gentlemen, we are here today at the request of the farm labourers of Tolpuddle. They have a grievance about the wages being paid to them by you, their employers. As I understand the matter, they have approached Magistrate Pitt and asked for the dispute to be decided by a Justice of the Peace. Apparently the men are under the misapprehension that the law is able to intervene in such matters and order you and the other employers to pay them a certain wage. Nothing could be further from the truth. We are living in a free country. Farmers, in common with all other employers, are entitled to choose for themselves how much they pay their employees. Those who are working for them are obliged to accept that wage – whatever it may be. That is where the law stands on the subject, gentlemen.'

Turning his attention to the stunned Tolpuddle trio, James Frampton said, 'As you can see, there is nothing I or my colleagues on the bench can do to change matters one iota – were we of the opinion there was anything that needed changing.'

George Loveless was on his feet in an instant. 'We haven't come here to force new terms from our employers. We are asking no more than that they honour the agreement we have already made.'

'Do you have such an agreement in writing?' James Frampton put the question to George Loveless.

'We believed that the word of gentlemen did not need to be committed to paper. We trusted our employers to keep their word.'

'Gentlemen, do you recall any such agreement being concluded?' Once again Magistrate Frampton addressed his words to the farmers, over the heads of the three Tolpuddle labourers.

There was a general shaking of heads and the magistrate returned his attention to George Loveless. 'Were there any independent witnesses to this so-called agreement?'

'Yes. Reverend Warren was there. He told us that if we would go quietly back to our work we should receive the same for our labours as any other man in the district.'

Magistrate Frampton now turned his attention to the two clergymen seated side-by-side in the seats usually reserved for court witnesses.

'Reverend Warren, can you recall such a settlement being agreed?'

Thomas Warren frowned in apparent concentration. 'No, Your Worship. I have no recollection of such an agreement being reached in my presence.'

George Loveless would have pursued the matter, but Eli clutched his arm. 'Say no more, George. As you remarked earlier, there is no justice here for the likes of us.'

Rising to his feet, Eli said, 'I too was present when Reverend Warren promised he would be a witness to the agreement we reached. I have no doubt the God we both worship was there too – and Reverend Warren will one day have to answer to His witness. Come, gentlemen, I think we have wasted enough of Mr Frampton's time.'

Maintaining their dignity against a background of increasing ribaldry from the assembled farmers, Eli, George Loveless and Albert Brine walked from the courtroom into the clean sunshine of the Dorchester street.

'Damn fools! What else did they expect from James Frampton? Did they think he would take their side against all the farmers and landed gentry of Dorset? It's men like your father and George Loveless who will ensure that Methodism remains a poor man's religion.'

'Why?'

Wes put the question as he urged the ageing pony into a trot. They were on their way home from Dorchester. The three Tolpuddle men had been overtaken not a mile outside Dorchester. In answer to her question they had given Widow Cake details of their meeting with Magistrate Frampton and the farmers.

'They hold the stupid belief that because they are honest, and right is on their side, then everything is bound to go their way. If they weren't so busy shouting "Allelujah" all over the place, they'd realise that men like James Frampton have worked for hundreds of years to ensure poor men were never given any rights.'

'How did you come by your land and cottage, Mrs Cake?' Mary put the question to her employer.

'It was a piece of land that was granted to my husband's family when the landowners around Tolpuddle stole all the common land from the cottagers. "Enclosure", they called it. They passed an Act in Parliament giving away all the common land to the Lord of the Manor and his friends. My late husband's grandfather – or it may have been his great-grandfather – put up such a strong objection to their bare-faced robbery that he was granted the land

I now have. A few others did the same, but they were soon forced to sell their land because they were squeezed out by the Lord of the Manor. Grandfather Cake was made of sterner stuff. He hung on to what he had. We took it over when we came back from the war, although my husband never lived long enough to enjoy it.'

'I hope Arnold and I have some land in Australia,' said Mary.

'Lord help us, the girl's into dreaming about the future again. That reminds me, Wesley. You'd better take a trip to find out how Mary is going to get to Australia?'

'How will I find that out – and where?'

'I don't know, you're the one with the learning. Didn't Reverend Warren teach you about that?'

'Well, he never mentioned anything about going out to Australia. I doubt if he knows very much about it himself.'

'Then we'll need to find out. The next time he calls on me I'll ask him. What's the good of having a vicar if he doesn't take care of his flock and find out such things for them?'

At that moment they were hailed by one of two riders who wanted to overtake them on the narrow road. Wes pulled the pony and trap to one side and James Frampton overtook them impatiently, followed by his grand-daughter.

Neither rider offered thanks to Wes for pulling over so promptly. James Frampton trotted past without bothering to look at them. Josephine did not urge her horse into a trot until she had passed by and observed who was in the trap with Wes. She reserved her final look for him, and it was long and hard, before she applied her crop to the horse's flanks and set off after her grandfather.

'That young madam has too bold an eye for a girl of her age and breeding. Unless I'm mistaken that's Magistrate Frampton's errant grand-daughter.'

'That's right.' Wes had been aware of Josephine's gaze upon him, but had tried hard not to return it.

'She was eyeing you up, young Wesley. Wasn't she the girl who got you into trouble with Magistrate Frampton when I had my fall down the stairs?'

'Yes.'

Wes did not want to say any more. He was still worrying about what she had said to him in Dorchester.

'Then you'd better watch out, my lad. That look she gave you spelled trouble, if ever I saw it. She's after you – and I don't think it's to apologise for the way she behaved before, either.'

Chapter 9

The failure of the magistracy to uphold the agreement made between the farmers and their labourers caused a great deal of resentment in and around Tolpuddle. Yet there was nothing that could be done about it.

The harvest had already been gathered. The work force on each farm was pared to the absolute minimum in preparation for the winter months. Now there was little work except threshing to be done.

Those still in employment were aware that if they gave trouble to the farmers they would be dismissed, and their cottages were tied to their work. They would not only be out of work but homeless too.

In addition, each man lived with the uncomfortable knowledge that if he were dismissed there would be dozens of out-of-work farm labourers clamouring to take his place, at whatever wage the farmer chose to pay.

Farmers were also fully aware of the strength of their position as employers. Only six weeks after the Dorchester magistrates' court meeting, wages in the area were cut by a full shilling per week.

The pangs of conscience brought about by the violent deaths of the Cross family had finally been laid to rest.

'The farmers know there's nothing at all we can do about it,' said Eli, gloomily announcing the news of the pay cut to his family one suppertime. 'If we want to stay in work we have to accept whatever we're given. Magistrate Frampton told us so, and he's right.'

'Magistrate Frampton was speaking as an employer, not as a magistrate,' retorted Wes. 'You said so yourself at the time.'

'Whatever I said, it doesn't alter anything. We can't persuade men to do anything at the moment. They're desperate, yes, but they're also fearful of losing their jobs.'

'The farmers know that, but it might be very different in the spring. That's the time to do something.'

'Do what? I have a nasty feeling that Magistrate Frampton's

just waiting for us to "do something". As soon as we do he'll have the might of the law on us.'

'Trades Associations are legal now and it's what you've always said the men must have. Look . . .' Hesitantly, Wes put forward a suggestion he had been mulling over for days. 'Some time ago Widow Cake asked the vicar to find out what ships were sailing for Australia so a passage could be arranged for Mary. He's made enquiries and said that while Transports and a few other ships go there from Portsmouth and Plymouth, there's a fairly regular service from London. Widow Cake wants me to take Mary there before the really bad weather sets in. I've already spoken to Ma about it. She'll work at the cottage and in the dairy while I'm away. I'm well ahead of things in my work at the moment, but I'd like you to call in sometimes and do anything that needs doing. Meanwhile, I'll take Mary to London, put her on the boat – and then go off and find Richard Pemble. I'll give him the letter you and the others wrote about the Association, and ask his advice. He might have some ideas about what we can do. He'll certainly be able to advise us on setting up an Association. Would you like me to do that on behalf of the Tolpuddle farm workers?'

Eli Gillam was not a man who liked being forced into making hurried decisions. Frowning, he thought about Wes's suggestion carefully before replying, 'I don't know. I'll have to talk to George Loveless and the others, but it does sound a good idea.'

'It's better than *sending* a letter. They can go astray and end up being produced in court as evidence against you. In fact, it would probably be better if we forgot the letter altogether. Richard Pemble has managed to stay above the law but there have been ugly rumours that he's associated with "Captain Swing" and the rick-burners. If ever his premises were raided, copies of all the letters found there would be forwarded to the magistrates of the areas from where they were sent. This way nothing would be in writing to incriminate anybody in Tolpuddle.'

'I'll go around and speak to the others tonight. When do you think you'll be leaving for London?'

'The end of the week. It'll take Mary until then to stop dithering and do something about making the voyage to Australia.'

When Eli had gone from the room, Rachel spoke quietly to Wes. 'Didn't the Vye girl's mother marry someone named Pemble?'

'Yes, I think she did.' Wes was deliberately non-committal.

'There's no "think" about it, young man. You know she did. Did you ever meet this Pemble?'

'I met him once.'

'What sort of man is he?'

Wes shrugged. 'I didn't care for him particularly. I thought he was too ambitious, but perhaps that's the sort of man we want on our side. One who has no intention of ending this fight as a loser, and that's just what it is – a fight.'

'That's a very profound statement to make, Wesley Gillam.'

Rachel was silent for many minutes, before throwing a question at Wes that startled him for a moment. 'Did our Saul ever meet this Pemble?'

'I don't know . . . probably. Why do you ask?'

'Because I imagine our Saul was far more likely to be impressed by such a man than you.'

'Oh, I don't know. Saul w— is no fool.' Wes corrected himself just in time. He had been about to refer to Saul using the past tense.

Fortunately, his mother did not seem to notice. 'If you go to see this Richard Pemble, are you likely to be seeing young Saranna?'

'I might, if she's still around.'

'You two were sweet on each other at one time, weren't you?'

'Probably. Now, if you don't mind, I think I'll go on to bed. I want to be up early. I need to do all I possibly can at Widow Cake's before I go to London.'

In reality, Wes wanted to escape his mother's probing questions. He had a lot of hard thinking to do.

But Rachel's questioning was not over yet, although she had changed the subject of her questions to a less sensitive one.

'Who's paying for this trip to London, and Mary's voyage to Australia? I can't imagine the poor girl having two pennies to rub together.'

'Widow Cake's paying for everything.'

'That's unusually generous of her.'

'She *is* generous, Ma. You just need to get to know her, that's all.'

'You've changed your tune, Wesley. She used to be the most miserable, mean woman in the world as far as you and Arnold were concerned.'

'She still can be, sometimes. Then, just when you're thinking the worst of her, she does something to surprise you. Like paying for Mary to go to Australia – and giving money to help her and Arnold make a new start there.'

'She's a truly Christian woman, I'll give her that. Whether I'll still be saying the same after I've worked for her for a few weeks, I don't know.'

The next day Wes went to Southover to take a bull calf to Farmer Hooper. Widow Cake was building up a nice small herd of cows and did not need bull calves. This one would go into Farmer Hooper's beef herd.

Having delivered the calf, Wes had started on his way back when he heard a horse coming along at a canter behind him. The lane was muddy and contained many large puddles as a result of recent rains. Wes stepped off the muddy track on to the grass verge to allow the rider to pass by without splashing him.

Not until he was well on to the verge did he glance up at the rider as the horse was about to pass him.

It was Josephine Frampton. She recognised him at the same time.

'Well, well! If it isn't Wesley Gillam, once Moreton's most prim and proper assistant gardener.'

Wes stared at her defiantly, remembering that she had most probably sent Saul to the gallows. He also remembered how she had once tried to get him into serious trouble with her grandfather, but he said nothing.

Suddenly, Josephine swung to the ground from her horse. 'You've grown a lot since then. You've become a man. How much of a *real* man are you, Gillam?'

'Enough to do what I want to do.' Wes spoke defiantly, yet warily.

'Enough for whom, Fanny Warren – or me?'

'What's that supposed to mean?'

'My, we are touchy! Mind you, I'm not surprised. Not after what happened to her. Tell me, how many people knew that Fanny was carrying your baby when she killed herself?'

'Fanny wasn't carrying my baby – or anyone else's.'

'That isn't what she told me when she came asking my advice.'

'She came to you because she thought she might be carrying the baby of one of the men who attacked her when the mob came to the vicarage.'

'That's a good story! Yes, I like that. But how many people would believe it if I told them my version?'

'You won't tell anyone.' It was a statement, but Josephine took it as a question.

'That depends. There's a small copse up ahead. Come in there with me. You be especially nice and I might decide not to say anything – but you'll need to be *very* good.'

'I'm not going anywhere with you, Josephine Frampton.' Wes needed to work hard not to spit out the venom he felt for this amoral rich girl.

'Please yourself.' Josephine turned to her horse and prepared to mount once more. 'I've offered you a chance to do something you'd enjoy – and save yourself a whole lot of trouble. If you're not prepared to take advantage of such an offer, that's your problem not mine.'

'You'll say nothing about Fanny, or me, because you're not the only one with a story that people might want to listen to.'

Josephine paused in the act of mounting. 'What's *that* supposed to mean?'

'It means that I could tell a story about a certain well-bred girl who lured a man to a room in London with an offer similar to the one you just made me. The only difference is that someone burst into the room and killed the poor man for his money.'

Josephine had gone deathly pale. 'Wh-where did you get this story?'

'That doesn't matter. What *does* matter is that the Bow Street magistrate issued a warrant accompanied by a very detailed description of the girl who's wanted for the crime. It seems she was seen by one of the women in the house where she took the unfortunate victim. If she was caught, there's a very strong possibility that another girl by the name of Meg could be persuaded to give evidence in order to save her own skin. I don't blame her, either. It's a hanging offence. Have you ever seen a hanging, Josephine? Perhaps wondered what it must be like the moment the hood's pulled over your head? Yes, I think you probably have.'

Wes needed to control himself as his words brought back the memory of the moment Saul stood on the scaffold in those final moments.

'Who told you? They were lying to you . . .'

Wes shrugged. 'It's just a story I heard. I've never put any store by it myself, but if ever any lies are told about Fanny and myself, I think I should tell all I know. Wouldn't you agree?'

Trying unsuccessfully to hide the fear she felt, Josephine swung herself up to the side-saddle. Once safely seated, she looked down at Wes, eyes dark in her otherwise bloodless face. 'I don't know what Fanny ever saw in you, Gillam. Perhaps if she'd ever met up with a *real* man, she would still be alive today.'

'That's right, Josephine Frampton, she probably would. I doubt very much if she'd have deliberately put him in the hands of the hangman because of any quarrel she might have had with him.'

This was the final straw for Josephine. There was a very real fear in her eyes as she pulled the head of her horse around and rode off the way she had come.

Looking after her, Wes thought he would have no more trouble with her.

Chapter 10

The departure of Mary Riggs, bound for Australia, brought the populace of Tolpuddle out of their houses to bid farewell and see the simple young girl on her way, despite the early hour.

Accompanied by Wes, she was travelling in Widow Cake's pony and trap to Dorchester, driven there by Eli Gillam. In the county town, she and Wes would board the London-bound coach at eight o'clock, arriving in the capital city at six o'clock in the evening.

Mary was taking all her worldly possessions with her to Australia. She had not acquired very much more property since making her home with Widow Cake, and it was all carried in a single bag.

She was highly excited about setting off to be with Arnold, but the moment of parting proved too much for her. As the pony set off and the trap was jerked into motion, the villagers set up a cheer. Mary, overcome by the emotion of the moment, burst into tears.

The last view Tolpuddle had of Mary was of her being comforted by Wes as pony, trap and occupants disappeared from view along the road to Dorchester.

Mary had never travelled by coach before. She marvelled at the leather seats and the spaciousness of the interior, much to the amusement of her fellow passengers.

As a town clock began striking the hour, a guard blew a long blast on a gleaming brass horn. The driver cracked his whip over the backs of the four horses drawing the coach and it lurched forward. Rumbling over the cobblestones of the inn yard the vehicle emerged on to the road. They were London-bound, travelling at a speed which soon had Mary gasping.

As naive as she was honest, Mary answered the questions posed by her fellow-passengers with absolute openness. Long before the coachman called that the capital city was in view, every passenger on the coach had been told that Mary was on her way to Australia. Once there, she would be marrying a young man convicted by the now notorious Special Commissions set up to try protesting farm workers.

299

Wesley was embarrassed by Mary's willingness to talk about Arnold and his criminal conviction. He felt it was a subject on which she should have maintained a discreet silence. However, when the coach finally pulled up at its destination, he was given proof that his fellow-passengers had been deeply touched by her story.

As Mary's bag was being handed down from the coach's luggage rack, one of the men who had travelled from Dorchester with them placed a small but heavy draw-string bag in Wes's hand.

'Thank the young lady for her company on the journey today. I have just taken a small collection from the others. We would be grateful if you would give it to her with our best wishes for her future happiness in Australia.'

With these few words the man was gone. Wes was left with a bag that he was later to discover held a wedding gift of twenty-five golden guineas.

The last few miles of the journey had been through the busy and crowded streets of London. It had convinced Wes that England's capital city was not a place in which to seek accommodation at this cold hour of the evening. He decided to take rooms for Mary and himself at the coaching inn where they had disembarked.

It was a fortuitous choice. While Mary and Wes were taking their evening meal, the landlord of the inn came across to ask if they were comfortably settled. During the ensuing conversation, Wes told him that Mary was going to Australia to be married. He asked the landlord's advice on booking a passage for her.

'Well now, you couldn't have timed it better if you'd tried. Sitting over there on his own is Mr Calnan, the shipping and emigration agent. He's been here today interviewing a large party of missionaries who are setting off for Australia tomorrow. He's just about finished his meal, I'll ask him to come across and have a word with you.'

Ten minutes later Joseph Calnan came to the table and introduced himself, bowing gravely to Mary and extending a hand to Wes.

'Good evening. I understand you two young people are interested in taking passage to Australia?'

'Not both of us. Only Mary. She is going to Australia to be married. She has a letter from her future husband. Show him, Mary.'

Mary kept the letter on her person, happy to show it to anyone who expressed an interest. She produced it from her bodice now and, after futilely smoothing the crumpled paper with her hand, passed it to Calnan.

As he read the letter, the agent looked up sharply towards Mary. 'He's a convict! Of what was he convicted?'

'He was one of the farm labourers tried by the Government Commission sent to Dorchester.'

'Ah!' The agent seemed relieved. 'Then he'll no doubt be a free man by the time you arrive in Australia, young lady. That woeful miscarriage of justice has finally been recognised by our government. A pardon for all persons convicted by the Commissioners has been granted. That makes my task very much simpler. How do you intend travelling? In a cabin, or with the steerage passengers?'

'What's the difference in the price? Mary's passage is being paid by the widow woman who employed Mary and Arnold, and who still employs me. She's not a rich woman.'

'The *Enterprise* is sailing tomorrow. As she is already showing a profit I can offer you a steerage passage at six pounds, or a well-appointed cabin for forty-two. If you can possibly pay the extra I strongly advise a cabin. It is both healthier and far more comfortable.'

Wes winced. 'I don't know... forty-two pounds is a lot of money.'

'It's all right, Wes. I don't mind travelling as a steerage passenger. I really don't mind how I travel, just as long as I get to Arnold.'

Joseph Calnan had been watching Mary as she spoke and now he said, 'What type of work were you doing for this widow who employed you?'

'I worked in the house, in the dairy, and looked after Widow Cake as well. She couldn't get around very well and needed helping a lot.'

Nodding his head in apparent satisfaction, Joseph Calnan frowned thoughtfully. 'I think I might be able to help you, young lady. I have today arranged a passage for a party of Methodist missionaries. One of them, Mrs Webb, is an elderly lady. In my opinion she should never be travelling so far, but she is – and she's in need of a personal servant for the voyage. The girl who should have travelled with her ran away last night. It seems she was terrified at the thought of such a long sea voyage. If the idea appeals and you are both suited to each other, it could mean a free cabin passage for you.'

Mary clapped her hands together in sheer joy. 'That would be wonderful! Looking after someone would give me something to do on the voyage. I was a bit worried about having nothing to do all day.'

'Then you wait here, young lady. I'll go up to Mrs Webb's room and speak to her.'

When Joseph Calnan had left the dining-room, Mary said to Wes, 'Isn't that marvellous, Wes? I knew everything would work out all right once Arnold said he still wanted to marry me.'

'Don't get carried away just yet, Mary. You don't know whether you and this Mrs Webb will suit each other.'

'We will, Wes. I know it.'

Wes was less certain. Mary was neither the brightest, nor the speediest of workers. Her ways would not suit everyone.

Joseph Calnan was away for so long that Wes began to feel he had been right to sound a cautionary note to Mary.

It was at least twenty minutes before the shipping agent returned to them. His expression wiped out Mary's confidence immediately.

'Mrs Webb would like to see you both – but don't build your hopes too high, young lady. She is not enthusiastic about employing a girl who is on her way to marry a convict. When I mentioned that you have travelled from your home in Dorset with a young man she threw up her hands in horror. However, I told her that if I were travelling to Australia I would have no hesitation in employing either of you to look after me. She finally agreed to speak to you, at least. Come along – and don't let me down.'

Missionary Mrs Webb was seated on a chair in her room. With her were another woman and a man, introduced to Wes and Mary as fellow-missionaries, Alice and Arthur Mason.

Hanging on the back of Mrs Webb's chair was a walking-stick. Wes was immediately struck by the similarity of this woman to his employer, Widow Cake.

Because of this likeness, Wes replied to her as he would to Widow Cake when she said to Mary, 'I believe you are looking for employment in return for a passage to Australia?'

'No, ma'am,' said Wes firmly. 'Mary is taking passage to Australia to marry a man we have both known since we were all children together. It was Mr Calnan's suggestion that it might suit both you and Mary if she travelled there as your personal servant.'

'Can't the girl speak for herself?' snapped the elderly missionary. 'Who are you, anyway?'

'Wesley Gillam, ma'am. Widow Cake sent me to take care of Mary and arrange a passage on a ship for her. We travelled to London on the coach from Dorchester today.'

'Wesley? Are you a Methodist?'

'Yes, ma'am. My father is a lay preacher in the Tolpuddle chapel.'

'Eli Gillam?' The question came from Arthur Mason. 'I knew him when I was a preacher in the Blandford circuit. A most sincere and hard-working Methodist. Please give him my regards when you return home. Now there's a man who would make a marvellous missionary . . .'

'Are you a Methodist too?' Mrs Webb put the question to Mary after studying Wes for some moments.

'Yes, ma'am – and I've never missed one of Preacher Gillam's Sunday services. He preaches a fine sermon. Used to send me home shaking sometimes when I was a young girl.'

Mary received the same scrutiny as Wes before the seated missionary asked, 'What about this man you are going to Australia to marry? Why was he transported?'

'I . . . I don't rightly know, ma'am. They said he attacked someone when he was part of a riotous crowd. But Arnold never hurt no one, ma'am, no more would he. He's as gentle as a puppy – and kind with it.'

'Mary's right, Mrs Webb. I was there when Arnold was forced to go along with the crowd, and I spoke to the man he was supposed to have assaulted. He was a Dorchester clergyman. He admitted that Arnold never really attacked him. He wanted to withdraw his complaint, but the judge – the Commissioner – wouldn't let him.'

Wes gave Mrs Webb details of the 'crime' for which Arnold had been transported, ending, 'It wasn't justice, Mrs Webb. Everyone in the court and in Tolpuddle agreed that. It was just that the Commissioners needed to make an example of some of the farm workers.'

'That's quite right, Mrs Webb. I do believe all the farm labourers so convicted have now been pardoned. The young lady will undoubtedly arrive in Australia to learn that her husband-to-be is now a free man,' the shipping agent endorsed Wes's story.

In a manner that convinced Wes more than ever that this lady thought and acted like Widow Cake, Mrs Webb said, 'I *am* aware of what is happening in the world, Mr Calnan.' Unexpectedly she said to Mary, 'Wait outside the room for a few minutes. I would like to have a few words with this young man who has escorted you to London.'

When Mary had left the room, Mrs Webb said to Wes, 'Mr Mason has said your father is a Methodist preacher. I will expect you to answer my questions in a manner worthy of him. Is the girl simple?'

Mrs Webb was nothing if not blunt, but Wes thought carefully before replying. 'I wouldn't say she is exactly "simple", ma'am. She's not quick-witted and you won't find her conversation exactly sparkling. On the other hand, you'll not find a more honest and sober girl, and she's warm-hearted and generous.

She'll also work hard, although I've met those who could complete tasks given them more quickly.'

'I prefer to have a girl around me who moves at *my* speed. What do you think, Alice?' Mrs Webb put the question to Mrs Mason, who had said nothing so far.

'She seems a very pleasant young woman, Mrs Webb. Clean, too. I always think you can judge a young girl's character by the way she keeps herself.'

Mrs Webb sniffed expressively before fixing Wes with a fierce glance. 'What's your relationship with the girl, young man? The truth, if you please.'

'I am very fond of Mary – and of Arnold too. I came to London with her because, like Widow Cake, I am anxious about her making such a long voyage on her own. I was hoping to meet someone like yourself whom I might ask to befriend Mary during the voyage. If you don't wish to employ her I hope you may still do this – although it may prove difficult for you. Widow Cake is paying for her passage to Australia. Although she has entrusted me with a great deal of money for the purpose, I really can't spend it on a cabin. Mary would have to travel steerage.'

'This young lady seems to have gone through life making a great many good friends. Very well, Mr Calnan, I will pay for a cabin for her. In return, she will care for me during the voyage. You may ask her to come in again, if you will.'

With a much kindlier expression on her face than she had shown before, she said to Wes, 'You can return to Tolpuddle and your employer, confident that Mary is travelling with friends, Wesley Gillam. What is more, when we arrive in Australia I will ensure she is reunited with her young man. I will also see to it that the two of them are married in a proper and becoming fashion. If you leave your address with Mr Mason, I will write and inform you of her safe arrival.'

Chapter 11

Wes stood on the dockside waving goodbye to Mary until her tear-streaked face became indistinct. Soon the ship itself was lost to view in the early-morning river mist. It had not been an easy parting. At the last minute, the enormity of what she was doing suddenly came home to the simple village girl. On the dockside she clung to Wes until the missionary companions of her new employer gently prised her away and led her on board the *Enterprise*.

Feeling very emotional, Wes shouldered the bundle that contained a change of clothing and made his way from the dock area. Fortunately, he now had something new to occupy his mind. He was on his way to visit Robert Loveless, cousin of George Loveless, the Tolpuddle Methodist preacher and farmworker's spokesmen.

Robert Loveless lived in a small city house, about a mile from the dock area. He was not in and Wes found the man's wife decidedly unfriendly. She was even more scathing in her remarks when he explained he had come from Tolpuddle, home of Robert's cousin.

Sniffing disparagingly, the woman said, 'Oh yes! My husband has more relatives than a dog has fleas. There's not been one of them come here without wanting something. Money, as a rule.'

'George Loveless doesn't want money, just advice.'

'Well, you're unlucky. He's out of London and I don't expect him back for at least another week.'

Wes's hopes sank. He wanted to be back in Tolpuddle by then. 'I was hoping he might be able to give me the address of a friend of his . . . Richard Pemble?'

The sniff was louder this time and accompanied by a tightening of the woman's lips. 'Another of these "Union" men, are you? I've told my husband I don't want him having anything to do with such nonsense. I intend telling Richard Pemble the same when next I see him.'

'Do you know where I can find him?' Wes asked hopefully.

'He's most likely with some of his low-life friends in Bethnal

Green. Old Nichol Street, I think it is. Most probably in some beer-house. You can tell him from me that I don't want no more Union people coming to this house. I've always been respectable and I intend keeping my house that way.'

With this declaration of intent, the wife of George Loveless's kinsman banged the door shut. On the doorstep, Wes wondered how he would find his way to Old Nichol Street, Bethnal Green.

Locating the street where he hoped to find the Trade Association leader was not as difficult as Wes had feared it would be. Most people from whom he enquired knew where Bethnal Green was. The closer he came, the more people knew of Old Nichol Street. They were all generous with warnings of what he might find there.

'It's little more than a stone's throw from 'ere,' said his last guide ominously, 'but I wouldn't take that there bundle with you. You'd do well to empty your pockets of anyfing worth pinching as well. They don't even shake 'ands in Old Nichol Street, for fear of losing a finger or two.'

After all the warnings, the reality came as something of an anti-climax. There were a number of urchin children who took a keen interest in his arrival and gathered about him quickly. However, as soon as he mentioned the name of Richard Pemble, they seemed to accord him a grudging respect.

Wes was directed to a beer-house by a small woman with a gipsy-like appearance who wore a man's fustian cap and smoked a pipe.

'I doubt if you'll find 'im there, though, dearie. 'E don't spend as much time 'ereabouts as 'e did afore 'e was wed. But ask for Meg. She'll likely as not know where you might find 'im.'

The landlord of the beer-house wore a dirty leather apron and smelled of sweat and stale beer.

'Meg?' He repeated in answer to Wes's question. 'Who wants 'er?'

'I do. At least, I'm told she might help me to find Richard Pemble.'

'She'll know if anyone does,' agreed the heavily perspiring land-lord. 'But don't 'old yer breath while you're waiting for 'im. Very elusive is Dick Pemble, especially if 'e don't *want* to be found. That's Meg, sitting over in the corner wiv the young dolly-mop.'

Wes did not know what a 'dolly-mop' was, but he saw the two young women seated in a corner of the crowded room – and they had seen him. As he went towards them, the elder of the two motioned for her companion to make room on their bench seat for him.

306

'Hello, luv,' she said cheerfully as he approached. 'You looking for company? Take a seat, buy us a drink, and we'll listen to all your troubles.'

The cheeky cheerfulness of the girl made Wes smile. 'I've got no troubles worth talking about, but I'll buy you both a drink. Then perhaps you'll tell me where I can find Richard Pemble?'

'Sit yourself down.' The girl nodded to a serving-girl hovering nearby. 'Bring us two gins, luv – and an ale for the young gent. I'm always suspicious of geezers who buy me drinks and don't have any themselves. Why would you be wanting Richard Pemble?'

'I think he might be able to help with some problems we have back home.'

Meg had been eyeing him while he spoke, and now she said, 'You remind me of someone I know, but haven't seen for some time. Where do you come from?'

'From Dorset.'

'The bloke who looks like you comes from there. Place named Tolpuddle, I think. Saul's his name.'

Wes stared at the girl for some moments, struggling with his emotions. Meg had been involved with Saul and Josephine Frampton in murder and robbery. How was she associated with Richard Pemble?

Gathering his scattered wits, he said, 'Saul's my brother. My name's Wes.'

'I knew it! Soon as I set eyes on you. He spoke of you sometimes. Thought a lot of you, he did. I'm Meg – and this innocent young flower here's Polly. She's my sister. I've tried to keep her away from such places as this, but she wanted to come here. Much the same as you seem to be following in your brother's footsteps, I suppose. Well! This calls for a celebration. Girl!' She called to the serving-girl. 'Forget the glass of gin. Make it a bottle – and this is on me.'

In explanation, Meg said, 'I'm very fond of Saul, although he hasn't been in here lately. Have you seen him?'

Wes nodded. It was obvious Meg did not know of Saul's fate. 'I saw him a few weeks ago.'

'Is he still with that girl – Josephine, I think her name was?'

'No, not any more.'

'Good. He'll be better off without her. She was a hard nut, that one. Too hard even for Saul. I never did trust her. She has a lady's ways, but she's certainly no lady.'

'How long you staying in Bethnal Green?' The question was the first time Wes had heard the younger of the two girls speak.

Meg looked around at her companion. 'I'm sorry, Polly. I forgot you was here for a minute. She's only just come to live with me,'

Meg explained to Wes. 'She's had enough of our stepfather, same as I did years ago.'

'Will you be staying around here long?' The younger girl repeated her question.

'No. I have to get back to Tolpuddle. I had to bring a girl I've worked with to the docks to catch a boat to Australia.' Wes told the story of Mary and Arnold and both his companions murmured sympathetic words as he spoke.

'I don't envy her going on such a voyage,' said Meg when Wes had finished speaking. 'One of the girls from here was transported some years ago. Fourteen, she was, and they transported her for seven years. She was a girl who had her head screwed on the right way. By the time her sentence was up she'd earned enough money to buy a passage home again. The way she talked about it, the trip out was about the closest thing to hell anyone could find here, on earth.'

'That was probably because it was a Transport,' said Wes.

'Likely it was,' agreed Meg with a shrug. 'Anyway, it didn't teach her the lesson it should have. She was hanged last year at Newgate, for murdering her new-born baby.'

Polly shuddered. 'Can't we talk of something else?'

Meg put an arm about the shoulders of her young sister and hugged her. 'Too soft for this world, is Polly. I don't know how our ma managed to produce two of us so different.'

'Where are you staying?' Polly asked Wes the question, at the same time shrugging off her sister's arm.

'I haven't thought about it. I was hoping to find Richard Pemble and set off for home again right away.'

'He doesn't come here very often these days. Now he's gone all respectable, it seems he wants to forget all his old friends.'

'Do you know where I can find him?'

'Yes, down at Eltham village. That's in Kent.'

'How do I get there?'

Meg fell silent but Polly said, 'Across the Woolwich ferry's the best way . . .' In response to her sister's questioning glance, she added. 'I know where Eltham is because we went through it when I went hop-picking last year. I'll show you the way, if you like.'

'Oh no you won't, young lady. I'm not letting you travel that far from London. Not with anyone.'

'Oh, all right then,' Polly pouted. 'But I'll take him as far as the Woolwich ferry.'

'Not today, you won't. It's far too late in the day.'

To Wes, Meg said, 'Seeing as how Polly seems to have taken a fancy to you, you'd better stay in my place with us for tonight. It's not fancy, but it's better than anything you'll find here. You'll be sleeping on the floor, so don't get any ideas – unless you've got the money to pay for her?'

'Meg!' Blood rushed to Polly's face and she looked accusingly at her sister.

'Don't you "Meg!" me. I'll say the same to you as I've said to him. Don't go getting any ideas. You came to stay with me and learn how to earn a living. There's only one way to do that for girls like us. You'll never make it if you throw yourself away on the first good-looking young man who takes your fancy. Before you knew it you'd be stuck in one room with a man who'd keep you short of money, with a load of screaming, dirty-faced brats clinging to your skirts. If that's what you *wanted* you needn't have come to me.'

'Thank you, I'd be pleased if you could put me up for the night – on your terms. I'd also be pleased if Polly would show me the way to the Woolwich ferry tomorrow.'

'Blimey! Listen to him, will you? He talks nearly as posh as that Josephine his brother brought here to this very place. But we won't talk about her. We're celebrating something or another, ain't we? Come on, toff, drink up. When this is gone you can buy us another bottle. I've decided tonight's a night when I'm going to drown me sorrows.'

Chapter 12

'You'll be back tonight?' Polly put the question anxiously to Wes.

They were waiting for the ferry as it edged through the sluggish brown water of the Thames. Moments later the vessel bumped against the small ricketty jetty where she and Wes were standing, on the north bank of the river.

'Yes. But I need to head back to Tolpuddle as soon as I can. Widow Cake will want me to account for every hour I've spent away from work.'

He and Polly had built up an easy relationship during the brief time he had spent in London and on the walk to Woolwich. Too easy. There could be little future in it, for either of them.

Polly had done most of the talking along the way, pointing out various places of interest and revealing something of the hard life she and Meg had led before both had left home. Their father had died when Polly was no more than a toddler. A couple of years later their mother had married again. Their stepfather proved to be a drunkard and a bully. Mother and both daughters had been daily targets for his abuse. As soon as she could, Meg left home to make her own way in the harsh world of London's East End.

Polly had stayed at home nursing their mother during the latter years when she was ill, protecting her from the violence of her stepfather. Not until the recent death of their mother did Polly finally break free of him. When he discovered where she was living he sought her out and attempted to force her to return and take care of his needs. Some of Meg's men-friends had prevented him carrying her off and, in Polly's own words, 'Gave him an almighty bashing.'

'I'll wait here for you.'

'I won't be back until very late, Polly. Go on back to Bethnal Green.'

'I've got nothing to do there.' She shrugged. 'I'll wait here and watch the ships. I'll day-dream about the places they've been or just come from, and imagine I'll go there too one day.'

Stepping ashore from the ferry boat on the Woolwich side of the

310

Thames, Wes skirted a working party of prisoners from one of the hulks moored in the river. Dressed in drab grey uniforms of a coarse material, the men were chained together in groups of six. Wielding heavy hammers, they were breaking stones with which they were building a quay, rising from the stinking river mud.

Leaving the chain-gang behind, Wes glanced across the water. The river was wide here, but he could still see the small figure of Polly sitting on the river bank. He waved, but there was no response. She probably had her glance fixed on a magnificent East India Company merchantman, being towed upriver by a labouring paddle-wheeled tugboat.

Polly reminded him of Saranna as she had been when he first met her at the Dorchester fair, intent on buying a pig. He grinned at the memory. He wondered how much she had changed in the two years since they had last met. Whether she would recognise him immediately . . .

He found the cottage in Eltham village easily enough. Larger than the Vye cottage had been in Southover, it had a large and neat garden, filled with a wide variety of shrubs and flowers.

His doubts about whether Saranna would recognise him were dispelled the moment the door was opened to him – by Saranna herself.

'Wes!' Her hand went to her mouth and mixed expressions of shock, delight and dismay chased each other across her face. 'What . . . what are you doing *here*?'

Saranna had changed from the gawky, poorly clad girl he had known in Dorset. She was even taller than before – almost as tall as Wes himself. But she was nicely dressed now and far more attractive than he had ever imagined she would be.

'Who is it, Saranna?' The voice of Nancy Pemble, Saranna's mother, came from within the house.

'It's Wes Gillam . . . from Tolpuddle.'

'Well, bless me! Don't leave him standing at the door, girl. Bring him in! Let's all see him.'

Wes followed Saranna through a room to the kitchen where Nancy was drying her hands on the apron she wore. She gave Wes the kind of welcome he wished might have come from Saranna. When the kissing and hugging were over, she stood back and held him at arm's length. 'Well! Aren't you the young gentleman now? Handsome with it, too. My, it's a good job you came along before this young man grew up, Richard Pemble.'

For the first time Wes noticed Pemble seated at a table which had been partly hidden from view behind the open kitchen door. Across the table from him was a man probably in his mid-thirties with prematurely thinning hair and a slightly peevish frown. On the table between the two men were a number of printed papers and hand-written documents.

Stretching out a hand towards Wes, Richard Pemble said, 'I remember you. We met when Nancy was living at Southover. You're the brother of Saul, as I remember. How is he? I haven't seen him for a long time.'

Wes's carefully guarded composure almost broke at the question. He had thought the Association leader might have known of Saul's fate. 'We haven't seen Saul in Tolpuddle since before Saranna and her mother left. I heard he has a ladyfriend. I expect they're off somewhere together.'

'Probably . . . but I'm forgetting my manners. Wesley, I would like you to meet Alan.' Pemble nodded in the direction of his companion. 'He's my right-hand man in the Grand Association of labour that's beginning to take shape now. He's also Saranna's future husband.'

'Oh! Congratulations . . . to both of you.' Shaking hands with the man, Wes felt he was excelling himself in hiding his true feelings today.

'How about you, Wes? Have you married the Tolpuddle vicar's daughter yet?'

Now Wes felt he could slacken the grip on his emotions as he told Saranna and the others of the tragic death of Fanny, adding, 'She never really recovered from the attack on her, the night the men broke into her house and dragged her outside.'

'I'm sorry to hear that, Wes.' Saranna seemed genuinely upset. 'But are you still carrying on with your learning?'

'Only what I have time to do myself. I stopped going to the vicarage when Fanny died.'

'That's the spirit, young man. Never cease learning. It's all-important in today's world. The employers would prefer to keep their men ignorant, but they won't be able to hold back the tide for ever.'

'How is Widow Cake?' Nancy asked the question and Wes believed it was a deliberate attempt to change the subject.

Wes told of Widow Cake sending him with Mary to catch a ship for Australia. 'That's one of the reasons I'm here today,' he explained.

'What's the other reason?' Nancy gave her daughter a rapid, searching glance before asking Wes the question.

'I wanted to speak to Mr Pemble. My father and some of his friends in the village want information about starting an Association for the workers. They're having their wages cut despite all the promises the farmers made, and they need to do something about it.'

Speaking directly to Richard Pemble now, he said, 'I had thought I might find you in London – Bethnal Green was where I was sent. When you didn't come there I thought I had better come here.'

'Well, we're all glad you did, Wes. It's very nice to see you again. Now, you men can talk all you like about the Association later. Right now I intend feeding Wes and hearing the news of what's been going on in Tolpuddle. Sit down here. How's that Widow Cake keeping? Is she any more cheerful these days?'

'She's finding it harder to get about and her tongue's sharper than ever. Yet she gave me the money to pay Mary's passage to Australia. She also gave quite a large sum of money to Mary herself. Hopefully she and Arnold can get off to a good start when she gets there and he becomes a free man once more.'

'Free pardons are already on their way for all those sentenced in connection with the workers' protests. Our Association has been pressing members of government on the matter for a couple of years now. It's a sign of our growing power that they've begun to listen to us.'

'I should think so too,' said Saranna. 'Arnold wouldn't have hurt a soul, and there were a lot more like him. They should have spent their time looking for the men who attacked Fanny Warren.'

'I agree,' replied Richard Pemble, with a reasonableness born of long practice. 'The lawless element who attach themselves to our protests are becoming an embarrassment to the movement. Nevertheless, without them our Association would have lacked the backbone it needed in the early days. Most farm workers are as I imagine this Arnold to be. Slow to anger and reluctant to oppose those who take advantage of their temperaments.'

'Now then! I've already told you, talk about politics can come later. First it's the turn of Saranna and me. How are your mother and father keeping, Wes?'

The talk was of those who lived at Tolpuddle and Southover for the remainder of the meal. As he ate and talked, Wes compared the striking good looks of Saranna with the rather sulky expression that seemed to be a permanent feature of Alan's face. It was an expression that Widow Cake might have described as 'lacking in generosity'.

'Who's looking after Widow Cake now that Mary's gone?' The question was posed by Saranna.

'My ma's taken it on for a while, but she and Widow Cake are bound to fall out before very long. What will happen then, I don't know . . .'

Conversation was interrupted by a knock at the kitchen door.

Nancy called, 'Come in!' and two men entered the room, anxious to speak to Richard Pemble.

'This is Association business,' said Richard Pemble to Wes who had just ended his meal. 'I'll talk to you later and give you papers detailing how to set up a local branch of the Association. I'll also send someone down to speak to your father and his friends.'

Before Wes could thank him, Richard Pemble had bundled Alan and the two new arrivals from the kitchen into one of the other rooms.

When they had gone, Nancy said, 'I don't know, I'm sure. With all the comings-and-goings this place is becoming more like Southover every day! I expect they'll all want feeding too and I'm nearly out of everything. Saranna, will you go to the farm for me and buy two dozen eggs?'

She produced a basket from the shelf in the corner of the kitchen and handed it to her daughter.

'You go with her too, Wes. You can talk along the way. Then Saranna can tell me later about all the things I'm bound to forget to ask you . . .'

Chapter 13

'So you're really going to be married . . . to Alan?'

'That's right. Does it surprise you?'

Wes and Saranna were walking from the cottage to the farm to purchase eggs.

'I knew you wouldn't stay single for ever.' Wes shrugged unhappily. 'I'm surprised you're marrying a man so much older than yourself, that's all.'

'At least he's old enough to know his own mind,' retorted Saranna. 'He's also very clever. Richard says Alan will be the most important man in the Association one day.'

'I don't suppose you've ever offered to take him to the alley behind the Antelope Inn?'

Saranna remained silent for a while, then she said softly, 'That was unfair, Wesley.'

'Yes, it was. I'm sorry.'

'Why did you say it? Why did you want to remind me of something that happened so long ago?'

'I don't know,' he replied miserably.

'I think you do. You've come here thinking all you had to say was, "I'm sorry, I think I might have made a mistake all those years ago. Come back to Tolpuddle, work for Widow Cake again and perhaps we might start all over again." Isn't that it, Wes? Because I made it obvious how much I thought of you then, you thought I only needed to see you again and we'd be back where we were. Isn't that right?'

Wes said nothing. There was nothing he *could* say. In his heart he knew Saranna was right. He had not thought this reunion out in any detail. Yet pushed somewhere to the back of his mind had been a vain wish that things might somehow be as they once were.

'Life isn't like that, Wes. We can't go back because nothing is the same as it once was.'

'I know.'

They walked on in silence for a while before Saranna said quietly, 'Why did you change so suddenly towards me, Wes? When we were in Dorchester for Arnold's trial, I thought you and

I had become very close. Then, overnight it seemed, you changed. It wasn't me, I know it wasn't. It was you. Why?'

'I saw Saul the night we came back.'

'What has that to do with anything? I saw him too. In fact, it was me who insisted that he come to see you and your ma.'

'We spoke about you. He told me you were his girl. Even asked me to keep an eye on you for him, to make sure you stayed his girl.'

'You believed him? After what happened – what *nearly* happened between us in Dorchester, you believed I was *his* girl?'

'I'd always thought you were Saul's girl, Saranna. When he told me outright that you were, what could I do? He was my brother. Why should he lie about something that was so important to me. Something that he knew would affect my whole future.'

'Was I really so important to you, Wes?'

'Yes.'

'That's the way I felt too. I was very hurt about the way you changed so suddenly.'

'Yes . . . I'm sorry, Saranna. Very sorry.'

'Saul is the one who should be sorry. If ever I see him again, I'll tell him exactly what I think of him.'

'You won't see him again . . .' Wes hesitated for only a moment before telling her what had happened to Saul, and of the part Josephine Frampton was believed to have played, adding, 'This must be a secret between you and me, Saranna. My ma and pa don't know about it and I never want them to know. The only other person I've told is Widow Cake.'

'Wes . . . it's *awful*!' She touched his arm in a remembered gesture, but now it was prompted by sympathy, not affection. That hurt too. 'Have you seen Josephine Frampton since then?'

'Yes, she's back at Moreton now and she hasn't changed. She was out to make trouble for me again. Fortunately, Saul had told me something about her. I only had to mention it and she went off very quickly, all thought of making trouble forgotten.'

'It sounds as though it worked as well as pushing her in the river did.'

She half-smiled, but it vanished when she looked at Wes's face. 'I'm sorry, Wes. What with Saul and Fanny . . . you've had a rough time. Were you very fond of her?'

Wes did not reply for a few moments, then he said honestly, 'I liked her, yes. She was a very kind and gentle girl. But most of all I felt *sorry* for her. Her mother was so selfish she never gave a thought to what Fanny herself wanted. Her father was almost as bad, but in a different way. He so smothered her with his love that she never had a chance to be herself.'

'Poor Fanny.' Saranna was genuinely sympathetic. 'Whenever I saw her, I always thought she was a girl who had everything I would never have.'

'She had nothing. Nothing at all. She lived an empty life.'

'Has there been any other girl in your life since she died, Wes?'

He shook his head. He would have liked to say he had always hoped that a miracle would happen and one day *she* would return to Tolpuddle, but he remained silent. It would be an unfair thing to say. Especially now, when she was to marry someone else.

'No, no one.'

When the eggs had been collected and they were on their way back to the Pemble cottage, Wes asked, 'Are you happy living in Kent?'

'We have far more here than we had at Southover.'

It did not answer Wes's question, but he did not press her. 'Will you still live in Kent . . . when you're married?'

'I don't know.'

Saranna sounded no more at ease than Wes when discussing her forthcoming marriage. Feeling such a brief reply needed amplification, she added, 'Richard thinks Alan should go up North. To live there and help the Association's cause. Naturally, I'd go with him.'

The silence between them had grown to embarrassing proportions when Wes said, 'I wish we *could* turn time back, Saranna.'

'To where, Wes? How far back would you go?'

'To that night in Dorchester. I'd make certain things turned out differently for you, for me – yes, and for Saul too.'

'Unfortunately, life isn't like that. There's no going back and starting again.'

'No,' agreed Wes miserably. 'It's just wishful thinking, that's all.'

When they reached the cottage, they found the household in a turmoil. Richard Pemble and Nancy were rushing around finding clothes and stuffing them hurriedly inside saddle-bags.

'Something's happened in the North of England,' explained Pemble. 'The miners are in dispute with the pit owners and they want to link up with the Association. This could be the big opportunity we've all been waiting for.'

'Where's Alan?' asked Saranna.

'He's gone back to his house to pack a bag. We're travelling together. You'll need to hurry if you want to see him before we leave.'

Thrusting an untidy sheaf of papers into Wes's hands, Richard Pemble said, 'You'll find all the details you need about the

Association in here. As soon as I return I'll arrange for someone to come to Dorset to speak to you all there.'

Saranna had already gone from the house and as Richard Pemble went off in search of something else, Wes said, 'I must leave too, Mrs Pemble.'

'You can't go before you've said goodbye to Saranna. Just wait until Richard and Alan have left. There'll be time to relax a little then. I might even be able to find a bottle hidden away somewhere.'

'Thanks, but I think I ought to go. I've got what I came for – and Saranna won't mind. She has Alan now. I belong to the past. I should have stayed in the past and not come here today.'

'Are those your own words, Wes, or those of our Saranna?'

'It doesn't matter who said them. It's the truth.'

'Not entirely. True, there's no *going* back, for anyone. But you can never wipe the slate clean. Sometimes the past has a habit of catching up with you. When it does you need to turn and face it, not try to run away.'

When Wes made no reply, Nancy asked, 'What was it went wrong between you and Saranna, Wes? For a while, when we were at Southover, I was convinced you and she were going to make a go of things. I was very happy about it. What happened?'

Nancy's words did nothing to ease his misery and Wes said, 'There was a misunderstanding. It was all my fault, but I didn't learn I'd been wrong until a few months ago.'

'Is there nothing that can be done to put things right now?'

'I've explained everything to Saranna, but she's marrying Alan. It might have been better if I hadn't come here.'

'No, Wes. Whatever happens, I'm glad you have come here to see us. I don't doubt that Saranna is too, but I do wish you'd stay and say goodbye to her properly.'

Wes shook his head. Carefully folding the papers given to him by Richard Pemble, he tucked them in a safe pocket. After a warm hug from Nancy, he set off from the house, heading back towards Woolwich.

Watching him go from the doorway of her cottage, Nancy thought he was a forlorn figure, for all that he was a grown man now.

Talking quietly to herself, she said, 'You may think you've made a mistake coming here today, Wesley Gillam, but I don't. Our Saranna's walked with your ghost at her shoulder for these past two years. Now she's either going to have to send you back to where you think you belong, or do something about it – and I have a very good idea of what she'll do.'

Chapter 14

It was almost dark by the time the ferry from Woolwich grounded on the north side of the river. Polly was very relieved to see Wes.

Linking her arm in his, she said, 'I was beginning to think you wasn't going to come back after all. Did you find Eltham, all right?'

'I did – and completed all my business.' Thinking of the time he spent with Saranna, Wes thought he had probably completed far more business than he had contemplated.

'Does that mean you'll be going back to Dorset now?'

'That's right. I've got work to go to there.'

'Can't you stay for just a couple of days more? There's a whole lot of London to see, you know. I could show you. There's the Tower, the theatres up West where all the nobs go, lords and ladies too. We could go to the theatre if you wanted to. You'd like that. There might even be a hanging at Newgate. I saw six of 'em hung together there once.'

Wes shuddered as memories of another hanging in another place returned to him. 'I told you, I have to go home.'

'Well, you're not going to set off tonight, that's certain. If you step out we'll get to the beer-house while there's something going on there. You can buy me a gin for walking here with you and telling you how to get to Eltham village. I've worked up a thirst while I've been waiting for you by that ferry.'

By the time they reached the narrow, dingy streets of Bethnal Green, Wes was worried about the proprietorial attitude of Polly. It seemed to have increased out of all proportion while she had been waiting at the riverside for his return.

It was even more noticeable when they reached the Old Nichol Street beer-house. The small cramped drinking area was filled to overflowing with customers. Despite this, and the difficulty of even one person entering, Polly insisted upon maintaining her grip on Wesley's arm. It made it difficult for him to push a way through. By making others get out of their way, Polly ensured that the maximum number of beer-shop customers saw she had come in with Wes.

When they reached the table where Meg was seated, surrounded by a number of companions, the elder of the two sisters looked up. 'Where have you two been all day?' She looked bleary-eyed, as though she had been drinking for a long time.

'I've been with Wes,' Polly declared brightly.

Meg frowned, and Wes corrected Polly's statement instantly. 'I've been to see Richard Pemble. Polly waited for me on this side of the Woolwich ferry.'

'Oh, yeah. I remember now. You told me where you were going. Now you're back you can come and join us. We're having a party. This is Tim Sparrow. He's been a guest of His Majesty the King for a couple of years. Now he's back with his friends – for a while, at any rate. We're celebrating in true cockney style.'

'You mean . . . you've just come out of prison?' Wes eyed the squat, broad-shouldered man with close-cropped hair somewhat apprehensively.

'That's right, although it should have been your friend Richard Pemble in there instead of me.' Tim Sparrow eyed Wes through watery, red-rimmed eyes.

'Pemble's no friend of mine,' Wes corrected the other man hurriedly. Sparrow apparently had a grudge to settle with Saranna's step-father. He did not want to be included in the settlement. 'I just went to seek his advice for those in my village about setting up a branch of the Association.'

'Why were you sent to prison?' he asked the question hesitantly.

'Because I trusted Richard Pemble,' came the bitter retort. 'Smash up the threshing-machines,' he said. 'The farmers don't want them any more than we do. They have them only because the landlords are insisting. Like fools, I and about fifty others believed him. We were taken by the magistrate and his constables. In court the farmers were there to a man, pointing us out to the judge and telling him what they'd seen. You tell the men in your village that if they trust Richard Pemble they're likely to end up in the same place as I did.'

Tim Sparrow was quite obviously as cockney as Meg. Wes would have liked to ask why he had been so far from home, smashing threshing-machines on behalf of farm labourers. He decided such a question might not be well-received and so he said nothing.

'Well, you're out now, Tim, and you've a lot of catching-up to do – in more ways than one.' Winking meaningfully, Meg nudged the newly freed man. The gesture provoked a howl of bawdy laughter from his companions.

This was one party Wes would gladly have forgone, but Polly

had made those on one side of the table move along, making room for herself and Wes. She seemed settled in for the evening. Wes knew he could not return to Meg's house to collect his belongings without either her or her sister. Anyway, he would not be able to catch a coach to Dorchester at this time of night. There was nothing he could do before morning except drown his sorrows.

'A penny for 'em, Wes.'

'Eh?'

'I said, "A penny for 'em". Your thoughts . . . it's an old saying. You were miles away in your thoughts and I offered you a penny for 'em.' Polly frowned at Wes's apparent lack of understanding.

'You wouldn't be getting value for your money.'

In truth, he had been thinking of Saranna. Of the life she had made for herself and what the future held for her – and for him.

He did not know what the time was, although it seemed he had been in the beer-house for hours. The noise and the unaccustomed drink had numbed his brain. He wished he had insisted on collecting his possessions and making his way to the centre of London. From there he could have caught the first available coach to Dorchester.

'Aren't you enjoying yourself, Wes?' Polly needed to shout to make herself heard above the strains of a bawdy cockney song.

'I'm not used to crowds like this.' He waved an arm in a gesture that encompassed the whole room.

'I expect you're tired too. You've done a lot of walking today. Would you like to leave and go back to Meg's place?'

It was exactly what Wes wanted. He said so eagerly.

'All right. I'll go and get the key from Meg. By the look of things, she's not going to want to go home until sun-up.'

Outside, in the cool night air, Wes felt the world suddenly begin to swing about him.

'Here! You all right?' Polly clutched his arm in a moment of alarm.

'I'll be all right in a minute. I'm not used to drinking, that's all. My pa's a . . . Methodist preacher. He won't have drink in the house.' He had trouble pronouncing the denomination.

'No drink? Cor! What do you do in the country when you want to celebrate something?'

'We haven't had a lot to celebrate just lately.' The statement reminded Wes of his main mission to the house in Eltham. He felt in his pocket to make certain all the documents he was taking home were safe.

'How about girls? Don't you have a sweetheart at home?'

'No.' It came out too quickly. Too abruptly. 'I did have one, but she left the village a couple of years ago.'

'This village of yours sound a bit dull to me.'

'It's not. I like it – and I bet we live a sight better than anyone in London.'

Wes was having to concentrate on both his words and his feet. He was not enjoying the experience. The next moment he tripped over an uneven cobble-stone and would have fallen had Polly not saved him.

'I reckon you've been making up for lost time tonight, Wes. Never mind, I'll look after you.' Polly put an arm about his waist. Her shoulder beneath his armpit provided sufficient support for him to make reasonably accurate progress along the road.

'Here we are. Can you stand up by yourself while I open the door?'

''Course I can!' he said indignantly, and promptly stumbled again, over nothing discernible this time.

He made it up the stairs, although there was a moment close to the top when Polly thought he was about to fall backwards to the bottom.

They arrived in the tiny flat with Wes insisting he was less drunk than it might appear, to the accompaniment of Polly's amused giggling.

Without lighting a candle, they passed through the room where Wes had slept the previous night and into the small bedroom Polly shared with Meg.

'This is Meg's room . . .'

Wes tried to pull back, but with a strength that belied her slight frame Polly pushed him to the unseen bed.

'You'll sleep in here tonight. No . . . don't argue, Wes. Come on. Let's get these boots off. Gawd, but they're heavy. No wonder you've had trouble walking home.'

She pulled off his boots, socks and then his shirt. Wes drew the line when she undid his belt and fumbled at the fastenings of his trousers.

'All right, you do them yourself.'

'I'll just lie down a while first.' Wes lay back, his head on a flock-filled pillow. But he was still for only a few moments. The world began to spin around him at an alarming speed and he sat up abruptly.

'What's the matter?'

There had been just enough light coming through the window for Polly to see the sudden movement.

'Everything began to spin around me.'

'We'll soon put a stop to that . . .'

Before he could marshal sufficient wits to consider the implications of the brief statement, Polly was sliding into the bed
beside him – and he did not have to be sober to realise she
was naked.

'What . . .!'

'Shh! Lie on your side, you'll feel better – and take these
trousers off.'

Even as she spoke she was carrying out the task for him with an
expertise that might have provoked a question or two in his mind
had he been more sober.

'I . . . I don't think I feel too well.'

'You're all right, believe me. All you need is something to
occupy your mind. Here . . .'

Suddenly she was kissing him and touching him. Moments later
she had aroused animal feelings in him that overrode the effects
of the alcohol and his feeling of nausea. Then, displaying more of
the strength she had shown when getting him on the bed, Polly
pulled him on top of her and they began making love. It was over
as quickly as it had begun and Wes lay with his weight upon her,
gasping for air.

'You all right?' Polly spoke as she struggled to free the upper
part of her body from his weight.

'No. I think I'm going to be sick . . .'

'Oh Gawd!' Throwing him on to his side, Polly slipped from the
bed as he began making noises deep in his throat. She returned
just in time and thrust an evil-smelling receptacle beneath his
nose. It would have made him retch had he been feeling better
than he was.

Some time later he lay on his back, gasping for breath. In the
darkness, Polly asked, 'Are you any better now?'

'Yes.' The simple word escaped painfully from his throat.

'You likely to be sick again?'

'No.' The word was as painful as the previous one.

'Then I can get rid of this.' He heard the window open and the
next moment the contents of the chamber pot were thrown out to
the street below.

'You sure you're all right now?'

'Yes.'

'Then I'll come back and keep you warm.'

She slid into the bed beside him and snuggled against him.
After a few moments, she said, 'That was your first time, wasn't
it?'

'Yes.' Wes did not feel communicative. He knew he should be
ashamed of what he had just done. It was against all the teachings
of his father – and his ma had always issued vague warnings

against such things. But the feelings of guilt he had were not due to his parents but because of Saranna. It was absurd, he knew, but he felt he had betrayed her.

'I don't think I've ever known anyone as old as you who hadn't done it before.' Polly's hand was caressing his chest and stomach. 'We'll do it again in the morning. You'll feel better then.'

In fact, they made love again before morning. Polly seduced him for the second time soon after they had been woken by Meg and the 'friend' with whom she had been celebrating his release from prison.

Meg and Tim Sparrow were noisily admonishing each other to be quiet, Meg warning him not to wake her sister. At the same time she seemed to be falling over every item in the bedroom and giggling at nothing in particular.

In the morning, Wes woke to hear snores from the other bed, but Polly was not beside him. He rose and crept into the other room, clutching his clothing, but Polly was not here either.

Dressing swiftly, Wes took up his bag and left the house. It was quiet outside. It seemed the residents of Old Nichol Street kept late hours and lay in bed in the mornings. He wondered where Polly had gone so early. He should have stayed to see her, but was afraid she might have tried to prevent him from leaving. It was better this way.

He believed they would never meet again.

Chapter 15

Although Wes could have had no way of knowing it, his visit to Eltham had thrown Saranna's life into an unresolvable turmoil. For two years she had made a determined effort to forget him.

Before leaving Southover she had given her heart to Wes and offered him her body. Only her mother knew how distraught she had been on the long journey from Dorset to the family's new home in Kent.

It had taken a long time to build a protective shell about herself. The reappearance of Wes in her life showed her how futile the effort had been. The shell had proved as delicate as a wren's egg.

Alan Pate formed an important part of that shell. A bachelor, he lived in Eltham with his mother and had been a friend of Richard Pemble for very many years. He had helped to organise the 'Grand Association' which was Pemble's brainchild.

Pemble provided the enthusiasm and the fiery oratory needed to inspire and influence working men. Meanwhile, Alan worked away at the solid foundations of the Association and built steadily upon them.

Alan Pate was not a passionate man. His actions were dictated by logic, not by deeply held convictions. Trades Associations – the Union of workers – were in their infancy. They struggled feebly against the implacable hostility of employers and landowners, who alone chose government and judiciary. Yet Alan Pate believed the worker possessed the ultimate weapon – his labour. Without it the country would grind to a halt. It was Pate's theory that, properly harnessed, such power would prove irresistible, as it had in France.

In common with Richard Pemble, he believed the labour force of the country was finally becoming aware of its own strength. Any man capable of leading them into unity would one day be numbered among the most powerful in the land. He believed the moment was close at hand – and he intended to be that leader. He

325

needed Richard Pemble now, but one day he would surely step over him.

Saranna made her way to the home of Alan Pate, which was at the edge of Eltham village, and let herself into the house.

There was as much bustle here as there had been in the Pemble cottage. Alan's saddled horse was hitched outside and his saddlebags were being packed for him by his mother. As she worked, the Trades Association leader was grumbling because she was taking such a long time.

'Do hurry up, Mother. It shouldn't take this long to find a few clothes and pack a couple of bags.'

Mildly embarrassed at his peevish harassment of the elderly woman, Saranna asked him, 'Are you going to be away for long?'

'I don't know, why?'

'Well, I'd like to know whether you're likely to be away for a few days, a few weeks, or maybe months.'

'I'll be away for as long as I need to be, I suppose. How long is that Gillam boy staying in Eltham?'

Stung by his indifferent attitude towards her, Saranna shrugged, 'No doubt he'll stay as long as he wants to. Ma won't be in a hurry to chase him away. She likes him. She always has.'

'Do you like him too? Is that why you're so interested to know how long *I'll* be away?'

'Why, Alan Pate! I do believe you're jealous.'

'Me, jealous? I grew out of such stupidity before I completed my schooling. Anyway, I'd certainly not be jealous of some clodhopping son of the soil. He's probably left his village home for the first time in his miserable young life.'

'Alan! What's the matter with you? I've never heard you speak of anyone in this way before. Wes is a very clever young man. Everyone in Tolpuddle says so.'

'It sounds as though it's not only your mother who likes him.' Alan Pate spoke scornfully.

'That's right, I like him too. He was a good friend to us when Ma and I lived in Dorset.'

'No more than a "friend"? It wasn't a "friendly" look I saw him giving you when he thought no one else was looking. How well did you know each other?'

'I don't intend answering that question, Alan, and you should never have asked it. I haven't seen Wes for two years. As I've told you, we were friends, that's all.'

'I'm sorry to sound suspicious, Saranna, but one day I hope to be an important man in the Trades Association movement. The wife of such a man needs to be above reproach at all times.'

'Are you trying to say I won't make a suitable wife for you? Is that what you're telling me?'

'Of course not. You'd make a splendid wife for any man but you're still very young. You have a lot to learn. I look forward to being able to instruct you how you should behave, Saranna. I want to be proud of you. I *will* be proud of you.'

She was so incensed by his words, emotion threatened to choke her. Yet even while she quietly fumed, she remembered that Wes had not suggested she should change. He wanted her as she was. As she had always been . . .

But Alan Pate had turned his attention back to his mother once more. 'Have you almost finished packing that saddle-bag, Mother? I don't want to keep Richard waiting . . . No! Don't try to fold a shirt like that. How many times have I told you? Here, give it to me. It should be rolled neatly, like this, and put away carefully.'

'Yes, dear, I know you've told me. I forgot. I'm sorry . . . I'll try to remember next time.'

Saranna watched and listened in silence. When they were married this would become one of her tasks. To pack Alan's saddle-bags. No doubt he would teach her the right way to do this too.

She shook off the sudden niggling unease she felt. It probably had something to do with seeing Wes again. He had unsettled her – and Alan must have noticed it. That's why he had behaved in the way he had towards her. He was right of course. Alan was *always* right.

'You'll hurry back, Alan?'

Saranna crossed the room and grasped his arm affectionately.

'I'll need to stay there until my work is done, Saranna. I have already told you so.'

He shook off her hand casually and began fastening the straps of the saddle-bag. 'You'll heed what I've said? Keep young Gillam at arm's length. I must go now, I can see Richard already waiting. Your mother must be more expert at packing saddle-bags than mine . . .'

As Alan rode away, meeting up with Richard without so much as a backward glance, Saranna thought of Wes. He had always been reluctant to part from her. She shook the thought off. That had been a long time ago. Yet as she headed for home, the thought of speaking to him once more made her step lighter.

'I thought he might at least have waited to say goodbye to me!'

Saranna stood in the kitchen of the Pemble home, hands on hips, looking indignant. She had been upbraiding her mother for allowing Wes to leave Eltham without bidding her farewell.

'I couldn't tie him down, love. Besides, you were off bidding farewell to the man you're going to marry. Wes probably thought it didn't matter very much to you whether he went or stayed.'

'Of course it matters!' She realised immediately she was being too emphatic. 'He's a friend, a very good friend, and I wanted the chance to talk to him. Why was he in such a hurry to leave?'

'Friends don't question what others do. They accept that they have their reasons and look forward to the next time they will meet.'

Saranna looked sulky. 'We'll probably never meet again. Not ever.' Suddenly, her eyes felt very hot. She turned away from her mother quickly, but it had not passed unnoticed.

'From what Richard was saying, Alan's likely to be away for a few months. I haven't heard you breaking your heart about that.'

'What's that supposed to mean?' Snapping out the words, Saranna turned on her mother.

Putting down the piece of dry washing she had been folding, Nancy held out her arms to Saranna. She came to them after only a moment's hesitation.

'Sit down, Saranna, I'll make us a cup of tea. I think it's time you and I had a talk.'

As she settled the kettle on the hot coals of the kitchen fire, Nancy said, 'Perhaps I've set a bad example to you. I've married Richard in order to give me some security as I grow older – although it's not a one-sided marriage. He married me to give him the comforts he's lacked since his first wife died. We both knew this when we decided to marry. What's more, we've known each other for long enough to like and respect each other. To accept just how much, or how little, we're putting into the marriage.'

The kettle had boiled previously and as the lid began dancing merrily, Nancy used her apron to protect her hand from the heat. Lifting the kettle from the fire, she poured water on the waiting tea leaves.

As she replaced the kettle on the hob, Nancy said, 'It wasn't like that when I was a girl and met your father, Saranna. Where he was concerned I thought nothing out before I acted. All I knew was that I'd have swum the English Channel stark naked just to be with him. That's the way it should be for all young girls in our walk of life when they marry. It's the one chance of true happiness we'll ever have. If it's not like that you'll be committing yourself to a life of drudgery and servitude that's worse than anything you'll find in the house of an employer.'

As her mother spoke, Saranna remembered Alan's mother packing her son's saddle-bags. His assumption that it was her duty to do so, and his impatience with her when he felt she was not doing it to his satisfaction. When they married that task and many others would fall upon her.

Nevertheless, she said, 'There are all sorts of marriages, Ma – and Alan's going to be an important man one day.'

It sounded feeble, even to her, and Nancy said scornfully, 'So you're an expert on marriage now – and that without ever trying it! All right, so Alan *will* be an important man – but important to whom? To those who look and see only a Trades Association leader, perhaps. But how about the woman who darns and washes his clothes, keeps his home clean and brings up his children? Will you still think he's wonderful when you're having to put up with his bad manners and bad temper when he's not out being "important"? When he's doing all the one hundred and one things the men he leads will never see?'

'I don't understand, Ma . . . It sounds as though you're trying to put me off marrying Alan. Why haven't you said all this to me before?'

Putting a mug of tea on the table beside her daughter, Nancy reached down and took one of Saranna's hands. She squeezed her daughter's fingers painfully as she strove to make her point as forcefully as she knew how.

'Because Wes hadn't come back into your life – and I thought he never would. I'd forgotten how you and he used to look at each other sometimes. You've never looked at Alan that way, nor he at you. You've both somehow drifted together and reached an understanding.'

Nancy took a sip of her own tea. 'Yes, Alan Pate *is* a good catch for any girl. Most mothers would be satisfied with such a match for their daughter – but you're too much like me, Saranna. I want you to know the happiness I found with your pa. The sort where you can wake up in the mud of a mountainside after seeing your friends maimed and killed in yesterday's battle, having to crack back the frozen blankets about you. You know the next day's going to be the same, and the next, and the one after that. You're cold and you're hungry and heavy with child. You really don't know how you'll survive another twenty-mile march. Then your man looks at you and smiles – just for you. Because he loves you.'

Tears sprang to Nancy's eyes as she said, 'In that moment you're the happiest woman in the world. You know you'll do whatever needs to be done. God and the enemy willing, you'll be together again at the end of the day and it will all have been worthwhile.'

When Nancy finished talking she wiped the tears from her eyes and Saranna said softly, 'You must have loved him very much, Ma.'

'Yes, I did. I still do, for all he's been dead for nineteen years and I'm now Mrs Pemble. But that's how I want it to be for you, Saranna. I can't lead your life for you, any more than I've ever let anyone dictate mine. But I want you to think about what I've said. Alan *is* probably going to be very successful one day – but don't confuse achievement with happiness – *real* happiness.'

Saranna rose to her feet abruptly and hugged her mother. It was a warm, spontaneous and happy gesture, 'Thank you, Ma. Thank you for understanding . . . and for everything. I know what I have to do now. I suppose I always have, really, but I won't be able to do anything until Alan returns. I owe him that, at least.'

Chapter 16

'So you've decided to return to us? I wouldn't have thought it would take you four days to put a girl on a ship and find your way back here again. You travelled on a coach too. When I was following the army we'd march that far – and fight a battle with Napoleon along the way!'

Widow Cake's unreasonable greeting was almost the last straw for Wes. Battered by his experiences at the hands of both Saranna and Polly, he felt exhausted, humiliated, and not a little ashamed of himself.

'While you've been gallivanting about up there in London, I've had to put up with the couple of hours' work your father deigned to spare me at the end of each day. That's when he didn't have his precious chapel business to attend to. The only good thing was that he was here so seldom I didn't have to listen to those mournful Methodist hymns he sings for hours on end. They're enough to turn the cows' milk sour.'

'It won't take me long to sort things out, Mrs Cake, I'm sure my pa kept everything together.'

Amelia Cake made a derisive noise in her throat. 'You won't tell me if he hasn't. Well, don't just stand there looking simple – tell me about Mary. Did you manage to get her off to Australia? What was the boat called? Is she going to be safe travelling all that way on her own?'

Wes told his employer about the missionaries and the arrangements he had made for Mary, at the same time handing back the money Amelia Cake had given him to pay for Mary's passage to Australia.

'Well, I will say you carried that out well enough,' she said grudgingly. 'But you say you did all that in the first twenty-four hours you spent in London? Where have you been since then?'

Pushing the events of his last night in London to the back of his mind, Wes said, 'I went to see Saranna.'

'Did you now?' Amelia Cake gave him a searching look, observing the fatigue that had brought him close to the point of exhaustion. 'Well, it shows you've got some sense, at least, in that

331

head of yours. Tell me about it. Were you able to persuade her to come back to Tolpuddle?'

'No. I wanted to, but it wouldn't have done any good. She's getting married. The man she's marrying has far more than me to offer her, even though he must be twice her age.'

'What? You left it at that? Wesley Gillam, I swear you don't *deserve* the girl! Has more than you to offer, indeed! You should have spent every minute of the time you were with her persuading her that it's *you* who has everything to offer.'

The irascible widow shook her head despairingly. 'I don't know. The young men of today aren't made of the same stuff as their fathers, that's certain. I hope for all our sakes that no one makes war against us in the next few years.'

Wes stood before her saying nothing and Amelia Cake said, 'All right, off you go now – but don't be late in the morning. In spite of what you say, there's a lot that hasn't been tended to since you've been away.'

As Wes walked away, the widow called after him, 'While you're lying in bed tonight, think of what I've said to you about Saranna. If a thing's really worth having then it's worth fighting tooth-and-nail for.'

Wes arrived home ready for a meal and an early night in bed, only to find there was a meeting of the more militant of the farm labourers in the house.

Eli was holding forth to the others and when he saw Wes enter through the door, said joyfully, 'Glory be! The Lord must have sent Wesley here at this very moment to bring us hope. Wesley has been to London to speak to Richard Pemble, leader of the Trades Assocation there. Did you see him, Wesley? Did you speak to him of our troubles?'

'I did – and he gave me various leaflets and documents for us to read. Most of them merely say how necessary it is for every worker in the country to have an Association to take his part against the employers, but a couple of them give good advice.'

'Stand here, Wesley, on this chair. Let everyone hear what you have to say.' Eli vacated his place on the chair and motioned Wes forward.

For his part, Wes would much rather have gone straight upstairs to bed, foregoing even an evening meal, but he realised it was not to be.

He told the eager men about meeting with the Trades Association leader. He also brought in the name of Alan Pate, explaining that he was a younger man than Pemble. He added that Pate would one day play an important role in the movement which

332

appeared to be gathering momentum in other parts of the country.

'While I was talking to both men a call came for them to travel to the North of England. There was a dispute in the coal mines. The miners have formed their own Union, but they wanted the support of Richard Pemble and his Grand Association.'

There was an excited murmuring in the room. Even here, in far-off rural Dorset, the farm workers had heard about the militancy of the coal miners of the North East. If *they* had sent for Richard Pemble to help them, he must be a good man to take the part of the farm workers.

'It's one thing having all these bits of paper,' said George Loveless, waving some of them in his hand. 'But they aren't going to persuade the farmers to put our wages back up again. What do we do now?'

'I think we're going to have to wait a while longer,' said Wes. 'Before Richard Pemble left for the North he told me he'd send a couple of men from his Association to Tolpuddle. They'll want to speak with us and advise us what to do. I don't think he'll forget, but I believe we might have to wait until things are sorted out in the North.'

The news that nothing would be decided immediately did not go down too well, but it was generally agreed there was nothing else to be done. They needed the advice of men who had experience in such matters before setting up their own Association. The Union of working men had not long been made legal by Parliament. Such liberal thinking was still viewed with suspicion and worse by many landlords. Any Association needed to be seen to be well within the law. If it was not there were many men around Tolpuddle who would delight in taking swift action against them.

'I think we've come as far as we can tonight.' Eli's voice rose above the babble in the Gillam kitchen. 'We'll call a meeting again when we've all had time to study the papers Wesley has brought from London for us. The word will go around in the usual way. In the meantime, say nothing of what's gone on to any of those who employ you. Now, we've a finance committee meeting at the chapel in a few minutes. Anyone concerned please make your way there now. We're a bit behind time and don't want a long night to make us late for work in the morning, do we?'

The farm workers left the cottage in a happier frame of mind than when they arrived. Behind them, George Loveless said to Wes, 'What manner of men are these Association organisers, Wesley? Do *you* think they'll be able to do anything to help us?'

It was a question Wes wished might have been put off until he was feeling less tired and able to think more clearly.

'I'd like to say yes, but . . .'

He faltered and his father said, 'Go on, Wes, tell us honestly your opinion of these men. It's an important matter to us, remember.'

'Well . . . I'd be inclined to think very carefully about what they tell you. Both the men I met see the Association as a means of gaining a great deal of power in the land. Although I've no doubt they'll be able to advise you on setting things up, they won't be around when the trouble begins. We have to remember that the farm workers of Tolpuddle are not important enough in their scheme of things for them to risk their necks for us.'

Wes ate only a small, almost silent meal before going upstairs. He was lying in bed, looking at the ceiling, almost invisible in the dark, when there came the sound of the door opening at the foot of the stairs. A few moments later his mother's voice said softly, 'Are you awake, Wesley?'

'Yes, Ma. What is it?'

She came across the landing space to his bed and sat down on the chair. It occupied the space where Saul's bed had once been.

'I was watching you while you were eating. Is something wrong?'

When he did not reply immediately, she said, 'Something *is* wrong. Do you want to tell me about it?'

'There's nothing very wrong, Ma. Just me being foolish, that's all.'

'Foolish about what?'

'I went to Kent to see Saranna Vye while I was in London.'

Rachel's stomach contracted involuntarily. She had been aware for some time that Wes was an attractive young man who would not remain single for very much longer. All the same, this came as a great surprise.

'Well! I knew you were fond of the girl when she was here, and she of you, but I didn't think your feelings were strong enough for you to go and seek her out.'

'It couldn't be helped . . . no, that's not true. I think I knew when I went to London that I'd try to find her anyway. As it happened I didn't need to make any excuses to myself. I had to go to Richard Pemble's house to see him. He wasn't in London.'

'How is she?'

Wes was silent for a while. This reminded him of the nights when he was a young boy and would sometimes have a nightmare. His mother would sit with him and try to draw out his fears and worries.

'She's going to be married. To someone she's met in Kent.'

'Oh!' Rachel did not know whether she was relieved or disappointed. 'I wish her well. I know there were always stories going around about her when she lived at Southover, but I liked her. Has her getting married made you unhappy?'

'Yes. I've never stopped thinking about her since she left. If it hadn't been for this man, Alan, I think I might have asked her to marry me.'

Rachel gasped. 'And you've kept this quiet for these past couple of years? Why haven't you said anything? Why didn't you say something before she left these parts?'

When Wes failed to reply, Rachel said, 'Was it because you thought your pa wouldn't have agreed to your marrying her? You needn't have worried about that. I'd have been able to talk him round. Besides, once he got to know her he would have become as fond of her as I was. Oh, Wes, you are a *fool*!'

It was not said unkindly. Rachel felt the hurt in her son. He had kept his feelings to himself for all this time, then had his hopes dashed when he finally decided to do something about them!

For his part, Wes felt relieved that he had told his mother about Saranna – without revealing the true reason why he had done nothing to try to stop her when she moved to Kent.

He was also feeling guilty about the night he had spent with Polly. Altogether, this was one of the most miserable nights he could remember for a long time.

'Never mind, Wesley. Another girl will come along for you before too long. You take my word for it.'

Chapter 17

The girl whom Rachel Gillam predicted would one day 'come along', arrived much sooner than Wes would have wished.

For three months after his visit to London the farm labourers of Tolpuddle waited impatiently for the arrival of the Association officials promised by Richard Pemble. The men failed to arrive. In the meantime agitation for action grew steadily stronger.

The harvest had long been gathered in; soon threshing began. However, instead of there being plentiful work for the men and women of the area, as there had always been in the past, the hated machines had been brought in. The age-old opportunity to earn a meagre bonus from this chore was taken away from the hard-hit families.

There was also a strong rumour that there would soon be yet another cut in wages. In many cases this would bring the money coming into a household down to a mere six shillings a week.

Wes had been kept busy recording minutes of numerous angry meetings. It was of this he was thinking as he wielded a billhook on the hedge of one of Widow Cake's fields. The hedge was growing alongside the narrow lane but Wes failed to see the young girl who walked along it towards him from the direction of the village.

She was upon him before he looked up and saw her smiling. His astonishment was so great that he almost dropped the billhook to the ground.

'Hello, Wes. I bet you're surprised to see me, here in Tolpuddle?'

'Polly! How . . .? Why . . .? What are you doing here?'

'Well! There's a fine welcome after what happened the last time we met – even though you did walk out on me while I was off buying something for your breakfast. Don't I get a kiss from you? I thought you'd be pleased to see me – although you're not going to like the news I'm here to give you.'

'What news?'

He asked the question nervously. Ever since that night spent with Polly in her sister Meg's flat he had been haunted by the

336

fear that walked with every single man and woman who flouted society's rules on promiscuity.

Polly's next words made that fear a reality.

'I'm having a baby.'

Horrified, Wes asked, 'My baby?'

'What sort of question is that?' Polly asked indignantly. 'Of course it's your baby! You don't think I'd walk for nigh on a week to find you if it wasn't yours?'

Polly's words made Wes feel he was looking down a long dark tunnel that had no end. 'What ... what do you want me to do about it?'

'There's a fine question, I must say! What do you *think* I want you to do about it? First I want you to find a place for me to stay around here, and then you can set about arranging for us to be married. *That's* what I want.'

Wes was stunned by Polly's unexpected arrival and devastating news. As he struggled to assimilate the implications of her words, there came a shout from the cottage.

Standing at the gate brandishing a walking-stick, Amelia Cake demanded, 'Wesley! What do you think you're doing? I don't pay you to spend time chatting to young girls. Who is she, anyway?'

Glancing resentfully towards the other woman, Polly asked, 'Who's that old witch?'

'She's my employer.' Wes eagerly grasped the intervention of Widow Cake. 'You'd better come and meet her.'

Polly trailed after Wes reluctantly. As they approached, Amelia Cake took in the girl's cheap clothing. Polly's shoes, not made for tackling rough, unmade country lanes, were falling apart. Her dress exposed far more cleavage than any Tolpuddle girl would dare reveal. She also wore gaudy ribbons in her hair in a manner that was not usually seen outside London.

When he reached the gate, Wes said, 'Mrs Cake, this is Polly. She's from London. Her sister is a friend of Saul's. I stayed with them while I was in London.'

'Did you now?'

Amelia Cake spoke only the three short words, but Wes had the uncomfortable feeling that she knew exactly what staying with Polly and her sister had entailed.

'What part of London are you from, girl?'

'Bethnal Green. I don't suppose you've ever heard of it.'

'Then you suppose wrong. I stayed there for a while,' was the surprising reply. 'I was visiting a soldier's widow, like myself. It was when I'd just come back from the war. I can't say it's a place I'd care to live for very long. What are you doing here?'

'I came to find Wes.'

'Well, now you've found him – and stopped him working too. You'd better come inside. Wesley, carry on with what you were doing. I want that hedge finished before you go home tonight.'

Polly appeared reluctant to enter the cottage, but Amelia Cake opened the gate and waved the stick she carried at her. 'Come on, girl, you're nearly as slow as he is. I've been on my feet for too long already and there's a kettle on the boil inside.'

The next moment the cockney girl was following the widow inside the cottage. Meanwhile Wes returned to his work and attempted to gather his thoughts together.

His mind was in such turmoil that he narrowly missed striking off a finger with a blow from the stone-sharpened billhook. He made a conscious effort to pull himself together. Injuring himself now would help no one.

Wes bitterly regretted the events of the last night he had spent in London. He should have foreseen the possible outcome. It would be easy to make the excuse that he had been encouraged by Polly. It might have been true to a degree, but he was old enough to bear full responsibility for his own actions.

He would need to find somewhere for her to stay. It would mean speaking to his ma – and to Pa. Wes winced at the thought of it. He did not doubt that the Bible had a quotation on every page directed against young men who fornicated and found themselves in his situation. His father would know them all.

As he worked, Wes waited anxiously for Polly to come out of Widow Cake's cottage. When she did, he thought he might send her on to the village. To his own home. He quickly changed his mind. He would need to be there to make the explanations. Polly would have to wait until he had finished his day's work.

Much to Wes's surprise, Polly had not put in an appearance by the time the hedging was completed. It was now almost time for him to finish work for the day. All he had to do was carry a couple of heavy, fallen branches to the wood-shed, across the yard from the kitchen. Here it would remain, ready to cut up on a rainy day.

He was in the shed when he heard the kitchen door open. He braced himself as he turned, expecting to see Polly. Instead, it was Widow Cake.

Leaning on her stick in the shed doorway, she said, 'Have you finished for the day?'

'Yes, I was about to come to the house, to fetch Polly.'

'She's not going anywhere. The girl's decided to stay here, to help me. She's not a lot faster than Mary was, but she's got a tidy mind.'

Wes was filled with a mixture of relief and puzzlement. Polly was not the sort of girl to take to domestic work. He was also uncertain whether her background was such that it lent itself to working in someone else's house.

'Mrs Cake . . . I don't know very much about her. About what sort of person she is, I mean.'

'What you're trying to tell me is that you're not certain she's completely trustworthy, is that it?'

'I'm not trying to suggest that she's dishonest or anything. It's just . . . I don't know her very well, that's all.'

Amelia Cake's snort would have startled the pigs in the sty beyond the shed. 'I would have thought you knew her better than anyone else, young Wesley.'

In that moment, he was aware that either Polly had told the widow or the shrewd old lady had correctly guessed her reason for coming to Tolpuddle. He wondered how much the young cockney girl had said about all that had happened in London.

'I'd better go in and tell Polly I'm going home now.' Wes avoided looking at his employer.

'You'll do no such thing. I've left her working. You can see her in the morning.'

Wes nodded. He knew better than to try to argue with Widow Cake.

He was halfway across the yard before she called to him.

'Wesley!'

'Yes, Mrs Cake?'

'For the time being there's no need for you to say anything to your mother, or to anyone else, about Polly being here. You understand?'

Wes did *not* understand, but before he could say so, Widow Cake said, 'It doesn't matter whether you do or not. *I* don't want you to say anything to anyone. Is *that* understood?'

Wes agreed that it was.

'Good. If you want to have a talk with Polly you can get here early in the morning and have a good chat while you're showing her how to clean out the dairy. With a girl about the place, I want to start making cheese again. This time in sufficient quantity to give me a worthwhile profit. She might as well learn right away there's a sight more to living in the country than admiring the flowers and the trees. I think she might realise that life's a whole lot easier in London than it is here.'

Chapter 18

For some weeks, during which Christmas came and passed and the calendar moved on to 1833, Wes lived with the presence of Polly on his mind, day and night.

She did not make things any easier for him, although, at first her complaints were directed against Widow Cake. She worked Wes and Polly too hard; she was never satisfied; she failed to praise anything that was done for her . . .

'How is it you've put up with her for so long?' Polly asked Wes one day. It was a Sunday afternoon, the first dry week-end they had experienced for weeks. Polly had persuaded a reluctant Wes to take her for a walk.

'She's all right once you get to know and understand her.'

They were walking over the hill away from the village. This was despite Polly's wish that they might be seen together in Tolpuddle. She looked about her sulkily now. 'Where is everyone? There's not a house to be seen anywhere. Look at it, miles and miles of . . . nothing! What is there to do here?'

'Not a lot. What do you want to do?'

'Take me for a drink somewhere, Wes.' She clasped his arm. 'I haven't tasted a drop of gin since I left London.'

'You won't get a drink today. It's Sunday. There's not an inn open anywhere around here.'

'I don't want to drink at an inn. They're for old farmers and weary travellers. Isn't there a beer-house somewhere, Wes? Better still, a gin-house?'

He smiled. 'You won't find either of those around Tolpuddle. The nearest ale-house is probably at Dorchester. That's too many miles for an afternoon's walk.'

Polly dropped her hand from his arm. 'What do people do about here for a bit of fun?'

Wes thought about her question seriously for a while. 'I don't suppose we have a lot of fun, really. At least, not in the way town folk think of fun. We lead very quiet lives in the country. But there's a feast day coming up in Dorchester soon. Perhaps Widow Cake will let you go. All sorts of things happen there on that day.

They have a fair, performing bears, lots of stalls . . .'

His voice petered out as he thought of the last time he had enjoyed the entertainments a Dorchester fair had to offer. On that occasion he had shared them with Saranna.

They walked on together quietly for a while, then Polly gave him a sly, sidelong look, 'I know what we *could* do . . . we could do it here easy enough, there's no one around. Do you want to, Wes?'

The thought of what she was suggesting appealed to Wes's animal instincts, but when he looked at her much of the desire seeped away. In spite of all the efforts she was making to hide her condition, her pregnancy was beginning to show. It brought home to him the predicament he was in.

'We'd better turn back now. By the look of the clouds to the west there's rain coming in.'

Pouting as they turned back towards Widow Cake's cottage, Polly complained, 'You wouldn't have let a drop of rain put you off doing it that night in Old Nichol Street. You thought you was dying – yet you still did it.'

Wes made no reply and Polly asked suddenly and unexpectedly, 'Don't you like me any more?'

'Of course I *like* you. It's just . . . I didn't expect things to turn out like this.'

'You mean, you never thought you might one day have to marry me?'

'Yes, I suppose so,' Wes replied with painful honesty.

'Well, you *should* have thought about it. You *are* going to marry me and it had better be soon. You can do something about it this week. I want a proper wedding, mind. Standing in the church with a vicar and lots of people watching.'

Wes said nothing, but now the subject had come up, the thought of a wedding excited Polly. 'Being married to me won't be so bad, Wes. I'll look after you right. We could move back to London and let the baby be born there. Once it's arrived I'll be able to bring money into the house – so you won't have to work as hard as you do here.'

'I don't want to go to London. I hate it there. This is where I belong – and it's where you'll have to stay if you marry me.'

It was the truth. Wes's idea of hell would be to live and work in London. Whether he would enjoy Tolpuddle quite as much with Polly for a wife was another matter.

'We'll see. I'm very good at getting people to change their minds.'

They walked the remainder of the way back to Widow Cake's cottage in near-silence. When they spoke at all the initiative came from Polly and her talk was invariably about people she knew in London, all of whom were strangers to him.

The next night, unexpectedly, three barns were fired in the Tolpuddle district. The fires, too many to be accidental, took everyone by surprise. The farm workers were increasingly unhappy about their pay but nothing special had happened to provoke an incident such as this.

It was generally believed among the workers that the fires were the work of a gang of itinerant Irish labourers. They had recently spent a week in the area offering their services to farmers at rates even lower than those now being paid to local men. Eventually, after a great deal of ill-feeling had been generated, they had been run off by a group of farm workers, but not before there had been a brief but bloody fight between them.

The landlords, taking their lead from Magistrate James Frampton, took a far more serious view of the night's activities.

Frampton suggested it heralded the beginning of further agitation, similar to that which had erupted during the winter of 1831. He took immediate steps to swear in extra constables. Patrols were mounted along the lanes around Tolpuddle and all strangers found in the area were closely questioned.

Among those stopped and detained overnight were two officials of the Grand Association of Trades Unions. Richard Pemble's own Association had amalgamated with another, larger Union. This was the name by which it would henceforth be known.

Much as Magistrate Frampton would have liked to keep the two men in his cells for longer than a single night, it was not possible. Both men had alibis for the night of the arson attacks that would have stood up in any court of law. They could prove they were not in the vicinity when the barns were set ablaze. Both had been travelling to Tolpuddle from the Newcastle-upon-Tyne area when the fires were lit. Neither could be charged with any offence.

Furiously disappointed, James Frampton was forced to set them free.

When the men reached Tolpuddle they were fêted for their narrow escape but neither man felt in the mood to celebrate. They wanted only to conclude their business with the Tolpuddle farm labourers and return home as quickly as possible.

One of the men was Alan Pate.

On the evening of their release, the two Union men addressed an open meeting on Tolpuddle Green, standing beneath the same tree that had sheltered so many speakers before them.

Here, in a public place, they spoke only of the advantages to be gained by a Union of farm workers, and how such an Association had benefited other workers all over the country.

The actual details of what they should do and the form that membership should take would come later. After dark the two men would meet with a select number of would-be Trades Unionists at the home of Eli Gillam. The meeting was deliberately arranged at night, to prevent the authorities from recognising any of the men who attended and victimising them later.

Alan Pate had recognised Wes from the moment the earlier meeting opened, but he made no attempt to engage him in conversation. It was left to Wes to break the silence between them. Catching Alan Pate when he had just finished talking to the assembled farm workers, Wes asked after Saranna.

'You must know as much about Saranna as I do,' said the Trades Association official coldly. 'I have not seen her since the day I met you in Kent.'

'I left her on the same day,' said Wes. 'In fact, I was on the road while you and Saranna were still saying goodbye to each other.'

'Is that so?' Alan Pate looked at Wes in surprise. All the time he was in the North of England he had believed that Wes had stayed behind in Kent after he had left. It had rankled with him for all these months. 'You haven't heard from her since?'

'Why should I? You're the one she's supposed to be marrying.'

'I am the one she *is* marrying,' corrected Alan Pate. 'No doubt we will arrange a suitable date as soon as I return to Eltham.'

Wes was still standing with the Trades Union official when a farm worker from the Southover farm which shared Widow Cake's grazing land sidled up to him. Giving Wes a wink, he said, 'You're a dark horse, Wesley, and no mistake.'

Wes looked at the man uncertainly. 'I'm sorry, I don't know what you're talking about.'

'Go on, you may have kept it a secret 'til now, but I reckon it'll be all over the village in a day or two.'

'What will?'

'Why, the wedding between you and the young girl who's working for Widow Cake. I had to call at the cottage on my way home with a message for Widow Cake from Farmer Hooper. While I was there I got talking to the young girl – Polly, is that her name? I asked her what a young London girl like her was doing in Tolpuddle. Shouldn't have thought there was much for a girl like her, I said. But she told me she'd come here because you were going to marry her. Like I said, you've kept that very quiet. Even Widow Cake didn't seem to know anything about it when I mentioned it to her.'

'Allow me to be one of the first to congratulate you,' said Alan

Pate maliciously. 'No doubt it will be as much of a surprise to everyone at Eltham as it is here. It must be a time of year when marriage is in the air. I have some arranging of my own to do when I return. I have allowed things to take their own course for rather too long. It is high time Saranna became Mrs Pate.'

Chapter 19

The two representatives of the Grand Trades Association and six of the leading members of the proposed Tolpuddle Association sat up for much of the night. By the time dawn was threatening, they had thrashed out details of the organisation of the local branch.

It was decided they should not use the word 'Union' in their name. It was a word that was becoming increasingly popular throughout the country with the various workers' movements. Nevertheless, the two delegates from Richard Pemble advised very strongly against its use.

It had been learned by bitter experience that both landlords and employers reacted angrily to any organisation with the word 'Union' in its title.

Such a reaction was not so important in the industrial North where attitudes were more clearly defined. Disputes in that part of the country had always tended to be settled head on. Here, among agricultural workers, there was a less confrontational approach. They needed to create a different image.

It was decided their organisation should appear to be more in the nature of a 'Friendly Association', or a 'Benefit Society'. On the surface it was a minor matter; nevertheless it was one that would affect the whole future of the movement in Tolpuddle.

It was eventually agreed the Tolpuddle farm workers would call themselves 'The Friendly Society of Agricultural Labourers'.

This settled, the men went on to discuss such matters as the need for each new member to take an oath of secrecy when they joined, and the regalia to be used at the initiation ceremony.

Eli Gillam and George Loveless were not in favour of such a ceremony. Staunch Methodists, they were against what they considered to be 'unnecessary frills'. They wanted an Association that would link the farm workers in a common cause that would be to everyone's advantage, that was all.

The more experienced Union officials who had come to assist the Tolpuddle men assured them that such an initiation ceremony was necessary. It was intended to instil a sense of the importance of what they were undertaking into each new member. They pointed out that all societies of note, from the Orange Lodge presided over by the Duke of Cumberland to the smallest of Trades Associations, followed such a procedure.

Eventually, both men withdrew their objections. They could not know that the time was not far away when events would prove their misgivings to be well-founded.

Wes hurried to work the following morning, well aware he was half an hour late at least. Alan Pate and his companion had not left the Gillam cottage until sometime after four o'clock that morning.

Cautious men, they declared their intention of being well out of Dorset before the news of the meetings they had held became known to the local magistracy. They were fully aware they had stretched their luck to the limit, having already escaped prosecution at the hands of Magistrate Frampton.

Trades Associations were officially legal according to the laws of the land. In spite of this, local magistrates had an uncomfortable habit of invoking ancient and obscure by-laws. In this way they were able to shape the law to suit 'local needs', as interpreted by themselves.

'I'm sorry I'm late, Mrs Cake.' Wes had seen his employer in the cottage kitchen as he passed by the window and he paused to call in through the kitchen door. 'Pa and some friends were at the house talking until the early hours. I overslept. I'll make up the time tonight.'

He was closing the door again to begin his outside chores when she called, 'Come here, Wesley Gillam.'

Wes opened the door again, more slowly this time. He felt he knew what she wanted. All the way from home he had gone over in his mind what he was going to say to his employer about himself and Polly. The only thing he had decided was that whatever was said, it was not going to be an easy explanation.

'Before you set about anything else, I've a task for you. Go and get the pony and trap ready – and be quick about it. You're taking Polly to Dorchester to catch the eight o-clock coach to London. I wouldn't trust her to buy a ticket if I gave her the money, so I'll give it to you. You can buy it for her. Well, what's the matter with you? Don't stand there with your chin dragging on the ground. Get off and do it – and be quick, the coach won't wait for you.'

'But . . . I thought . . . How long is she going for?'

'For good. She can tell you all about it on the way to Dorchester. When you come back I'll tell you the truth of it. Go on, boy, move yourself.'

Polly was waiting for Wes by the gate when he brought the pony round to the lane at the front of the cottage. She looked pale but defiant when he lifted her tiny bundle of belongings into the trap and she stepped inside.

Amelia Cake was at the front door of the cottage to see them off, but Polly made no acknowledgement of her presence. She stared stiffly to the front when Wes flicked the long rein down across the pony's back and horse and vehicle set off along the lane.

Not until they had cleared Tolpuddle and were on the main road to Dorchester did Wes say, 'I don't understand, Polly. What's this all about? Why are you leaving?'

'Because I've had enough, that's why.'

'Enough of what?'

'Enough of you and your not wanting people to see me. I've not even met your ma and pa. Enough of that carping old bitch back there – and enough of the whole bleedin' countryside! There's nothing ever goes on here. I'm going back to London where there's a bit of life to enjoy. Cor! I'm looking forward to that first drop of gin when I get back to Old Nichol Street. I can taste it on me tongue now . . .' Polly licked her lips in anticipation.

'But what about the baby? Our baby? How are you going to manage on your own?'

'You got any money on you, to help keep me going for a while?'

'No. All I've got is the money Widow Cake's given me for your coach fare – although I don't understand why she should be paying your fare to go back home.'

'Look, if you give me that money, I'll walk home. She'll never know.'

Wes shook his head. 'I couldn't do that. But you haven't answered my question.'

'I didn't think you'd do anything to risk upsetting *her*. I don't know why I came here in the first place. I suppose I thought I might put some spark of life into you.' Polly shrugged. 'I was wrong.'

'You came here because of the baby and we still haven't sorted that out.'

'That's true, but it's my problem, Wes, not yours.'

Polly looked at Wes with an expression that could best be described as kindly contempt. 'You really believed the baby was yours, didn't you? I think you'd have married me, given enough time, even though you didn't want to.'

'You mean the baby *isn't* mine? But . . . that night?'

'Don't flatter yourself you was the first, Wesley Gillam. You weren't, no, nor the last. If I had to make a guess I'd say the baby's father is my stepfather, but I couldn't be sure of that, neither.'

Polly shrugged. 'I might have got away with it if it hadn't been for that crafty old bitch back in Tolpuddle. Got to admire her, though, she didn't beat about the bush. Came straight out and said she knew the baby couldn't have been yours. Said she knew just by looking at me that I was at least a couple of months farther gone than I was making out. Said she wouldn't let you marry me and it was no good my trying to blame you for it. She swore that if I did she'd have me up before the magistrate if the baby came so much as a day before I said it was due.'

They were on the outskirts of Dorchester before Wes said, 'Would you really have have kept me believing the baby was mine and made me marry you?'

'I might have done if you'd agreed to come back to London with me. I could never have spent the rest of my life living down here in the country.'

Polly gave Wes a wan smile. 'But we'll never know now, will we? Never know whether we might just have made a go of things.'

Wes watched the coach pull out of the Dorchester inn yard with Polly on board and he felt as though a great weight had been lifted from his shoulders. Life held some hope for him once more.

But first he had to return to Tolpuddle and face Widow Cake.

Chapter 20

Wes slept well that night for the first time in many weeks. During supper, Rachel Gillam told him he looked as happy as a dog who had stolen a large bone.

'I suppose it's got nothing to do with this foolish rumour about you and that new girl who's working at Widow Cake's house these days? Someone even told me in the village today she'd heard you were going to marry the girl! I think perhaps I ought to meet her and see for myself what she's like.'

'I don't know where folk have got such an idea, Ma. Anyway, you can tell them all they're wrong. Polly has gone back to London. I think she found things too quiet here in Tolpuddle.'

Wes had received a surprisingly mild reproof from Widow Cake when he returned to the cottage after seeing Polly off on the London-bound coach. She said only that he was foolish to get mixed up with a girl of Polly's 'type'.

The Tolpuddle widow seemed far more concerned with Wes's possible involvement with the newly formed Tolpuddle branch of the Friendly Society of Agricultural Workers.

When Wes asked her how she had learned of the new Society, Amelia Cake replied scornfully, 'Bless you, boy, you didn't think it could be kept a secret in a village like Tolpuddle, did you? Farmer Hooper told me all about it when he was here last night.'

The Southover farmer had called on Amelia Cake the previous evening to discuss grass keep for his cows on her land during the ensuing year.

'It's no secret that your father and the Loveless family are heavily involved. Everyone knows too about the men who came to speak about starting a Union here. If the farmers know about it, then so too does Magistrate Frampton – and he won't turn a blind eye to what's going on. It's just the sort of situation he would like to get involved in. A Union of farm workers being organised by Methodists! As for bringing men from London to tell everyone what to do . . .! I don't know who thought that one up. Their ways up in London are different to ours, whether they be men or women. *You* should have learned that lesson. At least, I hope you have. I don't want any more young girls coming knocking at my door looking for you – and I don't want constables, neither. I've come to rely on you, Wesley. Don't let me down.'

The mood of the Tolpuddle farm workers was in sharp contrast to the gloomy prognosis of Widow Cake. There was a distinct air of buoyancy abroad. The workers had heard the Association men from England's capital city confirm all their own leaders had told them of the benefits to be gained from union with their fellow workers.

To the unsophisticated farm workers it seemed all their troubles would soon be brought to a speedy end. All they had to do was join the Friendly Society of Agricultural Workers. They were about to become a force strong enough to put an end to the humiliation to which they had been subjected in recent years.

A man would once more earn enough to support his family. He could put behind him the indignity of having to beg for money from the parish.

Unfortunately for the farm workers, a few influential men had very different ideas.

One such man was Magistrate James Frampton of Moreton House. Another was Lord Melbourne, the Home Secretary – and soon to become Prime Minister of Great Britain.

Melbourne had long viewed the Union movement with alarm and suspicion. Soon after taking office he had appointed a professor of an Oxford college to investigate the Trades Unions and report on their activities.

The report was duly completed and submitted to Melbourne. It recommended that everything possible should be done to stamp out the spread of Trades Unionism.

The link between Frampton and Lord Melbourne was William Ponsonby, a gentleman of considerable means who lived in Dorset. Ponsonby was brother to the late wife of Lord Melbourne. Through him, Melbourne was considerably involved in Dorset affairs.

Consequently, the Home Secretary took more than a passing interest in the matter when James Frampton wrote to him, expressing concern at the sudden upsurge of Union activity in the Tolpuddle region. The magistrate asked the Home Secretary's advice on the matter.

The stage was being set for an incident that would bring the small Dorset village to the forefront of national affairs. It would also catapult a handful of villagers into the annals of Trades Union history.

None of this was in the mind of Wes as he cleaned out the cow-shed behind Widow Cake's cottage a few days after Polly had returned to London. It was a cold, dreary day. Wes was thinking of nothing more exciting than whether to wean one of the calves from its mother that day, or wait until the next.

Suddenly, he thought he heard Widow Cake calling to him from the house. He stopped and went to the door of the cow-shed and then he heard the call again.

'Wesley! WESLEY! Come quickly, boy.'

Dropping the long fork he was wielding, Wes ran towards the house. It sounded as though Amelia Cake was in some distress.

The widow called again as he crossed the yard and this time he shouted in reply, to let her know he was on his way.

He found his employer lying in a pool of water on the floor of the kitchen, her face contorted in agony. Beside her a heavy, cast-iron kettle lay on its side, steam rising from the small amount of water that still remained inside.

'Help me to settle in the other room, Wesley. Then go and fetch your mother for me. She's as good as anyone in the village . . . Oh! Mind my foot. The right one. I've scalded them both, but I dropped the kettle on that one. I . . . think I've broken something.'

'You shouldn't have tried to lift the kettle on your own. You should have called for me . . .'

'Don't you tell me what I should be doing in my own home, Wesley Gillam. What I should have is someone living in the house to look after me. But I haven't, so I've got to get on with things for myself.'

Amelia Cake was a heavy woman but Wes eventually succeeded in getting her from the kitchen to the other room and laying her back on the settle. Her right foot was bleeding and appeared to be badly swollen, but the suffering widow would not allow him to look at it.

'Just leave me and fetch your mother. She's probably the most sensible woman in the village, for all that she's married to that Methodist father of yours. Go on now – and run all the way. I don't want to suffer this pain for a moment longer than I have to.'

Out of breath when he arrived at East Farm, where his mother was working, Wes blurted out his tale to her and the farmer who employed her.

'How bad is it?' the farmer asked gravely.

'I don't know, she wouldn't let me look at her feet, but the water must have been boiling and it was a heavy kettle. She reckoned she'd broken something.'

'You get on up to the cottage,' the farmer said to Rachel Gillam. 'Amelia Cake probably won't thank me for it, but I'll send one of the boys on a horse to fetch a doctor from Dorchester.'

The doctor reached Tolpuddle late that afternoon. He confirmed that Amelia Cake had broken one, possibly two, bones in her foot. She was also badly scalded and cut, although Wes's mother had already treated both cut and scalds.

Amelia Cake refused to retire to her bedroom. At her insistence, Wes brought her bed down to the front downstairs room of the cottage. Here, from her bed, the injured widow could see from the window to the front gate and the lane beyond. This way she felt she would retain at least some control over what went on in and about her cottage.

'I don't know how we're going to look after her though.'

Rachel was talking to her son in the kitchen after the doctor had left. She was cooking a meal for Amelia Cake before she too went home.

'I'll stay here tonight,' said Wes. 'I'll at least be to hand if she needs anything in the night.'

'That's all very well,' said his mother. 'But what she really wants is a girl living in to tend to her needs. There are some things you won't be able to do for her. It's a pity that other girl left in such a hurry. Widow Cake could have done with her here now.'

'I expect we'll manage,' said Wes, steering the conversation away from Polly quickly. 'Perhaps you could call in tomorrow, before you go to work at East Farm? Leave something that I can heat up for her dinner – and for me, come to that.'

'I'll do what I can,' agreed Rachel. 'But I'm looking after a sick woman at East Farm, and I can't afford to let my work there suffer. We need the money coming in the way things are at the moment.'

'We'll manage,' said Wes. 'You'll see.'

Later that night he went quietly around the house as it grew dark, lighting candles in the hall and kitchen. Putting his head around the front room door he peered in to see if his employer was sleeping or awake. He had lit a fire in the room and could just see her.

At first he thought she slept, but as he was closing the door again, she called to him, 'Wesley, what are you up to? Come in here and light the lamp. I want to have a chat with you.'

Widow Cake's words sounded ominous. As he lit a taper from the fire and transferred a flame to the lamp, Wes wondered what she was going to say. It had become apparent to him for some time that his employer was becoming more infirm with every month that passed. More than once he had wondered what she would do when she no longer felt able to look after herself.

The latest accident had probably brought the matter home to her. She had been lying here alone for some hours. No doubt she had been thinking hard. Amelia Cake did not like wasting time. He wondered whether she had perhaps reached some decision on her future. If she sold up she would probably have enough money to go somewhere and be looked after in a modest fashion for the rest of her years.

Wes wondered where this would leave him.

'Is there any writing stuff about the house, Wesley?'

'Yes, there's some in a drawer in here. With the book in which I've been keeping your accounts.'

'Fetch it out – and quickly now. I want you to write a letter for me.'

This would be the moment. No doubt she wanted to write to enquire about someone taking her in. Wes fetched the writing things and laid them out on the table close to her bed. Then he drew up a chair and prepared to write.

'Are you ready?'

He nodded.

'All right, take this down. "I have recently had a nasty fall and burned and broken my foot. The result is that I'm now stuck in bed in my cottage. It's most inconvenient, especially as there is no one in Tolpuddle willing or able to look after me. I would be very grateful if you would consider coming to take care of me for a while, until I am back on my feet again. I know it might be inconvenient, but I would pay you well for your trouble. Thank you, Amelia Cake." How does that sound to you, Wesley?'

Wes had been writing at great speed, now he said nothing until he had the last words written down.

'That's fine, Mrs Cake. The only thing you've left out is the name. Who do I send it to?'

'Well, who do you think? There's only one person I know who could look after me properly. It's to Saranna, of course. Get it off to her first thing tomorrow. You've got her address.'

Chapter 21

After the months he had spent in the North of England, followed by the brief visit to Tolpuddle, Alan Pate returned to Eltham village tired but elated.

The situation in the North of England had been potentially very explosive and the leaders of the local Union were surprised to see the Union leader. They told Pate they had warned Richard Pemble it would be dangerous for any of the men from the London headquarters to be seen with them. If there was a confrontation with the employers – as seemed extremely likely at the time – the Southern officials would undoubtedly be blamed for the troubles.

Richard Pemble had not passed this information on to his deputy and Alan Pate knew it had not been an oversight. During the years he had been working as deputy to Pemble he had steadily gained in influence within the Union movement. This did not suit the senior man's own ambitions.

Richard Pemble hoped one day to become the undisputed leader of a national organisation that would have both strength and influence in the affairs of the country. Once his own Association was consolidated with other Unions it would make him a very powerful man indeed. It was possible he had decided the time had come to cut off the only man who might challenge his leadership.

Richard Pemble's ploy failed. Alan Pate succeeded in cooling the situation in the North and gaining the respect of the working men there. He even won a few grudging minor concessions from the employers.

Because of what he knew and suspected, there was a coolness between the two men when Pate returned to Eltham. However, they spoke at some length about Union affairs as he unpacked his bags.

Eventually, Alan Pate asked after Saranna.

'I'll call and speak to her as soon as I can. It's time we settled on a date for our wedding.'

'I'm very pleased to hear you say so,' said Richard Pemble

hypocritically. 'I'm sure Saranna will be too. I know she is anxious to speak to you. Come to the house for supper this evening. You two can have a chat then.'

Alan Pate went to the Pemble house for supper that evening. In the meantime, two representatives of a Thames Seamen's Assocation had arrived. They wished to discuss bringing their own Union under the umbrella of the larger organisation. As the men sat about the table discussing their business it became clear they would be talking until well into the night.

It was late in the evening when Alan Pate made his way to the kitchen where Nancy and Saranna were still working.

'I had been hoping to have a serious, uninterrupted talk with you this evening,' Pate said to Saranna. 'I would like to discuss our wedding arrangements with you.'

'I was hoping we might have an opportunity this evening to speak about our future. Perhaps we could take a walk somewhere, away from the house?'

'There's no time tonight. We're discussing important Union business in the other room. But what do you mean "speak about our future"? We both know what that is. It is merely a question of agreeing a time and place for the wedding.'

'No, there's more to it than that, Alan. I've been doing a lot of thinking . . . but we can't talk about it here.'

Alan Pate frowned. In his mind he had already arranged the future. Their wedding would take place in three months' time. Once they were married they would move in with his mother. He had formulated the duties Saranna should take on as his wife. He wanted to discuss them with her, but they would need to wait for another day.

He was an ambitious man. Saranna was already aware of this, of course. She would be pleased to know she had a part to play in his plans for the future. Saranna had already learned some of the social graces she would need as his wife. He prided himself that he could take credit for these improvements.

The fact that Saranna was Pemble's step-daughter would be of initial advantage to him too, of course, but one day Pate intended ousting the present leader and taking his place. He needed to impress upon her that her loyalties lay with him and not with her stepfather.

'I'll see if I can find the time for us to talk later tonight.'

Saranna shrugged. 'Don't put yourself out for me.'

As Alan Pate was leaving the kitchen carrying a jug of ale for his companions, he paused. 'By the way, before coming home I visited Tolpuddle, to advise them on a Union matter. While I was there I met young Gillam, the lad who visited here just before I went away. It seems he's getting married too. Rather soon, I believe.'

Having made this announcement, Alan Pate left the kitchen – but not before he had seen the effect his news had upon Saranna. Whatever she had said to the contrary, he was convinced there *had* been something between her and Wesley Gillam when she was living at Southover. He would insist she told him the truth once they were married. However, he did not intend allowing it to cause a hiccough in his plans for their marriage.

Alan Pate did not find the time to speak to Saranna that night and he spent the next few days in London. He was not deliberately putting off the discussion – but neither was he in any great hurry. He wanted the news of Wesley Gillam's impending marriage to thoroughly sink in before he discussed the future with Saranna. He believed she would then be more amenable to the suggestions he intended putting to her.

Seated in the kitchen of his Eltham village home, Richard Pemble was inspecting a large batch of letters which had arrived that morning. Drinking a cup of tea, he chatted to Nancy and Saranna. Nancy was baking bread while Saranna was cleaning a number of fire-blackened pots in a wooden tub.

Opening one of the letters, Richard Pemble read it and frowned. Turning it over, his puzzled look disappeared. 'I wondered what this was all about. It's not one of my letters at all. It's addressed to you, Saranna.'

As Richard held out the letter, Saranna brushed back a hank of hair trying not to touch her face with the dirty hand. 'Who's writing to me?'

'It's signed by Amelia Cake.'

'Widow Cake?' In her excitement, Saranna forgot her dirty hand. The second attempt to brush back her errant hair left a black smear on cheek and nose.

'What does she say? Is something wrong with . . . any of them? Read it to me, Richard.'

As Richard Pemble read the letter to her, Saranna knew Wes must have written it on behalf of the Tolpuddle widow and she tried to read a message from him into it. However, no matter how hard she tried, she could find no hidden meaning in the wording of the letter.

Nevertheless, the plea was clear enough, whether it came from Wes or from the injured widow.

'Poor Widow Cake, she does sound as though things are going badly for her at the moment. She must be really desperate to ask me to go back to her, after all this time.'

'Are you sure it's Widow Cake who wants you in Tolpuddle and not Wes Gillam?'

The thought had not occurred to Saranna. It did now and for a few moments she became excited. Then she remembered.

'Wes won't care whether I go to Tolpuddle or not. He's getting married. You heard Alan say so the other night.'

'You don't think Alan might have had a reason for telling you that Wes is going to be married?'

'No, I don't. The thought did occur to me, but I believe he was telling the truth. I'm sure he took great pleasure in telling me about it, but I don't think he would tell an out and out lie.'

'Are things all right between you and Alan? You are still going to marry him?' Richard put the question to his step-daughter.

Mother and daughter exchanged glances before Saranna replied to his question. 'No, Richard, I've decided not to marry him. I made my mind up while he was away. I wanted to tell him as soon as he returned, but he hasn't stayed around long enough for us to have a talk – about anything.'

'He's going to be very disappointed. I understand he's done everything except organise the vicar and invite the guests.'

'That's his fault. He should have spoken to me first,' Saranna said sharply. Looking across the room at her stepfather, she asked: 'You'll not be cross with me for turning him down, Richard?'

'Not at all. It makes life a lot easier for me, as a matter of fact. Alan Pate is becoming rather too large for his boots. I might need to cut him down to size. That would prove difficult if he were married to you.' He grinned. 'You're really doing me a favour – yourself as well, I don't doubt.

'Having sorted that out, what do you intend doing about Widow Cake's letter?'

Saranna brushed back her hair once more, leaving yet another black mark on her face. 'As soon as I've finished with this pot, I'll wash and get ready. I've nothing to lose by going to Tolpuddle – and there might be a whole lot to gain.'

Chapter 22

While Saranna was having the letter from Amelia Cake read to her in Eltham village, a letter of a very different kind was being composed in the study of Moreton House in Dorset.

Magistrate James Frampton had made many false starts, as the pieces of screwed-up paper strewn around the waste basket testified, but he persevered.

He did not find the right words until the sonorous tones of the luncheon gong resounded through the house. Frowning in concentration, James Frampton ignored the summons.

Some five minutes later Josephine came upstairs to his study. 'Luncheon is ready, Grandfather. Did you not hear the gong?'

'I heard it, but I am very busy. You and the others go ahead without me. I will have something to eat when I have finished here. This is urgent.'

As he was talking, Josephine had been picking up the incomplete letters and placing them in the basket. One was almost a full page and before placing it in the basket she read what was written with uninhibited curiosity.

'My word, you are corresponding with important people these days, Grandfather. Writing to the Home Secretary, no less!'

'Josephine! That is a confidential letter about a very serious matter.'

'I can see that.' She continued reading, unabashed by her grandfather's admonition. 'And I agree with you. You seem to be the only one in the district who is aware of the dangers of allowing the Tolpuddle men to carry on their plotting unhindered. Do you believe many of the villagers are involved?'

Pleased with the interest Josephine appeared to be taking in the matter of the Tolpuddle Unionists, James Frampton replied, 'From the information I have been gathering, it would appear to implicate practically every labourer in the place. It is so serious I am seeking the advice of Lord Melbourne on the matter.

'The Gillam family are involved in all that's going on, no doubt?'

James Frampton looked at her suspiciously. He had been so

relieved at her safe return to Moreton there had been no more talk of sending her and her mother to the house he owned on Dartmoor. Nevertheless, it did not mean the incident involving the Gillam boy had been forgotten.

'What do you know about their involvement in a Union?'

'Only what I've heard the servants saying. The youngest Gillam is undoubtedly responsible for a whole lot of the agitation that is taking place. He always was a trouble-maker. I took much of the blame for what was supposed to have happened in the garden all those years ago because I knew a lot about what had gone on between him and poor Fanny Warren. I kept silent rather than get her into trouble.'

Time had clouded many of James Frampton's memories of Josephine's lies and indiscretions. She was once more the grand-daughter on whom he had always doted. He also believed she had a clearer idea of truth and integrity than the farm labourer son of a Methodist preacher.

'If you hear anything specific about the activities of that particular young man, let me know immediately. The liberal law-makers at Westminster may have made it easier for those involved in Trades Associations to stir up trouble, but they are not going to get away with their ways in Dorset. It only needs one man to overstep the line and I will make an example of him that will cause every other farm worker to think twice before helping to stir up trouble in my area. Fortunately, in Lord Melbourne we have a Home Secretary who is like-minded. I await his reply and advice, with great interest. Now, run away and get your lunch. Tell the others I will have mine when this letter is completed.'

Josephine went away well satisfied with the seed she had sown in her grandfather's mind about the Gillams. She would like to have mentioned something about the activities of Wesley Gillam's elder brother, but had stopped short of naming Saul. Josephine was very much aware it was vitally important for her own well-being that no one looked too closely into the activities of the late Saul Gillam.

Josephine would not breathe easily until Saul's brother was out of the way. She believed it might merely be a matter of time now. A bold-eyed young footman had recently been taken on at Moreton House. His home was in Tolpuddle and he enjoyed talking to Josephine and telling her what was happening there. She would express particular interest in what Wesley Gillam was doing these days. The infatuated footman would do the rest.

Although his father was actively involved in the work of the Tolpuddle Friendly Society of Agricultural Workers, Wes had declined to join the Union. He had taken on a great deal of the paperwork for the organisation, but he was almost unique in not having had his wages reduced over recent years. Indeed, Wes was now earning ten shillings a week from Widow Cake, more than any other man in the village.

Because of this, he did not mind putting in extra hours now while she was off her feet at home. She really needed a woman to be in the house full-time to tend to her needs, but there did not seem to be a suitable one in the village. At least, not a woman who suited Amelia Cake.

Rachel Gillam tried to spend at least a couple of hours a day in the widow's house, but it was not enough to do all that was needed.

Every evening Wes took Amelia Cake a meal cooked by his mother. Before leaving again he built up the fires and ensured that all was in order.

This left him with little time at the moment to devote to Union affairs. He was not entirely sorry. He could see the need for a Union, it was the only possible means the farm workers had of standing up to their employers, but Wes was not happy with the way initiation into the Union was being conducted.

Due to the number of staunch Methodists involved in the Society it was hardly surprising that new members were obliged to call upon God to guide their activities. They were also obliged to denounce violence, obscenity and bad language.

Wes found these regulations quite acceptable. However, the Trades Association advisors from London had insisted upon a joining ritual with which he could not agree. A secret initiation ceremony.

The initiates were blindfolded and led into a room in which were placed certain awesome objects. These included a full-size painting of a skeleton, a sword and a Bible. Initiates were then prepared for the ceremony by a number of solemn-faced Society officials dressed in white surplices.

During the ceremony they were obliged to repeat various prayers and promises. Finally, they placed their right hand upon a Bible and swore an oath never to disclose any matters concerning the Society to anyone outside the organisation. When the ceremony was satisfactorily concluded, the men were officially declared members of the Tolpuddle Friendly Society of Labourers.

Those Methodists among the officials were uneasy about the form of the oath of secrecy. However, as it followed the pattern set for every Union Lodge in the country, they complied with the suggested format.

Wes could not attend any of the Society meetings because he had not taken the oath. Only afterwards would he be given the names of new members and carefully enter them in a ledger. Beside each name he would note whether or not they had been able to afford the one shilling joining fee.

The Tolpuddle Friendly Society was gaining in strength but as yet no one knew where their new allegiance was likely to take them. It was a game of which few men knew the rules. Those who thought they did never expected to be required seriously to oppose their employers.

Chapter 23

'I think I'll take a walk to the cottage and make sure Widow Cake's all right, Ma.'

Wes had brought in a final armful of logs from the wood-shed and stacked them beside the kitchen fireplace in readiness for the next day. Now he reached down his coat from the back of the door.

'Going up there at this time of night?' It was almost nine o'clock on a dark, winter night. 'If she's fast asleep she won't thank you for waking her. Besides, it's no more than three hours or so since you got home.'

'I know, but she didn't seem too good today. With you not being able to get up there for the last couple of days, she feels things are not getting done about the house. It worries her. I don't expect to be too long. If the light's out I won't even bother to go in.'

'She shouldn't need to rely on you helping about the house as well as doing your own work. She should get one of the girls from the village to stay up there with her until she's got back on her feet again.'

Wes smiled. 'That's what I've told her. Trouble is, she doesn't want those who are willing to work for her. Those she would have, refuse to go up there.'

'It's entirely her own fault,' declared Rachel. 'If she wasn't such a cantankerous old woman she wouldn't have such a problem.'

Slipping his arms into the sleeves of his coat, Wes said, 'Widow Cake's all right, Ma. She just needs a bit of understanding, that's all.'

Outside the door, he shrugged the coat collar up about his ears. It was going to be a cold night. There was a hint of rain in the air too.

As he walked up the hill, away from the village, Wes thought about his employer. Deep down, he was very fond of the irascible old lady and he worried about her. This latest set-back in her physical well-being had hit her very hard. She had not yet begun to rise above it in her usual, forceful way.

There was another aspect to her infirmity that he tried hard not to think about. If anything happened to her, or if she decided to sell up and live quietly somewhere else with someone to look after her, he would be out of work. The cottage and land would doubtless be bought up by neighbouring farmers.

If he were not working for Widow Cake, Wes would need to face the problem that had dogged Saul all his life: the difficulty in obtaining work because he was Eli Gillam's son. He would probably have to take a similar course to Saul and leave Tolpuddle.

Wes wondered where he would go. Certainly not to London. He would be hopelessly out of place among its maze of narrow streets constantly surrounded by bustle and noise.

All the same, Wes realised he was becoming increasingly isolated from those of his own age who lived in Tolpuddle. Only the previous week a young man who had been a childhood friend had married the miller's daughter and was likely to be a father before another two months had passed. Wes had known both of them well at one time, yet he had not even known they were courting.

Working for Widow Cake was partly to blame for his increasing isolation from village life and the friends he had there. The cottage was well outside the village and he worked long hours for his employer.

When he was at home there was a great deal of paperwork to be done for the recently formed Friendly Society. This entailed a degree of secrecy that added to his isolation from the other young men and women in Tolpuddle.

All these thoughts were going through Wes's mind as he neared Widow Cake's cottage. In truth, he was beginning to feel a sense of loneliness in his life.

The cottage came into view as he passed a small clump of trees, and Wes frowned. Not only did Amelia Cake appear to be still awake, but there were lights burning in all the downstairs rooms. This was most unexpected. Widow Cake could move from room to room, but only with great difficulty and in considerable pain. Wes always tried to leave everything she would need close at hand, so she did not have to move from the downstairs room where she slept.

As Wes drew closer he could see there was a lamp lit in the kitchen. Amelia Cake was certainly not up to doing anything in there. It would be dangerous for her to try to move the heavy pots and kettles even if she were not handicapped by the broken bones in her foot.

He had told her on more than one occasion that she must stay out of the kitchen. She did not like being ordered about, especially in her own house, but it was for her own good.

It was in this positive frame of mind that Wes entered the

cottage through the kitchen door. The lamp was on the table and the fire was burning brightly. In addition, the heavy kettle that had been the cause of Widow Cake's injury steamed gently on the hob.

For Widow Cake to have shifted the kettle in her condition would have been foolhardy and might well have proved fatal.

Amelia Cake might be angry with him for saying so, but she needed to be told in no uncertain terms.

'Mrs Cake! Where are you?'

Wes stormed from the kitchen to her makeshift bedroom. Giving a peremptory knock on the door, he opened it and walked inside without waiting for his employer's reply.

'Mrs Cake, have you been in the . . .?' Wes came to a halt and his jaw dropped open in utter astonishment. Amelia Cake was not alone.

'Saranna!'

Wes's amazement changed momentarily to an expression of sheer joy that made Saranna's heart leap. It also silenced the rebuke that Amelia Cake was about to deliver to Wes for entering her room in such a fashion.

'Hello, Wes.'

'When did you arrive? How . . .?'

'It must have been just after you finished work. There was an obliging driver on the coach from London. He dropped me off at Milborne St Andrew. I walked over the hill.'

'You young people might have the energy to spend half the night talking. I'm an invalid who needs some sleep, so you can go off and leave me in peace. What are you doing here anyway, Wesley? Why aren't you at home instead of wandering about the countryside at night?'

'I came to see how you were. I didn't think you were as well today as you should be.'

'Is it any wonder, when there's not a soul in Tolpuddle cares if I'm alive or dead? No one to come in to clean the house for me, or see if there's anything I want. I haven't even had a visit from Reverend Warren.'

'Well, you'll be all right now that Saranna's here.' The smile suddenly vanished from Wes's face. 'You are staying Saranna? For how long?'

'For as long as I'm needed,' she said, ambiguously.

'And while she's here, she'll be putting in a full day's work, Wesley Gillam. Don't get tiring her out tonight with all your fool questions.'

Turning to Saranna, she said, 'Seeing he's here, you might as well make him a cup of tea and then he can go home. Off you go now, the pair of you. I'm tired and I want to sleep – and snuff that candle as you go. Come the end of the week I'll not have one left in the house.'

Wes added two logs to the fire in Amelia Cake's bedroom before snuffing the candle and leaving. When he reached the kitchen Saranna had two cups of tea poured.

Handing the cup to Wes, she said, 'It's comforting to know there are some things in life that remain the same. Widow Cake is one of them.'

'She's older now,' said Wes. 'And I fancy her tongue has lost a lot of its edge. But how about you? Have you married Alan Pate yet?' He looked for a ring on her finger, but she had her hands clasped in such a way he could not see the fingers of her left hand. 'Doesn't he mind you coming to Tolpuddle to take care of Widow Cake?' A sudden thought came to him. 'That is why you're here? To look after her for a while?'

'That's right. I came in answer to her letter. I expect it was you who wrote it?'

Wes nodded. After a few minutes of silence, he said, 'You still haven't answered my questions . . . about Alan Pate?'

'No, I'm not married to Alan Pate yet. As for him minding . . . I don't know. He was so busy before I came away I never had time to discuss it with him. There was no time to discuss anything.'

Now it was her turn to ask the questions. 'How about you? When Alan came back to Eltham after being here he said you were to be married. Is it to a village girl?'

Saranna's question took Wes by surprise. He had forgotten all about Polly already. 'I . . . no, I'm not getting married. He was just repeating a stupid rumour that someone was putting around at the time.'

They sat in silence for a while before Wes said suddenly, 'I'm not thinking. You've had a long day and must be tired. As you said, Widow Cake doesn't change. She'll still expect you to be up and working at dawn tomorrow.'

'I will be. Is there anything I should know before tomorrow morning, Wes? Are there any extra things to be done? How about the dairy?'

'I'll tell you all about that in the morning. I've been doing most of it just lately. I'll carry on until you've got used to what's happening.'

Wes put his cup down on the table and stood fidgeting awkwardly for a few moments. Finally moving off towards the door, he paused to turn and say, 'It really is good to have you back here, Saranna. Things will start getting better now, I know they will.'

'Widow Cake came as close as she knows how to welcoming me

with open arms when I arrived. It's nice to feel wanted and . . . I'm happy to be back here too.'

Wes walked home feeling happier than he could remember for years. Saranna was back in Tolpuddle, in Widow Cake's cottage – and she was unmarried. In the space of little more than an hour his feeling of loneliness had disappeared and hope had taken its place.

Chapter 24

Saranna's return to Tolpuddle to work for Widow Cake meant life became very much easier for Wes. She took on much of the dairy work, as well as feeding the chickens and the various animals.

It was winter and there was not so much work to be done around the fields. Consequently, Wes spent more of his time closer to the house, cutting and splitting logs and carrying out repairs to the outbuildings. He was aware that there was now a degree of organisation inside the house that had been lacking for a long time.

Wes saw Saranna on a number of occasions each day. She brought him tea during morning and afternoon and, at midday, there would be hot soup awaiting him in the kitchen.

Whenever the opportunity arose they talked a great deal about their lives during the two years they had been apart. It was like gathering the fragments of a picture that had been torn into many pieces and scattered. Putting them together gradually, two whole pictures began to emerge. There were still many fragments missing, but enough had been gathered for each to have an idea what life had been like for the other.

If there was a common theme, it was a sense of the loneliness they had both experienced. This was so even though, in Saranna's case, there had been a constant flow of visitors through the Pemble house in Eltham village.

Wes gained the impression too that the agreement to marry Alan Pate had evolved more from a desire to belong somewhere, rather than a genuine love for the man she was to marry.

The only thing Wes was unable to establish with any clarity was whether the proposed marriage between Pate and Saranna would still take place.

However, unlike the time when Wes thought Saranna was Saul's girl, he felt he owed no debt of honour to Alan Pate.

Wes's new-found sense of contentment had not passed unnoticed at home and Rachel Gillam was shrewd enough to guess the reason.

'How are things going up at Widow Cake's now?' She put the question on one of the rare occasions when the two men in her family were sitting down to supper together in the kitchen of their small house.

'Fine now Saranna is there. There's hardly been a grumble from Widow Cake and the house and dairy are clean and working well. Not only that, I'm getting hot drinks from the house during the day. Things have never been better.'

'Good. It's about time there was someone permanent up there to take care of things.'

'I don't know how permanent the arrangement is. Saranna's certainly here until Widow Cake's foot has healed. After that, I don't know. I believe she has some ties back in Kent.'

'What sort of "ties"?' Rachel noticed that some of the cheerfulness had deserted her son as he spoke.

'I think she's expected to marry someone – Alan Pate, one of the men who came down here on Association business.'

'Him? Why, he must be at least twice her age.'

'Yes, he is. I don't think she really wants to marry him.'

'Has she told you so?'

'No, she hasn't said very much about him. Anyway, it stands to reason that she can't be all that keen on him. If she was, she wouldn't be here now.'

Rachel suspected that Saranna Vye may have had other reasons for coming to Tolpuddle. Reasons to do with Wes . . . but Eli was talking.

'Isn't she the girl our Saul was mixed up with? The one who used to live over at Southover?'

'She wasn't "mixed up" with Saul. He was friendly with both Saranna and her mother.' Rachel thought there was a little too much heat in Wes's reply.

'All the same, I think the best thing you could do would be to stay well clear of the girl. I seem to remember she had something of an unsavoury reputation.'

Aware of Wes's sudden anger, Rachel said hastily, 'And I seem to remember that was no more than malicious village gossip. Probably put about by someone with a daughter who couldn't match Saranna Vye for either looks or brightness. I took a liking to the girl when I met her. She must get very lonely up there with only a crotchety old lady for company most of the time. Invite her home here one evening, Wes. Make it this Friday. She can get Widow Cake's supper and come here to eat with us. It will be nice for her to enjoy a pleasant family evening, for a change.'

'I won't be here on Friday evening,' said Eli. 'There's a meeting of circuit preachers, over at Puddletown.'

'I know,' said Rachel. 'That's why I suggested Friday. I want the girl to be able to relax while she's here – not feel she needs to watch everything she says, for fear you won't approve.'

'You must meet her sometime though, Pa,' said Wes hastily before his father took offence. 'Not only is she a very nice girl, but her stepfather is Richard Pemble. She probably knows more about Trades Unions than any man around here.'

'We know all we need to in Tolpuddle,' said Eli pompously. 'We don't intend to change the world as some of these big city Trades Associations – or Unions, as they like to call themselves now – seem to want. All we're after is fair pay for a good day's work. If the only way we can get it is by forming a Trades Association, then that's what we'll do, but no more than that . . . Talking of the Association, we've a meeting to swear in some new members tonight. I'll give you the details for the ledger later. Why don't you take this opportunity to come along and join as well?'

'You know the answer to that, Pa. I'll not join any Association while I'm working for Widow Cake. If every farmer looked after their workers as well as she looks after me there'd be no need for any Association.'

'That's true. I don't mind admitting that I'd rather be gathering men to go about the Lord's business than asking them to swear an oath to take action against their employers if the occasion arises.'

After his father had left the house, Wes felt restless. He wandered about the kitchen, putting a log on the fire although it was not needed and staring through the window into the darkness outside. Eventually, he said, 'I meant to bring Widow Cake's ledger home tonight to do some work on it. I think I'll just go up to the cottage and fetch it.'

'To fetch the ledger? Or is that just an excuse to go up there and see Saranna Vye?'

'The ledger needs bringing up to date. I should have done it a week ago. It was overlooked in the excitement of Saranna coming back.'

'You like this girl, don't you, Wes?'

After a moment's hesitation, he said, 'Yes, I do, Ma. I like her a lot.'

'Does she feel the same way about you? But no, she can't if she's to marry another man.'

'I don't know how she feels, Ma. We haven't spoken very much about it.'

'Well, don't get too fond of her, Wes. Not just yet. I don't want to see you hurt.'

As he set off in the darkness for Widow Cake's cottage, Wes thought his mother's warning had probably come too late. He had fallen in love with Saranna all over again – and this time far more deeply than before. Anything short of marriage with her was going to leave him desperately hurt.

Wes had feared Saranna might have gone to bed early, but she was in the kitchen busily making pastry.

'I want to use up some of those apples you stored,' she explained, carrying on with her work after Wes had told of his purpose in returning to the cottage so late. 'They won't keep very much longer, so I might as well use as many as I can. There'll be a pie for you to take home if you think your ma would like it.'

'She'd be delighted. We had to cut down our cooking apple tree last year. We've only eaters left, and they went months ago. Talking of cooking reminds me, Ma would like you to come to supper on Friday night. She thought it would be a nice break for you.'

He said it casually, trying not to let her see how important her reply would be to him.

Saranna was rolling out the dough on the table. The rolling-pin slowed to a snail's pace as she said, 'Was it really your ma's idea, or is it one of yours?'

'It's Ma's,' declared Wes, honestly. 'We were talking about you – how you've made life much easier for me here. Ma said you must get fed up with only Widow Cake for company. She thought you might enjoy an evening down in the village, with us.'

'Does your pa know? As far as I remember, he never really approved of me.'

'That was years ago, Saranna. A great many things have changed since then.'

'As long as you remember that too, Wes. I'm not the foolish young girl I was then. There's no going back – for either of us.'

Saranna's words were not encouraging, but Wes managed a shrug. 'It's not a question of going back for me, Saranna. It's more a matter of facing up to the way I really feel – and that hasn't changed. If I hadn't believed you were Saul's girl then I would never have let you leave Tolpuddle. There can't have been many days since when I haven't regretted the way I behaved, but Saul told me . . .'

Wes made a gesture of frustration. 'Saul told me you were his girl. I believed him. As I told you once before, I didn't think he'd lie over something that was so important to me.' He shrugged again. 'As you say, we can't go back. I wish we could. I desperately wish we could.'

For a moment they stood in the kitchen just looking at each other. Then Amelia Cake's voice broke the spell.

'Saranna! Who's that you're talking to? Who have you got out there in the kitchen?'

370

Rubbing her hands together to remove the excess flour, Saranna grimaced and made her way from the kitchen, calling ahead to silence Amelia Cake's continuing harangue. Wes followed her.

'It's all right, Mrs Cake, it's only Wes. He came to collect the ledger. He says there's some accounting to be done.'

Behind her, Wes appeared, clutching the book in question.

'I'll say what's all right and what's not all right in my house, young lady. If Wesley had work to do in the ledger he should have taken it home with him when he went off this evening. I don't want him coming here in the dead of night frightening me when I'm trying to get off to sleep. Do you hear that, Wesley?'

'I hear, Mrs Cake. I had meant to take it with me when I went, but I forgot.'

'The road to hell is paved with good intentions, Wesley, as I'm sure your mother has told you many times. Remember that.'

'Yes, Mrs Cake. I'll leave you in peace now. Good night.'

Outside the room, Wes grimaced at Saranna. 'Your being here is doing her good. She's almost back to being the Widow Cake we all remember.'

In the kitchen, as Saranna returned her attention to the pastry on the table, Wes said reluctantly, 'I'd better go now, before she starts calling out again.'

Saranna nodded. 'I'm glad you came here tonight though, Wes. It was nice to have someone to talk to – and tell your ma I'd love to come to supper on Friday.'

The acceptance elated Wes, but there was no further encouragement for him from Saranna. Moments later he was on the path, walking towards the gate that led to the narrow lane.

He was at the gate when her voice reached him from the doorway where she was standing.

'Wes?'

'Yes.'

'I said we can't go back, and that's true.' She spoke softly, so he needed to strain to hear her. 'But I didn't say there was no hope for the future. Just be patient, Wes. Give me a little time.'

Chapter 25

On Friday evening, Saranna and Wes walked from Widow Cake's cottage to the village together after work. Saranna was pleased it was dark. She was extremely nervous about being invited to eat with Wes and his mother at their small house and felt it must show.

Much of her concern stemmed from the opinions she knew Eli Gillam had held about her, before she moved to Kent with her mother.

Wes had tried to reassure Saranna by telling her his father had changed his views about her. About many other matters too. Anyway, he would not be eating with them.

Saranna also feared being asked questions about Saul from Wes's mother. He did his best to quell these fears too when she spoke to him of them.

'Try not to worry about it. Just say that you haven't seen him, for however long it's been. That you don't know where he is now.'

'You don't think that might be the reason she's invited me to your home tonight? Because she hopes I might be able to tell her something about Saul?'

'No, of course not.'

'Then why has she invited me, Wes? Or is this really your idea?'

'It was Ma who suggested it. We were talking about you – how you're exactly what Widow Cake has needed for a very long time. Ma said it must be very lonely up at the cottage sometimes, with only Widow Cake as company for much of the day. She thought you might like to share a meal with us.' It was the third or fourth time that week Wes had needed to give her the same explanation, but she was still not convinced.

Slightly less apprehensive, Saranna said, 'It's a very kind thought. I always did like your ma.' She was thoughtful for a few minutes, before saying, 'Does she know about me and Alan?'

'Yes.'

It was a deliberately cryptic reply. Wes did not intend to allow thoughts of Alan Pate to spoil the evening ahead.

Saranna held the same view. She made no more mention of the

Trades Association leader for the remainder of the walk to Tolpuddle.

'Come on in, Saranna . . . My word! I don't think I've ever seen such a difference in a girl!'

Rachel Gillam made the comment as Saranna took off her coat.

'The last time I saw you I offered you one of my old dresses. Now I'd be more than happy to wear one of your cast-offs – although I'd need to lose at least half my weight before I'd get into one of them!'

Rachel gazed at her visitor with genuine admiration. Saranna had always been a pretty young girl, even when dressed in threadbare clothes that were too small for her. Now she wore a stylish, well-made dress and was far more mature. Her long dark hair was brushed to a shine that reflected the light from the lamp, and she was a very attractive young woman indeed.

Acting upon a sudden impulse, Rachel stepped forward and gave her guest a warm hug.

'It's very nice to see you, girl. Your being at Widow Cake's cottage has certainly made a difference to our Wes. He was finding it very difficult to be both farm worker and nursemaid for her.'

'Well, he must have made a good job of it. She doesn't stop singing his praises to me and, you must admit, that isn't at all like Widow Cake!'

For more than half an hour Saranna chatted to Wes and his mother, becoming even more relaxed. She helped with the table and serving out the food, in spite of Rachel's protests.

They were about to sit down to eat their meal when the door opened and Eli came in.

When Rachel expressed her surprise that he had come home so early, he said, 'The meeting was cancelled. It had been called by the District preacher from Dorchester, but they've had a serious outbreak of cholera there. Two of his lay preachers have gone down with the illness. He felt it would be foolish to risk spreading it farther afield. No one else at the meeting knew why it had been called and there was no sense having a meeting just for the sake of it, so I've hurried to be home in time for supper.'

Eli's unexpected arrival had dispelled the relaxed atmosphere that had built up during the evening. To break an awkward silence, Wes said, 'Pa, I don't think you've met Saranna before.'

'That's so.' Eli had given her a searching glance when he came in the house, now he shook hands with her gravely. 'But I have heard a great deal about you. You were a close friend of our Saul, I believe.'

'I wouldn't say that, Mr Gillam. He called at our house occasionally, that's all.'

'Have you seen anything of Saul lately?'

Rachel asked the question eagerly. It was the first time she had mentioned her elder son since Saranna's arrival. She had intended keeping him out of the conversation, if possible, but since Eli had broached the subject . . .

Wes tensed, waiting for Saranna's reply.

'I haven't seen him since I was living at Southover.'

'Neither have we. Wesley was the last one to see him. Saul got himself into a scrape, somewhere in Wiltshire. Wesley said he thought he was going up North somewhere. I do wish he would come home, or at least let us know what he is doing.'

It was Eli who changed the subject, much to the relief of Wes and Saranna. Still speaking to their guest, he said, 'Wesley tells me Richard Pemble is your stepfather.'

'That's right. He was in the army with my pa. They were very good friends. Richard kept in touch with Ma and me after he came out of the army. He would often visit us when we lived at Southover and a couple of years ago he asked Ma to marry him.'

'Richard Pemble kept his visits very quiet. I never heard word of his being in this area.'

'You weren't interested in Unions or Associations then, Pa. Not only that, I can remember your saying that Richard Pemble should use his talents as a Methodist preacher serving the Lord, not going about the country stirring up trouble.'

They were eating now and Wes spoke between mouthfuls of boiled bacon pudding. 'I met him once, over at Southover.'

'Did you now? I never knew you were also a visitor to Southover.'

'I went there a few times.'

'Of course you did.' Rachel thought it was time she contributed something to a conversation of such an explosive nature. 'It would have been surprising if you didn't, seeing that Saranna was working at Widow Cake's then too.'

'How long are you staying this time?' Once again the question was put to Saranna from Eli.

'I don't know. It depends very much on Widow Cake. How long it takes before she's well again – and what she wants to do when she's up and about.'

'She'd be a fool to let you go again,' said Rachel.

'Aren't you supposed to be marrying one of Richard Pemble's assistants? The one who came to Tolpuddle to advise us on setting up our own Association?'

'Eli! What do you think you're doing asking the girl such a personal question? That's her business, not ours,' Rachel admonished her husband.

'It's all right, Mrs Gillam. I don't mind answering questions about Alan. In fact, I *won't* be marrying him, but he doesn't know that yet.'

'Oh! And when did you make up your mind about this?'

Eli's glance shifted to his son, who was sitting staring at Saranna in undisguised delight, before returning his attention to the girl again.

'I'd decided before I came back to Tolpuddle. That's partly why I was pleased to get Widow Cake's offer. I would have told Alan at that time, but he was never around.'

'So as far as he's aware, you're still to be married to him?' Eli seemed anxious to pursue the matter with her.

'I suppose so. I doubt whether my ma or Richard will have told him.'

'I should think not! It's not the sort of news a man should hear from anyone else,' commented Eli disapprovingly. 'Especially when a man's busy doing something to help his fellow-men. I've never known the country in such a mess. Why, we have fifteen farm workers waiting to take the oath to join the Association and there are more applying every day.'

Saranna looked surprised. 'You're not still making new members take an oath when they join your Association?'

'Yes. Alan Pate was insistent on that.'

'Of course! I forgot he'd been away in the North of England for some months when he came here. He wouldn't have heard. They've stopped making new members take an oath in all the London branches of the Association.'

'Why?'

'I don't know. It came about after a meeting Richard had with all the London Association leaders and a couple of Members of Parliament who are sympathetic to the cause.'

'I wonder why?' mused Eli. 'I'll have to try to find out more. I have never been keen on making new members swear an oath. It's worded in a Christian way, but I would be happy to drop it from the initiation ceremony altogether. However, I suppose we'd better carry on with it until we learn more.'

The talk was of Union matters for a while longer until Rachel managed to steer it in another direction, talking of village matters and the changes that had taken place while Saranna was away.

Eventually, when the meal had long ended, Saranna said it was time she returned to Widow Cake's cottage.

'Thank you for having me,' she said to Rachel. 'I enjoyed my meal and I enjoyed the evening. It was nice to be with a family again.'

'Then you must come again, girl. As often as you wish. There'll always be something to eat and we'd love to have you here.'

'I'll walk back with you,' said Wes, taking down his coat and handing Saranna's to her.

'There's no need for that,' said Saranna. 'It's not far.'

'Nonsense!' said Rachel, quickly. 'We couldn't let a young girl like you walk home on your own. Wesley will go with you.'

When the door had closed behind Wes and Saranna, Rachel sat down on the wooden armchair, on the far side of the fireplace from her husband. 'There! Didn't I tell you that Saranna was a nice girl? Go on, admit you've been wrong about her all this time.'

'She's pleasant enough,' agreed Eli, grudgingly. 'She's a good-looking girl, too. Probably too good-looking for her own peace of mind. There's a great deal of temptation put in the path of an attractive girl. Not all of them have the strength to put it aside. Perhaps she's one who can. Perhaps not.'

'You'd better hope she can, Eli. I think that one day we are going to have her as our daughter-in-law.'

Chapter 26

Walking back to Widow Cake's cottage with Wes, Saranna reiterated what she had said to Rachel Gillam. 'I did enjoy this evening, Wes. Although I had a nasty few minutes when Saul came up in the conversation.'

'Yes, so did I. But you handled it very well. Mind you, it was a bit of a surprise Pa's coming home the way he did.'

'Oh, he was all right. Better than I thought he would be, but I must admit he makes me nervous. I was always on edge about what he might say next. Mind you, I never have been comfortable in the presence of men who are utterly convinced that their way of doing something is the *only* way.'

'Isn't Alan Pate such a person?'

'I suppose he is, although I didn't realise it at first. It's only lately that I seem to have noticed it for what it was.'

Saranna did not add that it was only since Wes's visit to Eltham that she had begun to make comparisons between the two of them.

'What you said back there ... does it mean you really aren't going to marry him?'

'That's right.'

'I'm glad, Saranna. Very, very glad.'

'Why?' She knew what she wanted his answer to be, but feared he would not be able to say it. That he would skirt around it as he always had in the past.

But this was not the same Wes she had known then. Torn between his feelings for her, and a mistaken loyalty to his brother.

'Because I want you to marry me, Saranna. I let you go once, I don't intend allowing it to happen again.'

'Oh!'

The positive manner in which he made the blunt statement took Saranna by surprise. This was a Wes she had not met with before. He had become a man. She hoped he had not changed too much.

'Do I have anything to say about this? Or have you decided everything for me, the same as Alan would do?'

Wes was almost as surprised as Saranna at being able to express his feelings so openly to her. 'You have everything to say about it, Saranna, but I wanted you to know from the very beginning how I feel about you.'

'Since you've been so honest, I'll try to be the same. Before I left Southover to go to Kent, I believed I loved you about as much as any girl could love a man. When you behaved the way you did, able to believe I was deceiving both you and Saul, I was very hurt. So hurt that I was glad to get away from here and everything it meant to me.'

They walked on in silence for a few paces, hardly aware of the soft flurry of cold rain that blew in on the wind.

'I've spent two years trying to forget you, Wes. I even found a man who wanted to marry me – and I let myself believe I wanted to marry him too. Then you came back into my life. Suddenly I saw things through new eyes, saw Alan in a different light, and I knew I couldn't marry him. When I tell him he's going to believe it's because I still love you. You might think the same – but *I'm* not certain. The only thing I'm absolutely certain of at the moment is that I can't marry Alan Pate.'

'You don't know how happy that makes me, Saranna. You will learn to love me again. You *must*. I just couldn't bear to see you walk away again.'

'I'm going to need time, Wes. Time to get to know you again. Time to get to know myself.'

They had reached Widow Cake's cottage now and they stopped at the gate from the lane.

'Good night, Wes – and thank you for the evening. Thank you too for listening.'

She did not object when he kissed her. It was a gentle, undemanding kiss and despite the emotions it stirred up deep within him, Wes knew this was the way it had to be for now.

'Good night, Saranna. Don't be too long making up your mind. We've wasted far too much time already.'

At Moreton House, James Frampton was hosting a dinner for a number of his fellow magistrates. The talk at table was almost exclusively of the upsurge of Union activity in Dorset. Every man there was anxious to put a halt to its increasing growth. Many suggestions were put forward about methods to suppress all such movements, wherever they arose.

The magistrates sat about a table that groaned beneath the weight of good food and wines. Pheasant, beef, pork and hare were the main dishes but there were many others, and as a glass was near-emptied it was immediately refilled.

It was perhaps symptomatic of the ailments of the country that not one of the magistrates even thought that a return to a living wage might resolve the problems they were discussing.

Towards the end of the meal, the Moreton butler entered the dining-room and made his way to the head of the table where James Frampton was seated.

Bending low, he said softly in the ear of his employer, 'Excuse me, sir. A letter has just been delivered by special messenger. I thought you might want to read it right away.'

James Frampton frowned in annoyance. 'Damn it, Weedon! You're employed to see I'm not troubled with such trifles. I don't want to know about it now. I'm at dinner with friends. Put it in my study. It can wait until morning.'

'I thought, in view of the present company, you might wish to read it straightaway, sir. The letter is from London and bears the seal of the Home Secretary.'

James Frampton's irritability vanished immediately. 'Bring it in here, man. Bring it here right away.'

The butler had anticipated his employer's reaction. He signalled to a footman who stood in the doorway, holding a small silver tray on which was the letter and a paper-knife.

The servant advanced to the table and James Frampton took the letter. Ignoring the paper-knife, he broke open the seal which had identified the sender to the butler. From the envelope he removed a single sheet of paper. The letter was headed simply, 'Whitehall'.

James Frampton scanned the paper first, then read it through in more detail. Suddenly beaming, he called to the butler, 'Weedon, clear the servants from the room, if you please. No one is to return until I give the word.'

The butler was the last to leave the dining-room. When the door closed behind him, James Frampton called for silence around the table.

'Gentlemen, it may please you to know that Lord Melbourne fully appreciates the gravity of the situation facing our country – and Dorset in particular. I have had a reply – an *early* reply – to a letter I sent only two days ago, informing him of the situation we face here. I would like to acquaint you with its contents.'

The magistrate looked about the room until he was assured he had the attention of everyone present.

'The letter is written by Viscount Melbourne's Secretary. He first of all acknowledges receipt of my own letter, in which I expressed the alarm felt by every man here at the rise of these Trades Unions. It seems His Lordship thinks we have acted wisely in bringing it to his attention . . .'

There was a murmur of approval from James Frampton's guests. When it had died away, he continued.

'Lord Melbourne calls our attention to a Statute, passed in the fifty-seventh year of the reign of King George III. If my arithmetic is sound, I believe that would be a Statute of 1817. He feels confident that this Act may well be of significance in this matter.'

James Frampton folded the letter and looked along the table in a self-satisfied manner. 'I sincerely believe, gentlemen, that Lord Melbourne has given his blessing to any action we feel may be necessary. Moreover, he has pointed us in the direction we should take.'

It was left to one of the magistrates seated at the far end of the long table to ask, 'What is this Act quoted by Lord Melbourne?'

Instead of replying directly, James Frampton rang the bell on the table beside his glass. In response to the sound the butler re-entered the room.

'Weedon, I want you to go to the library. Bring me the Statute book containing the Acts of Parliament passed in the fifty-seventh year of King George III's reign. Can you remember that?'

'I can, sir.'

'Good – and hurry, please.'

It was a full five minutes before the butler returned to the room with a book. When he placed it down on the table in front of James Frampton, he apologised for the delay, explaining that the book was on a shelf well beyond his reach. He had needed to find a pair of steps in order to reach down the volume.

'Thank you, Weedon. You may go now.'

When the butler had left the room, James Frampton opened the leather-bound volume and turned the pages until he found what he was seeking. Reading silently for some minutes, he finally looked up and called for quiet.

'Gentlemen, the Act draws to our attention other, earlier Statutes. I will need to refer to them before I am able to make a full recommendation to you. However, this particular Statute was enacted to prevent Seditious Meetings and Assemblies and the wording is perfectly clear. It states that members of a society or club who take an oath not required or authorised by law shall be deemed an unlawful combination. There are a number of Sections worthy of our attention, but I think that Lord Melbourne has combined his wisdom and high office to show us the way forward. I am confident we now have in our hands the means to strike a resounding blow against the Trades Unions. A blow that will reverberate around the kingdom and strike fear in the hearts of all those who oppose the structure of society which God Himself has ordained!'

Chapter 27

The discussions that followed receipt of Lord Melbourne's letter continued at Moreton House until well into the night. Nevertheless, when Josephine came downstairs after having a late breakfast in her room, she found her grandfather poring over Statute books in his study.

'My! It would seem that Lord Melbourne's letter has stirred up feverish activity.'

'What do you know of his letter? Who told you about it?'

'Really, Grandfather! Did you imagine you could keep it a secret – at Moreton? The messenger who brought the letter was sent to the kitchen for a meal. Cook could winkle a deaf and dumb man's life story from him in a matter of minutes.'

Despite Josephine's scornful statement, she had not received news of the letter from any of the kitchen servants.

Andrew Symonds was the footman who had carried the letter on a tray to the dining-room. He had read the wording on the seal as he carried it through. The information had been passed on to Josephine during a late-night liaison in her room, while the magistrates were still revelling downstairs.

'Has Lord Melbourne told you how you can put a stop to the farm workers forming a Union?'

'Yes.'

James Frampton pushed the letter across his desk towards her and she picked it up.

As she read, he said, 'Unfortunately, it's not quite as simple as it appears to be. In order to have the maximum sentence passed upon the men who are organising the Tolpuddle Union, it will be necessary to make use of three separate Statutes.'

When Josephine finished reading the letter her grandfather took it from her. 'It *can* be done, of course, but the prosecution must satisfy certain vital criteria. This would appear to be the stumbling block at the moment.'

'What do you need to prove?'

'First, that the oath was actually administered. Second, I must obtain the names of those who were present at the time. Such details can only be proven beyond doubt by producing a witness who was there at the time. In other words, one of the initiates – and they are a close-mouthed lot.'

'If you obtain this information and are able to convict them, what will be their punishment?'

'That's what I'm working on now. I believe if we satisfy all the requirements of the Statutes, they can be sent to Australia for seven years. To all intents and purposes, it means we will never see them in this country again.'

Her grandfather had given Josephine the germ of an exciting idea. Wesley Gillam possessed knowledge of her that could effectively ruin her life – if not put an end to it! If he were out of the way she would breathe more easily.

'I think I might be able to help you, Grandfather. The servants are often telling me of their relatives who have joined this Union. In most cases, against their will – or so they say. I will see if I can find one who might provide you with some useful evidence.'

That evening, Josephine and Andrew Symonds, the amorous footman, met in the summerhouse. It was the same small building where Fanny Warren had once hidden and witnessed the exchange between James Frampton's grand-daughter and Wes.

Tonight, their love-making had been a brief and unsatisfactory interlude. Josephine's lover had failed to meet her seemingly insatiable demands. He was feeling sulky, and she frustrated.

There was a lengthy silence between them while Josephine adjusted her clothing. It was eventually broken by Symonds. 'Are we going to meet here the same time tomorrow?'

'Not unless you think you'll be better than you were tonight. It will be a waste of both our time. I might as well have had an early night in bed.'

'It wasn't my fault. I'm tired. I work hard all day and I don't suppose I've had more than a total of five or six hours' sleep in the last three nights.'

'So? If it's all too much for you perhaps we shouldn't see each other again.'

In truth, Josephine was becoming bored with the footman. It had been fun to seduce him, knowing he had never been with a girl before. But he was taking their affair far too seriously. He was becoming tiresome.

'No, Josephine . . . *Miss* Josephine. I'm sorry. I'll be better next time. I promise.'

'Better than what?' Josephine's shrug was lost in the darkness. 'But since you're here tonight you can answer some questions for me. First, what do you know about Wesley Gillam?'

'Why do you want to know?' Symonds replied sulkily. 'You're not still sweet on him?'

'Who said I was "sweet" on him?' Josephine demanded.

'One of the gardeners told me you got him into trouble a couple of years ago.'

'You've been talking about me with the gardeners? How dare you!'

'It wasn't like that,' said the footman hurriedly. 'I . . . we saw you going out riding one day last week. The gardener said . . . He said he thought you were a very attractive woman, but then went on to say you'd got Wesley Gillam into trouble. That was all.'

'That was quite enough.' Josephine wondered which gardener Andrew Symonds could have been speaking to. Perhaps it was the tall, curly-haired one. The one she thought was rather shy . . . 'I don't like being talked about by the servants – and that includes *you*.'

'I wouldn't say anything about you to anyone, Miss Josephine. I promise. I . . . I'm far too fond of you for that.'

Dismissing his protestation, Josephine said, 'You still haven't answered my question. How well do you know Wesley Gillam?'

'What is it you want to know about him?' He still sounded sulky.

'Is he involved in this Union the Tolpuddle men are joining?'

'I suppose so. His father certainly is. I've heard that Wes is keeping their records, so I suppose he must be.'

'Do you know anyone else who belongs to the Union?'

'Most of the men in Tolpuddle and the villages around there have joined. My cousin is being sworn in this next Friday.'

'You mean he's taking the initiation oath?'

'I suppose so. He wasn't feeling too happy about it the last time we spoke. He's not sure he's doing the right thing, but he daren't back out now. Everyone else on the farm where he works has joined. He says they won't speak to him if he doesn't.'

'What's this cousin's name?'

'Edward Legg . . . You'll see me tomorrow night, Miss Josephine?'

'I don't know yet. I'll find some way to get word to you tomorrow.'

'There's someone else who'll be joining the Tolpuddle Union on Friday night. I think you ought to know about him.'

'Who?'

'John Lock, one of Mr Frampton's gardeners.'

'Why should he join? He's not a farm labourer.'

'That's what I told him, but he said we should all stick together against those who are trying to grind us into the ground.'

'Did he, indeed?' Josephine thought her grandfather would like to know about his disloyal gardener. She did not doubt he could be persuaded to give evidence against Wesley Gillam and the others.

'You've done well, Andrew. I might decide to see you here tomorrow night after all.'

'I'll see if I can find out some more information for you by then, Miss Josephine. I'll also try to get a good night's sleep tonight.'

'Good. I must go now. Give me a few minutes before you leave.'

Josephine was about to leave the summerhouse when Andrew Symonds called to her in a hoarse whisper, 'Miss Josephine!'

'What is it?' was her irritable response.

'I heard something else today that might be of interest to you, seeing as how you're trying to find out as much as you can about the Unions.'

'Tell me – but hurry up! I must get back to the house before someone misses me and they start looking for me in the garden.'

Josephine was impatient to be away. She had all the information she wanted from her lover. There would be no meeting the next night. Instead, she would find some way to have him dismissed from her grandfather's employ.

'It concerns Wesley Gillam. A Trades Union man from London arrived in Tolpuddle today. It's the same man who came a few months ago and told them how to form their Union.'

'What's that got to do with Wesley Gillam?'

'The Tolpuddle inn-keeper was here delivering some ale Mr Frampton had ordered. The Trades Union man is staying at his inn. One of the first things he did was to ask the way to Widow Cake's cottage. That's where Wesley works. I'd say it's proof that he's working for the Union in Tolpuddle.'

Josephine thought it would certainly damn Wesley Gillam in court, if he denied all knowledge of the Trades Union.

'Did the inn-keeper mention the name of this Trades Union man from London?'

'Yes. I remember it because it's an unusual name. Least, it is in these parts. His name's Pate.'

'*Alan* Pate?' Josephine had met him a couple of times when she stayed in London with Saul. She had spoken to him once but, as far as she was aware, he had not been told her name. There was certainly no way he could link her to Saul.

'You don't know him, surely?'

'I might have heard of him. If it's the man I think it is then I'll probably go and have a word with him.'

Josephine left the summerhouse without saying more.

Behind her, Andrew Symonds pondered uneasily upon the thought of Josephine going off to meet a man who came from London.

Without any logical cause, a wave of totally unreasonable jealousy swept over him. If Josephine went to the inn to speak to this man Pate, he intended being there too. In fact, he intended keeping a close watch on everything she did in future.

Chapter 28

Alan Pate called in at the London headquarters of his Association before returning home to Eltham village. He had just spent a week in Oxfordshire, helping farm labourers to form a new Lodge.

Richard Pemble was in the building, working alone in his office. There had been a cooling in relations between the two men but Richard called to him as he passed the open door of the office.

'Alan! I was hoping to catch you as soon as you returned. Come in, and close the door behind you.'

Alan Pate did as he was told and guardedly accepted Richard's invitation to sit down.

'How was your visit to Oxfordshire? Did you sort out their problems?'

'I did. I believe we are well on the way to having a strong Lodge there. They are suffering almost as much as the Dorset labourers.'

'I'm glad you were able to sort out their problems because they are all going to come to you in the future. I've decided to step down from the presidency of the Association.'

'You've what!' Alan Pate could not believe he was hearing right. 'But the Association is your brainchild. You founded it virtually single-handed.'

There was more than a touch of hypocrisy in Alan Pate's protest. He had been gradually building up his own power within the Association for many months and had almost reached the stage where he would feel confident in making a bid to oust his colleagues and take his place. Now Richard Pemble had made such a move unnecessary.

'I've had many years of organising Unions, Alan. I must have travelled thousands of miles around England explaining how things should be done and challenging the authority of employers and landowners. I've worked to have laws changed in our favour and tried to find a way past every obstacle that's been put in our path. Before that I was part of Wellington's Army, fighting the French in Spain and France.'

Leaning back in his chair, Richard Pemble clasped his hands

behind his neck and looked at the man seated across the desk from him. 'It seems to me I've spent most of my life fighting someone or another. Well, I'm a settled, married man now and I realise I'm not getting any younger. It's time I sat back and let someone else take over the battle.'

'I can't believe it,' said Alan Pate. 'The Association without you won't be the same. But what will you do? Surely you're not giving up the fight altogether?'

'No, I'm not. I've been asked to help the dockers and Thames rivermen set up a Union. I'll do that. However, much of it can be carried on from home. I'll stay on until the end of the next month, then hand everything over to you. I know I'll be leaving the Association in safe hands.'

Alan Pate had been taken totally by surprise, but he was highly elated. He had been working towards this moment for a very long time. A sudden thought struck him. 'Does Saranna know of this?'

'No.'

'I'd like you to say nothing until I've seen her. I want to tell her myself.'

'Of course. When you see her perhaps you'll pass on our love from her mother and me? Tell her we'd like to hear from her. She should at least let her mother know how she's getting on.'

'Tell her?' Alan Pate was bemused. 'What do you mean? Isn't she at Eltham?'

Feigning surprise, Richard Pemble said, 'You mean she hasn't told you? She went to Tolpuddle last week. It seems that widow-woman she used to work for there is ill. Saranna's gone back there to help her until she's well again. I felt certain you would have known, seeing that you and she are due to be wed.'

Alan Pate reacted to the news of Saranna's departure for Tolpuddle with a haste that was out of character for him. There were business matters to be attended to in London, especially now he was due to take over the presidency of the Association. But all this was ignored. He set off immediately to ride to Tolpuddle.

The thought uppermost in Alan Pate's mind was that Wesley Gillam was at Tolpuddle – and so too was Saranna. He believed the story of the sick widow was a falsehood. Whether it had been initiated by Saranna or Wesley Gillam he did not know – but he would find out.

He also suspected that all this was the result of Gillam's visit to the Pemble home at Eltham.

In truth, Alan Pate also felt slightly guilty because he had avoided Saranna for a couple of weeks. It had been deliberate. An attempt to 'teach her a lesson', because of her behaviour during the time when Wesley Gillam was at Eltham.

He thought that perhaps he might have taken things too far. She would need to understand that she could not behave with such irresponsibility when she was married to him, of course, but he would make it clear he was willing to forgive her on this occasion.

He felt confident that the news he would soon be taking over the presidency of the Association, together with an offer to make immediate and firm arrangements for their wedding, would bring her into line once more.

Alan Pate arrived in Tolpuddle at two o'clock the next afternoon and went immediately to the Crown Inn. Taking a room, he washed, shaved and changed before asking the way to Widow Cake's cottage.

Wes was bringing the cows in for milking when he saw the rider approaching the house. He recognised him immediately and guessed why the Trades Association leader had come to Tolpuddle. The thought that he might be about to lose Saranna struck fear in him.

He knew he would undoubtedly be taken to task by Widow Cake, but he abandoned the cows in one of the middle fields and hurried towards the cottage.

Alan Pate had been in the cottage for a few minutes by the time Wes arrived. Pate and Saranna were standing in the kitchen, on opposite sides of the table, when Wes came through the door.

The Trades Union leader's glance at Wes was cold and he failed to greet him, but Saranna gave him a welcoming smile.

'Isn't this a surprise, Wes? Alan has just ridden here from London. He has some incredible news. Richard has decided to retire from the presidency of the Association. He's named Alan as his successor.'

'I didn't come all this way just to tell you that, Saranna, as well you know. I'm here to find out why you left Eltham so hurriedly, without saying anything to me. I also wish to discuss the details of our wedding.'

'I could hardly tell you when you weren't there . . . but I suggest we talk about it privately, later.'

'We were private enough until a few minutes ago,' said Alan Pate, pointedly.

'That's enough . . .'

'Saranna! Who do you have in the kitchen? Come here, girl.'

Amelia Cake's voice from her downstairs sick-room reached the three people in the kitchen. The widow was able to leave her bed now and she spent much of her time resting in a chair before the fire.

Going only as far as the kitchen door, Saranna called, 'Wes is here, Mrs Cake. So is Alan. He's travelled from London to see me.'

'Don't stand out there shouting, girl. Come in here and bring them with you – though what Wesley is doing in the house at this time of day, I don't know.'

'I came to see you, Saranna, not to pay a social call on your employer.'

'You'd better come and see her now she knows you're here.'

'I don't see why? You'll not be working here long and you owe her nothing. Indeed, I think she is in *your* debt.'

'Saranna? Did you hear me, girl?' The voice from the sick-room had an edge to it now.

'Oh, come on. She won't keep you a minute.'

Saranna virtually pushed Alan ahead of her along the narrow, low-beamed passageway to the room where they were awaited. Wes followed after, almost as reluctant as the Trades Union leader to face the Tolpuddle widow.

'So this is the man you agreed to marry?' Widow Cake looked him over critically when Saranna had introduced him. 'He's older than I expected him to be. What has he come here for?'

Alan bridled at Amelia Cake's words and her manner of speaking about him, but not to him. 'I came here to speak to Saranna. To discuss our proposed marriage – in private.'

'I'll decide who discusses private matters in my house. It would have taken no more than a few minutes of your time to come along and let me know what was going on.'

'If it's inconvenient I don't doubt that the landlord of the Crown Inn can find a room where Saranna and I might have a private talk. Saranna can meet me there.'

'Saranna will meet you there only if I tell her she may. I pay her to look after me – *here*. If it's so important that you have this talk then you can go to the kitchen and close the door – but don't make it too long. Saranna has a meal to prepare for me. I don't like eating after dark.'

Wes was edging towards the door as his employer was speaking, hoping to leave the room with the others, but he should have known better.

'Wesley! You stay and explain what you're doing here when there are cows to be brought in and milked. When you leave you can go out through the front door, so you don't disturb this gentleman, seeing he's so keen on enjoying his privacy.'

Saranna and Alan left the room, the Union leader still smarting from the sharp tongue of Amelia Cake. Behind them Wes waited for the tongue-lashing he felt was sure to come.

Instead, Amelia said, 'Why is this Alan Pate here, do you know?'

'He's come to find out why Saranna left Eltham without saying anything to him about it beforehand.'

'Why did she?'

'From what she's said to me I gather he wasn't around to be told. In fact, it seems he wasn't at Eltham very often at all.'

'I see. What about this marriage nonsense? He's far too old for her. Surely she isn't seriously considering marrying the man?'

'She told me she wasn't the night she came to our place for a meal. But he has a lot to offer her. Richard Pemble has just handed the presidency of the Trades Unions Association to him. He's an influential man, and likely to become more so. The wife of a man like that would be someone of importance.' Wes shrugged resignedly. 'He certainly has more to offer Saranna than I have.'

'Since when has that been of importance to Saranna? Come on, answer me honestly, Wesley. You think you know Saranna well, what is she more likely to choose? A man she loves, or the social standing that comes with marrying a man she doesn't?'

'I think that if she were left to think about it she'd marry for love – but Alan Pate is a very persuasive man, and he *can* offer her a lot more than I can.'

For a long time, Amelia looked at Wes without speaking. Then she said, 'Go to the drawer over there, Wesley. The top one in the sideboard. You'll find an envelope inside. Bring it out.'

Puzzled, Wes did as he was told. Inside the drawer was a long stiff envelope.

'That's the one. Open it and read what it says.'

Wes did as he was told, as he read his expression registering disbelief and then amazement. When he eventually looked up at her, he said, 'I don't understand! Why?'

'Why? What sort of a reaction is that? Hasn't that solicitor written what I told him to? What does it say?'

'It says that when you die, this cottage and all your lands will pass to me.'

'That sounds clear enough to me. Now, do you still think Alan Pate has more to offer Saranna than you do?'

Wes could only shake his head, but Amelia was already speaking again.

'I'll go farther than that, Wesley Gillam. I'll send for that solicitor again – he's the one who came here to talk about defending Arnold Cooper, more than two years ago. I'll get him to draw up a new agreement. What I'll say is this: you won't need to wait until I die to take over this cottage and the land. If you and Saranna marry and agree to take good care of me here until I die, everything will be yours on the day of your wedding. What do you say to that?'

Wes shook his head in disbelief, 'What can I say? Mrs Cake, you're a wonderful woman – and I love you for it.'

'Hah! That's easy to say when you know full well you'll be marrying someone your own age. Right, off you go and tell her, before that pompous jackass turns her head with his own importance. Mind you, I don't think you have anything to worry yourself about. Unless I have very much underestimated Saranna, she will have seen through his self-importance and sent him packing already. Now get off – and don't forget to bring those cows in . . .'

Chapter 29

'What were you thinking of, leaving Eltham and coming here without a word to me of your intentions?' Alan's manner was both angry and arrogant when he spoke to Saranna in the kitchen.

'How could I tell you when you weren't there and nobody knew where I could find you? Had you told me of *your* intentions I might have been able to tell you what *I* was doing. Besides, you'd deliberately avoided me for days.'

'I had not been avoiding you,' he lied, 'I am a very busy man, Saranna. You must understand that. I fear I shall be even busier now I am to take over the presidency of the Association. When we are married . . .'

'I won't be marrying you, Alan.'

'Don't be absurd! Of course you're marrying me. This is no more than a foolish little misunderstanding. Certainly not serious enough to cause us to even delay the plans we've made.'

'*We* never made any firm plans, Alan. You were always far too busy. You've always assumed that I'll accept we should marry when your work allowed. Well, I suppose its all worked out for the best, really. You've given me time to discover that I don't want to marry you. I'm very sorry, Alan. I'm even more sorry that you had to come all this way to hear the news. I had intended telling you even before I had Widow Cake's letter but, as I've already said, you were never there.'

'Saranna, this is preposterous! I realise that having Wesley Gillam come back into your life has been a disruptive influence, but it will pass once you return to Eltham. Come back with me tomorrow – today, if you like. Put Gillam and Tolpuddle where they belong, in the past.'

'It has nothing to do with Wes – well, it *does*, but he didn't have to try to persuade me about anything. I'd realised for a long time that I didn't love you in the way I should, Alan. I thought it didn't really matter. That everything would be all right once we were married. I was deceiving myself. It's a mercy for both of us that I've found out in time.'

'You're not making sense, Saranna. Having me come here so

unexpectedly has confused you. I'll leave you now and return to speak to you tomorrow. Think of what I've said. Don't throw away the future I'm offering you in a moment of foolishness. Look about you now. Is this where you want to be for the rest of your life? Slaving away in someone else's kitchen? You're worth more than this, Saranna. You'll marry me and we'll try to put all this nonsense behind us.'

Alan left Widow Cake's cottage satisfied he had made his point to Saranna. She was confused now but, alone in her room during the night hours, she would think of what he had said and would realise he had far more to offer her than a mere farm labourer. Nevertheless, he would not be satisfied until she was removed from the influence of Wesley Gillam.

Wes saw Alan leave the house but drew little comfort from what he saw. The Union leader walked to his horse with an air of self-confidence that Wes found disconcerting.

He wanted to dash into the house, find out from Saranna what had been said, and tell her of the incredible news Widow Cake had broken to him. But he could do nothing immediately. He had to bring the four cows into the milking parlour, prepare them for milking and settle the heifers in another cow-shed for the night. He would have to wait until Saranna came out to do the milking.

Saranna did not keep him waiting for long. She did not feel like talking to Amelia Cake just yet. In fact, she did not feel like talking to anyone, but at least she could tell Wes so. It was far more difficult to silence her employer.

'Has he gone now, Saranna? Gone out of your life for good?'

'Not exactly. He's staying at the Crown in Tolpuddle tonight. He'll be back to see me tomorrow – when I've "come to my senses", is, I think, the way he put it.'

'Do you want me to go down there tonight and tell him you don't want to see him again?'

'No, Wes. That would only cause trouble. When he gets the same answer from me tomorrow he'll realise I mean what I say. I'm not going to marry him.'

'Has Widow Cake told you her plans for me – and for you too?'

'I haven't seen her since Alan left.'

Wes told her of being left the cottage and land in Widow Cake's will and Saranna gasped in delight. 'That's wonderful news, Wes. I'm absolutely delighted for you. I always knew she thought an awful lot of you.'

'She thinks a lot of you too.' Wes told her of Amelia's additional offer, conditional upon the marriage of Saranna to him.

She thought of Alan's supercilious remark about working in someone else's kitchen for the rest of her life. This certainly defeated *that* argument. But she was far more cautious in her reply to Wes.

'That's a wonderful offer too, Wes, but I'm not going to be pushed into making any decisions that will affect the rest of my life. Alan's just tried to do that. I'll make up my own mind, in my own time – and not until I'm absolutely certain it's what I really want.'

Saranna knew she had hurt Wes. He had been brought down to earth with a bump after receiving such wonderful news, but she would have been less than honest with him had she said anything else.

Alan Pate's plans for the day received a set-back as he sat having breakfast in the Crown Inn the morning after his reunion with Saranna.

One of the inn's maids entered the dining-room accompanied by a tall but portly man approaching middle-age. The maid, somewhat embarrassed, pointed to Alan and then left the room hurriedly.

Threading his way between the empty tables, the man came to where Alan sat eating alone. When the Union man continued to enjoy his breakfast, paying no attention to his uninvited companion, the other man coughed rather nervously, 'Excuse me, sir. You'll be Mr Pate – Alan Pate?'

'I think you already know the answer to your own question, having been brought to the room by one of the serving-maids. You have an advantage over me, sir. Who are you?'

'Charles Hammer, sir. Parish constable for this area.'

'I see.' Apparently unconcerned, Alan reached across the table and extracted a slice of lightly browned toast from a small rack. Applying a layer of butter, he cut the toast in four pieces and added one of them to the food remaining on his plate. 'Do you have some business with me, Constable?'

'I am afraid I have, sir. Magistrate Frampton would like to see you, over at Moreton House.'

'What about?' Alan Pate cut a piece of egg, placed it carefully upon the piece of toast and forked them both to his mouth.

'I don't rightly know that, sir. But I'd be obliged if you'd accompany me there.'

'Am I under arrest?'

'Bless you, no, sir! Mind you, I'm not saying as how you wouldn't be, if you were to refuse, you understand?'

'I'm not quite sure I do, Constable. However, if you can wait until I've finished my breakfast I *will* accompany you – voluntarily, you understand.'

'Of course, sir, and I'm much obliged to you. It's a mile or two to the house, so I'll take the liberty of having the stableman prepare your horse. I'll need to borrow one from the pound, so if you'll be good enough to wait for me – when you've had your breakfast – I'll be as quick as I can.'

At Moreton House, Alan was shown to the study by the butler who walked ahead of him, leaving the constable to bring up the rear.

In response to the butler's knock a voice called for them to enter and Pate was shown into a spacious room. When he saw Charles Hammer standing uncertainly behind Pate in the doorway, the magistrate frowned in annoyance. 'You may go now, Hammer. I won't need you again.'

'Yes, sir. Thank you, sir. Should I wait in the kitchen? Just in case . . .?'

'That won't be necessary. You may go.'

In spite of his outward show of self-assurance, Alan was relieved at the magistrate's words. If he were to be detained for any reason the magistrate would not have sent the constable away. He had done no wrong, but that had not prevented him and a great many other Union leaders being detained by magistrates in the past.

This man had held Alan Pate and his companion in cells overnight on the last occasion he had visited Tolpuddle. Alan did not trust him.

'Well, Mr Pate, I thought I had seen the last of you after we last met. It would seem I was wrong. What mischief are you plotting on this occasion?'

'I don't deal in mischief, Mr Frampton, only problems, and they are seldom thought up by the working men who bring them to me.'

'You are wasting your time promoting your Union activities here, Pate. I'll put my question to you more directly. What are you doing in Tolpuddle?'

'I am here on a purely private visit. It has nothing whatsoever to do with my work.'

'You'll pardon me if I treat your statement with a degree of scepticism, Pate. You see, I know you have visited the home of Mrs Cake. As she is a crippled widow who owns her own property, I doubt if you went there to see her. That would appear to leave only her sole employee, Wesley Gillam. He's a bright lad, I believe. Far too bright perhaps to be working as a labourer on

395

such a small landholding. But no doubt it gives him more time to dabble in Union matters.'

'Whom I see is entirely my own business.' Alan's manner was suddenly far less belligerent than before. Wesley Gillam was the *last* person he had wanted to meet in Tolpuddle. 'Anyway, Trades Associations are legal now.'

'True. Misguided though I personally believe such legislation to be, I have no quarrel with anyone who remains within the law. However, it is my duty to ascertain that they *are* within the law.'

'Of course, and all true Union men are eager to ensure that their members are good, law-abiding citizens. If Wesley Gillam is breaking the law my Association will not be a party to it. Having said that, I would stress that my Association cannot be held responsible for local variations in procedures.'

'True. But in order to clarify this matter, are you able to tell me what form the oath administered by the Tolpuddle branch takes?'

'No.' Alan Pate knew this to be the crux of the whole meeting. Word had reached the Association that there was a query about the legality of a member being forced to take any form of oath. Magistrate Frampton wanted to know for certain that an oath *was* being taken when new members were enrolled. 'You would have to ask Wesley Gillam the answer to that question. Local officials decide what oath an initiate must take.'

'I see. Very well, Pate. I will not detain you any longer. Thank you for your co-operation. You may go – but be very careful while you are in Tolpuddle. If I have reason to believe you have not told me the truth about your visit, we will meet again.'

'I doubt that, Mr Frampton. My Association was formed not to stir up unrest, but to eliminate injustice. While I am doing this I believe I serve England better than you and your fellows. But time alone will be the judge of that.'

Chapter 30

Alan had his saddle-bags packed ready for his journey back to London when he called at Widow Cake's cottage, later that same day.

Wes was sawing wood in the yard at the back of the house. Alan made his way to the kitchen door, passing Wes by without acknowledging his presence.

Saranna was in the kitchen when he knocked. Thinking it was Wes, she called, 'Come in. I'm only ironing.'

When Alan opened the door and went inside, she said in surprise, 'Oh! It's you.'

'That's right. You were no doubt expecting young Gillam. It must be a very cosy arrangement for you both.'

'We both work for Widow Cake,' said Saranna evenly. 'I've already told you so.'

Alan expressed his disbelief in a momentary tightening of his lips before he said, 'I'm here to see if you've come to your senses. If you have you may return with me to Eltham. I can leave my horse for sale in stables at Dorchester and we'll catch a coach to London.'

'I haven't changed my mind since yesterday, Alan. I'm sorry if I've interfered with your plans. But I'd be even more sorry if I felt it was *you* and not your pride I'd hurt.'

'You intend remaining here and marrying Gillam?'

'I'll stay here to look after Widow Cake. As to marrying Wes . . . I don't know yet.'

'You're being extremely foolish, Saranna. I am offering you more than most girls from your background can expect to gain in a marriage.'

'You may think so, Alan, but my ma said something to me that I will always remember. She said the greatest gift that can be given to girls with my background is to marry a man you love, and who loves you in return. His station in life or his wealth doesn't matter. What does matter is real, unselfish love. Can you offer me that, Alan?'

'Of course I can. I would hardly want to marry you if I wasn't fond of you.'

'Fondness isn't love. You find it difficult even to say the word. I'm fond of you too, but I've come to realise I don't love you in the way I should. That isn't the way a marriage should begin.'

'So you won't return to Eltham with me?'

'No.'

'Very well. I hoped you would have changed your mind. But think about it. We should still have a good marriage. However, don't make the mistake of believing I'll wait for you forever. I won't.'

'Don't wait for me at all, Alan. Find yourself a girl who'll share your ambitions and help you to achieve them. You'll realise then that what I'm saying now is right. I'm not the wife you are looking for. She's still out there somewhere, waiting for you to find her.'

Alan left the cottage, still without so much as a glance in Wes's direction. When he mounted and rode away, Wes hurried to the kitchen to speak to Saranna.

He found her looking pale and considerably shaken. Despite the confident and positive manner with which she had confronted Alan, it had been a considerable strain.

Saranna had been his fiancée for a year. It had not been easy to tell such a forceful man she was not going to marry him after all.

'What happened, Saranna? What did you tell him?'

'I told him I am definitely not going to marry him and said I hope he'll find himself a suitable wife.' She shrugged and even managed a weak smile. 'That's all there was to it.'

Her attempt at nonchalance did not fool Wes, but before he could say anything more, there was a call from Widow Cake's sick-room.

'Is that you I can hear out there, Wesley? Come here this minute and tell me what's going on.'

'Right away, Mrs Cake.'

To Saranna, he said softly, 'I'd wager that she never missed a word that was said in here.'

'Stop whispering, young man, and do as you're told. Or will I have to struggle out there to find out what's been going on in my own house?'

Entering Widow Cake's room, Wes said, 'Alan Pate's just left. I don't think he made things very easy for Saranna. I thought I might make her a cup of tea.'

'Is that so? You're very free with other people's goods – but I called you here to find out what was said between them. I could hear a man's voice in the kitchen and he sounded angry.'

'Saranna told him she definitely wouldn't be marrying him. By the look of him when he left he was none too pleased.'

Suddenly, a huge grin escaped him. He was far more relieved

that Saranna had made the break with Alan Pate than he wanted to show.

'Good! Good!' Amelia nodded her head frequently, in approval. 'Perhaps we'll all begin putting some commonsense back into our lives again now. Don't you dare allow her to go away again, Wesley Gillam.'

'I won't, Mrs Cake. I won't.'

'I'm pleased to hear it. Now go off and make that cup of tea. Tell Saranna to bring hers in here, with one for me. I want to chat to her too.'

The day after Alan Pate left Tolpuddle, Eli Gillam was taken ill. He had not been well for a couple of days, but had tried to shrug it off. On this day he woke up with a severe headache and was so giddy he could hardly stand.

He took to his bed, struck down by illness for the first time in twenty-five years of married life.

Rachel was extremely worried about him. She needed to go to work, but hurried home at midday to see how he was. Wes also looked in on his father when he brought milk down the hill to Tolpuddle for one of Widow Cake's cheesemaking customers.

Taking some milk to the bedroom for his father, he asked how he was.

'I feel as though I'm dying, Wesley. I've never had a day's illness in my life, yet here I am unable to stand for longer than a few minutes without falling over. It would have to happen today of all days. Eight new members are joining the Association tonight. I'm supposed to be there to help with the initiation ceremony.'

'Well, they'll just have to manage without you. Someone else will take your place. I'll go and tell George Loveless as soon as I finish work tonight.'

George Loveless was seriously inconvenienced by the sickness of Eli Gillam. 'It's very short notice to find someone else,' he said. 'Can you help us out, Wesley?'

'I'd like to, but I'm not a member of the Association.'

'Of course you're not. You do so much for us I'd forgotten that. Oh well, I'll have to ask my brother to help. Tell your pa I hope he's soon well again. Do you have any idea what the trouble might be?'

'No, but if he's no better tomorrow we'll think about getting a doctor to see him. Good luck with your initiations tonight.'

The next morning, Wes was having breakfast before going to work. His mother had taken a cup of tea up to his father, in the hope he might feel like drinking.

Suddenly there was a shriek from his mother. 'Wesley! Come here – quickly!'

Fearing the worst, he abandoned his meal and ran up the stairs. His mother met him on the landing at the top. 'Wes . . . you must fetch the doctor, quickly. Your father has come out in a dreadful rash. I fear it's smallpox.'

Wes looked in on his father who sat up in bed holding a cup of tea in one hand and running exploratory fingers over his face with the other. The skin on his face and what could be seen of his neck and chin were covered in ugly angry-looking spots.

Wes was as alarmed as his mother. 'I'll go right away. But . . . how are you feeling, Pa?'

'It's a strange thing, Wesley, but I feel much better than I did yesterday. Almost my old self again. It's as though all the badness has come out of me in the spots.'

At the foot of the stairs, Rachel Gillam was wringing her hands in despair, more agitated than Wes had ever seen her before.

'What he's saying about feeling better worries me more than ever, Wes. I can remember my grandmother talking about a small-pox epidemic they had when she was a girl. Her father died of it – and he said the same as your pa! He woke up one morning saying he felt so much better. Twenty-four hours later he was dead!'

'Don't get yourself in such a state, Ma. I'll call in and tell Widow Cake what's happening. Hopefully she'll let me borrow the horse. Then I'll call to see Rosie Amos before going for the doctor. She might have something to give Pa.'

Wes did not enter Widow Cake's cottage. Smallpox was a dis-ease that struck fear into people. He knocked at the door until Saranna opened it, then stood well back while he explained mat-ters to her.

She acted as go-between for Wes and Amelia Cake. As he had anticipated, he was banned from entering the cottage until his father's illness had run its full course. He would come to work and remain outside, coming no closer than the yard. Neither should he enter the dairy. He would drive the cows in from the fields at milking time and leave the rest to Saranna. He could take the horse – but he was to be back as quickly as he could.

Wes saddled the horse as swiftly as the reluctant animal would allow. He was leading it through the yard when Saranna came to the door.

'Take care, Wes. I hope your pa will be all right. Tell your ma that if there's anything at all I can do to help, she has only to ask.'

Wes rode away wondering about the likelihood that he would catch smallpox from his father. The chances must be high. He also knew that in the instances where it did not prove fatal it could

400

often prove to be a highly disfiguring disease.

He shook the thought from his mind and headed for the small home of Rosie Amos, behind the mill.

'Smallpox, you say?' Rosie was as alarmed as Widow Cake had been, but she was also puzzled. 'It's not usual for smallpox to strike at this time of year. I haven't heard of any other cases in the area either, but then, I don't know everything. I'll mix up a potion from dried snakeweed root. It's not successful in advanced cases, but it's the best thing I know. Call in and pick it up when you come back. I'll leave it on the doorstep. I'll also leave a saucerful of vinegar there. You can put a shilling inside in payment.'

The physician in Dorchester was as surprised as Rosie had been, repeating her comment that he had heard of no cases in his area. But he agreed to come immediately. On the ride to Tolpuddle Wes told him all he could about his father's condition, and what had been done for him. The doctor said very little in reply, but seemed very thoughtful.

Riding through the single street of Tolpuddle it was apparent that the news had gone around very quickly indeed. Women stood at their doorways talking. They called to their children to come and stand near them, well clear of Wes as he rode past with the doctor.

Wes's mother was watching for them. She opened the door for the doctor, while Wes took Widow Cake's horse and tethered it to the fence nearby.

As the doctor followed his mother inside the house, Wes heard him ask her how the patient was.

'He's still cheerful, doctor, it's worrying me . . .'

Wes took his time securing the horses, reluctant to go inside and hear the doctor confirm the worst.

When he did go inside the house the doctor was coming down the stairs. Much to Wes's surprise, when the doctor saw him he broke into a smile. 'Well, young man, we've both had a long ride and a great deal of worry for nothing – I'm pleased to say.'

'You mean . . . it isn't smallpox, after all?'

'Pox it certainly is – but *chicken-pox*, not its more serious cousin.'

'But . . . he felt so ill.' Overwhelmed by relief as he was, Wes was puzzled. 'I've never seen Pa like that before.'

'If your father had caught the illness when he was a small boy he would, as like as not, have shrugged it off in a matter of days. It's rather more serious for adults. At least, until the spots show themselves, it is. He can get up and lead a normal life again as soon as he likes. In fact, I'd advise it. A man can feel a fool if word goes about that he's been lying abed with chicken-pox.'

Chapter 31

'Chicken-pox! Chicken-pox! Only a Methodist minister would kick-up a fuss about such a trifling illness. Why, half the children in the village have had chicken-pox and they probably never even noticed!' Amelia banged on the floor with her stick to emphasise her words.

She was seated in her favourite chair beside the fire in the kitchen. It was the first time she had made it from her sick-room to the kitchen since injuring her ankle. She was berating Wes now as he carried in logs from the wood-shed and stacked them in the alcove beside the fireplace.

Wes remembered the doctor's words, but kept silent. Widow Cake was in one of her 'not-to-be-argued-with' moods, today.

'Well, I'm relieved it wasn't smallpox,' said Saranna as she brushed up fragments of moss and bark which had fallen from the logs to the floor. 'Quite apart from the pain and the danger to Mr Gillam, we wouldn't have been able to have Wes come inside the house for weeks.'

'By the look of the mess he's making with those logs, I'm not at all sure that would be a bad thing,' snapped the caustic widow. 'As for that father of his! I only hope he'll offer to pay for the use of my horse and the loss of his son's work for half-a-day. Not to mention the amount of hay the horse ate as a result of carrying Wesley all that way.'

When Wes left the kitchen and the door closed behind him, Saranna said, 'You shouldn't get on to Wes so much, Mrs Cake. You know very well he works many more hours for you than most men would.'

'If he spends more time here than he should, I doubt if it's for *me*. It's more likely to be because *you're* here. Anyway, you should have learned by now that you never tell a man how good he is. If you do, he'll sit back and rest on his laurels, telling himself how lucky the world is to have him. You make sure you keep Wesley on his toes when you've made up your mind to marry him. That way you'll get a sight more work out of him. Now, all this talking has made me tired. Hurry up and finish in here so I can sit in peace for an hour. You can find something to do elsewhere in the house.'

'I'm still happy it wasn't smallpox,' declared Saranna, doggedly. 'If it had been Wes would probably have gone down with it too and . . .' As Saranna thought of the horrendous implications, she found she could not utter them. 'It . . . it's just too horrible to even think about.'

'Oh well, if it's made you realise how fond you are of the boy then I suppose some good's come of it all, but for goodness' sake tell him and be done with it. Not only will it give him something to be happy about, but perhaps then we can all begin making plans for the future.'

The future was what was being decided in the Gillam household that evening. But this was the very near future. Christmas was only a few weeks away and Rachel unfolded her plans.

'Why don't we invite Saranna to spend Christmas Day with us?'

'That's a wonderful idea!' Wes was immediately enthusiastic. 'But she couldn't leave Widow Cake alone on that day. Couldn't we invite her to spend Christmas with us too?'

'I don't want that woman in this house. If she came here she would spoil *my* day.'

Eli was trimming a piece of leather, preparatory to putting new soles on his boots. He walked many miles in order to carry out his preaching commitments and wore out the soles and heels of his footwear every couple of months.

'You won't be here, unless it's to show your face for dinner and supper, so it won't make any difference to you. Wes is right. Even if Widow Cake hadn't been so generous to him, what with that will and everything, we couldn't leave her on her own up at that cottage. She's unable to hobble farther than a few paces on her own. It wouldn't be Christian.'

Rachel glared at her husband, daring him to disagree with her.

The leather cut to shape, Eli slipped a boot over the heavy iron last on the floor and hammered in the first nail with excessive vigour. 'Then I suppose you'd better invite them both, although I can't for the life of me see why we can't enjoy Christmas here on our own, the same as usual.'

Rachel smiled at Wes. The argument had been won. An invitation would be extended to Saranna and to Widow Cake. 'Wouldn't it be wonderful if our Saul came home unexpectedly for Christmas? That would make my day complete.'

Wes hoped his mother would not see the momentary expression of anguish that came to his face. Much of the time these days he was able to forget the dark secret he kept from his family. Nevertheless, it came back occasionally to haunt him.

But Rachel Gillam was busy mixing the ingredients for the Christmas plum pudding. She did not look up from the table as she said, 'I sometimes wonder if I will ever see him again.'

'We will all meet again, Rachel, in the Lord's good time. We hope it will be soon, in this life, but whenever He chooses, it will be a glorious reunion.'

'I don't want to spend Christmas Day with any Methodist preacher!'

Amelia Cake exploded in indignation when Saranna put the suggestion to her. 'I don't mind them not drinking. I've hardly touched a drop since I came home from the war. No, it's not that. I just don't believe it's necessary to be miserable in this life in order to ensure we'll be happy in the hereafter. Christmas is a joyful time. A peaceful time – and that's how I'd like to spend it. My only regret is that I'll not be able to go to church. It seems ages since I was last there. I don't like to think that the next time I go there will be to get buried. The Christmas service is the best one of all. I can remember all the greenery decorating the church and the children, all bright-eyed and happy because they've had their stockings and presents. I miss that.'

Later that same day, talking to Wes, Saranna told him of what Widow Cake had said. His disappointment that Saranna could not spend Christmas at his home was very gratifying to her, but she had an idea.

'Wes, more than anything else, Widow Cake would like to attend the Tolpuddle church on Christmas Day. If there is some way you can take her, I am sure I could persuade her to come to your house for dinner.'

Smiling at the sudden return of Wes's hopeful eagerness, Saranna added, 'She probably wouldn't stay for very long, but at least we'd both be there for a while.'

'All right,' Wes replied without hesitation. 'I'll suggest taking her to church in the pony trap. When we come out of the church we'll be almost home anyway.'

Chapter 32

Christmas Day dawned clear and bright. There was just enough frost to sprinkle a sparkling white sheen on the fields.

Walking through the village on his way to Widow Cake's cottage, Wes passed a house where he knew there were eleven in the family. From inside came the excited squeals of children.

He smiled sadly as he remembered past Christmases, when he and Saul would come downstairs at first light to inspect the contents of their stockings. Filled with exciting shapes, they would be hanging from the heavy wooden mantelshelf above the fireplace in the kitchen.

It was painful to think that the happy elder brother he had so looked up to in those days had ended his life on a Marlborough gallows.

But these were not thoughts for Christmas Day. Especially when he was to have dinner with the girl he hoped one day to marry.

Wes was dressed in his Christmas Day best. Widow Cake had driven a hard bargain in return for going to the Gillam House for lunch. He would have to attend the church with her. Saranna said it was probably because the widow was nervous about going out of the house for the first time since her injury.

Wes was looking forward to the day, despite this. In his pocket he carried two presents. For Widow Cake there was a fine leather bookmark, worked with her name. Made for Wes by the village saddlemaker, it would mark the place for each Sunday reading in the family Bible she kept on her shelf.

For Saranna he had something even more special: a finely worked silver crucifix on a chain, to wear about her neck. It was real silver, bought from a woman in the village with money he had saved over the years.

The woman had once worked for a generous, titled family in nearby Hampshire. Now she was selling some of the many gifts she had been given there, in a bid to escape the rigours of the poorhouse.

When he arrived at the cottage he found Widow Cake dressed

405

and ready. Seated on a chair close to the door, she made Wes think of a young girl, waiting to be taken on an outing.

Wishing Widow Cake and Saranna a 'Happy Christmas', Wes handed them their presents, saying hurriedly, 'I'll go and get the pony and trap ready now.'

'No, you won't, you'll stay here until I've opened my present.'

When Widow Cake opened the small packet, Wes explained, 'That's your name on there. It's a bookmark, made specially for your family Bible.'

'I may not be able to read or write, young man, but I can recognise my own name.'

Suddenly, the sheer pleasure of having a permanent object with her name on it overcame the harsh front Amelia Cake presented to the world. 'Come here, Wesley Gillam. Bend down so I can kiss you.'

It was the first such show of affection Wes had ever known her make towards anyone.

While it was going on, Saranna was unwrapping her own present. Lifting the crucifix free of its wrapping, she drew in her breath in a gasp of delight. 'Wes, it's *beautiful*!'

'You like it?'

'Like? Oh, Wes, it's the most wonderful present I've ever had.'

She kissed him now, but on the mouth, and it left him warm, pink and pleased.

'Put it around my neck and fasten it for me, Wes.'

When the chain and crucifix had been fastened about her throat, Saranna fingered it and said, 'I won't be a minute. I want to look at it in the mirror in my room.'

'Don't be long, we mustn't be late for church.'

When Saranna had gone, Amelia said, 'You've made her a very happy girl, Wesley.'

Touching his lips where she had kissed him, Wes thought Saranna had made him very happy too, but he said, 'I'll go outside and get the pony and trap.'

Loading Amelia into the small vehicle proved to be hard work. It left the widow breathless, but she recovered quickly. By the time they entered Tolpuddle village proper she was her usual self once more.

It was the first time she had been to the village for many months, but she missed nothing. Passing the cottage that had once been occupied by Arnold Cooper and his grandmother, she said, 'Huh! I see that whoever's taken over the Cooper cottage hasn't changed the curtains. It doesn't look as though they've been washed, either.'

In the small church, as the widow entered slowly, flanked by Wes and Saranna, she received nods of greeting from most of the villagers. They all had respect, if not affection, for the uncertain-tempered war widow.

Wes's presence in the church was also the subject of much sly nudgings among the congregation. They wondered what might have happened to make the son of such a prominent Methodist preacher attend the village church.

Saranna too came in for her share of attention. She had been known to most of the villagers when she lived at Southover. Few had seen her since her return. She had blossomed into a sophisticated and attractive young woman and she received envious glances from other girls and warm appreciation from the men.

In spite of his earlier misgivings, Wes found he enjoyed the service. He would have enjoyed it even more had he been seated next to Saranna, but Widow Cake sat between them. Nevertheless, they exchanged many glances and Wes saw Saranna finger the crucifix frequently during the service.

When it was over they filed out of the church to receive Christmas greetings from Reverend Thomas Warren.

'I am delighted to see you here, Mrs Cake,' said the vicar, grasping both her hands and shaking them gently.

'Perhaps now you know I'm still alive you'll pay a call on a disabled widow who's seen neither hide nor hair of her vicar since she broke her foot.'

'Ha, ha! It's also very refreshing to know you haven't lost a scrap of spirit, Mrs Cake.'

Reverend Warren extended a hand to Wes. 'I can't tell you how delighted I am to see you in my church, Wesley. Especially today. I hope it will mean a rebirth – a new beginning, for all of us.'

Following these words, Thomas Warren murmured a few pleasantries to Saranna, and then passed on to the next in line.

'Did you enjoy the service?' Saranna asked Widow Cake when the old lady was settled comfortably in the trap.

'Yes. Yes, I did. Reverend Warren has never been able to preach a good sermon, and he never will, but I found it a great comfort to sit in church and take part in the service. It brought back many memories to me. Some are happy, some sad, but most of all I felt close to all those I've loved in my life. Thank you for taking me, Wesley. You too, Saranna. It's made it a memorable Christmas for me already. Now I suppose we ought to be on our way and not keep that father of yours waiting, Wesley. He isn't the most patient of men.'

Eli was not waiting for them when they reached the house. He was still conducting a service in the village chapel. The Methodist lay preacher was a more powerful and wordy sermoniser than his Church of England counterpart and he allowed his sermon to flow.

By the time he arrived home, Amelia Cake was firmly ensconced in Eli's favourite chair by the fireside. Nursing a cup of tea, she was offering advice to her hostess on the time needed to cook a goose perfectly.

'The compliments of the season to you, Mrs Cake – and welcome to our house.'

Eli was still filled with the passion of the sermon that had warmed the hearts of his congregation. He had sent them home rejoicing in the marvels that the birth of the Saviour had given to the world on this day, so many years before.

'We've been through all that, Eli. However, it *is* kind of you to invite me into your home today.'

'It's a day for celebrating the generosity of the Lord who gave His only son to us, Mrs Cake,' said Eli in his most pompous manner. 'A day for giving.'

'Then someone had better give that goose another turn if we're to fully appreciate the meal that Rachel has worked so hard to provide. That reminds me. Wesley, go out to the trap. I left my basket under the seat. In it you'll find a pair of vases I've had tucked away at home for goodness knows how long. I thought that, seeing as it's Christmas, you might as well have them, Rachel. They're good ones, Bristol glass I think they're called. They belonged to my late husband's family.'

When Wes had gone from the room, Amelia Cake said unexpectedly, 'That's a fine lad you've got there, Eli. He's the sort of son I would have liked to have, had the good Lord so willed it.'

'He's always been a good son to us, Mrs Cake,' said Rachel proudly. 'I know he appreciates your generosity towards him too, and so do we.'

Glancing towards Saranna, Amelia said, 'I hope this young lady is listening and appreciates what a fine husband she'll be getting if she marries him.'

'Mrs Cake!' Highly embarrassed, Saranna said, 'Wes and I have never mentioned marriage to anyone . . .'

'There are some things that don't need to be said. Leave the "saying" to vicars and preachers, and the like. Marriage is about the way you feel about a person. I may be old and infirm, but I'm not blind. If ever I've seen two young people made for each other, it's you and Wesley. Don't you agree with me, Rachel?'

Taken by surprise by Amelia's blunt question, Rachel looked up at Saranna. Seeing how apprehensive she was, Rachel suddenly smiled at her. 'We've thought so for a very long time, haven't we, Eli?'

'You've been telling me so for long enough,' he corrected his wife. Looking across the room to where Saranna was watching him uncertainly, he added, with a sudden flash of intuition about the way Saranna was thinking, 'But I'm inclined to agree with you. I can't bring to mind any other girl I'd rather he married.'

Christmas dinner at the Gillam house turned out to be a great success, much to the relief of everyone. Soon after the meal was over, Amelia said it was time she returned to her own home and took some rest. It had been an unusually strenuous day for her and she was tired.

Eli said he too needed to leave as he had another service to conduct before taking the final service of the day in Tolpuddle church. He offered to drive Widow Cake home. In return, she offered him the loan of the pony and trap to ensure he met his commitments for the day.

Saranna remained with Wes and Rachel and that evening they balanced the religious scales by attending the evening service at Tolpuddle chapel where Eli preached another powerful sermon.

His look of pure pleasure when he saw them in the congregation told them that his day also had been a special one.

Later that evening, Wes was walking Saranna home to the cottage. It was a chilly evening, with a hint of drizzle in the air, but they were both happy.

'This has been a lovely Christmas, Wes. I think it's the best I ever remember. I somehow felt as though I was part of the family.'

Saranna gave a soft laugh. 'Even Widow Cake was part of that family, and I think she enjoyed herself too.'

'So do I. The thing that amazed me was the way she and my pa were getting along by the time we came to the end of dinner. You'd think they'd been friends all their lives! Then when he took her home and she let him use the pony and trap to go and preach at a Methodist service!'

They both laughed together. When it died away, Saranna said, 'I'm sorry I didn't have anything to give you for Christmas, Wes. I've been feeling dreadful about it all day. But I never thought of Christmas when I came from Eltham, far less that I would be spending it with you and your family. I've been nowhere to buy anything since I arrived.'

'You gave me the best present you could have given me, this morning. It made the day for me.'

Puzzled, Saranna said, 'What was that? I didn't give you anything at all.'

'You gave me a kiss. I couldn't have asked for anything I wanted more.'

They walked on in silence for a couple of minutes before

409

Saranna said, 'Did it really mean so much to you, Wes?'

'Yes.'

They were approaching Widow Cake's cottage now and Saranna suddenly stopped walking. When Wes stopped too, she stepped closer. Murmuring, 'A happy, happy Christmas, Wes,' she kissed him for the second time that day.

This time there was no Widow Cake present to embarrass him and the kiss lasted for a long time.

When they were both forced to break away in order to draw breath, Wes continued to hold her close.

'You're shivering. Are you cold?'

'No, Wes. I'm just . . . happy.'

He kissed her again. When they pulled apart this time, he said, 'I love you, Saranna.'

She hugged him even more tightly. 'I believe you really do, Wes.'

'You're the only one who's ever doubted it.'

They remained in each other's arms for a few more moments before Saranna said, in little more than a whisper, 'I love you too, Wes.'

He could hardly believe he was hearing right. 'Say that again . . . please.'

'I love you, Wes. I love you very, very much. I always have.'

'Then you'll marry me?'

'Whenever you want me to.'

Wes was so happy, he felt like shouting to the whole world that they were to be married. After kissing and hugging Saranna for a long time, he said, 'Come on, let's go and tell Widow Cake. She deserves to be the first to know.'

Chapter 33

Wes and Saranna decided they would marry in the spring of 1834. Rachel Gillam was overjoyed at their news. Eli too approved of the marriage. The Christmas meal with Saranna had finally dispelled the earlier prejudice he had entertained against her. His only regret was that it would have to be a church wedding and could not be held in the Tolpuddle chapel.

There was much agitation throughout the land to allow weddings to be solemnised in the non-conformist Churches. A certain amount of sympathy had been expressed in Parliament for the idea, but no laws had yet been passed.

Amelia Cake's reaction to the news of her employees' intended wedding was typically less euphoric, yet she too registered her unqualified approval of the marriage, and added that it was about time they both came to their senses.

During the next few weeks Wes was unable to go anywhere in the village without having someone stop him and offer congratulations on his forthcoming wedding. Eli Gillam was a popular preacher on the Methodist circuit and his son was well-known to everyone.

Then something occurred to put a dent, at least, in his feeling of well-being. On his way home from work one evening, after dark, Wes thought he detected a movement in a doorway, close to his home.

He took little notice; village girls and boys carried on a great deal of their courting in doorways. Then, as he passed by, a man's voice called softly, 'Wesley Gillam?'

'That's me.'

Wes did not recognise the voice. Not until the man stepped forward and was touched by the light from a nearby window did he realise who it was. His name was Andrew Symonds and his family had moved back to Tolpuddle in recent years after working elsewhere. The family were church-goers with a house at the far end of the village. Wes knew little about them – except that the young man who was speaking to him had worked at Moreton House for James Frampton until very recently. Only that day Wes

411

had been told Symonds had been dismissed.

'What can I do for you?' Wes asked the question after a few seconds when the other man failed to follow up his original question.

'I think it's more what *I* can do for *you*. You know I've been working at Moreton House?'

'Yes. I hear you've been dismissed, but you shouldn't let it worry you too much. You're probably better off away from there.'

'I was dismissed because Miss Josephine told her grandfather I was insolent. I wasn't. I like her far too much ever to be insolent to her. I thought she liked me, but she couldn't have done, could she? If she had, she wouldn't have lied about me.'

The manner in which Andrew Symonds spoke reminded Wes of Arnold – but Symonds was not as easy-going as Wes's unfortunate friend.

In a voice filled with resentment, he said, 'I'll get even with her, don't you worry. I know how.'

'It's not worth even thinking about it, Andrew. Her grandfather is a magistrate and he has a knack of bending the law to suit himself and his family. Think yourself lucky to be away from there. Miss Josephine tried to get me in trouble a few years ago by telling lies about me. I was very nearly sent to prison. I don't think she's ever forgiven me for getting away with it.'

'She hasn't. Miss Josephine's been asking me a lot of questions about the Society of Farm Workers and about you too. Especially about you.'

'Me . . . and the Society? Why?'

Wes was puzzled. Why should Josephine want to tie him in with the Society? Unless Magistrate Frampton was planning something against the farm workers' organisation and wished to include Wesley with it. But Andrew Symonds was speaking again . . .

'I don't know exactly what it's all about, but I think that's why Magistrate Frampton had the Association man there a week or two back.'

'Which Association man would that be?'

'Him who stayed at the Crown, in the village here.'

'Alan Pate? Why should he go to Moreton House?'

'I don't know. When I spoke about him to Miss Josephine I got the feeling she knew him, 'though I don't know how she could. Anyway, she got quite excited when I told her he was staying in Tolpuddle.'

Wes realised that Andrew Symonds had revealed far more about his relationship with Josephine Moreton than he realised. He must have known her very well for them to be talking about such matters.

He thought he knew what their relationship had been. It was proof, had he needed any, that Josephine had not changed despite the passing of the years.

She must have come to know Alan Pate through Saul and his activities. Yet surely she would not talk openly to Pate and risk having her past brought out into the open? However, if Alan Pate had been to Moreton House . . . It raised serious implications for the Tolpuddle Friendly Association.

'Thank you for warning me, Andrew. I don't think you'd better say anything to anyone else about this. It might make Magistrate Frampton angry with you.'

'Don't worry, she won't make any trouble for me – but I might make some for her.'

Andrew Symonds slipped away in the darkness, leaving Wes wondering what course the ex-footman's revenge was likely to take.

'Is something bothering you, Wes? You're not having second thoughts about marrying me?'

Saranna put the question to him when she came out to the cow-shed the next morning. Unnoticed, she had been watching him from the doorway as he washed down the cows, prior to milking. It was clear to her that he had something on his mind.

'Something's bothering me, yes, but it has nothing to do with our getting married – unless it's because I don't want anything to come along to prevent it happening.'

Finishing off the cow he was washing down, Wes told her about his meeting with Andrew Symonds.

'Do you think he was telling you the truth? Why should she go to such lengths to try to get you into trouble? It's a few years now since you got the better of her at Moreton House. Surely she isn't still angry about that?'

'No, I think it's something far more serious. I believe Magistrate Frampton is planning some kind of action against the Farm Labourers' Society. If she believes I'm a member she might think it's a good opportunity to get me out of the way once and for all.'

'But why should she go to such lengths over *you*? It doesn't make sense.'

'Yes, it does. I know something that would put *her* in prison for a very long time. It could even take her to the scaffold. She would be very happy if she thought there was a chance of having me sent away from Tolpuddle for a long time.'

Wes repeated the story told to him by Saul the night before he was hung. He added, 'I don't know how much of it is true. Most of it, I suspect. It certainly frightened her when I told her I knew

413

about it and threatened to inform the Bow Street magistrate if she tried to cause any trouble for me.'

'And so it should! I heard rumours about this when I first went to Kent. Richard spent a lot more time in London than he does now and was talking to Ma about it one night. The Bow Street Runners were involved in the case. They made life very difficult for a great many of those who lived around Bethnal Green for weeks because they'd heard someone from there was involved. They never got anywhere with their enquiries because word went around that Meg was mixed up in it somewhere. She's well liked in the area.'

Mention of Meg reminded Wes of her young sister. He had not thought of her for a long time and was embarrassed that he should be thinking of her now. But Saranna was too concerned to notice.

'What are we going to do about it, Wes? We can't allow her to involve you in any plans Magistrate Frampton might be making against the Association.'

'There's nothing we can do right now, because we don't know what he intends. Anyway, I'm not involved with the Society. But Josephine is terrified that her secret might come out. Now I've told you what I know about it. If anything does happen to me, perhaps you can use the knowledge to help in some way.'

Wes moved on to the last cow in the line-up. 'Mind you, it's quite likely that Andrew Symonds has got it wrong. He's very bitter about Josephine at the moment and is looking for sympathy wherever he can find it. Let's hope that Magistrate Frampton doesn't intend doing anything about either the Association or me.'

Chapter 34

A little over a week after Andrew Symonds had given Wes warning of Josephine Frampton's questioning, Saranna was at the Gillam house. She had finished her day's work at Amelia Cake's cottage and was helping Rachel prepare an evening meal.

Wes sat in a corner of the kitchen frowning over Widow Cake's account books, working by the uncertain light of a yellow wax candle.

Suddenly the door opened and Eli came in. Rachel was fond of saying that whenever Eli entered the house it was like releasing a bull in a small pen. He always entered with a rush and seemed able to be in every place at once.

Tonight was no different from usual, except that he was waving a sheet of stout paper in front of him. Crossing the room to where Wes sat, Eli slapped the piece of paper down on the small table in front of him.

'Here, read this and tell me what you make of it! It's Magistrate Frampton's doing, I'm certain of it, but I don't for the life of me know what it is he's playing at.'

Wes picked up the piece of paper. It was heavily printed on one side and the word CAUTION at the top of the page immediately caught his eye. Midway down the page, in letters almost as large, it stated 'Will become GUILTY OF FELONY and be liable to be TRANSPORTED FOR SEVEN YEARS'.

At the foot of the page, again in letters that leaped from the paper, were the words: 'CONVICTED OF FELONY and Transported for SEVEN YEARS'.

The notice was endorsed by no fewer than nine of the county's magistrates. Among them was the name of James Frampton.

Now Wes studied the notice's wording, printed in smaller letters between the headlines. As he read, he occasionally looked up at his father in consternation. The notice was a warning aimed at those who joined or who intended joining Unions, or Associations, to which they bound themselves by taking 'unlawful oaths'.

According to the notice it was illegal to become a member of such a Union; to take any oath; administer an oath; or even to fail to reveal that such an oath had been administered.

There was much on the notice couched in legal jargon that would need careful reading, but the message was clear enough. Despite the laws of the land which had removed the restrictions on Trades Unions, the Dorset magistrates seemed to have found a sizeable loophole in the legislation. They had decreed that the members of the Tolpuddle Friendly Society of Labourers were breaking the law.

'What do you make of it?' Eli asked his son.

'Where did you get it?'

'It was nailed to a tree at the east end of the village, but they're all over the place. No one can fail to see them. How many men can actually read them is a different matter, but I don't suppose any magistrate will worry about that.'

'I think it will have to be read, re-read, then read again before it even begins to make sense – but it sounds alarming. Magistrate Frampton's been working on this for a very long time. He won't have acted without being quite certain he's got everything right. The question is, what are you and the others in the Society going to do about this?'

'It's difficult to see what we can do. We've cast our die. There can be no turning back now.'

Listening in growing dismay to the discussion, Rachel said, 'This doesn't mean you'll be taken to court and perhaps sent to prison, does it, Eli? You and our Wesley too?'

'Wesley's done nothing. He isn't even a member of the Society. For the rest . . . We were given to understand that Trades Associations are legal now. Alan Pate and the other man from London assured us this is so. They said Trades Unions and Associations are allowed by specific Act of Parliament.'

'The initiation oath!' Saranna said suddenly and loudly, causing the others to cease talking and look at her in surprise.

'Don't you remember, Wes? When you told me the members were made to take an initiation oath on joining the Tolpuddle Society, I was surprised. They've stopped it in most Associations and Unions everywhere else in the country. That notice mentions "illegal oaths". That must be why the others have stopped taking an oath.'

'But there's nothing in the oath that could possibly offend anyone. It's more like a prayer than anything else. We deliberately made it so.'

'I doubt if the wording matters very much. It's an oath. That's sufficient excuse for the magistrates to take some action if it's not allowed.'

'What are we going to do?' Wes asked of his father.

Eli picked up the notice. 'I'm taking this to the chapel. George Loveless, James Brine and some of the others will be there tonight. We'll discuss it and see what everyone thinks.'

Later that evening Wes and Saranna were walking back to Widow Cake's cottage. They were discussing the notice once more. Wes had one of them in his pocket, taken from a fence post at the entrance to the lane.

'This notice could be no more than an attempt to frighten the workers who've joined the Society. On the other hand, they *might* have broken the law by taking an oath, however innocent it might be. Whatever the reason, it's pretty obvious that Magistrate Frampton has decided it's time he made a move against the Association.'

Wes put an arm about Saranna. 'I'm worried about it. I'd hate anything to happen to Pa. I'm worried enough to take a copy of the notice to Richard Pemble and ask his advice.'

'He's no longer a member of the Grand Association, Wes. Alan is in charge now.'

'I can't very well take the notice to him and ask his advice! Especially as we know he's been to Moreton House. I don't suppose there's anything sinister in that, but I can't see his doing anything to help *me*. Anyway, Richard Pemble knows far more about Union matters than anyone else in the country. He'll be able to advise us.'

'*I'll* take the notice to Uncle Richard,' said Saranna, unexpectedly.

'You . . .? Why?'

'I want to tell my ma that you and I are getting married. We need her permission because I'm not twenty-one yet. I also hope to be able to persuade her to come to Tolpuddle for the wedding.'

Wes was not happy about Saranna going to Eltham village. Alan Pate was there. Wes believed he would make another effort to persuade Saranna to change her mind about not marrying him. He did not seriously believe it would make any difference, but it might prove unpleasant for her.

'It makes sense, Wes. You must see that?'

'Yes, I do,' he said, grudgingly. 'I just don't like the idea of your going there on your own.'

'I don't like the idea of being parted from you either,' Saranna gave him a hug. 'But I think the magistrates' notice is a big worry. We must find out what Uncle Richard thinks about it before Frampton makes his next move.'

'When were you thinking of going?'

'It's got to be as quickly as possible, Wes. I believe I ought to speak to Widow Cake tonight and travel on tomorrow's coach from Dorchester.'

'As soon as that!' Wes was dismayed.

'Yes. The more I think about it, the more convinced I am that we must move quickly. Frampton isn't likely to give the Society time to find a way around his warning. If he's confident enough to put up a public notice I think we can assume he's already gathered enough evidence to act. Come on, let's go inside and tell Widow Cake what I'm doing. We must also make some arrangements for looking after her until I return.'

Chapter 35

Saranna's coach journey from Dorchester to London was not without incident. Wes used Widow Cake's pony and trap to convey her to Dorchester. Along the way he expressed concern about the thick dark clouds which blurred the transition from night to day. He predicted that snow was on its way.

As it happened, a wide strip along the South coast stayed free of snow, but it was a different story farther inland. Long before the coach reached Salisbury, snow was falling heavily and settling on the road.

Sitting inside the vehicle, Saranna was aware that the speed of the coach was becoming slower and slower. Snow lay like a thick blanket on the road. Muffling the sound of the horses' hooves, it cushioned the wheels from the rough surface, absorbing all noise.

Saranna thought it eerie. It felt as though she was riding in a ghostly coach, passing silently through half-seen villages and hamlets.

When they were still some miles short of Salisbury, the driver was steadying the horses down a fairly gentle incline, when the coach began to slide slowly sideways.

There was no immediate panic. Those inside merely looked at each other in silent apprehension and waited for the driver to bring the vehicle under control once more.

Unfortunately, before the horses could obtain purchase on the snow-covered road, the two nearside wheels dropped in a ditch and the coach lurched sideways.

As one of the two other women inside the vehicle began to scream, the coach toppled sideways.

It was prevented from falling fully on its side by a snow-covered hedge, but the vehicle came to rest leaning at an acute angle. All the passengers had slid down the leather seats to one side. The woman who had screamed was crying out that she was being crushed.

'It'll be all right. Don't panic in there.'

The voice of the driver came to them from outside. 'We'll have you righted in no time . . .'

The 'no time' turned out to be half an hour, by which time some twenty or thirty men and boys had gathered about the coach and four powerful cart-horses had been roped to the team of steaming coach-horses.

With much shouting of advice and counter-advice, screeching springs and complaining woodwork, the coach was slowly heaved clear of the ditch and pulled to the road.

Unfortunately, the accident had damaged one of the axles and the coach had an alarming motion when it was pushed along the road by the many helpers.

Peering in through the door, the driver said, 'Everyone all right in here?'

Relieved to be out of the ditch and upright once more, even the woman who had screamed and who had been quietly sobbing throughout their ordeal, nodded in assent.

'It'll be a bit uncomfortable, but we'll get the coach to the next village. It's only a quarter of a mile along the road. There's an inn where they'll put us up until the weather improves and the coach is repaired, or another brought to take us on.'

'How long will that be?' The question came from a florid, heavily built man who carried much of the weight that had reduced the woman in the coach to tears.

'Your guess is as good as mine, sir,' replied the driver. 'It depends very much on the road up ahead of us.'

'That just isn't good enough,' declared the large man unreasonably. 'I am carrying an important letter for Lord Melbourne, the Home Secretary, and am expected to deliver a reply to Dorchester by Monday at the very latest.'

'We'll all do our best to get you through,' said the driver, seemingly unimpressed with the importance of the other man's errand. 'But if you want to be certain, then I suggest you try to hire a horse in the village and ride on to London.'

'Don't be stupid, man. I couldn't possibly ride a horse in such conditions. You must have the coach repaired and press on.'

'I'll certainly try, but we won't be going on today, that's certain. I'll not risk my other passengers for the sake of a letter – no matter how important it is.'

The florid man had to be content with this reply, but did not accept it gracefully. For much of the day he sat in the lounge of the inn where the passengers were lodged. Drinking steadily, he stirred himself only to call for another brandy, or to weave his way to the stable yard. A coach-builder had been found and he was soon busily renewing the broken axle. The messenger to Lord Melbourne was checking on his progress.

Late in the afternoon, Saranna came downstairs and saw the

messenger heading for the yard yet again. Following, she stood beside him, watching the hardworking coach-builder putting the finishing touches to his work.

'It must be most frustrating for you,' she said to the large man conversationally.

'Damned frustrating! If you'll pardon my language, miss.'

'Is the letter very important?'

'Of the *utmost* importance, I assure you. Indeed, the security of our realm might very well hinge on the letter I carry here.' The large man patted his ample waistband, suggesting a hidden belt. 'But nothing can be done until I return with a reply.'

'There's no one in Dorchester important enough to take on the task of saving the country.' Saranna was scornful. 'And saving it from *what*, I ask?'

'From subversives, miss.' The messenger was indignant. 'Not that you'd know about such matters, but there are forces abroad in England today intent on breaking down law and order. Subversives. Very dangerous men.'

'Oh! And what qualifications do you have to be entrusted with such a letter?'

'I'm a solicitor's clerk, miss. I work in the magistrates' court – and this letter is from the magistrates themselves.'

The messenger was telling Saranna more than she had hoped for, but he had said nothing specific yet. 'Why does a reply have to be back at Dorchester by Monday?'

The messenger tapped the side of his nose, winking at her at the same time. 'If I told you that you'd be as wise as me, miss. All I'll tell you is that those subversives are going to get a big surprise if the reply to this letter is what the magistrates are expecting.'

Saranna tried to extract more information from the magistrates' messenger, but he had told her all he intended saying. Possibly it was all he knew. When it became apparent he mistook her persistent curiosity about the message he carried for interest in himself, Saranna abandoned her questioning and returned to her room. She felt she had learned enough to prove she had not underestimated the importance of her journey to Richard Pemble.

No more snow fell during the night and the coach was able to resume its journey at first light. The Dorchester magistrates' messenger was suffering as a result of the drink he had consumed during the unscheduled stop. He sat in a corner of the coach hardly uttering a word all the way to London.

Saranna reached her home after dark that same evening and received a rapturous welcome. Nancy Vye was overjoyed at seeing her daughter again. Her added delight when Saranna told of her forthcoming marriage to Wes left room for no other subject of conversation for the first hour of her homecoming.

Not until the hugs, laughter and tears were over was Saranna able to pull the somewhat crumpled notice from her bag and pass it on to Richard Pemble.

A quick scan through its message was sufficient for the Union man to realise its importance.

'Where did you get this?'

'Similar posters are attached to trees and fences throughout Tolpuddle. In many of the villages around there too, I suspect.' Saranna told him of the messenger and his boastfulness. 'What do you think it means?'

'I know exactly what it means. The Dorchester magistrates intend arresting those Tolpuddle Society men who have administered the oath to initiates. It's happened before. They're using an Act of Parliament that refers to other Acts going back some forty years – to the time when the fleet mutinied at Spithead. It was never intended to be used against men who join a Union. The cases that have been brought so far have stopped short of using the full weight of the Acts. The men who have been taken to court have merely been fined.'

Tapping the notice, he said grimly, 'Reading this – coupled with what your talkative messenger said – it seems to me that Frampton and the other magistrates intend making an example of the Tolpuddle men. This should really be passed on to Alan, Saranna.'

Richard Pemble rubbed his chin and looked at his step-daughter. 'Unfortunately, I'm afraid he has little love for anyone in Tolpuddle. Neither will he have any stomach right now for a confrontation with the Dorchester magistrates. His Grand Association is in trouble and likely to collapse about his ears if he can't pull it together in a hurry.'

Saranna looked at Richard Pemble shrewdly. 'You knew that would happen when you allowed him to take over the Association.'

'I believed it might,' agreed her stepfather, totally unrepentant. 'But he has only himself to blame. By spending so much time trying to oust me and strengthen his own position, he tore the Association apart. But that isn't going to help the Tolpuddle men.'

'What can they do to help themselves?'

The question was put to him by Nancy who had been listening to their discussion.

'In order to bring this case to court, Magistrate Frampton must have found someone who took the oath and is willing to give evidence against the others. They must try to find who it is and persuade him not to speak against them. Without him, the magistrates can't do a thing.'

'What if it's too late for that? What if he's already sworn his evidence before the magistrates?'

Saranna was seriously worried. Eli Gillam was one of those who was in the habit of administering the oath to new recruits to the Tolpuddle Society.

'It mustn't be too late. He must be found and stopped at all costs.'

'Will you come back to Tolpuddle with me and help?' Saranna thought she knew the answer even before Richard Pemble replied. Her stepfather was not a man who allowed himself to become involved personally in such disputes. He preferred to give his advice from a safe distance.

'I would like to be able to,' he said, managing to sound regretful. 'But my watermen are involved in some delicate negotiations with their employers at this very moment. I need to be here to guide them. What I *will* do is write a list of the actions the Tolpuddle men must take on their own behalf and you can carry it back to them.'

Nancy Vye was alarmed. 'You'll not be going back to Tolpuddle for a while, Saranna? You'll stay here for a few days?'

'I can't, Ma, much as I'd like to. The messenger on the coach said he had to be back there by Monday. That means something is likely to happen soon afterwards. I must try to get there before everything goes wrong for Wes's father and the others.'

Chapter 36

Saranna reached Tolpuddle on her return journey twelve hours too late to thwart James Frampton's plans to destroy the Tolpuddle Labourers Friendly Society.

When George Loveless, the Methodist lay preacher and colleague of Eli Gillam, left his home to go to work on Monday, 24 February 1834, he found Constable James Brine awaiting him outside the cottage. Brine had replaced Parish Constable Hammer – and he was an altogether more efficient law-enforcer.

It was unusual for the constable to be abroad at such an early hour, but Loveless nodded to him and would have walked on had Brine not stepped into his path.

Surprised, George Loveless said, 'What do you want with me?'

'I have a warrant for you, from the magistrates.'

The farm worker had expected some action to be taken against the Society men, but he had not been expecting this.

'What are its contents, sir?'

Thrusting the document into Loveless's hands, the constable sounded embarrassed as he said, 'Take it yourself, you can read it as well as I can.'

Scanning through the wording of the document, George Loveless looked up and said, 'There are five other names here.'

Apparently ignoring the question, the constable said, 'Are you willing to go to the magistrates with me?'

'To any place, wherever you wish me.'

'Then we'll go and pick up the others.'

Walking around Tolpuddle, five more men were collected by the constable in a similar manner to Loveless. James Loveless, younger brother of George; Thomas Standfield with his son, John; James Hammett, and a namesake of the constable James Brine.

All were asked the same question the constable had asked George Loveless and all agreed to accompany him to see the magistrates.

The relatives of the six men were not so ready to accept their arrest. The screams of Harriet Hammett, young wife of James, brought every man and woman in the small village to their doorways. Among them were Eli Gillam and Wes.

'What's going on?' Eli asked his fellow preacher as the party followed the self-conscious parish constable along the road that led to Dorchester.

'We've been arrested, Eli. Constable Brine is taking us to the magistrates in Dorchester.'

'Arrested on what charge?' Wes walked alongside the Tolpuddle men.

'Administering an illegal oath.'

George Loveless lengthened his stride to catch up with his five companions and Wes dropped back. He was both relieved and confused. The constable had not called at the Gillam cottage – but why not?

Rachel's relief was less complicated. 'Thank the Lord! Thank God!'

She held the apron she wore up to her eyes. 'They didn't come for you, Eli. *You* haven't been arrested.'

'No, but six good and honest men have and I'm concerned for them.'

Outside, in the village street, the women and a few of the men stood in stunned groups as the six arrested men vanished from view along the Dorchester road in company with Parish Constable Brine.

The largest group stood around the inconsolable Harriet Hammett. Her cries might have been even louder had she known her husband would not return to her for five long and bitter years.

As they walked along the road behind the constable, George Loveless and his companions commented quietly among themselves on the absence of Eli Gillam from their party. They wondered why he, one of the busiest of the group in recent years, had not been arrested.

They learned the answer to their question in Dorchester. Upon their arrival in the town they were taken to the house of Magistrate Wollaston – the half-brother of James Frampton.

Ushered into a large room, they found Wollaston here with James Frampton. Also in the room, looking extremely ill at ease and unable to meet the eyes of his fellow farm labourers, was Edward Legg, the cousin of Andrew Symonds, late-footman at Moreton House.

Now the reason why the six men had been arrested and Eli Gillam had not became clear to George Loveless. Edward Legg had turned informer – doubtless under considerable pressure from James Frampton. He would identify the six men as being present at the oath-taking when he was inducted into the

Tolpuddle Labourers Society. Eli had been absent on that particular occasion, due to his bout of chicken pox.

The brief proceedings went much as Loveless thought they would now he realised what the six men were up against. Legg identified them as having administered the oath and James Frampton duly recorded the identification. Loveless protested in vain that, as far as he was aware, he and the others had not violated any law.

'That will be for the court to decide,' snapped James Frampton. 'You are committed to prison to await trial on the charges for which you have been arrested. Take them away, Constable Brine.'

After trying in vain to meet Edward Legg's glance, George Loveless was led outside with the others. Escorted by a number of Dorchester constables now, the six thoroughly dejected men were taken to Dorchester gaol. Here they were stripped, had their heads shorn and were locked up together in a large cell.

Such treatment alone should have alarmed the six men had they been more aware of prison procedures. They were not being treated as men arrested on a minor charge, but as felons, already convicted of the charges they faced.

Most of the snow had disappeared between London and the South coast and the coach carrying Saranna arrived in Dorchester on time. It was a crisp, cold night and, as no one had anticipated her arrival, she walked the seven miles to Tolpuddle.

She realised immediately she entered the village that something was amiss. There were lights in every cottage and there seemed to be much coming-and-going between the various households.

Saranna went to the Gillam house before going to Widow Cake's cottage. Here she received a warm and relieved welcome from Rachel.

'You don't know how pleased I am to see you, Saranna. We heard there'd been some bad snow on the London road after you'd gone and we were worried about you. It was as much as I could do to stop Wes riding off after you, to make sure everything was all right.'

'The coach had its problems,' admitted Saranna. 'But what's been happening in Tolpuddle? Everyone seems as busy as though it were daylight.'

'You may well ask,' said Rachel, and told Saranna of the happenings of that morning.

'So I'm too late.' Saranna produced the letter from Richard Pemble, in which he suggested the Tolpuddle labourers should exclude the oath from their initiation ceremony. 'The only grain of hope I can offer now is that Richard has sworn to call upon every Union and Association in the country to raise their voices in support of the Tolpuddle men, should they be needed.'

She placed the letter on the table in the kitchen. 'Where is Wes now?'

'With his father, at the chapel. There's a meeting of the Tolpuddle men. Lord knows they earn little enough, but every man in the village has promised to put money into a fund to pay for the defence of the men who were taken off this morning. Surprisingly, some of the farmers have also offered their support. Mind you, I think most of them are secretly pleased at what's happened. They'll go along with anything that might stop the men demanding higher wages.'

'I'll go down to the chapel to see Wes now, and take this letter with me. There might be something in it to give them some encouragement at least. I should think they're in need of it after the happenings of this morning.'

'Stop and have a cup of tea and something to eat first, girl. You'll be famished after your journey. Tired too, after walking from Dorchester, I dare say.'

'Could you save something for me until I come back from the chapel, Mrs Gillam?' Saranna gave her future mother-in-law a tired smile. 'You see, I've missed Wes too. I don't think I could sit still long enough to eat, knowing he's only such a short distance away and I haven't told him I'm back.'

As she prepared a meal for the return of Saranna, Wes and Eli, Rachel thought of Saranna's words. It gave her a great deal of comfort and she thanked the Lord for His goodness. The world of so many women in Tolpuddle had been turned upside down by the events of the day. Yet she was able to look forward to the marriage of her youngest son to a girl who was not only intelligent and good-looking, but one who thought the world of him.

Rachel thought she must be one of the few women in the village that day who had any reason to be happy.

Chapter 37

'Are you saying that Wesley Gillam is not among the men who were arrested at Tolpuddle?' Josephine Frampton was absolutely furious. 'I told you that of all the men in the village he is the one who most deserves to be arrested. He is one of the most active of the Union men. I *told* you so.'

She stood in her grandfather's study, hands on hips, confronting him. He had just returned from Dorchester well-pleased with his day's work and informed her of the arrest of six Tolpuddle men. He'd expected her to applaud his actions; instead, she had exploded into anger.

'Servants' gossip may have Gillam linked with the Union, my dear, but he was not present when my informant was inducted into this dangerous Society. But why are you so concerned with this one young man? The little *contretemps* you had with him was some years ago now. Such matters are best forgotten.'

'He told lies about me, and so did Fanny Warren. Whenever I happen to meet him now I feel he's secretly laughing at me.'

Josephine pouted. 'Besides, I'm a Frampton. Like you, Grandfather. I don't like anyone getting the better of me – of *us* – in anything.'

'You're a Frampton all right, my girl. There's no doubt about that. Your father would have been proud of you.'

James Frampton was feeling content in spite of Josephine's outburst. He had sprung the trap on the Tolpuddle Labourers Union – or Friendly Society, or whatever they cared to call it. The name meant nothing. They were all involved in the same thing: subversion.

He felt he had done his duty by the gentry of Dorset. The matter had also brought him to the attention of Viscount Melbourne, who was being tipped as a future Prime Minister of Great Britain. There was a strong possibility that this single incident could bring a baronetcy into the Frampton family . . .

'I have another interesting piece of information for you, Grandfather. It might even help you to arrest Wesley Gillam.'

Josephine's words brought James Frampton back from his day-dream of family honours and recognition for the work he had done to protect the English way of life. 'Oh? What is this fascinating piece of information?'

'One of your own gardeners is a member of this Tolpuddle Union.'

'A Moreton gardener! Who is he? Tell me his name and I'll dismiss him today . . .'

'I thought you might prefer to keep him on – providing he's prepared to go to court and say what you want him to say, of course?'

'It doesn't matter what I *want* him to say. If he is a member of this Association and he wants to remain at Moreton House as a gardener, he will go to court. Tell them what he knows about the initiation ceremony and the oath he took. Who is he?'

'His name is John Lock. I don't think you'll find it difficult to persuade him to appear as a witness for you. From what I've heard he's frightened both of losing his position here and of finding himself on a ship to Australia. He hopes to marry one of our maids. From what I know of the little minx, she's not likely to remain faithful if he remains in prison for longer than a single night.'

As James Frampton hurried away to summon the unfortunate employee, Josephine thought her affair with the curly-haired Moreton House gardener was proving extremely satisfying in more ways than one.

When Wes and Eli journeyed to Dorchester to visit the imprisoned men, they learned that matters had advanced a stage further. They had been arraigned before a number of magistrates, sitting in closed court inside the prison. As a result of this hearing, they had all been committed for trial at the next Assizes.

'But how can they possibly have any evidence against you?' asked a bewildered Eli. 'It isn't illegal to belong to a Trades Association and there was nothing in the oath the men took that was in any way treasonable.'

'I don't think that matters any more,' said George Loveless, sounding more despondent than at any time Eli could remember. 'They are set to crucify us all, Eli. Justice has been pushed aside in their determination to secure a conviction against us. When they searched me they found a key to the box I keep in the bedroom at Tolpuddle. My wife came in to see me yesterday. The constables have been there and taken the box. Inside were the rules of the Society, a subscription book and a number of letters to other Societies. My wife says the magistrates' men were delighted with their find. No doubt they'll use them against us in court.'

'We've been in touch with Richard Pemble,' said Wes, trying to sound an optimistic note. 'He's sending a letter to every Union in the country and assures us of their wholehearted support. He also says you need have no concern for your defence. They are willing to supply sufficient funds to ensure you have the best counsel in the country. You're not alone in this fight. Thousands of working men in the country are gathering behind you.'

'That's as may be,' said George Loveless wryly. 'But it's only the six of us festering here, in gaol. I've never known anywhere like it! I preach the Word whenever I can, but this place is full of so many men who have given up all hope that it's difficult not to follow the same path.'

'Have faith in the Lord,' said Eli. 'Remember, he went through many such periods of doubt in His life. He'll be with you now, of that you can be assured.'

'My faith in the Lord has never wavered,' declared George Loveless. 'It's my faith in those who administer justice that is at a low ebb.'

On the way out through the prison corridors, Eli and Wes found the prison chaplain waiting to talk to them. Introducing himself, he said, 'I believe you have been to visit the six misguided men from Tolpuddle?'

His words caused Wes to bridle immediately, but Eli replied to him evenly enough. 'We have been visiting our unfortunate friends, yes.'

'I spoke to them myself only yesterday and tried to make them see the error of their ways. I regret I was subjected to abuse from George Loveless in particular. He is quite unrepentant.'

'Really? Perhaps you could tell me of what he should be repenting, sir?'

'Of being idle and spreading discontent. Of ingratitude towards the master who keeps him in employ. Of disloyalty to our government. Ministers of the realm are going to great lengths to ensure that the inhabitants of this country, whatever their station in life, can sleep safely in their beds at night. Need I say more?'

'No, sir.' Eli spoke, looking the chaplain in the eye. 'Even a donkey needs to bray only once for the world to know he's an ass.'

Ignoring the chaplain's startled indignation, Eli continued, 'I have known George Loveless – this idle, discontented man – all his life. He spent hours at night, toiling by candlelight, to teach himself to read and write. With no help from his "generous" master, himself a Methodist who now pays George the princely sum of seven shillings a week, he has built up an impressive library. A library of books on theology, sir, a subject on which I have found no man to be his equal, whether they be bishop or fellow-preacher. As to spreading discontent, I dare to suggest he has brought great comfort and tranquillity into the lives of men who might otherwise have been subjected to the cold mercy of those who choose to work in this place.'

Eli's gesture encompassed the gaol in which they were standing.

'As for disloyalty to this government . . . Would the government give of their time and labours to form a Society to help the labourer in time of trouble? Support his family if he falls sick, or is thrown out of work by circumstances over which he has no control? Does the government offer its support because the farmers are giving him a wage insufficient to feed, clothe and house his family? You have no need to search for a reply, sir. We both know the answers to my questions.'

Wes had never seen his father in such a forceful mood as he was now. It seemed to him he had grown in stature while the chaplain had shrunk. But Eli was not through yet.

'No, sir, the government has behaved with far less loyalty to George Loveless and the others than it has the right to expect from them. Loveless has spent a lifetime bringing the word of God to ordinary people. For this, and for attempting to succour them at a time when neither government nor Church seems to care whether they live or die, he has been arrested. His preaching and his actions have done nothing to endanger country, Church, or his master. On the contrary, he has sought to give them means other than revolution by which to seek redress from their wrongs. For this he will undoubtedly suffer the full fury of a merciless and unjust judiciary.'

Eli looked defiantly at the chaplain who appeared stunned by his words. 'I fear I have detained you too long, sir, and I have no wish to have the stench of this place in my nostrils for a moment longer. I bid you good day. May the Good Lord we both profess to serve bless you and help you to discover anew the compassionate teachings of His only son.'

Outside the grim high walls of Dorchester gaol, Wes turned to his father and said, 'I wish George Loveless and the others could have heard you putting the chaplain in his place, Pa. It would have heartened them greatly. I think I was more proud of you then than I have ever been before.'

'Thank you, Wesley. Unfortunately, the words of a Methodist preacher or of a Church of England chaplain will make no difference at all to the outcome of this matter when it is heard in the Assize Court. I fear there are too many men whose minds are as closed as is the chaplain's. It is my opinion that anything said on

431

our friends' behalf will be so many wasted words. The fate of
George Loveless and the others has already been decided – by the
government in London.'

Chapter 38

'Your ma is going to be hard put to manage on the wages your father is getting, when you and Saranna are married.'

Widow Cake made the observation to Wes in the kitchen of her cottage. He was making good use of a spell of heavy rain by working indoors and white-washing the kitchen walls. Saranna was working upstairs in the bedrooms.

'Yes. We've discussed it, but Ma says they'll manage while she's still working at East Farm.'

It was something that had been worrying Wes, but he had tried to put off thinking about it until he and Saranna were married.

'No doubt they will, but how long is that going to last? Molly up at East Farm has been ill for a long time and I believe she's sinking fast now. What happens when she's gone? Especially now the daughter's come back to help out. They won't need anyone else.'

'I don't know, I'm sure. But as long as Farmer Priddy doesn't cut Pa's wages any more I'll still be able to put enough into the house for them to keep going fairly comfortably.'

'It's no way for a young couple to begin their married life, having parents acting as millstones about their necks. Living here will make it easier for you and Saranna, but you'll still want to save and get a few things of your own together.'

'We'll manage.'

'Everyone *manages* when they have to, but that's not what I'm talking about.'

In an apparent change of subject, Widow Cake said, 'Talking of managing, could you cope if we took on another half-dozen fields and started running sheep, as well as the cows?'

The question took Wes by surprise. 'Where would you get more fields?'

'From Aaron Stokes. We've been good neighbours for many years. He hasn't bothered me, and I haven't troubled him. We've both enjoyed it that way. Now he's decided to sell up.'

Aaron Stokes was a recluse who had not been seen in Tolpuddle village for many years. He owned the property to the north of

Widow Cake's land and grew or bred everything he needed on his small farm. Eccentric in his ways, Aaron could occasionally be seen in his fields wearing his only outdoor garment, a long sleeveless coat made from a single cow hide.

'He's been near-crippled with arthritis for the last couple of years. He struggled over here last night to tell me he's finally decided to give up the farm. In his time he's fallen out with the manor, the Church, and every farmer and landowner in the district. That's why he's offered his land and cottage to me at a price I'd really be a fool to refuse.'

'Where will he go?'

'It seems he has a sister almost as peculiar as he is. She lives over Cheselbourne way, not many miles from here. He's going to live with her and they'll most probably take on someone to come in and look after them. It's the best thing for him. Her too, probably. But you haven't answered my question.'

'I'll need help, Mrs Cake. It's been hard at times to keep things working well here since we lost Arnold. Especially since we began building up the cow herd.'

'But you don't think it's a bad idea?'

'It's a very good idea. I'll have to find out exactly what we're getting, so I can plan it all out, but I think it should work out well. It's very exciting.'

'Good! Aaron's calling in to see me again after dark tonight. I'll tell him that I'll buy his farm. You can sit down this evening and write to that solicitor in Dorchester. Get him to draw up an agreement and we'll have Aaron sign it, before he changes his mind.'

'If you like, I'll drop the agreement in to the solicitor on Monday. It's believed the Tolpuddle men will come up for trial on that day. I'd like to be there to hear at least part of the case and bring back news to the village of what's happened to them.'

Widow Cake appeared to be giving the matter some thought. She finally nodded her head. 'All right. There's not too much to be done outside in this weather, anyway. I think you'd be better advised to keep well out of whatever's going to happen to them – but I doubt if you'd take any notice of me anyway.'

Incarcerated within the high, stout walls of Dorchester gaol, the six men from Tolpuddle lost count of days and dates. For them only day or night brought about change in their monotonous routine.

Sometimes a wife or friend would make the journey from Tolpuddle to Dorchester, but it was not guaranteed they would be allowed in to see the men. Visiting was permitted very much on the day-to-day whim of the prison governor or the chief gaoler.

The accused men were not even told that their trial was imminent until one day they were taken in chains from the gaol to the court in the County Hall.

Once here, they were lodged in claustrophobic cells beneath the courtroom. High-walled, but barely four feet wide, the cells had neither windows nor any form of lighting. An imaginative man could come to believe he had been entombed and forgotten . . .

As if this in itself were not bad enough, a fire was lit in the gaolers' room and fed with wet and green brushwood. It seemed the chimney needed sweeping because it was not long before the acrid, choking smoke began seeping inside the dark, narrow cells.

The Tolpuddle men choked beneath the courtroom in company with a young woman accused of attempting to smother her new-born bastard child, and three young men charged with theft.

Meanwhile, upstairs in the court itself, a Grand Jury was sworn in. Their duty was to listen to the evidence against the prisoners and decide whether they had a case to answer to before a judge and petty jury.

The answer to this question in respect of the Tolpuddle six was never in doubt. The foreman of the grand jury was William Ponsonby, brother-in-law of Lord Melbourne, the Home Secretary.

Just in case this gentleman proved incapable of influencing his fellow jury members, included among their numbers were James Frampton, his son Henry, step-brother Charles Wollaston, and other magistrates whose signatures had been on the warrant calling for the arrest of the Tolpuddle men.

Such a gathering hardly required the views of the judge to reach a decision. Nevertheless, the learned Mr Baron Williams was determined that his words too should be recorded for posterity. Himself an ex-Whig Member of Parliament, he reminded the Grand Jury members of the dangers of allowing Trade Unionism to flourish unchecked in the land.

Despite such overwhelming odds gathered against the six Tolpuddle men, both judge and jury had extraordinary difficulty in extracting the evidence they required from farm labourer Edward Legg and John Lock, the Moreton House gardener. Both men seemed to have forgotten much of the evidence they had recited at the magistrates' hearing.

Nevertheless, the outcome was at no time ever really in doubt. After only the briefest of deliberations, the Grand Jury duly informed the judge they had found a 'True Bill' against the accused men.

Having thanked the Grand Jury for performing their duties in such an exemplary manner, Mr Baron Williams announced that he would try the six men on Monday, 17 March.

None of the men in the courtroom, certainly not one of the unfortunate members of the Tolpuddle Friendly Society of Labourers, could have imagined the importance this day would have.

They could have no way of knowing that 17 March 1834 would be the day when the relationship between worker and employer would change forever.

Chapter 39

The solicitor to whom Wes took Widow Cake's letter promised to deal with the matter of the transfer of Aaron Stokes's land to Amelia Cake as quickly as possible. He would have a deed of sale drawn up and take it himself to Tolpuddle. There he would fill in any additional details that might be required.

This business settled, Wes was about to leave the solicitor's office when he met Mr Fielding. This was the counsel who had unsuccessfully defended Arnold Cooper in the same Dorchester courtroom where the fate of the six Tolpuddle men would be decided.

'Hello ... young Gillam, is it not? Are you here as a witness in the trial of the labourers from your village?'

'No. I came to deliver something for Widow Cake, but I'm hoping to get to court and hear the trial. I know all the men involved well. I hope we might all return to Tolpuddle together.'

'I fear there's very little chance of that happening, young man. Without wishing to become involved in an argument about the rights and wrongs of the matter, it is my understanding that the magistrates who had them arrested have built up a very tight case against them.'

'Yes, that's what Widow Cake said,' agreed Wes gloomily. 'But I'll go to court and hope for the best.'

The two men began walking towards the courtroom together and Fielding said, 'The case has aroused a great deal of interest throughout the whole country. I doubt very much if you will get into the court in the normal course of things. You'd better come with me.'

It was evident that the counsel was right as they approached the courtroom along the High Street. Men and women filled the street before the building. Among them, Wes recognised a number of wives and relatives of the accused Tolpuddle men.

All were clamouring to be allowed entrance to the courtroom, but they were being firmly kept out by court officials. At the door the officials drew to one side to allow Mr Fielding into the building. They would have barred Wes had he not said, 'Mr Gillam is with me. Kindly allow him to pass.'

437

Once inside, the counsel suggested Wes should find a place for himself on the public benches.

'Are you involved in the case?' Wes had not thought of asking him before.

'No. I represent the young girl who is accused of trying to suffocate her baby daughter but I intend remaining in court for the Tolpuddle trial. I believe there is a great deal at stake. Not only for the Tolpuddle men, but for the legal system too.'

Mr Fielding defended his client successfully. Her acquittal gave Wes hope that the trial of the Tolpuddle men might follow a similar course.

When their names were called the men came up from the cells and Wes was appalled at their appearance. The hair on their heads had only just begun to grow and gave them an unfortunately villainous appearance. They were also red and watery-eyed from the gaolers' fire, which was still being fuelled by green wood. In addition, George Loveless had a cough, also caused by the fire, which frequently broke in upon the proceedings.

A number of the members of the Grand Jury were present in the court, seated in a high enclosure, looking down upon the Petty Jury, as though overseeing their deliberations.

The Petty Jury, like that of its peers, had been carefully selected. Each man was a farmer, a number of them tenants of the men who sat above. One would-be juror had been rejected by the prosecution because he was a Methodist. It was thought he might have been biased in favour of the six men in the dock.

There was little sympathy for the men from the jury box, and perhaps only Wes among the spectators who really cared what happened to them. Looking about him, Wes could see none of the men's relatives in here. It seemed they had failed to gain entry to the trial.

The six men were being charged only with administering an oath. One that was neither required, nor authorised by law. However, such was the devious process of the law that the authorities had been allowed to permute the facts. As a result, no fewer than twelve charges were laid against the bewildered men.

After the prosecution had outlined its case, the procession of witnesses to the box began. Among the first were John Lock and Edward Legg. Their evidence here was even more vague than it had been before the Grand Jury. Only by a combination of bullying and unashamedly biased questioning was Baron Williams able to draw enough evidence from them to satisfy himself – if not the defence counsel.

Next to enter the dock were the proprietors of a shop in Dorch-

438

ester. It was alleged that James Loveless had handed to them two designs to be painted for use in the initiation ceremony. One was of Death, the other of a skeleton. The statements elicited from the shop owners did nothing to prove an oath had been read, but it impressed upon the jury the alleged satanic nature of the ceremony.

Finally, the prosecution called upon the governor of Dorchester Prison; a tithingman; James Frampton's bailiff – and James Frampton, the Moreton magistrate, himself.

These four gave corroborative evidence that a key had been found in George Loveless's possession when he was searched in prison. It was ultimately found to fit the lock of a box in his house wherein was a letter about the election of the Society committee. There was also an account book containing a list of the members and the money they had paid to the Tolpuddle Friendly Society.

None of the material evidence produced in court was able to substantiate the charges that an illegal oath had been administered by the men standing in the prisoners' dock. Yet, despite protests lodged by the defence counsel, their evidence was admitted.

The laws of the land did not allow the six men to give evidence in their own defence, but their counsel put up a spirited defence on their behalf. They pointed out to the court that the charges on which the men had been brought to court were based on an act that had been framed many years before. Its object then was to prevent sailors at the Nore from taking part in mutinous acts.

The defence case lasted for some hours. Not until the end of the speeches were the prisoners asked if they wished to say anything.

Five of the six Tolpuddle men had barely been able to follow the legal arguments that had been made on their behalf and against them. Only George Loveless handed down a brief written note which was duly passed to the judge.

In the note he had written: 'My Lord, if we have violated the law, it was not done intentionally. We have injured no man's reputation, character, person, or property. We were uniting together to preserve ourselves, our wives, and our children, from utter degradation and starvation. We challenge any man to prove that we have acted, or intend to act, different from the above statement.'

It was a reasoned if unavailing plea, a final desperate attempt to avert the vengeance of the formidable forces mustered against the six farm labourers from Tolpuddle.

The outcome of the case was not in doubt from the moment Mr Baron Williams commenced his summing-up. In it he pointed out to the jury that such societies as the men were promoting were calculated to shake the very foundations of society and lay the country open to great peril from within. The jury had, he declared, only to look at what had happened in France during the lifetime of many of those in court . . .

It took the Petty Jury less than half an hour to reach their verdict. The six Tolpuddle men were 'Guilty as Charged'.

When the upsurge of sound in the tiny courtroom provoked by the verdict had been brought under control, the principal actors in the day's drama waited for the judge to pass sentence upon them. Instead, much to everyone's surprise, Mr Baron Williams announced the men would be returned to their cells to await his deliberations. Not until these had been concluded would he pass sentence upon them.

As the spectators surged from the court to pass on the outcome of the case to those waiting outside, Wes fought his way to where Mr Fielding sat with some of his colleagues at a table before the now empty Bench.

Seeing him coming, Mr Fielding rose to his feet and met him, guiding him through a side door that led through the building and out into an alleyway at the side of the court.

Behind them they could hear uproar from the members of family and public crowding about the main court entrance.

'That's better,' said the counsel, shivering in the cool evening air. 'At least we can hear ourselves speak out here.'

'Why didn't the judge pass sentence on them today? Why has he put the case back to await his "deliberations"?'

'That's a matter for some speculation, Wesley. Some of my colleagues say it is because one of the defence counsel has complained that the whole hearing was a complete farce and he intends lodging a protest with the Lord Chancellor's office. Mr. Baron Williams would want to avert that. He has only recently been elected to the Bench. Indeed, I believe this is the first case over which he has presided. He would not wish there to be a complaint about his conduct on his very first Assizes. Others think it might be that His Lordship is contemplating showing mercy to the convicted men and wishes to study the case in more detail to ascertain if there are any grounds for leniency.'

'What do you think?' Wes asked the friendly counsel.

'I would give little hope of leniency, Wesley. Judge Williams's summing up was not that of a man who intends being merciful. I cannot offer the faintest glimmer of hope to your unfortunate friends.'

The counsel was proven tragically right. Judge Williams left the men in the tomb-like cells beneath the courtroom for two days, before having them brought back to the court in order that he might pass sentence upon them.

Fixing them with a stern eye that caused their near-defeated spirits to sink even lower, he dismissed George Loveless's plea, saying that he could not accept that they had meant no harm, nor that they intended no offence. 'Your intentions', he said, 'can only be known to yourselves.'

He went on to warn them that legal punishment is not to seek revenge against those who broke the law, but to set an example and act as a warning to others.

'Accordingly . . .' and here Mr Baron Williams fixed them with a glance that showed neither compassion nor mercy, '. . . I am bound to pass upon you the sentence which the Act of Parliament has decreed. The sentence is that each of you be transported to such places beyond the seas as His Majesty's Council in their discretion shall see fit for the term of seven years.'

Chapter 40

Eight days after their conviction at Dorchester five of the convicted Tolpuddle men were transferred from Dorchester gaol to the prison hulks in Portsmouth harbour. Only two days later they were unwilling passengers on the convict Transport *Surrey*. Their journey to exile and hardship in New South Wales had begun.

George Loveless did not sail with them. Taken ill as a result of the foul conditions in the cells beneath the Dorchester court-room, he had been transferred to the Dorchester prison hospital. Not until mid-May did he set sail in the *William Metcalfe* en route to his own exile in Van Diemen's Land.

Meanwhile an unprecedented campaign commenced against the convictions and the swingeing sentences passed. Newspapers throughout the land unexpectedly took up the cause. Meanwhile, Unions from one end of the country to the other met to decide what form their own protest should take.

Tolpuddle was torn between those who were outraged at the sentences meted out to the farm labourers and those who grieved for their transported relatives. Only a very few, those who lived in manor and vicarage, and one or two farmers, voiced approval of Judge Baron Williams.

However, many who approved of the convictions had reservations about the severity of the sentences. They admitted the labourers could have known nothing of the existence of the obscure law under which they were charged, far less that they were breaking that law.

Two days after the trial had been reported in the national newspapers, a letter arrived in Tolpuddle addressed to 'Wesley Gillam, care of Widow Cake'.

Tearing open the envelope, Wes opened out the single sheet of paper and began reading the contents in front of his employer and Saranna. As he read, his face registered a variety of expressions. Puzzlement was followed by disbelief, replaced as swiftly by consternation.

'What is it, Wesley? Who's it from?' Amelia Cake's impatience finally got the better of her.

442

'It's from Richard Pemble.'

'The Union man? Saranna's stepfather?'

Amelia's interest waned. 'Watching your reactions as you read it, I thought it might be something of interest.'

'It is,' said Wes. 'He wants me to go to London. To address a meeting that's to take place there in three days' time.'

'You? Are you certain that letter's not meant for your father?'

'Quite certain. Richard Pemble says he doesn't want any form of preacher. It would frighten away more people than it would attract. Neither does he want anyone who's in a Union. He wants someone who knows the six Tolpuddle men and is young enough to say something fresh about them and their conviction. Something those at the meeting won't have read about them already.'

'You'll go, Wes? You'll go and say what needs to be said?' Saranna entered the conversation for the first time.

'I know nothing about speaking to a lot of people – any type of people.'

'You must go. Richard will help you – and there's no one more fitted to speak on behalf of the convicted men. As Richard says, you know the men who were sentenced and you've written letters to other Unions for the Tolpuddle Society. You also know better than anyone else about the work that's gone into forming the Tolpuddle Society.'

'Don't I have any say about how my employees are going to spend their time? Or do I just pay out their wages and watch this place go to rack and ruin because you're never here?'

'I'm sorry, Mrs Cake. It's just . . .'

'It's just that you intend going to London, whatever I have to say about it,' snapped Amelia. 'As for feeling sorry . . . who *should* you be feeling sorry for? A poor widow who has no one she can rely on for more than twenty-four hours at a time? Or a group of grown men who should have known better than to try to stand up to the likes of Magistrate Frampton and his friends?'

'The Society was formed to help their families, Mrs Cake.'

'Ha! A fine job they've done of it. There are four families in the village without a father to support them. Fifteen children likely to go hungry because there's no money coming into their houses. Tell me how joining this Society has helped them – if you can?'

'What happened in Dorchester wasn't justice. Any more than it was justice that had Arnold sent away.'

Wes looked at Widow Cake with an expression that was part-defiance, part-resignation. 'Do I take it you're saying I can't go to London?'

'You don't "take" anything. I'll make it clear enough what I want you to do without your "taking" it. Of course you can go. I'd be up there myself with you if I was fit enough. But you can tell that father of yours I'll expect him to come up here and put in some real work in your place – and I don't want to hear him singing any of those Wesley hymns while he's here. If he needs to sing hymns before he can work, I'll teach him some good Church of England ones. Hymns with a bit more tune, and a lot less "Hallelujah!" Anyway, you'll need to get up to London pretty quickly if you intend being there in time to speak. Oh, and tell your father I want him up here tomorrow. I want to speak to him – and to your mother as well. I want them *both* up here. Now you'd better tidy things and get off home. You'll need to get things ready and catch the morning coach from Dorchester.'

Bemused by the speed of events and Amelia Cake's whirlwind organising, Wes was halfway out of the door before she called him back.

'Wesley! Just say what you need to say at this meeting and then come straight back. I don't want any more young ladies pitching up on my doorstep looking for you in a couple of months' time . . .'

Wes ducked out through the doorway hurriedly, aware of the questioning look Saranna was giving him.

He hoped Amelia's unguarded remark might have passed unnoticed. He should have known better.

It was after dark before he completed all the chores about the cottage. He was walking to the village accompanied by Saranna when she suddenly said, 'What's all this about young girls pitching up on Widow Cake's doorstep after you'd been to London?'

Wes felt his cheeks burning and was relieved it was dark. 'Oh, you know Widow Cake and the way she talks. She was talking about Meg's sister. When I was in London I happened to mention that Widow Cake could do with someone to look after her now that Mary has sailed for Australia. The next thing I knew was that Polly turned up here. She didn't last very long, though. The country life didn't suit her at all.'

'Is that all? Are you quite sure she didn't come to Tolpuddle expecting to look after someone a little more exciting than Widow Cake?'

'Of course she didn't. I told you, she came here hoping Widow Cake would employ her. But they didn't suit each other.'

'Was this the girl some of the villagers expected you to marry?'

'Marry? I shouldn't think so. Polly was far too much of a city girl to want to marry a country boy like me.'

'Hm! I'll believe you this time, Wesley Gillam, but you'd better take heed of Widow Cake's warning. Keep away from those London girls. If one of them turns up on the doorstep this time you'll have me to answer to – and then you'll realise that Widow Cake has a silken tongue compared to mine when I'm riled!'

When Wes arrived in London, he made his way to the address given him in Richard Pemble's letter. Much to his relief, it was in a respectable residential part of central London.

The house was in a street of tall, terraced buildings. Each had steps leading up to a front door with railings on either side and a railed area in the basement, from whence came the sounds of a busy kitchen. Wes thought it was probably a house of the type he had heard referred to as a 'gentleman's town residence'.

Feeling more nervous than he had for the whole of the long journey from Dorchester, Wes tugged timidly on a bell pull beside the door. In the silence that followed, he thought he heard the tinkle of a bell somewhere deep within the house.

After waiting for some minutes, he was wondering whether to ring again when he heard movement from the other side of the door.

A moment later it opened. Wes had been expecting a servant to open it to him, but was confronted by a young woman of about twenty-five years of age who smiled at him from the doorway.

'Good evening. Is there something I can do for you?'

Her accent and bearing were not those of a servant, but reminded Wes of Fanny Warren. Perhaps it was for this reason that he suddenly found himself tongue-tied.

'Er . . . yes . . . I think so. Richard Pemble asked me to call here.'

The young woman made a sound that signified exasperation. 'Richard is always sending young men and girls here. I suppose you're seeking work, like the others? Well, I'm afraid I have nothing to offer you – unless you have a good writing hand?'

'I can write well enough,' said Wes. 'But . . .'

'Come on inside. I'm Dorothy Osborne.'

Suddenly the woman noticed the bag on the doorstep beside him. 'I can offer you work and accommodation for a couple of days only. I can't promise you anything beyond that. Oh, do come in!'

Wes picked up his bag but then stopped halfway in through the doorway. 'I'm sorry, I fear I haven't made myself very clear. Richard Pemble suggested I might come here and address some meeting. My name's Wesley Gillam.'

When this piece of information failed to make any impression on the young woman, he added, 'I'm from Tolpuddle.'

It was as though he had suddenly stumbled upon a magic password. The young woman squealed with delight. 'From

Tolpuddle! Come in. Come in. Of course! You're the young man Richard was telling us about. He was not at all certain you would be able to come. Oh! We're *delighted* to have you here with us. You must think me terribly silly. I was chattering so much, I hardly gave you a moment to explain your business. I am so *terribly* sorry.'

As Dorothy Osborne continued to chatter away she was leading Wes along an airy, high-ceilinged passageway, heading towards the rear of the house. Eventually opening one of the many doors on either side, she preceded him into a huge room.

There must have been at least a dozen baize-covered tables in there. At almost every one of them a young man or woman sat busily writing. Most were young, but Dorothy Osborne called to an older, scholarly-looking man who sat at an elegant desk in the centre of the room.

'Robert, this is Wesley Gillam, the young man from Tolpuddle. He's here to speak at our rally. Wesley, this is Robert Owen.'

The man stood up and greeted Wes warmly. At the same time, he was aware that the others in the room had stopped working and were looking at him with a keen interest.

'Welcome to London, Wesley. We are very pleased indeed to have you here.'

Indicating the others in the room, he said, 'As you can see, we are not allowing the country to forget your colleagues. We are busy sending out letters and circulars, calling for support in our campaign to have their sentences commuted.'

'Do you know any of the convicted men?' The question was asked by Dorothy Osborne.

'All of them. Their families too. Tolpuddle is only a small village. Unfortunately, I was the only one from Tolpuddle to get in to witness the trial . . .'

'You were actually *there*? You are able to tell us about it at first hand?' Now it was Owen's turn to show excitement.

Minutes later Wes was giving details of the trial to everyone in the room. They left their work to gather around and listen attentively to what he had to say. For more than an hour Wes told of the court hearing and answered the many questions posed by the male and female campaigners.

Finally, Dorothy Osborne called a halt to the questioning, pointing out that he had spent the whole day in a coach travelling from Dorchester and must be in need of rest and refreshment.

'However,' she said to Wes, 'you can be quite certain that everyone here will resume their work fired with new enthusiasm as a result of your account of witnessing this gross injustice.'

There was a loud murmur of assent and Wes could feel the

excitement and resentment in the room as the small group went back to their work.

Accompanied by Robert Owen, he was led from the room and Dorothy Osborne said, 'That was a wonderfully stirring and moving account of the suffering of those poor men. The meeting is scheduled for the day after tomorrow, but I wonder if we might use your time to the full tomorrow? A great many newspapers are sympathetic to our cause. They would be delighted to interview you.'

'I'll do all I can while I'm in London,' declared Wes. Remembering Widow Cake's warning, he added: 'But I *am* a working man. I must get back to Tolpuddle as soon as possible after the meeting.'

'Of course. It's most encouraging to know there is at least one employer in Tolpuddle who isn't frightened to support the labourers.'

Wes thought of Amelia, and smiled. 'Yes, I suppose I *am* fortunate. Widow Cake fears nothing and no one. No one at all.'

Chapter 41

Although Wes was sleeping in the big London house he woke as early as he would in Tolpuddle. He was washed and dressed before he heard the servants going about their business.

Finding his way to the kitchen, he had a cup of tea with the servants working here. He discovered, much to his surprise, that he was regarded as something of a celebrity among them.

It was a totally new experience. After giving it due consideration, he decided it was neither a justified, nor a comfortable, mantle to wear.

Wes also learned that the house in which he was staying belonged to Dorothy Osborne, inherited from her father. She had been involved in Trades Union matters for some years, using her considerable fortune to further the cause.

Robert Owen, he discovered, was a man of humble beginnings who had worked his way through the cotton mills of Scotland to become a wealthy mill owner. Philanthropist and social reformer, it was almost inevitable that he should become an influence in the Trades Union movement.

Wes realised he was in illustrious company, here in London.

After almost an hour spent listening to servants' gossip and information, Wes was located in the kitchen by Dorothy Osborne who took him upstairs for breakfast.

The campaign helpers began to arrive at the house while Wes ate, and it marked the beginning of a very busy day for him.

He was taken to visit other houses where the occupants were busily making up posters and manning printing presses from which thousands of leaflets were being turned out.

It came as a surprise to him to learn what a huge amount of support there was in the capital for the convicted Tolpuddle men – and it seemed this was gathering considerable momentum with each passing day.

Wes wished the six unfortunate men could somehow be made aware of the tremendous efforts being made to secure their release.

Shortly before noon, he was returned to Dorothy Osborne's

house to face newspaper reporters. He told his story, giving the backgrounds of the six men, and then faced a barrage of questions from the assembled journalists before Robert Owen finally called a halt.

'Gentlemen, I think Wesley Gillam has given each of you enough information to fill a page or two in your newspapers. I do hope you will give it the coverage it deserves in order that we may secure the speedy release of the ill-used labourers of Tolpuddle. If you require any more information, I have no doubt you will learn it at the grand meeting we have arranged tonight at the National Institution.'

As the journalists filed from the house, Wes was taken to another room where, much to his delight, he found Richard Pemble and Nancy awaiting him.

The greeting from Saranna's mother was as warm as though she had been in her own cottage. After hugging and kissing him, she said, 'You don't know how delighted I am that you and Saranna are to be married, Wes. I've known for years that she loved you. I suspected for almost as long that you felt the same way about her. Well, it's taken a long time for both of you to realise it for yourselves, but that's probably all to the good. You and Saranna are a little older now and able to cope with life better.'

'Talking of coping,' said Richard Pemble, grasping Wes's hand, 'Robert tells me you've fired all our volunteers with enthusiasm with your talk to them yesterday about our Tolpuddle brothers.'

'I hope all that everyone is doing will help George Loveless and the others in some way,' said Wes. 'They should never have been convicted in the first place.'

'True,' agreed Richard Pemble. 'George Loveless and the others are being made martyrs to the cause of Trades Unionism. Fortunately, this whole sorry business is showing signs of rebounding upon the government and the employers. Throughout the length and breadth of the country the Unions are rallying their strength and gathering new members. By joining together they are discovering they have the power to fight the injustices the labouring classes have suffered for generations – and there is no doubt we are going to win.'

Listening to Richard Pemble now, Wes realised that his first impression of the man had been the right one. Richard Pemble was an ambitious Trades Union man. The fate of the Tolpuddle men meant less to him than the use he could make of their plight. No doubt this was important for the future of the Trades Union cause, but it was not the reason Wes had come to London.

'I'll leave you to fight the Union's cause,' he said. 'I've come here in the hope of doing something to help free George Loveless and the other Tolpuddle men. It's the injustice of *their* convictions that I thought we were fighting.'

'Of course we are,' said Richard Pemble soothingly. 'And we'll win their fight too – but injustice didn't begin at Dorchester, and it will not end there.'

'You go off and talk politics with your friends, Richard,' said Nancy, firmly. 'I'm taking Wes outside for a walk. I want to talk to him about Saranna and the wedding. You can all have him back in about half an hour.'

Once out of the house, Nancy linked arms with him and said, 'I thought you might like to get away from everyone for a while.'

'I'm grateful to you. I know they all mean well, but I find all this talk of fighting for "the cause" a little wearying.'

It was the truth. Until now, Wes had not realised the pressure to which he had been subjected from the moment he arrived at Dorothy Osborne's house.

Thinking about it, he said, 'I feel like an autumn leaf, caught up in a high wind.'

'Never mind. We can both forget about Trades Unions and newspapers for a while. Let's talk about the wedding – but, first of all, how is Saranna? When she came home I seemed hardly to have time to talk to her before she rushed back to Tolpuddle again.'

'She's keeping well and asked me to give her love to you. As for the wedding . . . we haven't had a lot of time to talk about it in any detail. Hopefully we will be able to arrange it for the end of next month, but I'll write and give you all the details as soon as we have something definite.'

Talking as they walked about the streets of London, the half hour Nancy had promised the Union organisers became an hour and a half. They returned to find the organisers of that evening's meeting beginning to panic.

The remainder of the afternoon passed in a whirl of interviews and advice from Richard Pemble. There were only brief interludes of sanity when Wes was able to spend a few minutes in Nancy's company.

In no time at all, it seemed, it was time to leave the house and take a carriage to the hall where the meeting was being convened. Along the way it was plain for all his companions to see that Wes was becoming increasingly nervous. Eventually, Nancy took hold of his hand. She did not release it until they reached the hall and it was time to climb down from the carriage.

As the small party walked into the hall, flanked by Union helpers, Wes's nervousness very nearly became panic. As he and the others walked out on the stage situated in the well of the hall, a roar went up like nothing he had ever heard before.

'Would you believe there are almost ten thousand people here tonight?' A delighted Robert Owen had to shout the information in Wes's ear in order to be heard above the enthusiasm of the assembled throng. 'It's a far larger crowd then we had anticipated. It's fortunate we thought to have a speaking-trumpet available. You're going to need it to reach those at the back of the hall.'

The introductions seemed to drag on for ages while Wes began to perspire in anticipation of the ordeal to come.

Fortunately, his nervousness vanished when he stood up and began talking of the men he knew, and about the court proceedings he had seen and heard.

At times the roars of approval, or howls of disapproval, drowned his words and he was forced to pause until order was restored. At such moments an awareness of the size of his audience threatened once more to overawe him, but it did not.

When he reached the end of his talk he received an ovation of thunderous applause that seemed unending. While it continued, Robert Owen came forward to shake his hand, as did Richard Pemble. Even Dorothy Osborne came forward to kiss him on the cheek and offer her congratulations.

The remainder of that evening passed in an atmosphere of unreality for Wes. So many people wanted to meet him. At times there was so much talk about him it seemed his head would never stop swimming. Things only partially resumed a degree of normality when he returned to the house of Dorothy Osborne and ended the night having a few drinks with his hostess, Nancy, Richard Pemble, and a few more of their friends.

The following day passed in a similar whirl, only this time there seemed to be more social events than working ones. He was quite relieved he would not be staying in London for another day.

Early the next morning Wes boarded a fast coach bound for Dorchester. He was sent on his way by Nancy and Richard Pemble, Robert Owen and Dorothy Osborne.

The scholarly philanthropist had suggested he should stay in London for a few days longer – a week, perhaps – but Wes declined the suggestion. Quite apart from Widow Cake's reaction if he remained in the capital for anything like a week, he found that all the unaccustomed talking he had done in the couple of days in London had seriously affected his voice. It would be a few days before it returned in sufficient strength for him to talk normally once more.

Wes was satisfied he had carried out the mission he had come to

London to accomplish. It had been a very successful few days. Through the newspapers and his talk to the vast audience at the National Institution he had told the true story of the six victims of anti-Trades Union prejudice.

All he wanted now was to reach Tolpuddle as quickly as possible. To be with Saranna and return to a normal life once more.

Chapter 42

'I told you Wesley Gillam is heavily involved with Trades Union affairs. You should have included him on the warrant when you arrested the others.'

Josephine Frampton was tight-lipped as she looked accusingly across the desk at her grandfather. Between them was a stack of newspapers, brought to Moreton House by a servant from Magistrate Wollaston in Dorchester.

The front page of every newspaper was filled with details of a great rally in London, addressed by Wesley Gillam of Tolpuddle. On their inside pages the newspapers carried interviews given to journalists by the young Tolpuddle man.

Some newspapers also carried details of the lives and backgrounds of the six Tolpuddle men so harshly treated by the courts – all based upon information given to them by Wesley Gillam.

'Gillam was not at the induction meeting,' explained James Frampton irritably. 'He could not be charged with any offence.'

The magistrate was as enraged as Josephine at this remarkable upsurge of public sympathy for the Tolpuddle men. He felt it might have died away after only a few days had it not been fuelled by Gillam.

The boy had been a damned nuisance since the day he rode his horse across the Moreton lawns.

'I could not arrest him without having any evidence against him.'

'How much evidence do you need, for goodness' sake! He goes to London sponsored no doubt by the Trades Unions and there spends his time arousing sympathy for men who have been justly convicted in a court of law. Then he tells every newspaper in the country how he has been involved in Trades Union affairs, writing letters for them and so forth. What more do you want?'

'There should be something in all that, I must admit.'

For a few moments James Frampton lapsed deep into thought. 'I'll go through the papers that were found in the Loveless house. See if I can find anything of use to a magistrate.'

'Of course you'll find something! Besides, any judge who reads the newspapers couldn't fail to convict him of something. Wesley Gillam is more involved in the affairs of the Trades Unions than any of the men who are now on their way to Australia.'

Wes was happy to be back from London, although never again could he expect to be fêted in the way he had over the past couple of days. It was an experience he would never forget.

Much to his surprise, there was no one at home when he reached the Gillam cottage. It was most unusual. It was possible his father was at a Union meeting, or perhaps at the chapel, but his mother rarely left the house after dark.

Dropping the bag containing his London clothes in his room, he left the house and made his way to Widow Cake's cottage.

Entering the kitchen he found both Saranna and his employer here.

'Wes!' Saranna ran to him and hugged him delightedly. It was the welcome he had been looking forward to on the long walk from Dorchester.

Finally holding her off at arm's length, he grinned. 'The last woman to do that was your ma.'

'You've seen her? I'm so glad. How is she?'

'She's fine and sends her love.'

'We expected you home yesterday,' Widow Cake brought him down to earth.

'Well, we *thought* you might be home then,' corrected Saranna. 'But we guessed you'd been busier than you expected when the man from the *Dorset County Chronicle* came looking for you. He said your talk was reported in all the London papers and told us you're now a celebrity. You addressed a crowd of thousands, he said.'

'Well, as far as I can see it's done nothing to get the Tolpuddle men out of prison and back with their families.'

Widow Cake's gloomy observation brought Wes back to earth.

'It will, Mrs Cake, I'm convinced of it. It seems the whole country is on their side. Questions are due to be asked about them in Parliament today. London is talking of nothing else.'

'I'll believe it when it happens.' It seemed she was determined at all costs not to appear in any way cheerful.

Changing the subject, Wes said, 'I called in at home on my way here. There was no one there so I came straight here. I can't think where Ma could be.'

Saranna and Amelia looked at each as though sharing a secret and Wes asked, 'Is something going on? Do you know where my ma is?'

'We know where they *both* are,' said Saranna. 'You're not the

454

only one who's been doing things to change the world, Wesley Gillam. Mrs Cake's been making a few changes here too.'

Saranna was keeping an expressionless face and Wes was not certain whether what she had to say would be good or bad news.

'It's not Pa? He hasn't done something to annoy you?' He directed the question at his employer. 'I'm sure he didn't mean anything . . .'

'Well, he won't stop singing those confounded hymns,' said Amelia. Then her face broke into a smile at Wes's worried expression and she said, 'Oh, tell him, Saranna, for goodness' sake. Put him out of his misery.'

'Your ma and pa are up at Aaron Stokes's cottage. The solicitor came to see Mrs Cake while you were away. She's bought the cottage and land and Aaron moved out the very same day.'

'That was quick,' commented Wes. 'But what's it got to do with Ma and Pa?'

'They're going to move into Aaron's cottage. It will need a bit of cleaning and smartening up, but it's larger than the one they're in now and they'll be a lot more comfortable.'

'That's wonderful news – especially for Ma. She's always wanted somewhere larger than the cottage in the village. Mind you . . .' Wes spoke sadly. 'Now she'll spend more time talking of Saul returning. Of being able to have his own room.'

A sudden thought struck him. 'Before I went away we were talking of bringing in sheep and making more use of all the land we have now. We agreed we'd need another man. Where will he live?'

'I've already got another man – and he'll be living in Aaron's cottage.'

'With Ma and Pa?' Wes was puzzled. His parents would not be pleased about such an arrangement.

'No, just with your ma.' Amelia was enjoying her little game.

Saranna came to his rescue. 'The new man *is* your pa, Wes. He's coming to work for Mrs Cake and will no longer have to worry about having his wages cut at the whim of the local farmers.'

Eli Gillam was well-pleased about his move to Aaron Stokes's old cottage and did not find the prospect of working for Amelia Cake at all daunting. They both had harsh things to say about each other, yet beneath it all there was a mutual respect between them.

His wages would be higher too. He would be back on the weekly wages paid to agricultural labourers in other parts of the country. Not only that, Eli knew that one day Wes was to inherit Widow Cake's property. It would mean he would be working for his son. It was the next best thing to working for himself, which had always been an impossible dream for him.

He would also be gaining a daughter-in-law in a matter of weeks. It did not matter that the law did not allow them to marry in a Methodist church. They were at this moment attending a service in the village church to hear the banns being called for the first time. John and Charles Wesley had themselves been ordained in the Church of England and would have their followers worship there. All was well and life was good.

Wes and Saranna had taken Amelia along to hear the banns being called and, as usual, she thoroughly enjoyed the service.

As Wes, Saranna and the widow were leaving the church after the service, Wes saw the village constable, James Brine, standing on the church path, but he took no notice. It was part of a parish constable's duties to ensure that nothing interfered with divine service on a Sunday.

Reverend Warren was congratulating Wes and Saranna on their forthcoming wedding, telling them he would like to see them and discuss the service and what would happen on the day. As they spoke the vicar became aware of the constable apparently moving closer to the church porch.

'What is it, Brine? If you have something to discuss, leave it until everyone has gone. Then you may come in and see me in the vestry.'

'It's not you I'm waiting to see, Reverend Warren. My business is with him.' The Tolpuddle constable jerked a thumb in the direction of Wes.

'What business do you have with Wesley?' snapped Widow Cake. 'I should have thought the Tolpuddle men would have had their fill of you and your "business". George Loveless and the others will certainly be regretting the day they put their trust in you.'

'I was only doing my duty, Widow Cake. Same as I am today.'

'What is it, Brine?' Even Reverend Warren seemed anxious for the village constable to go. 'Say what you want, then leave us in peace, if you please.'

'Like I said, Reverend, my business is with Wesley Gillam.'

'Then tell me what it is,' said Wes. 'It's time I was getting Mrs Cake home.'

'I'm afraid someone else will have to do that.' Pulling a piece of paper from his pocket, James Brine said, 'I have a warrant here for your arrest, signed by Magistrate Frampton.'

Saranna gasped in dismay and there was a disbelieving silence from everyone standing nearby who heard the constable's words.

'Arrest me for what? I've done nothing wrong.'

'According to the warrant it's for much the same sort of thing as

George Loveless and the others were arrested. Only in your case it says you did maintain correspondence or intercourse with an unlawful combination or society. That's what it says here, it isn't any of my business to understand it. My duty is to arrest you and convey you to Dorchester prison to await a hearing before the Dorchester magistrates.'

Chapter 43

The Sunday that had begun so well for Wes rapidly became a nightmare. It also seemed for a while that the parish constable was likely to be lynched. When he announced he was arresting Wes someone ran to the nearby Methodist chapel. Word was shouted in at the chapel door of the arrest and worshippers spilled out to swell the angry crowd gathered in the churchyard.

Although five of the Tolpuddle six who had so recently been transported were Methodists, and this was the church, every villager had been incensed by their arrest. For a while it seemed the parish constable was likely to suffer a severe beating. He was saved by Reverend Warren and the young man he was arresting.

'I'll have no violence within my churchyard,' warned the vicar. 'If there is any trouble there will be more warrants coming to Tolpuddle and I will be forced to bear witness against all those who are here now.'

Adding his own weight to the vicar's words, Wes attempted to calm the angry villagers. 'It's all right. Go home now. Violence will serve no one. This is a mistake. It has to be. I'm not even a member of the Friendly Society.'

Even as he was speaking, Wes wished he was as confident as he sounded. George Loveless and the others had done nothing wrong, yet they were now on the high seas, heading for seven years of exile.

It was also now rumoured that one of the men, James Hammett, had not even been present at the oath-taking ceremony for which he had been sentenced to seven years' transportation. Justice did not favour the men of Tolpuddle and he had been mistaken for his brother who *had* been present on that fateful night.

Urged to point out the mistake by those arrested with him, Hammett had refused. His brother's wife was heavy with child. She needed her husband with her . . .

Overriding Saranna's declared intention of accompanying him to Dorchester, Wes sent her home with Amelia Cake and set off with the man who had arrested him.

Constable James Brine was not in the least bit grateful at

having been saved from the angry Tolpuddle villagers. On the road to Dorchester, he declared, 'It's a good thing you were able to stop your friends from attacking me, Gillam. If they'd as much as laid a finger on me you'd be facing even more serious charges when you came to court.'

'They weren't my friends,' corrected Wes. 'They were your enemies.'

This was all that was said between the two men on the seven-mile walk to Dorchester. Wes had no inclination to talk. He was too busy trying to think what might have led to the warrant's being issued against him.

He *had* written letters for the Society, but surely that was not sufficient to have him brought to trial and convicted?

Perhaps it had something to do with the talks and interviews he had given in London?

He continued to give the matter much consideration – and time and again his thoughts came back to Josephine Frampton. He remembered the look of sheer hatred on her face when they had last met.

Surely she could not have been instrumental in having him arrested? It seemed improbable, yet, remembering what she had achieved in the past, Wes was forced to admit she was quite capable of anything.

Saranna thought so too when he expressed his thoughts to her. She had come to Dorchester to visit him in prison, charming her way past gaolers who insisted that as a remand prisoner he was not allowed to receive a visitor until he had been examined by the magistrates.

'Josephine has a lot of influence with her grandfather,' she said. 'If she wanted you imprisoned she'd find some way of arranging it through him.'

Saranna was worried. Josephine must be very determined to have Wes out of the way if she really had gone to such lengths to bring him to court. If she had gone so far she was equally capable of persuading someone to give perjured evidence against him.

But her main aim was to try to reassure Wes and she said, 'Don't worry. Widow Cake came into town with me. She's seeing Mr Fielding right now, asking him to take on your defence. Your father drove us in, but once we'd spoken to the gaoler he realised he had no chance of getting in to see you so he's gone off to wait for Widow Cake.'

'I doubt if Mr Fielding will be able to do very much to help me. After witnessing the trial of the Tolpuddle men, I'm convinced there's no justice to be found in Dorchester.'

'You mustn't think that way Wes. You know what Widow Cake is like when she's roused. She's absolutely livid about the charge and the way you were arrested. She'll move heaven and earth to get you off. You're news too where the newspapers are concerned. Magistrate Frampton and his friends won't get away with anything this time.'

'Whatever happens I'm likely to be in here for a very long time. The Assize Court has only just finished sitting. There won't be another until the autumn.'

For the remainder of the brief time she was visiting Wes, Saranna tried very hard to cheer him up. It was not easy. The gaol was a depressing place. The only advantage Wes had over most of the other inmates was having a cell to himself.

Although neither of them was aware of it, this was deliberate. It was thought that by being separated from the others, Wes would be unable to communicate with friends in the Trades Unions.

He found his bed of straw uncomfortable that night and he lay awake for many hours listening to the gaol sounds. Far from being made happier, he was thoroughly depressed as a result of the visit from Saranna. The thought of what he would be missing if he were gaoled or, worse still, transported, plunged him into the depths of despair.

As he lay waiting for elusive sleep to come, he could not help thinking how his fortunes had changed. A few days before he was being fêted in London and looking forward to being married to Saranna. Now he was in gaol trying not to listen to the night sounds of the other prisoners, and awaiting trial on charges he did not understand.

The next evening, Saranna told Widow Cake she was going to the village to visit Rachel Gillam. Wes's parents would be moving into Aaron Stokes's cottage the following week. Rachel was busy packing up her things ready to load on the cart that would take them there.

However, Saranna had no intention of visiting Rachel. Instead, she took the road that passed by Southover and led to Moreton House. She was paying a call on Josephine Frampton.

It was a four-mile walk and it was growing late by the time Saranna arrived at the home of James Frampton. Despite the hour there was a light in almost every window of the solid-looking mansion. She could see much activity in the kitchens as she passed by the windows on her way to the servants' door.

She needed to knock on the door a number of times before it was opened by a flustered maid. Peering into the darkness, the maid said, 'Yes? Who is it, please?'

'It doesn't matter who it is. I have a message for Miss Josephine.'

The maid tried hard to identify the caller, but Saranna deliberately stood well back, away from the light escaping through the doorway.

'Miss Josephine is in the drawing-room with Mr Frampton's guests. There's a party going on.'

'I don't care about that. You tell her there's someone will be waiting for her to come out through the front door. Tell her it's a friend of Meg's, from London.'

Having delivered this cryptic message, Saranna moved backwards into the shadows, well out of sight of the inquisitive maid.

Saranna waited for twenty minutes before she saw Josephine slip through the front entrance of Moreton House.

'I'm here,' she called softly. 'Standing in the shrubbery on the other side of the drive.'

'Who are you?' Josephine queried uncertainly. 'And what is this about Meg?'

'It's nothing about Meg. I said only that I was a friend of hers. And I am. We have no secrets.'

'What is it you want? If it's money, you'll need to wait until tomorrow. I have none on me and will not be able to obtain any tonight.'

'You can keep your money. I'm here to talk about Wesley Gillam.'

After a long pause, Josephine queried, 'What about him?'

'I would have thought you knew that very well. He's been arrested.'

'What has that to do with me? My grandfather is the magistrate. What he does is none of my business.'

'I think it is. I believe it's you who's been putting ideas in his head about having Wes arrested.'

'Who are you?' Josephine asked once again. 'What have you to do with Wesley Gillam?'

'I'm a friend of his. A very good friend. So good that if anything happens to him I intend travelling to London to speak to the magistrate at Bow Street. I'll tell him that the girl he's been looking for these past three years can be found here, in Moreton House. How much money was the man carrying when he was murdered? It was quite a lot, I believe. At least, Meg said it was. She's prepared to turn King's evidence against you. In fact, when she hears what happened to Saul, I know for certain she'll be delighted to.'

'What is it you want from me?' Josephine spoke in a whisper, but her fear was evident.

461

'I want Wesley Gillam freed from gaol and the charges against him withdrawn.'

'I can't do that. I told you, my grandfather is the magistrate. What he does has nothing to do with me.'

'Then I think you'd better make it your business. If Wesley goes free you can forget I ever called. Forget about what happened in London – if you can. But if Wesley Gillam is found guilty and sentenced to imprisonment, or transportation, I swear you'll go to gaol too – at least, until they hang you by the neck until you're dead.'

'Wait! Please, I'll do everything I can, but let's talk about this. I can find you money, if that's what you want. Do you hear me? Come back . . .'

Josephine's pleas were wasted. Her visitor had disappeared into the night as mysteriously as she had appeared.

Chapter 44

The daily prison routine had barely begun. Beyond the door of Wes's cell the inmates of Dorchester gaol were stirring in preparation for the monotony of another day. Suddenly a key rattled in the lock of the cell door and it swung open with an agonising screech that echoed far along the dark, damp corridor.

A gaoler entered the cell and said cheerfully, 'Come on, Gillam. No good you lying there thinking lovely thoughts of what you'd be doing if you weren't in here leading such a lazy life. There's someone wanting to see you.'

Wes started up. 'Who? Surely not Saranna at this early hour?'

'I don't know who this Saranna is, but it's certainly not her. It's Magistrate Frampton who's waiting to see you – and if you know what's good for you, I wouldn't keep *him* waiting.'

Wes was taken to a large room bare of furniture except for a huge table and two chairs. The chairs were occupied by James Frampton and a small man with red-rimmed, watery eyes. They sat on one side of the table, Wes was told to stand on the other.

The magistrate wasted no time on niceties. 'Gillam, you know why you've been arrested?'

'No.' Wes spoke defiantly.

'You were told the nature of the felony with which you are being charged?'

'I was told something that made very little sense to me.'

'I was told.' Frampton dictated to his companion and the watery-eyed man added the words to a sheet of paper that lay on the table in front of him.

'Is there anything you wish to say to me, Gillam?'

'Yes. When will I be released and allowed to return home?'

'Nothing to say,' said the magistrate in an aside to the clerk.

To Wes, he said, 'You will be taken from here today to Salisbury. There you will be tried at the Assizes which begin tomorrow. That's all.'

James Frampton stood up, ignoring Wes.

Shaking off the warder's hand as he tried to lead him away, Wes asked, 'Why am I going to Salisbury?'

'Because Mr Fielding has been given leave for you to be tried there. If I had my way you'd stay here, in Dorchester, until you rotted.'

With this observation, Magistrate Frampton stalked from the room, his myopic clerk scurrying after him when he had gathered up all the papers from the table.

Wes was given very little time to ponder on the reason why his counsel had arranged for him to be tried in Salisbury and not Dorchester. Less than an hour after his brief appearance before Magistrate Frampton, he was on his way north-eastward to Salisbury. Travelling in an unsprung, closed van, the thirty-five miles felt more like a hundred.

That same day, shortly after noon, a much more sophisticated carriage, pulled by a pair of spirited horses, drew to a halt outside Widow Cake's cottage. Mr Fielding, Wes's counsel, alighted.

Saranna saw the barrister through the window and came running out of the cottage.

'What's the matter? Has something happened to Wes?'

'Yes, but I trust it may prove to be to his advantage. I have succeeded in arranging for Wesley's trial to be moved to Salisbury Assizes. Unfortunately they commence tomorrow, which leaves us with very little time. I'm on my way there now. I thought I would call here first, to see if you wished to attend. If so, I can take you there – if you can be ready right away.'

'Give me ten minutes,' said Saranna.

Running inside the cottage, she breathlessly told Amelia Cake what was happening.

'Tell Mr Fielding to come inside for a while,' said Amelia.

'But . . . he's in a great hurry!'

'His time is being paid for by me. Tell him to come in. Bring him into the front room.'

The widow's foot had healed enough for her to sleep upstairs once more, leaving the 'front room' free for entertaining the occasional visitor of Mr Fielding's importance.

The barrister was a tall man and he needed to stoop to pass through the door. He had hardly straightened up when Widow Cake said, 'You've succeeded in having Wesley's trial shifted to Salisbury, I hear?'

'That's right, Mrs Cake. I'm on my way there now.'

'Good. He'll have a fairer hearing there than he'd have got at Dorchester. All the same, I want to be there to make quite certain.'

'You're coming too? I want to be away quickly, Mrs Cake. It's a long way and I have matters to attend to when I arrive there.'

'I'll be ready in half-an-hour. Saranna . . . You be ready in ten minutes and then you can run down to the village and tell Rachel Gillam. She'll no doubt want to come too. Tell her to leave word for Eli. I want him to attend to things up here while we're away. Go on, girl. Mr Fielding's in a hurry.'

Mr Fielding and the three women reached Salisbury before dark. Although the Assizes were due to begin the following day, there were few cases to be heard. It proved no problem for the women and Fielding to find accommodation at an inn close by the courts.

It was not until the following morning, at breakfast, that they discovered they had been sharing the inn with James Frampton and his granddaughter.

Mr Fielding inclined his head to the Moreton magistrate, but received only a frosty acknowledgement. Josephine did not recognise any of the Tolpuddle women and, after a brief glance in their direction, she began eating her breakfast in a desultory way, as though she was not enjoying it. She looked pale and out of sorts.

They met again briefly in the courtroom where Fielding arranged for the three women in his party to sit in the front row of the public gallery. Josephine sat in the row behind.

Everything here followed very much the same pattern as it had when Widow Cake and Saranna had attended Dorchester court for Arnold's trial. But the proceedings today lacked the air of excitement and expectation that had attended the trials of the men involved in the Captain Swing riots.

The court filled only gradually and there were still vacant seats in the public gallery when the judge arrived to take his place on the Bench, flanked by the mayor and the county sheriff.

When he had taken his seat, Mr Fielding left the table where he was sitting and came across the courtroom to whisper to Amelia Cake, 'Do you recognise the judge? It's His Honour Judge Kennedy – Sir William Kennedy when you last met him. He was the prosecuting counsel in the case against Arnold Cooper.'

Saranna gasped, 'Do you mean it's the man Mrs Cake put out of his room at the inn? That's not likely to be to our advantage.'

Judge Kennedy had been watching the movement in his court. He now fixed his gaze upon the Tolpuddle widow. With a gesture of his hand he silenced the clerk of the court who was about to speak.

Looking across the courtroom to where Widow Cake sat, he said, 'I trust you were able to find suitable accommodation last night, madam?'

'I did, thank you.'

'Good. I believe the last time we met it was your intention to use your stick to some effect upon the learned judge because you disagreed with the court's verdict?'

Totally out of character, Amelia Cake felt it politic to remain silent.

'May I ask in which case you are taking an interest today? It is possible I will find it necessary to request that your stick be held in safe-keeping until after I have delivered my verdict.'

'I'm here to see that Wesley Gillam receives more justice than did Arnold Cooper.'

Judge Kennedy looked down at the list on the bench in front of him and frowned.

'Wesley Gillam? I see no Gillam here.'

Mr Fielding stood up immediately. 'May it please Your Honour . . . I represent Mr Gillam. The case has been moved from Dorchester, at my request. It has all been arranged in rather a hurry. I understand he has yet to appear before Your Honour and the Grand Jury.'

'Thank you, Mr Fielding. In order that the interested persons shall not need to wait too long, I will have the Grand Jury called during the lunch recess.'

'Thank you, Your Honour.'

Judge Kennedy nodded to Fielding, and then to Amelia Cake.

Saranna felt there was a faint glimmer of hope. 'You know, I think he might be more sympathetic to Wes than I dared hope,' she whispered to Amelia.

'I don't know why you should feel that. Take my stick, indeed!'

The first case to be heard by Judge Kennedy did little to justify Saranna's optimism. Two men came before him charged with wounding a gamekeeper with intent to resist arrest when caught poaching. Both pleaded guilty.

One of the men, aged somewhere in his middle-thirties, was sentenced to hang. The other, a lad of seventeen years, was transported for life. This case was over before lunchtime and the judge, sheriff and mayor rose from their seats, gave a bow to the court, and departed through a door behind the Bench.

Chapter 45

Uncertain what the day that lay ahead would bring, Wes was filled with grave apprehension. He had not seen Mr Fielding since his arrival and no one had told him what was expected of him.

His cell was an improvement upon those beneath the Dorchester court, but it was still highly claustrophobic. He had no inkling of the time and was momentarily startled when the bolt on the outside of the cell door was drawn and the door swung open.

'Come on, Gillam. The judge wants to see you.'

Wes was heavily shackled, hand and foot, and stumbled awkwardly in the wake of the gaoler. A couple of minutes later he was pushed into a room containing the Grand Jury, comprised of more than twenty stern-faced jurors. To one side of them stood James Frampton.

'Stand here!' The gaoler pushed him into position facing the jurors. Wes was glad he had not had his head shaved. At least he felt he looked reasonably respectable.

The judge eyed him with some interest, but his first words were to Magistrate James Frampton. 'Mr Frampton, you have brought charges against the prisoner, alleging he maintained correspondence with a society which has been deemed unlawful by reason of administering an illegal oath to its members. Before we examine the various Acts of Parliament to which you refer in your indictment, may we hear the evidence you have to present to the Grand Jury in support of the charge?'

'Your Honour, the prisoner recently went to London at the invitation of a Trades Union to speak at a meeting of Union supporters...'

'Just a moment, Mr Frampton. You can produce evidence that Gillam was invited by a Trades Union?'

'It was reported in a newspaper...'

'I regret, that is not admissible evidence, Mr Frampton. I repeat, do you have firm evidence of this?'

'No, Your Honour.'

'Then the Jury will please disregard this statement. Please continue, Mr Frampton.'

'I have letters from a number of Trades Unions quite obviously replying to letters sent by Gillam to them from the Tolpuddle Labourers' Friendly Society.'

'I see. You can produce evidence that the Trades Unions to which you are referring are illegal organisations as defined in the various Acts of Parliament you invoke?

'Not *written* evidence, Your Honour. However, the Tolpuddle Society has been declared illegal in the Assize Court in Dorchester . . .'

'As I recall the case, it was the *oath* given to its members that was declared illegal,' corrected the judge. 'But, be that as it may, you will be providing oral proof, no doubt, that Gillam has been writing to the Tolpuddle Society.?'

'Not *to* the Society, Your Honour, but certainly on its behalf.'

'With all due respect, Mr Frampton, I can see nothing in any of the Acts quoted by you which makes it a criminal offence to write on behalf of an illegal organisation – even were you able to satisfy myself and the Grand Jury beyond all reasonable doubt that such an offence had taken place. Please put before the Grand Jury all the *evidence* on which you felt it your duty to issue a warrant for the prisoner's arrest?'

For almost half an hour Magistrate Frampton tried to convince the Grand Jury that the 'evidence' he had against Wes was sufficient to secure a conviction against him in the Assize Court before a Petty Jury. He made an attempt to introduce the friendship of Wes with the six convicted men of Tolpuddle, but fell into tight-lipped silence when Judge Kennedy refused to allow him to elaborate on this. The Judge declared sharply that it had no relevance to the case against Wes whatsoever.

The final minutes of the hearing were taken up with a discussion of the Acts of Parliament upon which Frampton had based his charges. Wes understood little of this, but he was becoming increasingly heartened by the way the examination was proceeding. Unlike the judge who had presided over the trial of the Tolpuddle six, Judge Kennedy seemed intent on purveying true justice.

Finally, Judge Kennedy told Magistrate Frampton he might be seated while he addressed the Grand Jury.

'Gentlemen, you have heard what Magistrate Frampton has had to say about the charges he has brought against Wesley Gillam. You have also heard my comments on the quality of the evidence produced to you in support of those charges. If you still feel it is a case that should be heard in court before a Petty Jury, it is your privilege to recommend such a course. On the other hand, if you, in your wisdom, feel there is a decided lack of substance in the charge, then it is your duty to endorse the indictment as *ignoramus* and the accused will be discharged forthwith.'

The Grand Jury were out of the room for only fifteen minutes. In answer to the Judge's question, they handed him the indictment.

Scrawled across the document was a single word: '*Ignoramus*'.

White-faced with fury, Magistrate James Frampton stalked from the room, after paying the briefest mark of respect to the Judge who had effectively thrown out his indictment.

Wes was aware he had been acquitted of the charges levelled against him without having to say a word in his defence and without being required to stand in the dock in the Assize Court. However, he did not know what he should do now.

It was Judge Kennedy who solved the problem for him. 'You may remain here, Mr Gillam. Some of your friends are sitting in court. I am about to begin the afternoon session and I will inform them you are here – and may I offer you my congratulations, and also my apologies? The charges for which you were arrested should never have been brought against you.'

By the time Judge Kennedy made his way into the courtroom, the officials were becoming restless. He was extremely late for the afternoon session. Even now, it seemed he was not ready to proceed with the cases on the list.

Looking across the courtroom, he called to Widow Cake, 'Mrs Cake. I am very pleased to inform you there will be no need to confiscate your stick today. Mr Gillam has just made an appearance before the Grand Jury. They are of the opinion that a satisfactory case cannot be made against him. He is free to return to Tolpuddle with you. Mr Fielding will escort you to the Grand Jury room. I hope you do not feel your journey has been wasted?'

Struggling to her feet, Amelia Cake said, 'You have my gratitude, Your Honour, but anyone who knows Wesley Gillam is aware he never did anything against the law. It was only that fool Frampton who got it into his head that he had. I don't know why you put up with him as a magistrate. He once got it into his head that someone had tried to murder me in my own house – when all I'd done was to fall down stairs! He might have a big house and important friends, but he certainly doesn't have any common sense.'

Amelia's observations brought laughter from the public gallery and smiles from the officials in the well of the court.

Behind the widow, Josephine Frampton closed her eyes and swayed in her seat, so great was her relief. In her lap she clenched her hands so tightly she drew blood from one of her palms. She was aware that it was not only Wesley Gillam from whom the shadow of conviction had been lifted.

470

Chapter 46

The humiliation experienced by James Frampton in the Grand Jury room at Salisbury courthouse was as nothing compared with the ordeal suffered by his granddaughter a few nights afterwards.

Most of the lights were out in the main house at Moreton and many of the servants were already in bed when the whole house was aroused by the sound of desperate screaming coming from the garden.

Magistrate Frampton had been working late in his study and was among the first to dash from the house, brandishing a horse pistol. Other servants were ahead and behind him carrying lanterns. They headed towards the summerhouse which appeared to be the scene of the anguished cries.

When the magistrate arrived he was shocked to see his granddaughter being led from the summerhouse. She was completely naked and had a great deal of blood on her hands, arms and face.

'What is it? What's going on, Josephine? Have you been attacked?'

Instead of replying, she took refuge in hysteria. 'In there. He was in there. He attacked us with a knife.'

'Us? Who were you with? You, girl . . .' He addressed one of the servants. 'Take off your coat and give it to Miss Josephine.'

The servant obeyed his command, even though it left her in a state of undress too. She had been about to get into bed when the disturbance began and had slipped a coat on before leaving the house to learn what was happening.

'Mr Frampton, sir – I think you ought to come here. But keep the ladies away, sir.'

One of the footmen came from the summerhouse, a lantern shaking in his hand.

'What is it?' Magistrate Frampton advanced cautiously, the pistol held firmly in his hand.

'It's John Harvey, sir. He's naked too and he's badly hurt. It looks as though someone has tried to cut his throat. Stabbed in the back too, by the look of it.'

There were shocked exclamations from the gathering circle of

471

servants about the summerhouse. Ignoring them, Magistrate Frampton followed the footman inside the small building.

John Harvey, a young, curly-haired gardener, lay on his face in a pool of his own blood. He was barely alive – and was as naked as Josephine.

James Frampton's first thought was that the gardener had somehow lured Josephine into the garden and attacked her, but he could see no knife lying about. Neither were there any clothes – if one of her shoes, lying in the centre of the summerhouse, was disregarded.

It did not need an excessively intelligent man to work out what had happened. Josephine had been in there with the gardener. The pair must have been naked when someone else burst in upon them, almost murdered the gardener, cut Josephine badly in the same attack, and made off with their clothes.

Turning to the footman who had first found the badly wounded gardener, James Frampton said, 'Find one of the stableboys and send him for a doctor. Quickly now!'

His first priority was to keep the gardener alive. He would warn the staff of Moreton about saying nothing in the morning. This was a scandal that needed to be kept as quiet as possible. It would be impossible to do this if the gardener died on the premises and a murder inquiry needed to be launched.

Much to James Frampton's relief, his efforts were rewarded. The young gardener lived long enough for him to be sent to his home in a small village on Dorset's south coast. The fact that he died there two weeks later did not matter. By that time Josephine and her mother were in the Frampton-owned cottage on Dartmoor, well away from any scandal.

Nevertheless, news of what had happened at Moreton soon circulated about Tolpuddle and there was a great deal of bitterness at the manner in which the Moreton magistrate had protected the already tarnished reputation of his errant grand-daughter.

But the happenings at Moreton House were far from everyone's thoughts two weeks later, when Wes stood beside Saranna in front of the altar of Tolpuddle's small church. The ancient build-ing was packed to capacity for their wedding.

Nancy and Richard Pemble had travelled from Kent for the occasion. There was also a sprinkling of journalists to record the event for the national newspapers which had printed reports of Wes's success in London.

Amelia Cake sat next to Eli Gillam, beaming as though it was the marriage of her own son. Her magnificent wedding present to bride and groom had been the deeds to her lands and property. Wes would never need to work for another employer during his lifetime.

The only complaint Amelia was heard to utter on this happy day was in respect of Eli Gillam's voice. After all the years she had spent complaining about the Methodist hymns he was always singing, she had discovered when he stood beside her in church that it was his voice and not the hymns that were at fault.

As she left the church, walking behind Wesley and Saranna Gillam, she swore that if she heard him singing once more she would buy a donkey to sing a duet with him.

'Ah! A donkey is a blessed animal, Mrs Cake,' said Eli, too happy about the events of the day to allow anything she said to upset him. 'One carried our Lord on his last journey to Jerusalem, and don't forget it was one of the first animals the son of God saw when he came down from heaven on that Christmas Day many years ago.'

'That's as may be,' snapped Widow Cake. 'If he'd tried to sing him a lullaby, the child would probably have gone back again. But there are times when I wonder whether that might have been such a great tragedy. Think about it. No bishops or vicars – and no Methodist preachers to challenge their preaching. Perhaps it would be a far more peaceful world to live in!'

In front of them, Wes and Saranna heard the exchange and smiled happily at each other. It was certain that Magistrate Frampton would never again attempt to take action against either Wes or the Labourers' Friendly Society, but life in Tolpuddle would never be dull as long as Widow Cake held a place in their lives, and a special corner in their hearts.

Epilogue

For the first few years of his married life, enthusiastically assisted by Saranna, Wesley Gillam continued to play a prominent part in the continuing campaign to free the six Tolpuddle 'martyrs', as the unjustly convicted men became known.

During these years, Trades Unions throughout the land grew in strength as a direct result of the trial and conviction of the Tolpuddle men. They joined together in their determination to have the men pardoned and returned from Australia.

In April 1834 a crowd estimated at between 35,000 and 200,000 gathered in London. (The estimates varied, depending on whether the source of information had its origins in government or the Trades Union movement). The assembly set out from Copenhagen Fields, in Islington, and marched in good order to Whitehall. Here, Lord Melbourne refused to accept a petition containing 300,000 signatures, calling for the release of the Tolpuddle Six.

Agitation for the men's release continued unabated, but met with little success. Then, early in 1836, a sympathiser to the cause made a remarkable discovery. The Duke of Cumberland, in his capacity as head of the Orange Lodge, was in the habit of administering an oath similar in form to that which had convicted the Tolpuddle farm labourers.

Cumberland was the brother of King William IV.

Gleefully, supporters of the 'martyrs' clamoured to have the royal duke indicted. The public outcry had immediate results.

On 14 March 1836 Lord John Russell informed Parliament that it gave him great satisfaction to announce that His Majesty had been pleased to grant a free pardon to the Tolpuddle Six.

Justice and common-sense had belatedly prevailed. But Australia was very many miles away from Whitehall and communications were poor. James Hammett, the last of the six Tolpuddle men to be returned to his homeland, did not set foot on Dorset soil again until August 1839.

Hammett was also the only one of the six to remain in Tolpuddle. He is buried in a quiet part of the churchyard in the village he loved, his grave a place of pilgrimage for thousands from every walk of life.

Others who knew him then lie nearby, their resting places unmarked, their deeds long forgotten.